ROAD TRIP WITH THE BEST MAN

SOPHIE PEMBROKE

THE MAVERICK'S BRIDAL BARGAIN

CHRISTY JEFFRIES

MILLS & BOON

First Published in Great Britain 2018
by Mills & Boon, an imprint of HarperCollinsPublishers,
1 London Bridge Street, London, SE1 9GF

Road Trip with the Best Man © 2018 Sophie Pembroke
The Maverick's Bridal Bargain © 2018 Harlequin Books S.A.

Special thanks and acknowledgement to Christy Jeffries
for her contribution to the Montana Mavericks continuity.

ISBN: 978-0-263-26502-6

38-0618

MIX
Paper from
responsible sources
FSC™ C007454

FSC
www.fsc.org

This book is produced from independently certified FSC™
paper to ensure responsible forest management.

For more information visit: www.harpercollins.co.uk/green

Printed and bound in Spain
by CPI, Barcelona

ROAD TRIP WITH THE BEST MAN

SOPHIE PEMBROKE

For everyone who ever wanted to take
to the open road and find themselves.

It's never too late.

CHAPTER ONE

DAWN FEATHERINGTON STARED down the aisle at the perfect floral arrangements tied to each row of chairs set out on the grass. The string quartet was playing Pachelbel's *Canon*—again—the officiant smiling serenely at the foot of the pagoda steps. The late-afternoon sun shone down on the manicured lawns of the Californian coastal mansion Justin's mother had insisted would be the perfect venue for the two hundred and fifty guests they needed to invite, lighting up the delicate white ribbons and lace strung around the pagoda.

Everything looked perfect. Until she turned her attention to the expectant guests, all waiting slightly less patiently than they had been twenty minutes ago, and felt her stomach twist.

Because the only thing missing now was the groom.

Dawn ducked back behind the screens that the venue staff had put in place to keep the bridal party's arrival a secret until the last moment. Behind her, her four sisters whispered amongst themselves, their rose-pink silk bridesmaid dresses rustling with them. She couldn't hear what they were saying, but then she didn't really need to.

Can you believe this is happening again?

No. They were wrong. Justin loved her, he wanted to marry her. He'd hated even having to spend last night in a different hotel—although he'd insisted they had to, for tradition's sake. He'd be here any moment. Probably.

Dawn bit back a sigh. It wasn't as if this exact thing had happened before, anyway—whatever her sisters were whispering. She'd never got *quite* as far as the altar with any of the others. They'd all called it off before it reached this point.

Two broken engagements—one at the rehearsal dinner, but that still wasn't the actual altar, right?—three long-term cohabiting relationships that had never even got as far as the ring and now Justin. Forty minutes late for his own wedding.

It wouldn't be *quite* so bad if every single one of her boyfriends hadn't gone on to marry someone else within twelve to eighteen months. Including, in one particularly soul-destroying case, marrying her own sister.

'The Dry Run.' That was what her sisters called her. Dawn was the woman that guys tried out settling down with before they picked the woman they *actually* wanted to spend the rest of their lives with. And for some reason that woman was never Dawn.

But Justin was different. Wasn't he?

From the moment they'd first met, she'd felt it. She'd been at a work event, one held at an estate not unlike this one, with vineyards stretching back from the gleaming white house. She'd been standing on the terrace, looking out at the sunset, when he'd approached her and made some comment about the hosts that she could barely re- member. All she had taken in was his smile and his charm. They'd talked all evening—well, okay, mostly he'd talked, but he had so many interesting things to say! Then, the next day, he'd sent flowers and a note to her office, ask- ing her to meet him at some ridiculously exclusive bar across town.

She went, and the rest was history. They'd announced their engagement four months later and, now, here they were.

Or rather, here *she* was. Justin's whereabouts were still a mystery.

The whispering behind her grew louder and Dawn turned to see the best man, Justin's older brother Cooper, striding across the lawn from the main house towards them. He wasn't smiling. Then again, she hadn't seen him smile yet in the twenty-four hours since they'd met, so that might not actually be a sign.

Dawn sucked in a breath and braced herself.

'He's not coming.' Cooper stood a few feet away, his expression blank. As if he hadn't just torn her whole world apart with three little words.

She'd suspected that Cooper didn't like her since she'd first met him at the rehearsal dinner. But then, he'd never seemed particularly enthusiastic whenever Justin had talked to him on the phone either. And, really, what best man didn't make the effort even to attend the engagement party?

'Way to break it to her gently,' her sister, Marie, said sharply. She wrapped an arm around Dawn's shoulders as their other sisters made sympathetic cooing noises.

Dawn would probably have felt a lot more comforted if Marie hadn't married her ex-boyfriend two years ago.

She could feel all the usual emotions swelling up inside her—the anger, the despair, the gaping emptiness—but she clamped down on them. No. This wasn't going to happen again. It couldn't.

And, if it did, she wasn't going to give any one of her perfect sisters—or Justin's sanctimonious brother—the chance to see it break her.

'Is that for me?' Dawn pointed to the envelope in Cooper's hand, proud of how steady her voice was. Her finger didn't even shake.

She could almost believe she wasn't actually dying on the inside.

Cooper gave a short nod and handed it over—but not, she noticed, before removing a second envelope. One that had his name on it.

Apparently Justin had more to say than just to the bride he'd stood up.

Focusing on keeping her hand steady, she took her letter and untucked the envelope flap. So like Justin, to write an old-fashioned letter. He wasn't the sort to dump a girl by text message—like her second fiancé—or even by email, like boyfriend number three. Justin was a gentleman.

Or he had been, until now.

Inside the envelope she found a single sheet of creamy paper covered in his block print writing —one that Dawn was pretty sure Justin must have taken from the elegant writing desk in his mother's immaculate front room. She scanned the words quickly, then folded it up again and pushed it back into the envelope, making sure not to let her expression change at all.

They were *not* going to win.

'Right. Well, it seems we won't be having a wedding today after all.' Her voice didn't even sound like her own.

'Oh, Dawn!' That was her mother, of course, who'd come to find her father to see what the delay was. 'Oh, not again, honey!'

Dawn kept her gaze fixed on Cooper's face, even as he raised one eyebrow at the word 'again'.

'Will you help me tell the guests?' she asked neutrally.

'I believe that unfortunate task does fall to the best man, traditionally,' Cooper said.

Traditionally. As if this happened at everyone else's weddings, not just hers.

'Great. Okay, then.'

'Do you want me to send them home?' Cooper asked, his voice as bland and unemotional as ever. 'I believe there was a dinner planned...'

And an open bar, actually. That might be important later.

Dawn thought of the tables of canapés and champagne, the four-course meal that Justin's family had insisted on paying for. There wouldn't be any refunds at this point, of course, but it wasn't as though the Edwards family couldn't afford it. And a lot of these people had travelled a long way to be with them on their not-so-special day.

Well, the least she could do was feed them. And give them a good story to tell on the dinner-party circuit.

'No,' she said as firmly as she could manage. 'I'll go tell the venue to get the bar open and prepare to serve dinner. Everyone else should enjoy the day, at least. Excuse me.'

And with that Dawn hitched up her heavy, lace-covered skirt and made for the mansion as fast as she could in her satin heels.

She needed a drink, and a toilet cubicle to hide in, fast.

That way, no one would be able to see her fall apart.

Again.

Cooper watched his brother's jilted bride make her way towards the ridiculously fancy mansion she'd chosen for what was supposed to be her big day. She seemed strangely composed for someone who'd just had their entire future torn away from them.

Which, given the contents of the note Justin had left for him, probably shouldn't have been such a surprise.

I can't go through with it, Cooper. I'm sorry for all the upset this will cause Mother, but I know you'll understand.

You see, this week I've found that I just can't shake the feeling that Dawn has ulterior motives for wanting to marry me. I thought she loved me as much as I loved her. But now I'm worried she loves my money a lot more. I can't face her—not now. I need some time away to think everything through, figure out the truth about our relationship, our feelings.

If I'm wrong I'll make it up to her somehow. But I can't marry her when I'm not one hundred percent sure that it's the right thing to do.

I'm heading up to the beach house for the week to think. I'm sorry to place this on you, brother, but I knew you would be the only one to understand exactly what I'm going through...

Yeah, Cooper understood. Apparently neither Edwards brother was any good at spotting a gold-digger until it was too late.

At least Justin had got out before he reached the altar, which was more than Cooper had managed.

Justin had done the right thing. Even if it kind of screwed up Cooper's plans for kicking back, getting hammered on high quality whisky and maybe even seducing an attractive guest to help him forget how much he hated weddings. Traditionally, he supposed he should have lined up a bridesmaid, but since they all appeared to be A: married and B: sisters of the bride, he was happy to spurn tradition on this one.

Although maybe his plan, such as it was, wasn't completely ruined—especially since Dawn intended to let the celebratory part of the day go ahead despite not having anything to celebrate.

He just needed to break the news to the dearly beloveds gathered for the non-event.

Couldn't be any harder than facing his father's shareholders after that debacle with Melanie and the Reed takeover, right? Or telling his parents that he'd been conned by the woman he loved and they were all about to get screwed in the divorce courts.

Yeah, this was nothing.

Cooper took a deep breath and walked down the aisle, thankfully alone.

'Ladies and gentlemen, I have some sad news for you all.' Everyone's attention was instantly on him, of course, and Cooper smiled his best reassuring smile. 'I'm afraid that there will not, after all, be a wedding here today.' The expected whispers and groans went up from the crowd. Cooper knew better than to expect real disappointment from any of them. More likely they were mentally preparing their gloating renditions of this story for anyone unfortunate enough not to be there to witness it. Goodness knew there'd been enough stories told about him after his divorce, not all of them even close to the truth.

Not that he cared. What difference did it make to him what people said about him anyway?

But he didn't want them saying that stuff about Justin.

'The bride has requested that you all still stay for dinner, however,' he added, and a more enthusiastic murmur went up at that. 'And I believe the bar will be open imminently.'

Then he stepped out of the way to avoid the stampede.

'Cooper? What's happening? Dawn's parents are in pieces over there, and her sisters…well. Where's Justin?' A dark-haired woman in a too-short pink dress pushed through the crush to get to him. Cooper frowned at her for a moment before recognising her as someone he'd been introduced to at the rehearsal dinner two nights before. Not a bridesmaid, so not one of Dawn's numerous sisters. American, so not Dawn's family, either—apart from her mother's transatlantic twang, they all had the same regional British accent that she did. A friend, then. There hadn't been many of those at the dinner—it had mostly been family. So she had to be… No, he had nothing.

'I'm sorry, have we met?' He smiled his most charming smile, but received only a scowl in return.

'Yes. Last night. I'm Dawn's friend, Ruby.'

'Right. Ruby. Of course.' Yeah, no way was he going to remember that more than a few minutes this time, either. Why waste time on people who weren't going to matter to him in the future? And, since Dawn was no longer going to be his sister-in-law, he didn't need to worry about it.

'So? Where's Justin? Where's Dawn, come to that?'

'Last I saw, Dawn was heading into the venue to demand they open the bar early,' he replied. 'And Justin… I can't say exactly where he is. But I know he's not coming.' And if for some reason his brother lost his mind and suddenly appeared to try and make up with his bride—if he decided that his love would be enough for both of them, even if Dawn's had never existed—well. Then Cooper would be there to stop him. To keep them apart until Justin came to his senses again and appreciated his lucky escape.

'The bar?' Ruby shook her head, turned on her heel and stalked away from him towards her gold-digging friend—stopping briefly to talk to Dawn's confused parents on her way. Maybe they'd been in on it together, he thought absently. Well, Dawn might not be a heartbroken jilted bride, but if nothing else she had to be bitterly lamenting the loss of all that money. The thought made him smile.

Love, Cooper knew from bitter experience, could make

a man act crazy. Justin had done the right thing, and Cooper would make sure he kept doing it.

There was no way he was going to let his little brother make the same awful mistakes he had.

Dawn had found the perfect hiding spot: in the ladies' room on the second floor, furthest from the bar. There were at least two other bathrooms between there and the ballroom where the not-wedding breakfast would be served, and Dawn couldn't imagine *anyone* traipsing this far away from the complimentary alcohol if they didn't have to.

She was completely alone, just as she needed to be.

'Dawn?'

Completely alone except for Ruby, that was.

'In here,' she said, unlocking the door with a sigh. Ruby, she'd learned over the last couple of years since they'd become friends, never took silence for an answer.

Ruby bustled into the bathroom, slamming the door shut behind her and handing over the bottle of Prosecco she was holding.

'Okay, can someone please explain to me what the *hell* is going on? Because that idiot of a best man was basically useless.'

Reaching into the tiny clutch bag she'd retrieved from her sister Elizabeth on her way back to the mansion, Dawn pulled out the letter from Justin and gave it to Ruby. It wasn't as if *she* needed to read it again, anyway. The words were already burned into her brain.

Dearest Dawn,

I'm so sorry to do this to you, darling, but I know I have to be fair to both of us, to give us both our best chances at a happy future.

I can't be there to marry you today. Please don't

*ask me why, simply know that when I asked you to
be my bride it was because I truly believed that our
futures lay together. But the world changes more
quickly than we can sometimes imagine.*

*Cooper will help you with our guests, and explain
everything to my parents.*

Once again, I'm so sorry, Dawn.

With love and affection,

Justin

Dawn watched as Ruby read the letter, her eyebrows
jerking higher with every line. *Yeah, that was my reaction
too.* Well, that and her heart cracking in two.

Time to open the Prosecco.

'So, he can't tell you why he didn't show up, he ditched
the whole problem onto his idiot brother and still claims
he's being *fair* to you?' Ruby sounded incredulous.

'Yes, apparently I have been jilted at the altar for my
own good.' Dawn took a swig from the bottle and passed
it back to Ruby. 'At least that's an excuse I haven't heard
before. I mean, with Richard it was because he realised
he wasn't ready to settle down after all—although he did
settle down six months later with a redhead he met on his
"finding myself" trip around India, incidentally. Harry
decided he was gay, after he'd been living with me for
three months.'

Ruby stifled a giggle at that. Dawn ignored her and
carried on ticking off her disastrous prior relationships
on her fingers.

'Patrick left me for a job in Dubai, where he claimed
I'd be desperately unhappy so he couldn't ask me to go
with him. Ewan cheated on me with his ex-girlfriend and
Trevor married my sister instead.'

'Girl, you have the worst luck with men. You should try women instead.'

'Don't think I haven't considered it.' Dawn sighed. 'I just… I don't understand what's wrong with me.'

'Nothing is wrong with *you*,' Ruby said fiercely. 'Trust me, it's those men who are the fools here.'

'Except every one of them managed to settle down with someone else after they got shot of me,' Dawn pointed out. 'And now Justin… I mean, he just didn't even bother to show up. And he can't tell me why. That's…it's not enough.'

'You need closure,' Ruby said sagely, returning the bottle of Prosecco to her.

Closure. That sounded good. Closing the book on her absurdly cursed love life and moving forward instead. Understanding the mistakes she'd made, or what it was about her that made finding her happy-ever-after so impossible. Because this? This wasn't what all those fairy tales and happy endings had led her to expect from life. And she wanted better for her future.

She wanted to find someone to share her life with. Someone who'd stick by her through the ups and downs, someone to come home to after a hard day at work, someone to *love* her just as she was.

Really, how hard could it be if all four of her sisters had managed it? Not to mention every cousin, friend and family acquaintance she had, except for Ruby. Dawn had attended so many weddings in the last ten years, they'd all started to merge into one.

And now it had been her turn at last and everyone had been so *happy* for her. And relieved, she knew—her family wasn't good at hiding their emotions that way. They'd been relieved that *at last* Dawn was through that terrible run of bad luck and they could all stop worrying about her and get back to being blissfully happy themselves.

Except now it was all ruined.

'Your parents were looking for you,' Ruby said, her voice softer. 'And your sisters. Plus, well, everyone you've ever met.'

Yet Ruby was the only one who'd actually managed to find her. Not that Dawn was particularly surprised by that. Ruby *knew* her—had seen right through her the first day they'd met and declared that they were destined to be best friends. And so they were.

'I don't want to see them.' She loved her family, really she did. And she knew they loved her. But she couldn't take the pity in their eyes one more time. That disappointment and—worse—that sense of inevitability. And she *really* didn't want to hear her mother's, 'Not every woman is meant to be a wife and mother, Dawnie,' speech. Because she *knew* that—of course she did. And if she'd chosen to be alone, to forge her own path through life, that would be great. But she hadn't.

Six times now, she'd thought she'd found true love. She'd thought she'd found forever.

And six times she'd been wrong.

She took another, longer gulp of Prosecco, the bubbles stinging her throat as they went down.

Maybe her mother was right. Maybe it was time to concede defeat. To dedicate her life to being that crazy aunt who was always off on adventures, posting photos of her in exotic places with handsome men she never stayed with long enough for them to let her down.

It wouldn't be a bad life.

'What do you want me to do?' Ruby asked. 'Just say it, and I'll make it happen.'

Ruby, Dawn decided, was the best friend a girl had

ever had. Life would be so much easier if she could just fall in love with Ruby. Well, as long as Ruby loved her back, which wasn't at all a sure thing. She wasn't exactly Ruby's type—she preferred blondes who played guitar, if her last three girlfriends were anything to go by. So, no, even Ruby couldn't be her happy-ever-after. Not in a romantic way, anyway.

But she was still the best friend ever.

'I need to get out of here,' Dawn said. 'I need to figure out what happened. What I do next. I don't want anyone to worry about me or anything but I can't stay here. I need to go find…closure.'

Ruby gave a sharp nod. 'Closure it is. Give me five minutes. And finish that bottle while you're waiting.'

CHAPTER TWO

THE PARTY WAS in full swing, the celebratory spirit apparently undimmed by the fact that there hadn't actually been a wedding for them to celebrate. Cooper stayed in the bar long enough to make sure that the venue had everything in hand, then grabbed a bottle of beer from behind the bar and headed out into the darkening evening to find some peace and quiet, his best man duties *done*.

The terrace at the front of the mansion was expansive, elegant and, most importantly to Cooper, empty. Apparently none of the other guests felt inclined to survey the view that Dawn had been *so* taken with that she'd had to book the venue on sight, despite the fact it was convenient for practically nobody. His mother, at least, had seemed pleased with her choice.

Cooper sighed, well aware that the day had turned his already bitter heart just a little more sour.

Even if the wedding *had* gone ahead, he doubted he'd have been in much of a mood to celebrate today. He'd given his prospective sister-in-law the benefit of the doubt when the save-the-date cards had come out—in fairness, it was unlikely that Justin would have mentioned that the date she'd chosen was the anniversary of Cooper's divorce. Chances were that his brother hadn't even realised or they'd have picked another day. But the fact remained that it was now officially three years since he'd disentangled himself from that messy web of lies and false love and, while his freedom probably *should* be something to be happy about, it seldom felt like it.

But at least his brother hadn't made the same mistake. That was something to celebrate. With a small smile, Cooper raised his beer bottle to the sky and silently toasted Justin's lucky escape.

Then he frowned, peering over the edge of the terrace at the sweeping driveway below. Out there, in the shadows of the swaying trees, he spotted a willowy figure. One in a very distinctive white lace dress.

'Where is she going now?' he murmured to himself as he watched Dawn trip over her train and reach out for the nearest tree to steady herself. Was she drunk?

And, more importantly, was she going after Justin?

Without thinking, Cooper put aside his beer bottle and sprung over the edge of the terrace, landing in a crouch on the packed ground. He strode across the driveway to where was parked the vintage robin's-egg-blue Cadillac convertible he'd hired for Justin to drive away in for his wedding night. It had been his own, personal present to his brother—something far more meaningful than a second toaster, or even the speech he'd written to give to the assembled crowd. The car was a memory that only he and Justin shared. A dream, or a promise, they still had to fulfil.

'When we're grown-ups, we'll be able to do whatever we want,' he remembered saying when Justin had been only seven to his ten. 'We'll get the coolest car ever—'

'A Cadillac?' Justin had interrupted.

'Yeah, a Caddy. And we'll drive it all the way across America together. Just you and me. It'll be the best adventure ever.'

They'd never done it, of course. Life had got in the way. But renting the car for Justin for this day, the start of the rest of his life, had felt like a reminder never to give up on his dreams, just because he'd been tied down by love, family and the business.

Except now he wasn't, of course. Justin had run and left him to clear up the mess.

Like a drunk woman in a wedding dress trying to break into his incredibly expensive hire car.

'Do you really think you're in any condition to drive that?' Cooper crossed his arms and leant against the far side of the car, glaring over to where Dawn was trying to unlock the driver's side door.

'Do you really think it's your place to try to stop me?' Dawn asked, eyebrows raised. She didn't *sound* drunk, but Cooper was hard pressed to think of another reason she'd be stealing his car.

Yeah, okay, so he was thinking of it as *his*. Since Justin clearly wouldn't be using it for his planned honeymoon road trip with Dawn, it seemed stupid not to make the most of the already paid-for rental. He could take it up the coast, maybe, for a couple of days, until he needed to be back in the office.

Once he'd evicted the woman in white who was trying to steal it.

'Since it's my name on the rental agreement, I think it's exactly my place.' Cooper was gratified to see that his statement at least gave her small pause. 'Where are you planning on taking it, anyway?'

'To find some answers,' Dawn said, her head held high. Her long, pale neck rose elegantly up from the white lace monstrosity of a dress to where her dark hair was curled and braided against the back of her head, tilting her chin up with its weight. She looked every inch the English aristocrat—rather than the low little gold-digger Cooper knew she was.

Her words caught up with him. 'Answers? You mean you're going to find Justin?'

Dawn slammed her hands against the unyielding metal of the car door. 'Of course I am! Did you even read the letter he left for me? Could he have been any more vague? So, yes! Yes, I'm going to go find him, and figure out what the hell happened so I can get my life back on track!'

As it happened, Cooper *had* read the letter—if only to be sure that his brother wasn't leaving things open for a blissful reunion with his gold-digging bride. Which meant… 'Except, of course, Justin didn't tell you where he was going. Don't you think you should take that as a hint that he didn't want you chasing after him?'

Dawn's eyes narrowed. 'No, he didn't tell me. But I'm willing to bet he told *you*. So, spill, Cooper. Where is your brother?'

Damn.

She didn't really expect him to tell her outright, but maybe she'd get lucky. Maybe there'd be a clue or something that would lead her to Justin.

Cooper's expression went blank, obviously trying to avoid giving anything away. Dawn sighed. Still, Justin couldn't have gone far, right? Not if he'd left those notes for Cooper and her that morning. Especially since their bags for the honeymoon, according to the carefully planned and laminated schedule for the day, should be in the boot of the very car she was trying to unlock. Stupid vintage cars and their stupid vintage locks. Why couldn't Cooper have hired them something with central locking, at the very least?

Wait. *Were* the bags in the car? She hadn't checked.

Ignoring Cooper's lack of reply to her question, Dawn

hurried around to the boot of the Caddy—trunk, she supposed, since it was an American car—and fiddled with the key Ruby had pinched from Cooper's bag for her until the boot popped open.

Empty.

The boot, trunk, whatever you wanted to call it, was empty.

'Where're my bags?' she asked in a whisper.

Cooper followed her round to stand beside her, and they stared at the lack of suitcases together. 'There should be bags?'

'Yes!' Dawn could feel the desperation leaking out in her voice. 'We packed all the bags for our honeymoon and put them in Justin's car yesterday.' They'd had a late lunch together back at Justin's hotel before Dawn had headed off to spend the night with her sisters at their hotel across town. Justin had been a staunch believer in the 'bad luck for the groom to see the bride before the wedding' thing and, quite honestly, Dawn hadn't wanted to tempt fate either. Which seemed doubly stupid now. 'He was supposed to transfer them to *this* car this morning. I figured he'd have at least left mine when he dropped off those bloody letters earlier.'

'He didn't.'

'Well, I can see that!' Dawn's voice was getting high and squeaky now, and she didn't even care.

'No, I mean he didn't bring the letters here. I found them both this morning—they'd been slipped under my hotel room door in one envelope, with my name on it. I thought they were the notes for my speech I'd asked my secretary to drop over and just shoved them in my jacket pocket. I only checked them once we realised that Justin still wasn't here…'

'So he never even came here this morning,' Dawn said

softly. 'So all my things…they're still in his car. Which is probably wherever he is.'

Her clothes. Her ridiculously expensive wedding-night lingerie. Her toiletries. Her honeymoon reading. Her *passport*. All she had with her here was a tiny clutch bag with some face powder, a dull nude lipstick she'd never wear in everyday life, a spare pair of stockings, her phone and her credit card, in case there was a problem with the open bar at the venue. Even last night she'd borrowed things from her sisters and had worn the 'Mrs Edwards' pyjamas they'd bought her—which she hoped they burned as soon as they got back to the hotel.

She had *nothing*. Not even a husband.

'I'm sure your family can—'

'No!' Dawn cut him off before he could even *suggest* she crawl back to her family, broken and in need of help. Again.

She'd done that too often in the past. This time, she needed to fix things herself.

Yes, she had nothing. Yes, this was basically the worst she'd ever felt in her whole life.

But that just meant that things could only get better from here on. Right?

At least, they would if she *made* them better. If she took charge of her life for once and stopped waiting for a happy-ever-after to save her.

'Okay, I need you to tell me where Justin is,' she said as calmly as reasonably as possible. 'He has my belongings. My passport was in his travel wallet with his, ready for our honeymoon. If he's not going to marry me, then I need to check out my visa, figure out what I do next, and in order to achieve that I need my stuff.' And she needed closure. She needed Justin to look her in the eye and tell her what had gone wrong. What had changed since lunch time yesterday that had made him run?

She needed him to tell her what was wrong with her so she could *fix* it and bloody well make her own happily ever after, with or without a man.

But, somehow, she suspected Cooper would react better to the more practical approach.

'Look,' she said when he hesitated. 'You want me out of your brother's life, right? I mean, that much has been obvious since you called to not congratulate us on our engagement.' *Are you sure about this?* was what he'd actually said. *Isn't it a bit fast?*

She had no idea where that instant dislike for her had come from, but Justin had told her he was like that with any girl he got serious about, so she was willing to bet it was more of a Cooper problem than a Dawn one.

'It's not what *I* want that matters,' Cooper said. He left the fact that Justin obviously wanted her out of his life unsaid, which was possibly the nicest thing he'd ever done for her.

'My point is, it's quite hard for me to, say, up and leave the country to start over somewhere else while Justin has my passport.' Never mind that she had no intention of leaving the States if she didn't have to, especially since it would involve her traipsing back to Britain and her parents with her tail between her legs. If Cooper needed to believe that she was on her way out of Justin's life to tell her where he was, then he could believe that.

He didn't need to know that her passport wasn't the only thing Dawn wanted from Justin. The answers she needed were none of his business.

Cooper sighed, his broad shoulders sinking slightly as he realised she wasn't going to give up. Dawn stood firm, staring him down, not giving him a second to rethink that realisation.

'Listen, Dawn, Justin said in his note that he needed to get away, he needed time to think. To refocus himself, he said. He needs to be away from *everyone* right now—family, friends and especially you. You need to give him that time.'

'Time to think,' Dawn echoed, a thought of her own crystallising in her brain.

'Exactly.' Cooper sounded relieved. He shouldn't. 'Why don't you spend some time with your family, while they're over here, try and relax too? I mean, this must have all been very stressful for you.' The disbelief was strong in his voice on that last point, but it didn't matter. He'd already told Dawn what she needed to know.

There was only one place Justin went when he needed to get away from everything and think. He'd told her on their third date at that hot new restaurant that served everything with kale.

She knew where she needed to go.

'I could do that,' she said agreeably. 'Or I could head over to your family's beach house in the Hamptons and find Justin.'

Cooper's eyes widened, just enough for her to know she'd guessed right.

'I think I know which I'd rather do, don't you?' Dawn smiled triumphantly and enjoyed seeing Cooper's face fall.

At least she'd come out on top *once* today.

'I didn't say he was at the beach house,' Cooper said as soon as he gathered his wits again. How could she possibly know that? He felt in his pocket to make sure the letter Justin had written him was still there. He wouldn't have put it past Dawn to have pickpocketed it from his jacket when they were investigating the trunk of the Caddy. She'd obviously already stolen the car keys from his bag, so thievery wasn't beyond her. Not to mention the millions of dollars she had hoped to take his brother for.

Dawn slammed the trunk closed. 'You didn't have to. I know my… I know Justin.'

For a moment there, Cooper almost thought he heard sadness in her voice as she failed to find a word to describe his brother in relation to her. He wasn't her husband, that was for sure. And she couldn't possibly still think of him as her fiancé, or even boyfriend, now, could she?

Except he had a very bad feeling that if Dawn went to the beach house to find him she'd go out of her way to convince Justin to be exactly that once again. That was what a gold-digger would do, right? She'd invested too much time and energy in Justin as a prospect to give up now. She'd probably even try and talk him into eloping to Vegas and making things official as soon as she had her passport back.

Her passport. She didn't have her passport. And she wasn't a US citizen or a permanent resident, so she would need it to fly across the country to the Hamptons where Justin was holed up.

He would have flown, Cooper realised. Anything else would have been crazy. Which meant he'd probably already be there, and Dawn's belongings were in some long-stay car park at the airport, locked in his car. Even if she had the keys, she'd have to hunt through several thousands of cars to find his. But that, he suspected, wouldn't stop Dawn from heading to New York State to find Justin.

'Even if he is at the beach house—and I'm not saying he is,' he added quickly, off Dawn's smug smile. 'Say he is there. How, exactly, are you planning on joining him, given that he has your passport?'

That wiped that smile off her face. But only for a moment.

Grinning widely, she held up the keys to the Caddy. 'I'll drive.'

Since she hadn't been able actually to open the door a few minutes ago, Cooper doubted that she was capable of driving forty-eight straight hours or so across the entire continental US, but the determined gleam in her eye still gave him pause.

'Really. You, all on your own. Across the whole of America. Alone.'

'If I have to,' Dawn said stubbornly. 'If that's the only way to get to Justin, yes.'

Yeah, this wasn't about her passport at all, was it? She wasn't setting off on this absurd road trip to get her stuff and hightail it back to Britain.

She was doing this to get Justin back. And he simply could not allow that.

'Give me the keys.' He held a hand out across the bonnet.

'No!'

'The car is hired in my name,' he said patiently. 'If I call and report it stolen, the cops will have caught up to you before you even get out of the state. Besides, how much have you had to drink?'

'Not much,' she mumbled, sounding less certain. 'Fine, then I'll hire another car.'

'With what proof of ID?'

'I'll take my dad's rental.' She was getting desperate now, he could tell. And that was bad. Desperate people did desperate things.

'No,' he said, making what might possibly be the worst

decision of his life. 'We'll take this car. Now, give me the keys.'

'We?' Dawn asked, dropping the keys into his open palm.

Cooper crossed to the driver's side and unlocked the car.

'We,' he confirmed. 'And I'm driving.'

CHAPTER THREE

DAWN WOKE UP as they drove through what she thought must be San Francisco.

They.

She and Cooper.

How the hell had that happened?

She kept her eyes closed, so Cooper wouldn't know she was awake, while she tried to figure it all out.

It might be Ruby's fault. These sorts of things—crazy, unpredictable, ridiculous things—usually were. If she hadn't forced that Prosecco on her then Dawn would have been clear-headed enough not to get into this position. Possibly. Okay, fine, but at least she'd have been able to open the car door the first time and drive *herself* away from her nightmare of a not-wedding.

Of course, if Cooper hadn't intervened, she wouldn't have known where she was going, and who knew how long it would have taken her to figure out that Justin had run off with her passport and suitcase?

Justin.

Of course. It was *Justin's* fault. All of it.

She felt a little better for deciding that, so risked opening her eyes.

'Sobered up yet?' Cooper asked without looking at her. 'There are some painkillers in the glove box.'

'I had, like, *two* glasses of Prosecco, Cooper.' Even if they hadn't actually been in a glass. And probably not as good as the champagne Mrs Edwards had ordered to go with the wedding breakfast her guests would be sitting down to eat around now. 'I wasn't drunk.' Was that the only reason he'd insisted on driving her? Because he thought she was too drunk to do it herself?

Cooper sighed. 'Well, there goes the only justification I could come up with for this crazy road trip.'

'What's crazy about it?' Shifting in her seat, Dawn tried to get comfortable and work out the kink in her neck from sleeping with her head against the window. How long had they been on the road, anyway? If the bright lights around them really were San Francisco, it must have been about an hour since they'd left the venue.

'Everything,' Cooper said flatly.

Dawn ignored him. Clearly he didn't understand about closure. He didn't understand her. And that was fine—why should he? In a day or so she'd have what she needed and he'd be out of her life for good. Right?

Wait. Frowning, Dawn tried to pull up a mental image of the map of the USA she'd had on her wall as a teenager, when she'd planned to escape the stifling perfection of her family and run away to her mother's homeland, the States, as soon as she was old enough.

She couldn't exactly remember *all* the particulars of the interstates and roads, but she did remember one crucial thing: America was big.

Really big.

And the Hamptons were right on the other side of it from where she'd planned to get married today.

She shuffled around in the leather passenger seat of the Caddy again, trying to get her skirt into something resembling a comfortable position. American cars might be bigger and arguably better than the rest, but *no* car was truly comfy when wearing several thousand dollars' worth of lace and silk. The voluminous skirt would have looked wonderful walking down the aisle, or dancing the first dance, but Dawn felt it was rather wasted being crammed into the front seat of what was clearly Cooper's dream car.

'How far exactly is it to the beach house, anyway?' she asked as nonchalantly as she could. However far it was, it was where she needed to go.

But she had a nagging feeling it might take a little longer than the day or so she'd imagined when she'd suggested driving there.

'About three thousand miles,' Cooper replied, equally casually. 'Give or take.'

'Three thousand miles.' Dawn swallowed. Hard.

'Give or take,' Cooper repeated. 'About forty-eight hours of solid driving, mostly along Interstate 80.'

'You've done this before?' That was good. If he'd driven this way before, then it was clearly doable and not quite as insane as it sounded in her head.

'Never,' Cooper said, and Dawn's spirits sank again. 'Justin and I always planned to do a coast-to-coast road trip one day, though. Had it all planned out and everything. We were going to do it over a couple of weeks one summer. Hire a vintage Caddy like this one, really make the most of it.'

And instead he was making the trip with her—his sister-in-law who wasn't. Dawn wanted to ask why he and Justin had never taken their trip, but the closed expression on Cooper's face stopped her.

Well, that, and the phrases 'a couple of weeks' and 'forty-eight hours of solid driving' echoing around her head.

'We're going to need to stop overnight, then,' she said.

'Over *several* nights,' Cooper corrected. 'Even if we split the driving, we'll both need to rest. Plus this car is a classic, vintage model. It's been refurbished, of course, but still. It's not exactly covered for non-stop cross-country travel.'

'How many days do you think it will take us?' Dawn asked, staring at the hard planes of his face, the set jaw. Two days ago, she'd never even met this man. Yesterday she'd realised he seriously disliked her. And now it looked as though they were going to be spending an awful lot of time together.

Maybe this wasn't the best idea she'd ever had.

Cooper shrugged, never taking his eyes off the road. 'Maybe four or five. If we really push it.'

And longer if they didn't. Possibly a lot longer if anything went wrong with the car.

Dawn tried to remember how much space she had left on her credit card. Motel rooms for a week were going to add up fast. Not to mention food, petrol and everything else. She forced herself to take deep breaths and stay calm. The last thing she needed was Cooper figuring out how much she was freaking out.

She just had to stick to the plan. Get to the Hamptons, get her stuff back and find the closure she needed to move on. After that, this whole trip would just be a memory—like a half-remembered, crazy dream.

One more breath, and she felt the calm settling over her again. That was better.

Then she looked down at the puddle of lace and silk she was sitting in and cursed Justin one more time for good measure.

'In that case, I'm really going to need to find some new clothes.'

* * *

'It's not too late to turn back, you know.' Cooper could tell she was getting cold feet. She was British—what did she know about great American road trips? Or how *long* they took? For some reason, tourists always seemed to underestimate the size of this country. And he could totally use that to his advantage now. 'I mean, we're only an hour or so out. It would be no big thing at all to turn round, head back to that lovely mansion you picked and get back to your regularly scheduled life. You can tell your family you just needed to get some space, so you went for a drive. No one's going to think anything's odd about that, not after the day you've had.'

Cooper did his best to sound sympathetic, rather than gleeful. He might have always wanted to do a big coast-to-coast road trip, but this wasn't exactly how he'd pictured it—even if the car was perfect. No, the best thing for everyone involved was for Dawn to give up now and go home.

'In fact, we're still going to be closer to the wedding venue than to the beach house for another....' he glanced down at the dashboard '—one thousand, four hundred and seventy miles. I mean, we haven't even crossed the bridge to Oakland yet. Perfect time to turn round.'

'No.' Just the one word, but Cooper could hear a world of stubbornness behind it.

'You know, I could call Justin and ask him to courier your passport and stuff to you,' he pointed out, entirely reasonably, in his opinion.

'Still no.'

Damn. He must have laid it on a bit thick. He'd been so sure she'd been about ready to back down from this crazy stunt. What was she really hoping to achieve? To prove to Justin how much she truly loved him so he'd forget that, until she drove across the country, he knew she'd only wanted to marry him for his money? Did she really think that would work?

Cooper sighed. The worst part was, she might be right. After all, if *he* wasn't afraid Justin might fall for the big romantic gesture, he wouldn't be turning onto Interstate 80 at the San Francisco-to-Oakland bridge right now.

The problem was that Justin had always been the romantic one—even if he'd been the only one to see through Rachel the one time Cooper had let down his walls long enough to fall in love. Justin still believed in love and happy-ever-afters in a way that Cooper never had—and certainly hadn't since he'd learned the hard way that the only thing other people wanted from him was his money and influence.

But Justin... Justin had always been easily swayed by a beautiful woman—just like their father. And Dawn was, Cooper could admit, objectively speaking a beautiful woman. With that dark hair and pale skin, not to mention those bright green eyes...

Of course, every woman looked beautiful on her wedding day. Which was no doubt the reason Dawn had decided to chase after Justin in her wedding dress and full make-up—to make maximum impact.

Cooper smiled to himself. At least he could be pretty certain that the dress and make-up would look rather less impressive in a week's time, when they finally reached the Hamptons and Justin. And, since he was the one who knew where they were going, he'd have to do his best to make sure that any new clothes she did manage to get her hands on wouldn't be half as alluring.

'You know, I've always wanted to take a proper road trip too.' Cooper glanced over and saw that Dawn had kicked off her shiny satin high heels and rested her feet against the dashboard. Her perfectly painted toenails peeked out from under the edge of her wedding dress, glossy red.

He looked away. 'Have you really?' As of five minutes ago, he'd bet.

'Absolutely,' Dawn said, nodding enthusiastically. 'And really, there just isn't enough of Britain to count as a *proper* road trip. You can drive the whole thing in a day or so. No, you have to come to the States for a real road trip experience like this.'

'And what constitutes a "real road trip experience" in your mind?' Cooper asked sceptically.

'Uh, well…snacks, obviously. And music. You need a soundtrack.' She looked dubiously at the ancient radio the Caddy boasted. Cooper suspected that if it picked up anything it would be radio waves beamed straight from the fifties, giving them a steady diet of Elvis and Buddy Holly. The car's engine and working parts had all been updated enough that he trusted the Caddy to make the distance he needed, but the interior and aesthetics were most definitely of its time—radio included.

'What else?' he pressed.

'Stopping to eat in diners—like, proper, authentic American ones, with pancakes and burgers and stuff.'

'Are you hungry, by any chance?' Cooper asked. 'Because that's the second food item on your essentials list so far. And you've only come up with three things.'

'Kooky roadside attractions!' Dawn shouted. 'That's what a road trip needs! I mean, that's what I've always imagined for my dream road trip.'

That she'd clearly come up with five minutes ago as a way of convincing him she was going through with this. Right. 'Roadside attractions,' he repeated dubiously.

'Yeah, you know—like the world's biggest ball of twine. That sort of thing.'

'The world's largest ball of twine is in Kansas,' Cooper replied automatically, and regretted it almost instantly. 'We're not going through Kansas.'

Dawn stared at him. He tried to pretend he hadn't noticed. 'How do you even know that?'

He shrugged. 'I know things.' Such as the world's largest ball of twine made by one person was in Minnesota, which they also weren't going through. But he wasn't telling her that.

'You like kooky roadside attractions too!' Dawn declared. 'Well, this is perfect, then. We can bond over them on our road trip.'

She sounded so pleased with herself for figuring out something about him that Cooper had to pour cold water on her optimism.

'Not much point in bonding though, really, is there?' he pointed out. 'Not when you'll be out of my life, and my brother's life, the moment you get your passport back. Right?'

Because that was the deal here. He wasn't helping her win Justin back. He was making sure she never even had the chance to try.

And, the sooner she accepted that, the better.

'Right.' Dawn dropped her feet from the dashboard and shoved them back into the stupid, uncomfortable wedding shoes her sister had insisted she buy.

For a moment there, she'd let herself get carried away with the trip. With the escape. Running away was so appealing right now…but she wasn't. She was running towards something.

Justin.

Not to win him back, exactly, whatever Cooper thought. But to figure out the truth.

She had to remember what she was in this for: closure. Not kooky roadside attractions.

Well, maybe one or two. They *did* have to take breaks, after all.

Speaking of which…

'Do you think we could stop somewhere soon?' she asked. 'Not to turn around or go back or anything. But you were right. I *am* hungry.'

Breakfast and mimosas had been hours and hours ago, and she hadn't been able to stomach lunch, when the ceremony was supposed to start at two. All she'd had since Justin's non-appearance was half a bottle of Prosecco, a couple of canapés and a breath mint—all courtesy of Ruby.

Cooper made an impatient noise in the back of his throat. 'We can stop when we get to Sacramento.'

'Sacramento?' Dawn didn't want to admit that she had no idea where that was but…she really had no idea where that was.

'It's only another hour or so from here,' Cooper told her.

Dawn wondered if her stomach might start to eat itself before then.

'So, you know this route pretty well, then?' she asked, more to distract herself from her growling stomach than anything else.

'It's mostly one road,' Cooper answered. 'Just follow the I-80 to New Jersey, and from there I'm practically home.'

'Right. You live in New York.' Too far to consider flying over to meet his brother's girlfriend in California, of course.

'When I'm in the country.' And too busy to bother anyway. Even if he worked for the same family company as Justin, somehow Cooper managed to make it more all-consuming.

What was it Justin had always said about his brother?

'He doesn't need love, he has work. It's basically the same thing for him.'

How sad that must be. Sure, Dawn was all for job satisfaction—that was what had brought her out to the States in the first place. Her company had needed someone to take over the marketing of one of their products on this side of the Atlantic, and they wanted someone who understood the true Britishness of it, as well as how to sell it to the locals. With her American mother and very British father, Dawn had been perfectly positioned for the job.

But a job wasn't a life. It was something to do in between the more meaningful parts—the parts of a life that involved other people. Relationships, family, friendships, love.

The part of her life that had used to be all about Justin until that afternoon.

Suddenly her job was looking a lot more appealing.

'So, what is it you love so much about your job?' she asked. Maybe she could learn something from Cooper. Such as how to forget all about the more painful aspects of her existence for a while.

'You mean apart from the money?' Cooper asked drily.

Dawn raised her eyebrows as she looked at him. 'Given it's your family business, I'm pretty sure you'd still have plenty of money even if you didn't work yourself half to death.' The Edwards family had made the rich list every year for the last hundred, after all.

'Who says I work myself that hard?'

'Your brother.'

A muscle jumped in his jaw at her statement, but he didn't respond.

'So I figure, if you're working that hard it has to be for more that money. So is it love of the job? The challenge of it all? Or...?' Another option occurred to her. One far more fitting to her own situation. 'Or is it an escape?'

Because that would explain it. But what was he trying to escape from?

'You know, it's funny. My brother never told me all that much about you at all. Whirlwind romance, was it?'

Dawn looked away at his obvious attempt to turn the questioning round on her. 'I wouldn't say "whirlwind".'

They'd been together over three months before Justin had proposed. That wasn't whirlwind, was it?

'And a short engagement too.' He glanced away from the road to raise an eyebrow at her.

'Well, my work secondment was almost over, and if I wanted to stay, well, we had to make some decisions quickly.'

'I'm sure. Of course, I know my mother was scandalised at having to try and plan a whole wedding in so short a time.'

'We were lucky her name opened a lot of doors when it came to finding a venue,' Dawn admitted.

'You mean her money.'

'Both, probably.' Of course, that had also meant that Mrs Edwards had had the first and final say on where they held the wedding, what it looked like and who they invited.

'Hmm.'

Dawn frowned. 'Is there something you're not asking me? I mean, something you want to know?' Because it felt very much like he was skirting around some accusation she couldn't quite grasp. 'Wait—did you think we *had* to get married? You know, for...old-fashioned reasons?' The kind of reason that would have had her father on Justin's doorstep demanding he marry his daughter now he'd ruined her.

'You mean, did I think you were pregnant? No.' Cooper's words were blunt, unemotional, but the image they brought up stung Dawn's heart all the same.

She'd imagined it, even if he hadn't. Her life with Justin. A family of her own. All of it.

And now it was never, ever going to happen.

Turning in her seat, Dawn stared out of the window at the lights and landscape rushing past. San Francisco Bay stretched out under them as they crossed the road bridge back to the mainland, on the interstate at last. The road that would take them all the way across the country. All the way to Justin and closure.

'You might as well try and sleep some more,' Cooper said suddenly. 'I'll stop in Sacramento so we can eat. Then it's your turn to drive.'

Her turn. Right.

'You're sure you don't just want me to drop you off somewhere so you can fly home?' she asked. 'I promise I'll look after the stupid car.'

But Cooper shook his head. 'No. We're in this together now.'

'Why?' Who in their right mind would want to take this trip with her?

'I have my reasons.' And obviously no interest in sharing them with her.

Dawn sighed and rested her head against the window again. If she needed to drive on the interstate, she really should try to sleep.

Besides, apparently she had plenty more days ahead of her to figure out exactly what Cooper was getting out of this crazy road trip.

CHAPTER FOUR

AT LEAST SHE didn't snore. Cooper supposed that he should be grateful for small mercies, given the current situation. The car was running fine, the interstate was as clear as it ever was and Dawn didn't snore. She did, however, sleep all the way to Sacramento, a full hour and a half's drive. Not that he was complaining. He was a long-time fan of his own company and rather less keen on hers.

As the road swung towards the north of Sacramento's centre, Cooper kept an eye out for any decent looking place to grab a coffee and maybe something to eat. He'd promised Dawn, after all, and besides, his own stomach had started to remind him that it was a long time since lunch—and there hadn't been much of that, anyway. He'd been saving himself for the wedding breakfast—not expecting to be on the road by the time everyone else sat down to eat it.

Spotting some familiar lit-up signs, he signalled to leave the interstate and pulled into a parking lot shortly after. The retail park wasn't huge, but it had both chain restaurants and stores. Since he hadn't exactly packed for this trip either, he could do with picking up a few things—and getting the hell out of the tux his mother had insisted he wear. Suits were one thing—Cooper could appreciate the value of a good suit. But bow ties were simply never going to be his style.

He glanced across at his companion and the wide lace skirts covering every inch of the passenger seat. At least he had to be more comfortable than she was. And that corset style top looked actually painful.

Yeah, they should stop and change. If nothing else, pulling up at a motel with a bride in a few hours' time was just going to look tacky.

'Dawn?' he said softly, then repeated it louder when she didn't stir. 'Dawn.'

Her eyes flickered open. 'Are we there?'

'We're in Sacramento,' he said, unsure if she was awake enough even to know where she was asking if they were. 'Come on. We can pick up some supplies and get something to eat before we carry on.'

She nodded, but her eyes were fluttering closed again. Cooper rolled his eyes and climbed out of the car, slamming the door loudly behind him.

That woke her up.

He locked up then took off towards the nearest store that looked as though it would stock everything they needed for the next few days. When he reached the door, he glanced back and saw Dawn struggling to catch him up, her wedding dress tangling around her legs and hampering her movements.

'Honeymoon over already, huh?' an older guy asked, stacking carts by the door.

Cooper ignored him. Yeah, they really needed to get some different clothes.

Inside, the harsh overhead lighting turned Dawn's lace dress almost a pale yellow, but they were still getting plenty of stares from the other shoppers.

'Let's split up,' he suggested. The whole bridal thing

was making him uncomfortable, and she wasn't even *his* bride. 'It'll be quicker.'

Dawn nodded her agreement. 'Fine. I saw signs for the bathrooms at the front of the store, so I can get out of this dress too.' She looked almost as happy as him at the prospect. 'Where shall I meet you?'

'The burger joint across the way?' Cooper had a sudden, unusual hankering for a proper burger and the place looked big enough that they should be able to seat them, even if it was busy. 'Whoever gets done first can get us a table.'

'Works for me,' Dawn said, shrugging as she headed off towards the women's clothes.

Cooper moved around the shop quickly and efficiently. Years of business travel—and the occasional lost suitcase—meant he knew exactly what he needed to survive a few nights on the road, and at least this time he didn't need to replace any of his suits. A couple of pairs of jeans, some tee shirts, a slightly thicker zip-up top, underwear, socks, sneakers and essential toiletries, and he was done. They might not be of his usual quality or brand, but they'd do for a few days. He headed to the tills to pay, then straight to the restroom to change, hoping they'd at least be clean.

He felt better just for being in casual clothes. With autumn still a few weeks off, it was definitely *far* too hot for a tuxedo in California. And if he had to take this stupid road trip, he at least wanted to be comfortable doing it.

Pushing open the door, he headed back out to the front of the store, planning to stash his discarded clothes and the rest of his new purchases in the car before heading across to check out the burger bar menu. But when he stepped out into the small corridor outside the restrooms, he found Dawn waiting for him—still in her wedding dress.

'Let me guess,' he said, drily. 'You neglected to pack

your wallet and now you need money from me.' How predictable. But Dawn wouldn't be the first woman to use him as her personal ATM, and as long as it meant that she couldn't worm her way into the family's finances longer term he was willing to live with it. Especially as even he knew that wedding dresses didn't have pockets.

But Dawn blinked at him with confusion, then held up a bag of clearly already paid-for shopping. 'I had my credit card in my clutch bag. I just can't undo this dress on my own.'

Oh. *Oh.* 'You need my help.'

'Please.' She looked pained just to have to ask him, but she turned and presented her back to him all the same. 'If you could just loosen the corset ties enough, I should be able to wriggle out of it myself.'

As she spoke, the doors to the main store opened again and two large men walked through, their curious eyes fixing instantly on Dawn and her wedding dress.

Cooper scanned the doors leading off the small corridor. He was *not* undressing a woman in public, with an audience to boot.

'In here,' he said, giving her a gentle push towards the baby-change room and hoping it wasn't already occupied by a squalling infant with a dirty diaper.

Fortunately, it was free. Cooper locked the door behind them before addressing the issue of Dawn's gown.

'How did you even get into this thing?' he asked as he fumbled with the corset laces at the back of the dress.

'I had help,' she said drily. 'Lots of help.'

'Your bridesmaids?' How could a dress possibly be as complicated as this? There must be a better way of getting her out of it. What if he pulled on that end of the lace? Would that make it better or—?

'Ow!' Dawn cried as the dress tightened around her middle.

Right. Worse.

'Yes, my bridesmaids,' she went on as Cooper quickly went back to loosening the laces the slow and boring way. 'My four sisters, all of whom had their own wedding day experiences to draw on to tell me *exactly* how I was supposed to do things.'

She didn't sound particularly pleased about that, Cooper noticed.

Finally, the last of the laces gave way and the wedding dress parted at the top, leaving the long, graceful curve of Dawn's back uncovered. No bra with the strapless dress, he realised. Cooper found himself staring at the expanse of bare skin, his fingers still gripping the edges of the dress, wondering if she was wearing anything at all under the wedding gown...

Dawn glanced back over her shoulder at him, her green eyes wide and innocent as she held the top of the dress tight against her chest.

Cooper blinked and stumbled back. What was he doing?

'Right, you're out,' he said, reversing towards the door at speed. 'I'll, uh, wait for you outside.'

'Thanks.' Dawn gave him a grateful smile—one without any hint of come-on or desire in it—and he cursed himself again for his most inappropriate thoughts. 'But why don't I meet you over at the restaurant like we planned? This might take me a few minutes.'

'Right. Stick to the plan.' Cooper unlocked the door and slipped through it without opening it too far, to try and preserve Dawn's modesty.

Then, once he heard her lock it again from the inside, he strode away as fast as he could towards the burger bar across the parking lot. It was Dawn's turn to drive next. Maybe a beer would help him erase the image of his brother's fiancée's skin and the unexpected urge he'd felt to touch it.

Dawn let out a long breath as she locked the baby-change room door and heard Cooper's footsteps rushing away. For a moment there, she'd seen something in his eyes she couldn't quite identify but, whatever it was, it had caused him to tense up completely.

She sighed. They had a long way to go on this road trip. She couldn't afford awkwardness between them.

Still, getting out of the damn wedding dress would help. It wasn't even as if the lace and silk concoction was one *she'd* chosen. Her gown had been picked by committee—the only dress out of the hundreds she'd tried on that she, her mother, Justin's mother and all her sisters could agree on.

And now it was just another reminder of this most terrible day.

Dropping the dress from where she held it against her bare breasts, Dawn shoved the fabric down over her hips and stepped out of it, suddenly feeling free again. With a smile, she dressed quickly in the new underwear, denim skirt and pink tee shirt she'd bought—cheap, cheerful and easy to wash and wear again. She'd picked up a pair of white sneakers too, along with extra undies, a couple of other thin tee shirts and a sweater for if the evenings grew cooler. None of it had cost much individually, but all together it made her even more nervous about the price of motel rooms on the road and the remaining credit left on her card.

Next, she pulled out the pack of cleansing wipes she'd bought and set about removing every trace of the make-up her sister Beatrice had carefully applied that morning.

Normally, Dawn wouldn't have expected it to last so long but, given the trowel Bea appeared to have applied it with, maybe she wasn't so surprised.

'You want it to stay in place all through the photos, Dawnie. Just leave this to me.'

Finally, after removing forty-eight hair grips—Dawn had counted—she pulled out the new hairbrush from the bag and began brushing out the artful curls and braids her other sister, Jennifer, had insisted on. Then she tied it back into a simple ponytail to keep it out of her way, finally feeling like herself again.

She shoved everything else back into the bag her purchases had come in—all except the wedding dress, which was too huge and unwieldy to fit. She'd have to lug it over to the restaurant as it was.

Unless she didn't.

Dawn eyed the rubbish bin in the corner of the room. It was obviously designed for nappies and other baby-related rubbish, but it was larger than she'd have expected. Maybe even large enough for a ridiculous quantity of silk and lace.

She hesitated, biting down on her lip as she held the wedding gown against her. She shouldn't. It was a horrendous waste of money and craftsmanship, and even sentiment.

But, on the other hand, the dress was a stark reminder that *nothing* about her wedding day had gone to plan. From the preparations being railroaded by her family and Justin's mother, to Justin not actually *showing up*, why on earth would she want to keep the dress as a reminder of the day she *hadn't* got married?

So, she shouldn't. But she was going to.

Biting back a gleeful grin, Dawn crammed her wedding dress into the bin and pressed the lid down on top. Then, feeling a hundred pounds lighter, she grabbed her shopping bag and unlocked the door, striding out to begin her life over again.

Starting with dinner with her non-brother-in-law, and ending when she finally looked Justin in the eye and understood why he'd jilted her at the altar.

After that? All bets were off.

Cooper had secured a table near the window, so he could watch for Dawn crossing the parking lot to join him, but in the end she still took him by surprise.

As a petite, fresh-faced young woman slid into the booth seat opposite him, her dark ponytail bobbing cheerfully, he opened his mouth to tell her that he was waiting for someone—before he realised it was Dawn.

He snapped his jaw closed again and stared.

'What looks good here?' Dawn asked, her attention already on the menu, rather than him.

But Cooper's gaze was fixed on her unfamiliar face.

When he'd first seen her, dressed in a tailored dress that showed off her figure, and a matching jacket that he knew his mother would approve of, he'd known her type instantly. The glossy, carefully waved hair, the perfect make-up, the nude heels… She was the sort of woman he'd dated for years, the sort of woman he'd *married,* come to that. She'd even looked a little like Rachel, now he thought about it.

Maybe that was why he'd been suspicious of her from the start.

But now, with her face scrubbed clean until her cheeks shone pink, her hair pulled back from her face and wearing a short denim skirt, pale pink tee and sneakers…she looked like a different person.

One far too young to be marrying his brother. Or conning him out of his fortune, for that matter.

Which was probably why she'd got as far as she had, of course. Justin wasn't an idiot. He'd have spotted a gold-digger a mile off if she'd been obvious about it.

Suddenly, his brother's last-minute revelation and flight made more sense to Cooper.

'Do you have your UK driver's licence with you?' he asked, ignoring her question about the food.

Dawn frowned at him over the top of the menu. 'Actually, yes. I keep it in my phone case. Why?'

'Because I'm not sure you look old enough to drive in that outfit, and if we get pulled over I want to know how much trouble we're in.'

Her face cleared at his words and she laughed—high, bright and far happier than he'd expect from a woman who'd just been jilted by the love of her life.

'That's why I have it,' she admitted. 'I've been ID'd so often in bars since I arrived in this country, and I couldn't face being turned away from the bar at my own wedding.'

'How old are you, anyway?' he asked, suddenly curious. He knew so little about this woman who had almost been his sister-in-law. And, looking at her now, he wondered how much of the stuff he *did* know was an act, an attempt to be the sort of bride Justin would expect.

'Twenty-eight,' she said promptly. 'And, yes, I know, I look younger. I'm actually the third-eldest of my sisters.'

'How many of you are there?' He had a vague image of a gaggle of women all wearing the same pink brides-maid dresses, but he hadn't actually stopped long enough to count them.

'Five, including me.'

'So you're right in the middle.'

'That's right.' Dawn's smile was too tight, which made him question what part of this conversation she felt un-comfortable about. Her entire family had flown out for the wedding, so she couldn't be embarrassed by them. Could she?

'You don't get on with your sisters?' he asked, probing the obvious wound. If he was stuck travelling with Dawn for the next handful of days he might as well use the time wisely, learning as much about her as possible, to help keep Justin safe from any attempts on her part to win him back.

'Oh, no. I love my sisters.' Dawn didn't sound entirely convinced by her own words.

'But?'

She gave him a weak smile. 'You know siblings. They always think they know what's best for you.'

'Most of the time, I've found that they do.' He thought back to Justin's comments about Rachel the week before Cooper had married her.

Are you sure it's the real thing, Coop? That she's in love with you, not just the idea of being part of the Edwards legacy?

And here he was, playing exactly the same part for Justin. He just hoped he could do a better job of it. That Justin would believe him, even though Cooper hadn't believed his brother last time.

That still rankled, he knew. Cooper's lack of faith in Justin had caused a gulf between them that neither brother seemed to know how to cross. But maybe now, having lived the same experience, they would find their way back to each other again. Cooper hoped so.

He'd never blamed Justin for what had happened with Rachel, only himself. The same way he'd never blamed his mother for introducing him to Melanie and asking him to mentor her as she learned the ropes of the company.

His mother couldn't have known that wasn't all her beautiful young friend was hoping to learn, and Cooper had been so inexperienced and keen to show off his place in the company that it hadn't even occurred to him that Melanie might have ulterior motives. That she was less interested in *him* than his knowledge of company secrets. Or that she'd use everything he showed her and take it back to her boyfriend's rival company—leaving Cooper to deal with his furious father and desperately trying to rebuild trust with the board.

Which only made the whole situation with Rachel more galling. Having been taken in once, he'd thought he was too cynical, too knowing, to fall for the same tricks again. Until Rachel had swept into his life, blinding him with her polish and beauty. Suddenly he was spending his fortune on keeping her in jewellery and designer clothes, on being seen in the right places and with the right people. And Justin was the only one who'd called him on it.

Time to return the favour.

'Come on,' he said, lifting the menu again and studying it. 'We need to get a move on if we're going to make it to Reno before we stop for the night.'

The sooner they made it across the country, the sooner he could help Justin extricate himself from his gold-digger fiancée—for good.

CHAPTER FIVE

DAWN HADN'T DRIVEN much since her arrival in America—but she was damned if she was going to let Cooper know that. This was *her* road trip he was gate-crashing, so *of course* she was going to drive most of it. On the right side of the road and everything. She just needed Cooper to add her to the insurance first. One quick phone call and she was good to go.

At least, now she was no longer weighed down by her wedding dress, driving wasn't the impossibility it would have been before. So all she had to do was figure out the controls and dashboard of the vintage Cadillac and try not to crash into anything between Sacramento and Reno. How hard could that be?

Cooper gave her a quick primer on the car as she started the engine, and she nodded as if it all made perfect sense. She'd figure it out once she got on the road, she was sure.

'And I just stick on the I-80?' she asked, wanting confirmation of the route in case he fell asleep while she drove. It seemed kind of ridiculous that one road could take them all the way across the country, but Cooper nodded.

'Until we hit New Jersey later in the week, pretty much. Although we'll probably want to turn off into Reno to find somewhere to stay tonight.'

'Right, then.' The car jerked into motion, juddering out

of the parking space Cooper had chosen. Dawn was glad she didn't have to reverse the ridiculously long car just yet. Getting it to go forward was tricky enough.

'You'll get used to it,' Cooper told her, stretching out his legs as best as he could in the passenger seat, his arms folded across his broad chest. He might look less formal in jeans and a tee shirt, but somehow Dawn couldn't help but feel he was no less intimidating. 'Just need to gentle her along.'

His eyes fell closed as the car jumped forward again. He couldn't really be planning to sleep, could he?

He'd been quiet over dinner, barely even contributing to the conversation after his questions about her sisters. She'd kept up a constant chatter to start with, uncomfortable with his silence, but there were only so many observations she could make about the restaurant, the menu and the food before she ran out of things to say.

At least, things that weren't to do with her abysmal love life, or questions about Cooper's own life that she knew without asking he would never answer.

Justin, she remembered, had told her everything there was to know about himself on their first date. Everything he thought mattered, anyway. He was an open book, he'd said, and she'd loved reading him. Loved learning all his quirks and ticks. What he liked, what he didn't. How he felt—about the world, about his life, about her.

She remembered the first party he'd taken her to as his date—one held at a business partner's property down in southern California. She'd felt so out of place in her usual party dress, which suddenly seemed a little drab and simple next to the designer outfits of the other women present. And then she'd managed to put her foot in it hugely when a stranger had asked how she liked the wine and she admitted it was a little sharp for her—only to learn that the man asking was, in fact, the vintner. By the end of the night she'd been miserable and desperate to go home, sure that Justin had to be regretting ever inviting her. But Justin had simply smiled, kissed her and told her that she'd know what not to do next time. Then, the next day, he'd made her an appointment at a dress shop in town so she could buy something more appropriate to wear for the party he wanted her to join him at that weekend.

It had just been so easy to fall into sync with him because he didn't hide anything away. His expectations, feelings and opinions were always on show. Dawn had never had to guess with Justin.

But he'd never talked much about his brother. Which was a shame, because she couldn't help but feel that understanding Cooper better would make the next few days go a lot smoother. Even though Justin had spoken at length about his childhood, his parents and his friends, Cooper had hardly ever even come up in conversation. Why had she never noticed that before?

She let her gaze drift over to the elder Edwards brother, still prone in the passenger seat, taking in the parts of him that felt familiar. His nose was ruler-straight, just like Justin's, and his dark hair the same colour. But there were so many differences, too: Cooper was taller, broader and his jawline much harder. But with his eyes closed she couldn't see the biggest difference between the brothers—the dark, harsh, bitterness she always saw in Cooper's eyes.

What had caused that? And, whatever it was, did it explain why he'd agreed to drive across the country with her to find Justin?

What did he think she was going to do when she got there that she needed a chaperone?

Shaking her head, Dawn frowned down at the steering wheel, took a deep breath and prepared to try again. Really, this was no different from when her father had taught her to drive over ten years ago. She just needed to practise. Practice, her mother had always told her, made perfect.

Which didn't explain why, after all her practice at relationships, another man had walked off and left her. Again.

But she wasn't thinking about that. She was thinking about the open road and the future.

'Are you planning on leaving the parking lot at any time tonight?' Cooper asked without opening his eyes.

Setting her jaw, Dawn pressed down the accelerator and began to drive.

Her future was waiting, after all.

'Cooper? I'm guessing this is Reno?'

Dawn's words jerked him awake—which was the first sign that he'd fallen asleep in the first place. He hadn't expected to, given the way the car had been lurching around as Dawn got used to driving it, but apparently she must be a fast learner, because he didn't remember much of anything after they'd left Sacramento.

He opened his eyes in time to see the Reno arch lit up almost overhead, announcing that they had arrived at 'the biggest little city in the world'.

'You wanted to stop here tonight, right?' Dawn asked, glancing away from the road for a second to look at him. Then her gaze was fixed back on the traffic in front of them, her hands, pale in the light from the illuminations overhead, gripping the steering wheel tightly. If she'd been doing that for the full two hours since he'd fallen asleep, they must be aching by now. No wonder she was ready to stop for the night.

'Yeah,' he said, peering out of the window at the lit-up hotel and casino signs they passed. She must have pulled off the interstate and into the city while he was still asleep—another sign that she really needed to stop driving. He'd intended to spend some of the drive on his phone, finding them a hotel for the night, but since they were already here they might as well go and knock on reception desks until they found somewhere suitable. 'We'll find somewhere safe to park this thing, then hunt down a couple of rooms for the night.' The last thing he needed was someone stealing their hired Caddy before they'd even got any further than Nevada.

He'd never spent much time in Reno before, and he didn't intend to spend much time here now. Neither he nor Dawn were there for the gambling or the entertainment—it was just another stop on a journey he hadn't fully intended to make. They'd find a hotel, get some sleep and be on the road again first thing. But as he strode along the lively streets—lit up with music, illuminated signs and chatter—Cooper realised that Dawn was no longer beside him.

'Dawn?' He spun round, trying to spot her in the crowds. It was nearly eleven at night, but the streets of Reno were still packed with people. Had she given him the slip? Cooper swore as he realised that she was still in possession of the keys to the Caddy. She could be racing off towards Justin, alone, right now. Maybe she'd been faking her tiredness, her need to stop for the night, just to lull him into a false sense of security so she could ditch him.

'Sorry!' Dawn popped up beside him, his racing heart jumping at her sudden re-appearance. 'I got distracted by one of the bars—they had a band playing and, well, I'm a sucker for live music. It's been forever since I saw a band live! Justin was never really interested. Sorry again,' she added, frowning at him as he realised he hadn't responded.

He'd been so sure she had gone.

Why *hadn't* she gone?

Cooper would have done. Why risk being tied down to

him, the one person who could reasonably be expected to stop her from convincing Justin that she loved him and that they should still get married, when she had a chance to go it alone?

'Cooper?' Dawn's frown deepened. She reached out and touched his hand, and the feel of her fingers against his skin jerked him out of his reverie.

'I think I saw a suitable hotel down this way,' he said, waving vaguely in the direction of a side street. 'You should stick close.'

'Right. Will do.' Dawn gave him a sharp nod and stayed right by his side as he led her towards the lights of what thankfully turned out to be a halfway decent hotel. Even better, it had two free rooms left, right next to each other, and Cooper took them without even checking with Dawn, handing over his credit card happily as the slot machines of the casino downstairs rang out merrily, signalling that someone had just won big.

What did it matter if the hotel wasn't as luxurious as he'd normally expect—or as she had obviously hoped to grow accustomed to by marrying Justin? They'd be on their way first thing anyway.

He handed Dawn her key card and she bit down on her lower lip as she took it.

'I can pay for my own room, you know,' she said. 'I'm not expecting you to foot the bill for this whole road trip or anything.'

Ah. So *that* was how she was going to play it. Suddenly, it all made sense.

Dawn was going to use this trip together to get him on her side. To convince him that she truly did love Justin, not just his money. Starting by offering to pay her own way.

It was a decent plan, he had to admit. If Justin hadn't

already told Cooper about her gold-digging ways, maybe he'd even have fallen for it.

Although, given his history with Rachel, probably not. Even she'd gone Dutch on dinner at the start—but it had only lasted until he'd fallen for her and started insisting on paying for everything out of love. She'd stopped offering after that—and from there it had been only a small step to demanding presents to prove his love.

The fact Dawn thought she could manipulate him like that, the way Rachel had, made his shoulders tense.

'You can pay tomorrow night,' he said coldly as he turned and headed for the lifts. 'I'll see you back here at eight-thirty. Sharp.'

And with that he left her alone in the lobby with her bag, even though her room would be right next to his. He didn't want her getting the wrong idea about this trip, after all.

The last thing he wanted was Dawn thinking that the two of them could become *friends*.

This was *not* how Dawn had expected to be spending her wedding night.

Letting the hotel room door swing shut behind her, Dawn leant against it and surveyed the small double bed, the tiny fridge in the corner and the TV on the wall. The window looking out over the street was ajar and she could hear the noise and laughter of downtown Reno filtering up through it.

Not exactly the four-poster bed in the luxury boutique hotel on the Californian coast that she'd booked for her and Justin's first night as man and wife.

Dropping her carrier bag of meagre belongings on the floor, she pulled her phone out of her pocket and stared at the screen. No missed calls. No messages. No voicemails.

No word from Justin at all, except that infernal note he'd left her.

Dawn tossed the phone onto the bed and sank down to the floor, wrapping her arms around her knees. She was exhausted, but she knew she wouldn't sleep, even if the hotel bed wasn't as uncomfortable and the blankets as scratchy as they looked.

What was she doing? Racing across the country to try and find something to make herself feel better? To restore her broken confidence?

After picking herself up and starting again so many times before, when was she going to accept that this just wasn't the life she was supposed to lead? She should have known better than even to try again after the last time, and the time before that.

And *Justin*. Gorgeous, rich, successful, *happy* Justin. How could she have imagined for a second that he could really stay that happy spending the rest of his life with her?

She'd tried so hard to fit in with his lifestyle, to be the sort of woman he'd be proud to have on his arm. She'd filled her wardrobe with those neat but expensive shift dresses he liked her in and binned all her old jeans, especially the ones with the holes in the knees. She'd stopped scraping her hair back and started spending time actually styling it in the mornings, wearing more make-up than a brush of powder and some lip balm when she remembered, or brightly coloured lipsticks when she wanted to make an impact.

She'd favoured neutrals over colours, even though they made her feel washed out and bland, because he'd told her that his mother believed that bright colours on a woman looked trashy. She'd read up on things he was interested in and learned to understand the markets and investments well enough to follow conversations at dinners in fancy restaurants. Hell, she'd even gone skiing with him and his friends, running up her credit-card balance even more to buy all the required equipment for the week, despite the fact that she hated the cold and had never skied before.

She'd given him her all. And it hadn't been enough.

She wasn't enough.

Sighing, Dawn pushed herself up off the floor and rummaged in the carrier bag for the new toothbrush and toothpaste she'd bought when they'd stopped. She hadn't wanted to waste any of her remaining dollars on non-essentials, so there wasn't much else in the bag, but at least she'd thought to pick up a cheap charger for her phone.

Now, when Justin didn't call, she'd know it was because he didn't want to speak to her and not because she'd run out of battery. *Yay.*

Okay, she wasn't going to think about him any more. Not tonight, anyway. She was going to wash, get changed and get into bed. She needed her sleep if Cooper wanted her to drive again the next morning.

Of course, as soon as she'd finished cleaning her teeth and stripped off her skirt and tee shirt, she realised the thing she'd forgotten to buy at the shop.

Pyjamas.

'Damn it.' Frustration taking over, she threw her bag towards the bed, missing and sending the bedside lamp crashing to the floor as the ceramic base smashed. The light fizzed and went out, and she stared at it in the semi-darkness, the room only lit now by the illuminated signs outside her window.

Her anger drained away. She'd have to pay for that. Literally. With money she barely had.

This whole thing was a mistake.

'Dawn?' The banging on the door accompanying her

name snapped her out of her reverie. 'Are you okay in there?'

Cooper. Of course—his room was right next door. God only knew what he thought she was doing in there.

'Fine!' she called back, kneeling to gather the pieces of the lamp. 'Sorry, just knocked something over. Nothing to worry about!' Her voice was too high, too desperate, and he obviously heard it.

'Open the door, Dawn,' he said after a moment.

Sighing, she pulled on her pink tee shirt again, hoping it was long enough to cover at least the top of her legs. She might not know Cooper well yet, but she knew enough to be certain he wasn't going away until she opened the door.

'I broke the lamp, that's all,' she said, pulling the door wide to show him. He hadn't changed yet, she noticed, so was still wearing his jeans and tee shirt, making her feel woefully underdressed. 'I'll pay for it myself when we check out.'

She watched as his gaze took in the darkened room, the lopsided lampshade then, very briefly, her bare legs. Clearing his throat, he stared at her face instead.

'You're not hurt?' he asked.

She shook her head. 'Just been a very long day.'

Cooper gave a short nod. 'Get some sleep. I'll see you in the morning.'

And he was gone, leaving Dawn alone with her broken lamp and her imaginings of what might have been if Justin had only showed up that afternoon.

CHAPTER SIX

SOMEHOW, COOPER FELT more tired the next morning than he had when he'd fallen into the lumpy hotel bed the night before. Ideal for a long day of driving, really.

He'd like to blame the poor-quality mattress, or the noise from the casino below, or even the tiny bottle of rum he'd liberated from the mini-bar before he'd fallen into bed. But, if he was honest with himself, he knew *exactly* what had kept him awake the night before.

Dawn Featherington.

Not the woman herself, of course—there'd been no sound from her room after the almighty crash that had had him worrying she'd thrown herself though the window without opening it. His heart had raced as he'd stormed out of his room and into hers, only to find her pink-cheeked and embarrassed but unhurt. At least, physically.

She hadn't been able to hide the tear tracks on her cheeks, though, or the redness around her eyes. Her long, bare legs might have distracted him for a second—really, who wouldn't have been distracted by those?—but mostly he'd seen her distress, even in the poorly lit room.

And he knew, absolutely, that it had nothing to do with a broken lamp.

Ever since he'd read Justin's note, he'd been assuming that Dawn was just like Rachel. His ex-wife had set the bar for unfeeling, manipulative gold-diggers, but after seeing Dawn last night he was sure there was something more to this story.

Maybe it was just the frustration of seeing all her efforts come to nothing when Justin hadn't shown up for the wedding. But Cooper couldn't help but feel he was missing something about her. *Could* she really have loved him?

Groaning, Cooper rolled out of bed and prepared to meet Dawn down in the lobby. At least he had another few days on the road to figure out what he was going to do when they finally caught up with Justin.

A shower and a change of clothes helped him feel a lot more human, and seeing Dawn waiting for him by the reception desk, looking through leaflets for local attractions, relaxed him a little too. He hadn't really expected her to run off on her own this time, but there was always the chance. He didn't want her going after Justin alone. Not until he was sure about her motives.

She was wearing the same skirt she'd bought yesterday with a bright, sunny yellow tee shirt this time—one that didn't look as if it would cover *any* of her legs. Not that he was thinking about her legs. Much.

Engaged to your brother, Coop, he reminded himself. *Also probably after the family money. Forget the legs.*

'Ready to go?' he asked, lifting his own bag as she turned around. 'We can grab breakfast on the road.'

She nodded, shoving a couple of leaflets into her plastic bag as she picked it up.

'I spoke with Reception about the lamp,' she said as they stepped out into the sunlight. 'Gave them my credit card details.'

'They probably have breakages like that all the time. I wouldn't worry.' Although she clearly was, for some reason. Some reason he suspected that was bigger than just a broken lamp.

And it was up to him to figure out what it was. To understand this woman before they reached the Hamptons.

Good job he had plenty of time and an enclosed space to do it in, otherwise he'd have been screwed. Understanding people, and their motives, had never been his strong suit. As evidenced by his marriage, if nothing else.

They stopped at a coffee shop to grab to-go cups and doughnuts before heading back to the car.

'It's going to be a hot one today.' Dawn stared up at the bright blue sky as he opened the door. 'Shame the Caddy was built before air-conditioning became an automatic add-on.'

'The Caddy is a *classic*,' Cooper said, instantly defensive. 'Besides, it's a convertible. No need for air-con. Not when you have the wind in your hair.'

'And bugs in your teeth,' Dawn muttered.

Cooper ignored her. *Clearly* this Brit couldn't understand classic American design.

He took the first shift behind the wheel, wishing that the car had cup holders, instead of him needing to hold his coffee between his thighs. Not that he'd mention that disappointment to Dawn, of course. She had too little respect for the car as it was.

'You should name her,' Dawn said as he pulled back onto the interstate minutes later.

'Name who?' he asked, not taking his eyes off the road.

'The car. Since you love her so.' There was a forced sort of jolliness to her voice, and Cooper wondered if she was trying to put the previous night behind her.

'I don't name cars,' he said flatly.

'Well, maybe you could start.'

They drove in silence for a while, the only noise the

rustle of the doughnut bag. Until, just as he finished the last of his coffee, Dawn spoke again.

'Cassandra,' she said. 'Cassie for short.'

'You're actually naming the car.'

'Well, you weren't going to.'

'Not Cassie.' That wasn't…regal enough for a car like this.

'Calliope.'

'No.'

'Carly?'

'Definitely not.' She glanced over as he shuddered at the suggestion. 'High school ex-girlfriend,' he explained.

'Ah. Not Carly, then.'

She was quiet for so long that he thought she might have actually given up on the idea.

Until she said, 'Claudia.'

Cooper considered. Then, against his better judgement, he smiled.

'Claudia it is.'

A new day. A new start. A new Dawn, even.

That was what Dawn had been telling herself since she'd woken up. It was no longer her wedding day. Which meant that the rest of her life started now.

Even if she was going to spend almost the first week of it on a road trip with her almost-husband's brother.

She'd picked her sunniest yellow tee shirt, plucked up all her courage to speak to the reception staff about the broken lamp and accepted that breakfast was going to comprise mainly of sugar and caffeine. Hell, she'd even persuaded Cooper to lighten up enough to name the car.

Claudia was an *excellent* name, although she still maintained there was nothing wrong with Cassandra, either.

The only problem was, that kind of cheeriness took effort. It meant constantly distracting herself from everything she'd lost.

And Cooper wasn't helping with that.

She tried to start all sorts of diverting conversations—about cities he'd travelled to, his work, his family—but got nowhere. Somehow, Cooper managed to answer even the most open-ended of questions with a definitive yes, no or sometimes just a grunt. What was it with this man and small talk?

She even reached for the radio once or twice, but Cooper's glare put her off the idea. Apparently he *really* wasn't a morning person.

Justin hadn't been either, so maybe it was a family thing. Whenever they'd gone away together, he'd objected to her getting up at the break of dawn, ready to explore. In his mind, weekends and holidays were for sleeping late, then staying out later that night. Dawn, on the other hand, hated wasting so much of the day. Still, since they hadn't lived together, and Justin didn't like week-night sleepovers, it wasn't as if it had been a problem every day. Dawn had managed to adjust to his schedule, more or less, whenever they'd stayed out of town together. And, when she couldn't, she'd just used her quiet, alone morning time to read up on fun places they could go and explore when Justin *did* get up. Or if she ever came back alone, if he had other plans for the day.

She frowned to herself at the memory. Why had they always had to do what *Justin* wanted, anyway?

Maybe it was time to start demanding she get to do what *she* wanted for a change. Starting with this road trip.

'So, where shall we stop next?' she asked Cooper, after they'd been on the road for a couple of hours. Sugar for breakfast really wasn't her thing, and she was aching for some savoury food, even if lunchtime realistically was still more than an hour away.

But Cooper just shrugged, forgoing anything even approaching an answer this time.

'I thought you had this route all mapped out.' Dawn reached under her seat for the road atlas she'd found the day before. It was old, but she could always double-check the details with the travel app on her phone.

'I wasn't exactly planning on taking this trip, remember?' Cooper said, not even glancing her way.

'Well, neither was I, buddy,' Dawn grumbled under her breath. 'You can thank your brother for that one.'

That did earn her a look, but one she couldn't quite read.

'I guess I just figured you'd done all the planning for when you meant to take the road trip with Justin,' she said. Although, if he hadn't, that meant she could start choosing some of their stops. She could insist they went where *she* wanted to stop. It was strangely liberating.

Then she frowned again, as another question occurred to her. 'Why *didn't* you take that road trip?'

'I got married that summer instead.' Cooper's words were even, unemotional, but Dawn could tell there was a whole big, messy story behind them. One that would definitely distract her from thinking about Justin—if she could get him to tell it.

'I didn't know you'd ever been married.' In fact, it was hard to imagine Cooper stopping glowering long enough for anyone to fall in love with him, but she didn't mention that.

'It didn't take,' he said flatly. But Dawn saw the way he glanced down at his left hand, as if he were still expecting to see a wedding band there.

'Justin never said.' Which was strange, although not unimaginable. Justin had always shied away from the subject of Cooper. Maybe this was why. 'Can I ask what happened?'

'No.'

'Right.' Of course not. 'I just thought—'

Cooper interrupted her with an exasperated sigh. 'Would you like to spend the next thousand miles or so discussing possible reasons Justin might have had for not turning up to marry you yesterday?'

'I suppose not,' Dawn admitted. Although, in some ways, that was *exactly* what she wanted to do. Just not with Cooper. What she really needed was Ruby, a bottle or two of wine, a bowl of potato wedges with sour cream and sweet chilli sauce and several uninterrupted hours to dissect exactly what had gone wrong in her relationship.

Justin's brother was no substitute for that.

And none of it changed the fact that the only person who could give her the actual answers she needed was Justin himself. Who was still—she did some quick mental arithmetic—forty-one driving hours away.

Yeah, she was definitely going to need to stop for lunch before then. But at least she got to choose where.

Leaning forward, Dawn rooted around in her bag for the leaflets she'd picked up at the hotel, fanning them out as she looked for a likely place to stop and eat. If Cooper wasn't going to distract her, she'd occupy herself by planning their journey. Her way.

Checking their location on her phone, and matching it up with the ancient road atlas she'd found in the glove box, she narrowed down her choices, putting some leaflets aside for later in the trip. Eventually, she held up one with the picture of a giant polar bear on the front.

'Elko, Nevada,' she said triumphantly.

'Excuse me?'

'That's where we should stop for lunch,' Dawn explained.

'Elko, Nevada. Home of the world's largest dead polar bear.' It was spontaneous, quirky and all the things she hadn't been lately. Totally out of character, really. Except...it didn't feel that way. It felt as if maybe this *could* be her character, if she let it.

As though this was the Dawn she'd been looking for.

'Why would we want to eat lunch with a dead polar bear?' Cooper asked, eyebrows raised. 'And besides, I thought we decided that we weren't stopping for kitsch roadside attractions on this trip.'

'We have to eat some time,' Dawn said reasonably. 'Why not take a peek at White King while we're at it?'

'White King?'

'That's the polar bear's name.'

Cooper sighed. 'Of course the polar bear has a name.'

'You're the one who named the car Claudia,' Dawn said with a shrug.

'I didn't—' Cooper bit off whatever argument he was about to make, and Dawn hid her grin. Baiting Cooper was far more fun than learning about his secret marriage, anyway. 'Fine. How far is Elko?'

Dawn bounced a little in her seat as she consulted her phone. 'About another hour and a half. We'll be there right in time for lunch!'

'Perfect.' Cooper's voice was bone-dry. 'A picnic with a polar bear. Just what I always dreamt of.'

'I knew you'd love it.' Dawn settled back into her seat with a satisfied grin.

Maybe this trip wouldn't be so unbearable after all.

Cooper stared up at the giant, glass-encased polar bear. He had to admit, he'd never seen bigger. Not that he'd actually been *looking*.

'Apparently, White King is ten feet four inches tall

and weighs two thousand, two hundred pounds.' Dawn straightened up from reading the plaque beside the bear.

'I could have read that myself, you realise,' Cooper said.

Dawn gave a light shrug. 'It's more fun to learn these things together.'

Fun. Last he recalled, that wasn't what this road trip was about. Although, he had to admit, Dawn was a better travelling companion than he'd expected. She hadn't complained about the long hours in the car, or demanded to stop for bathroom breaks every thirty minutes. And she hadn't pressed too much to discover his secrets. It felt more as though she was using meaningless small talk—and polar bears—to distract herself from the end of the journey.

Which was interesting in itself.

'What I don't get is why this creature is *here*.' Cooper gestured around him at the casino and hotel that housed the giant bear, which seemed to have nothing to do with the Arctic Circle, as far as he could see.

Dawn peered down at her leaflet again. 'Apparently it was something to do with a competition to find the biggest polar bear, back in the fifties.'

Of course it was. Didn't everything come down to competition in the end? To proving you could be bigger or better or greater or richer than everyone else?

Cooper turned away from White King and sought out the bar menu instead. Cheap and cheerful was what they were going for, apparently.

'Hot dogs?' he suggested, and Dawn hesitated for a moment before nodding.

Then she grinned. 'It says here they'll bring your food to the slots, if you ask.'

Cooper frowned. 'So you're a gambler? Did my brother know?' Because that was exactly the sort of information that might have driven Justin away on his wedding day.

A rich husband would certainly have solved the issue of any outstanding debts at the poker table…

But Dawn just laughed, as if he had to be joking. 'I've never actually been in a casino before. Not counting sleeping above one last night, of course. Justin and I talked about eloping to Vegas at one point, but…' She shook her head as she trailed off.

'But he wanted a proper family wedding, I assume.' Justin wouldn't have deprived their mother of the chance for a society event of the year, however stupidly in love he was.

'Actually, it was me.' Dawn flashed him a small smile. 'I knew my parents and my sisters would never forgive me if I just showed up married one day. And, besides, I'd waited long enough for a big day of my own.' She shrugged. 'Why skimp on it, right?'

'Especially when your fiancé has the money to give you your dream wedding,' Cooper replied. Of course she'd want the spectacle. What was the point of marrying into money if she couldn't show it off? Eloping would have defeated the object. If she was anything like Rachel—and, from Justin's note, he had to assume she was, even if she didn't always seem it—an elopement would have suggested a hasty mistake. She'd have wanted to show the world that she'd completely won Justin over, made him fall absurdly in love with her, before she dropped him and ran off, laughing all the way to the bank.

Dawn's smile stiffened. 'Yeah, well, weddings are always a compromise, aren't they? I mean, there's so many people to keep happy.'

Why would she care about that? That was the part that Cooper couldn't figure out. Unless it was all part of the act, of course.

Rachel had designed every aspect of their wedding, and had kept control of the reins with an iron grip. The day hadn't been theirs, it had been hers, and everyone there had known it.

But, now that he thought about it, he hadn't seen much of the Dawn he'd come to know over the last three days in the arrangements for and Justin's and her wedding. And the guest list had been easily three-quarters full of people he knew his mother must have invited.

What he couldn't figure out was whether that meant she was less good at screwing his family over than Rachel, or more. Because, from speaking to his family after Justin's no-show, they'd seemed even more surprised—if not exactly disappointed—that the wedding hadn't gone ahead than Dawn had been.

'So, what do you think?' Dawn asked, her smile still a little too forced. 'Want to show me how to use these machines while we wait for our hot dogs? Perhaps White King here can be our lucky charm.'

Cooper stared across at the ringing, beeping, irritating machines. It wasn't exactly *his* idea of a fun time, but at least it was something different from staring at the interstate for hours on end. Salt Lake City, where they'd decided to stop for the night, was still another three hours or more away, even if the traffic was good.

He rolled his eyes. 'Fine. Let's go get some change—as soon as I've ordered these hot dogs.'

Dawn's beaming smile was almost enough to make him forget why they were there in the first place, and the childish way she clapped her hands with glee was enough to make him doubt the only things he knew about her all over again.

She was a liar. She was after Justin's money.

So why was he having so much fun travelling with her?

CHAPTER SEVEN

'I'M PAYING FOR the hotel tonight,' Dawn reminded Cooper as the lights of Salt Lake City appeared on the horizon through the windscreen. Hopefully he'd take the hint and find somewhere affordable.

Cooper looked up from the hotel app on his phone. 'Planning on using your winnings from the historic commercial casino?'

'Ha! You'd better hope not, or we're sleeping on the streets tonight.' White King had, sadly, proved to be less of a lucky charm than she'd hoped.

'Yeah, I wouldn't turn to a career in professional gambling any time soon.' He scrolled through the pages of vacant hotel rooms on his phone, and Dawn tried to concentrate on the road rather than the prices on the screen. She'd have to check her card balance online when they stopped. Maybe she could up the credit limit...

'Okay, I've got us two rooms at a motel on the outskirts,' Cooper told her. 'Nothing fancy, but I figured we'd grab dinner first anyway, then just show up in time to sleep.'

Nothing fancy. In Cooper's world, that could mean anything, but at least it sounded as though he hadn't purposefully booked the most expensive place he could just to mess with her.

He had to know that she wasn't from the same sort of

world as his brother and him—he'd met her family, after all. With five girls all at home, money had never exactly been abundant in the Featherington house—although, until she'd met Justin, Dawn had never felt badly off. Still, compared to the Edwards' world of beach houses in the Hamptons, vineyards in California and the ability to fly first class everywhere, Dawn supposed *most* people would feel kind of broke.

Of course, it was more her credit card bill that made her feel particularly poor these days. Because, while Justin had always been generous, he just hadn't always got that keeping up with the Edwards cost money. He'd happily pay for flights, holidays and dinners, but it wouldn't occur to him that the outfits he liked to show her off in, or the drink she needed to order at the fancy restaurant bar and sip slowly until he showed up an hour late for dinner, blaming work, were rather more expensive than she was used to paying for. Apparently Top Shop and a bottle of cider were *not* the Edwards' way.

She'd tried explaining it to Justin once or twice, but embarrassment meant she'd bungled it, hinting around the edges of the problem but never fully articulating it. Justin had just patted her hand and said how nice it was to date a girl with an actual job for a change, one who wasn't always looking for new ways to spend his money because she had her own.

But Dawn's job, good as it was, definitely hadn't paid for the same sort of lifestyle Justin was used to.

She just hoped Cooper was a bit more reasonable in his hotel expectations.

'Take a left off here,' Cooper said, glancing between the road and the map on his phone. 'There's a pancake house along here we can eat at, and the motel's not far after that.'

'Pancakes for dinner?' Dawn asked as she signalled. 'Aren't they more of a breakfast thing?'

Cooper shrugged. 'Why limit ourselves?'

'Fair point.'

The thing was, Dawn mused as she tucked into her chicken and mushroom cream sauce pancake a short while later, that until this week she'd always been more of a salads girl. At least, since she'd come over to the States. Firstly because her sisters had teased her about American portion sizes, and joked that she'd be as big as the other four of them put together by the time she came home again, and she'd really wanted to prove them wrong. And then, of course, having spent all that money on expensive clothes of the sort Justin liked, she really couldn't afford not to fit into them any more.

Besides, Justin liked her in bikinis, and they took a certain amount of self-discipline to look good in. Especially given the fact that most of the other women he introduced her to had nothing else to do with their time *but* make sure they looked good in bikinis. Dawn couldn't commit time or money to a personal trainer for three hours a day, plus nutritionally balanced meals delivered daily from a world-class chef, but she could order a plain salad when she ate out, and go for a run once in a while. So she had.

Until this week. Since Justin had failed to show up at the altar, she'd eaten a burger, doughnuts, hot dogs and now pancakes.

And she'd loved every delicious mouthful of them.

One thing was for certain—whatever happened with Justin, she was never going back to limiting herself to boring, tasteless food again.

They ate quickly, both tired and ready to get to the motel after a long day guiding Claudia across the country. Dawn drove the last mile or two to the motel, Cooper calling out directions from the satnav on his phone. As he guided her into the car park, Dawn let out a sigh of relief. The motel looked clean and respectable enough, but not as though it was going to break the bank. If they stuck to places like this, and she could get another five hundred dollars on her credit limit just in case, she should get away with paying for every other night's accommodation.

Of course, what she'd do after that was another worry entirely. One she'd deal with after she'd dealt with Justin.

'Let's go check in,' she said, breathing easily for the first time since they'd left White King behind. 'I've been dreaming of a bed to myself for the last hundred miles.'

Which, she decided later, was probably what had jinxed the whole thing.

'Yes, I am *absolutely* sure that I booked two rooms.' Cooper scraped a hand through his hair and glared at the teenager behind the motel desk who apparently had flunked maths every year since the first grade. 'Two. Not one. It's a fairly simple concept.'

'Yeah, but see, the thing is—' the boy started.

'The thing is *I need two rooms*!' Cooper roared, making the boy behind the desk jump. He'd feel guilty, except he was too exhausted to feel anything except tired. And maybe annoyed.

Dawn's hand on his arm caught his attention, and he turned to look at her.

'Let me?' she asked softly.

Cooper sighed and stepped back. 'By all means.'

'Hi!' Dawn beamed at the receptionist, looking perky and pleasant and nowhere near as tired as Cooper knew she had to be after driving all afternoon. 'So, my friend here booked us two rooms for tonight. Can we have them, please?'

'That's the thing! He didn't.' The boy leant over the desk, obviously relieved to be dealing with someone who would actually let him finish a sentence. Something that Cooper was fairly sure was a mistake, as the end of the sentence was usually, 'No,' in his experience.

'He absolutely did,' Dawn said. 'On your chain's booking app.'

The boy pulled a face. 'Oh, man, we've been having all sorts of problems with that thing. See, what he booked was one room for two adults.' He turned the computer screen so Dawn could see it, and Cooper watched her face fall. 'And that's the only room we have left.'

'Of course it is,' Dawn muttered, so low that Cooper had to strain to hear her. 'Because my life is apparently cursed.'

'So, uh, do you want the room?' The boy looked between the two of them, room key in his shaky hand.

This was ridiculous. Cooper reached across and plucked it from his hand. 'Which room?'

'Two-oh-two,' the boy replied, smiling with obvious relief.

Cooper grabbed his bag and motioned to Dawn. 'Come on.'

'So...we're sharing a room?' Dawn asked as they headed to room two hundred and two.

'Apparently so,' Cooper bit out.

'Right.' She did a quick double-step to catch him up, and Cooper realised he might be walking a little fast.

He was just so damned annoyed with himself. Or at least with the stupid booking app.

Spotting the number on a door, he halted suddenly, Dawn skidding a little beside him as she did the same.

Please let there be two beds. Please.

It was a long shot, he knew, given the quality of the

motel, but Cooper had spent a long day in the car, and the few days before that hadn't been exactly relaxed, plus he'd hardly slept the night before. All he wanted to do was crawl into a soft bed and sleep for twelve solid hours. Was that so much to ask?

Apparently so.

The door swung open to reveal one bed that could charitably be called a small double and an even smaller, lumpy-looking couch under the window.

Perfect.

Sighing, Cooper stepped in and flung his bag onto the floor by the couch. 'You take the bed,' he said, because he might be grumpy and exhausted but he was still a gentleman. 'I'll crash on the sofa.'

He was about to sit down on it and loosen his shoes when Dawn said, 'No.'

'No?' He looked up. Her expression was pure stubbornness, and he was just too tired for this.

'I'll take the sofa. I'm shorter—I'll fit better. You take the bed.' She folded her arms across her chest as if she was waiting for him to argue.

He *should* argue. That was the gentlemanly thing to do. But he really wanted that bed...

No. 'Don't be silly. I'll take the couch.'

'I am not being silly.' Dawn's eyes grew harder, and he realised he might have chosen his words poorly. 'I'm being practical. The sofa is too short for you to sleep on, and it's your turn to drive first in the morning, so you need the rest more than me. I can sleep in the car tomorrow before I have to drive.'

When she put it like that, it did kind of make sense.

'Fine, if you insist.' Cooper gave her a tired smile. 'Thank you.'

Dawn nodded sharply. 'But I'm using the bathroom first,' she said, and flashed him a grin.

Maybe tonight wouldn't be too unbearable after all.

This was unbearable.

Dawn shifted between the lumps in the sofa's cushions, tugging the extra blanket they'd found in the wardrobe a little tighter around her. Just feet away, she could hear Cooper's slow, even breaths. At least one of them was getting some sleep. The bed, she thought rationally, probably wasn't all that comfortable either, given the general quality of the motel. But it had to be less awful than the sofa from hell.

Maybe she shouldn't have made such a fuss about giving him the bed. If she'd just let him play the gentleman, she could be curled up there asleep right now. Except then he'd have been grumpier than ever in the morning, and she didn't want to subject Claudia to his aggressive driving. Or herself to his glowering looks and sharp comments, come to that.

Sighing, Dawn turned over again, praying she'd find a comfortable position. She was being unfair to Cooper, she knew. So he wasn't thrilled to be spending his holiday on a road trip with a woman he barely knew. That was understandable. And actually, over the last day or so, he'd started to lighten up. They'd even had a beer each with their pancakes when they'd stopped and, although they'd been too tired to talk much, there had at least been a weary comradeship building between them, she thought.

Until the whole room debacle, anyway.

There was, she realised now, a third option for sleeping arrangements—one that neither of them even seemed to have considered. It had only occurred to Dawn once she was settled on the sofa with a spring stuck in her back.

They could have shared the bed.

For one brief, blissful moment, Dawn let herself consider how it might feel to lie on an actual mattress, with enough space to stretch her legs out the whole way. With a real duvet, instead of this scratchy, itchy wool blanket. With Cooper's arms wrapped warm around her and…

Wait. No.

Where the hell had that come from?

A place of sleep deprivation, Dawn decided, as she turned her back on the bed and stared, wide-eyed, at the cushions of the sofa.

She was not thinking about Justin's brother that way. And, actually, she really wasn't. What she was imagining was warmth, comfort and another person beside her who wasn't just there because…

Why *was* Cooper there, anyway? What was it about her that made him want to drive cross-country just to be there with her when she saw Justin again? She was under no illusion that Cooper was doing this to get them back together again, so he must be planning to make sure that Dawn didn't try to win Justin back.

But why? What was it he disliked so much about her?

She sighed. Another mystery to add to the list of things she didn't understand about Cooper Edwards. One she definitely intended to solve before they reached the Hamptons.

Just as soon as she got some sleep.

When the alarm on his phone went off at six a.m. the next morning, Cooper cursed it for a solid minute while grappling to find the snooze button. Why was he getting up at six in the morning when he was supposed to be on *holiday*? He'd booked a whole week off, something he hardly ever did, to relax after playing best man for his brother. That week had been designated for lazing in the Californian sunshine with a couple of quick work visits to the vineyards to check on things and do a taste test or five. Nothing that required six a.m. starts.

Then, as the alarm went silent, he blinked at the yellowing motel ceiling and remembered.

No wedding. Road trip. Stupid hotel booking app.

Dawn.

Turning onto his side, he looked over at the sofa, only to find it empty. He frowned, until the sound of the shower running in the attached bathroom caught his attention and explained Dawn's absence.

Yeah, that couch must have been *really* uncomfortable if she was already up and moving. He'd have to make sure she got some sleep in the car, or there was no way she'd be fit to drive in the afternoon. And he had a feeling she was the sort to be grumpy when she didn't get enough sleep—much like himself—and he'd like to keep things friendly, since they were stuck together.

Wait. Friendly? Since when had he wanted to be *friends* with Dawn Featherington? Hadn't he planned on avoiding that very thing?

From the shower, her voice rang out, singing something from some Disney movie or another, and Cooper held in a sigh.

There was one thing he hadn't counted on when he'd agreed to this road trip.

He hadn't imagined, for a moment, that it might be *fun.*

And it wouldn't be, with anyone else.

He groaned, rolling over to bury his face in the pillow as he thought back over the past couple of days.

The problem was that he'd been expecting Dawn to be someone else. Someone with high expectations, and doing a lot of whining when he didn't meet them. He'd expected her to be annoyed at the long hours in the car and never offer to drive, horrified by the tacky motels he kept choosing for them to stay in and disgusted by the idea of hot dogs for lunch and pancakes for dinner. He'd expected Dawn to fleece him for nights in five-star hotels and insist on dressing up for dinner in the fanciest restaurants.

He'd expected Dawn to be just like his ex-wife, Rachel.

Instead, he'd got the woman who wanted to stop off to see giant polar bears, and drove the Caddy with the sort of love and affection he showed her himself. And had actually *named* her, come to that.

He hadn't been mentally prepared for Dawn. That much was clear.

That was one of the reasons he'd set his alarm so early. Because, when they'd settled into their room together the night before, just for a moment he'd imagined them heading out and grabbing breakfast together the next morning. He'd thought of suggesting they take in Gilgal Gardens before they hit the road, because if she thought the giant polar bear was quirky she really hadn't seen anything yet. He'd even considered, just for a moment, suggesting they share the damn bed.

But then he'd remembered his brother's note, remembered who she really was, interest in kitsch roadside attractions aside. So when he'd opened his mouth to say goodnight, he'd found himself saying, 'I want to hit the road by seven. We can stop for coffee and breakfast on the way. It's ten and a half hours to Lexington, and we can make it in a day if we don't hang around.'

That was what mattered. Getting to Justin quickly and ending this.

Then he'd turned over in the bed, his back to her couch, already regretting the overreaction that meant spending over ten hours stuck in Claudia's overheating seats the following day.

He regretted it even more now, as the alarm went off again, and he levered himself out of bed to wait for his turn in the shower. But then he remembered what roadside surprises Interstate 80 had for them today and he couldn't help but smile.

Maybe this road trip had started out as an obligation. But did that really have to mean it couldn't be fun too?

CHAPTER EIGHT

By the time Cooper was done with his shower, and had packed up his few belongings, Dawn was already waiting for him in the lobby, paying the motel bill for the night before. Cooper faltered slightly as he approached when he realised what she was doing. Yes, she'd said she would, but he hadn't actually believed it.

The woman made no sense. The only possible explanation that fitted with Justin's letter was that she was trying to prove him wrong—trying to show Cooper that the money wasn't important to her, so that he didn't interfere with her plans to win Justin back.

The only problem with that theory was that Cooper had been with women like that before—women who liked to live the high life on credit to enable them to move in the circles that meant they could find a rich husband to pay it off. And Dawn, with her hair scraped back in a high ponytail, wearing the same denim skirt as yesterday with another cheap and colourful tee shirt, did not fit that mould.

His instincts told him that Dawn wasn't trying to be anything right now. She was just being herself. And that made no sense at all. So either his instincts were wrong or there was something else going on here that he didn't understand.

Who the hell was this woman Justin had run out on?

And why did it bother Cooper so much that he couldn't read her the way he read every other woman he met these days?

'Ready to go?' Dawn asked, smiling cautiously at him, probably in response to the frown he could feel creasing his forehead.

'Yep. Let's go see how Claudia fared for the night, shall we?' He tried to make his words friendly, and saw Dawn's shoulders relax a little for the effort.

Claudia was as steady and reliable as ever, and Cooper slipped behind the steering wheel with relief. This, at least, he understood. The classic car, the open road, travelling to reach a destination—that all made sense.

The woman in the seat beside him, less so.

He swung into a drive-through to pick up coffee and breakfast muffins before they left the city, then headed back out on the interstate. Dawn seemed quieter this morning—maybe more tired than ever after her night on the couch. She dozed for a bit, but even after she woke up she didn't seem to have much to say.

After about an hour, the silence grew a little too oppressive as they drove through the hills out of Utah into Wyoming. Cooper switched on the radio, hoping for something not terrible, and grinned when Elvis crackled through the speakers.

'Seems appropriate,' Dawn said, returning his smile. 'Claudia, the open road and Elvis. I'm basically living the American cliché right here.'

'If it were the nineteen-fifties, maybe,' Cooper admitted. 'This is more of a nostalgia trip than reality, I think.'

'You're probably right. Still, it's nice to imagine.' She sounded strangely wistful as Elvis sang of lost love and heartache.

'So, is this what you were imagining when you moved

Stateside?' Cooper asked, curiosity getting the better of him. 'Being an all-American housewife, baking apple pies and driving places with the hood down?'

Dawn laughed. 'Do you think I'd have agreed to marry Justin if it was? That's not exactly the sort of lives you guys live, is it?'

'No, I suppose not.' With the Edwards brothers, it had always been work hard and play harder. Until Rachel, of course. Then, for Cooper at least, it had become 'work hard and forget'.

'But… I guess… I grew up on stories from my mum— she's American, did you know?' Dawn said, and Cooper nodded to show he remembered. 'She grew up here in the sixties, and apparently her mother was very much that all-American housewife you talk about. Her family were quintessential middle America, I guess. All the clichés you can imagine.'

'So what took her to England?'

'My dad. They met when he was over here on a road trip of his own, actually. They fell in love fast, and her parents thought she was crazy when she said yes to his proposal after only two weeks.'

'Hardly surprising,' Cooper pointed out. He'd proposed to Rachel after only a month—and look what an almighty screw-up that had turned out to be.

'But she stood her ground. They got married less than a month later and moved to England together.' She paused and Cooper waited, knowing that couldn't be the end of that story. 'My wedding-that-wasn't was the first time she'd been back in almost forty years.'

Cooper's eyebrows shot up. 'Wow. Talk about burning bridges, huh?'

Dawn gave a small, embarrassed-looking shrug. 'I guess my grandparents *really* didn't approve of the marriage. But, the thing is, she talked about her life here, growing up, so often that it felt real to me. And so when I got the opportunity to come and work over here it felt like a no-brainer, you know?'

'Did you track down any of your family?'

'No,' Dawn said, turning to look out of the window. 'My grandparents both died years ago, and Mum was an only child. So there didn't seem much point, really. I wanted to come here for me, to see what it was really like. And then I met Justin.'

'And fell madly in love.' Cooper didn't try very hard to keep the sarcasm out of his voice, but Dawn didn't even seem to notice.

'Yeah. I did.' She smiled down at her hands shyly, as if embarrassed by it. 'The funny thing is, everything happened so fast it was almost scary. And Justin… His world wasn't mine, and sometimes I felt so out of my depth. But then I realised it couldn't be half as terrifying as what my mum had been through for love. So I just let myself go with it. Of course, with hindsight…' Her smile turned rueful.

'Would you do things the same?' Cooper asked. 'If you'd known how things would turn out?'

Dawn bit down on her lip before answering, obviously giving the question far more thought than Cooper thought it deserved.

'Yes,' she said eventually. 'I think I would.'

Would she have done things the same? Would she have risked getting stood up by Justin on her wedding day all over again, and then taken off cross-country with his brother on a crazy road trip?

Who in their right mind would bring all that on themselves *twice*?

Well, she would, it seemed. Because, try as she might, Dawn couldn't imagine living her life in a way that didn't take that sort of chance to find a 'for ever' love. Couldn't imagine *not* jumping at the chance for happiness.

Was that how her mother had felt all those years ago? Suddenly, Cooper's question made her feel closer to her mum than she had in years.

'It's funny,' she said, smiling. 'All these years, I've thought I was nothing like the rest of my family—especially my mum and my sisters. But maybe I have more in common with them than I think.'

'You all fall in love too fast?' Cooper asked, and she knew he was being sarcastic, but he was also *right,* so she nodded.

'We all take a chance on love,' she amended. 'Some of us more often than others.'

'Ah, so you've done this a lot, then?' Cooper's tone wasn't surprised—more as if she was confirming something about herself that he'd long suspected. Although why he'd been thinking about her past romantic entanglements Dawn couldn't imagine.

'Not *lots,* exactly.' Dawn winced as she wondered what the exact definition of 'lots' was, anyway. 'Let's just say I haven't always been particularly lucky in love.'

'I noticed,' Cooper said drily.

Shifting in her seat, Dawn looked past him out of the windscreen rather than continue the conversation. Then she frowned.

'What is *that*?'

Cooper didn't even look before he answered. Apparently he'd known this was coming.

'It's the giant head of Abraham Lincoln.' There, on the side of the road, a huge statue stood over them, judging them.

'That's…kind of what I was afraid you were going to say.' Dawn stared out at the looming figure high over the interstate, staring down at the traffic. 'Um, why is it there?'

Cooper shrugged. 'Hard to say. I think it used to loom over the Lincoln Highway, which at least made some sense. Then it got moved, well, here.'

'Because that is a totally normal thing to do,' Dawn said, staring out of the window as Cooper drove past the giant bronze head.

Huh. America.

Maybe her mum had been right to get out while she had the chance.

'This is the country of extremes,' Cooper pointed out. 'Extreme wealth, extreme poverty, extreme temperatures…'

'And extreme statues,' Dawn finished for him. 'I get it.'

'Just wait until you see what's coming up next.' Cooper smirked at her, then turned his gaze back to the road.

Dawn didn't have to wait long. About fifteen minutes by Claudia's clock—although she had no idea how accurate that was.

'Okay, that's less bizarre than the giant head,' she admitted. 'But what *is* it?'

'It's a tree. Don't you have those in Britain?'

'Not growing out of solid rock in the middle of the road we don't.' At least, not that she'd ever seen.

They were in the middle of Wyoming, with bright blue skies and scorched brown earth all around them, the interstate a river of grey in the landscape. And there, right in the centre of I-80, stood a tree. Lopsided and windswept, and maybe a little stunted, but a living tree. Growing right out of a piece of what looked like granite.

'That takes some perseverance,' Dawn said as they sailed past the plucky little tree. 'I mean, the road even goes *around* it.'

'Story goes that when they were building the first railroad along this route the railroad men were so impressed with that stubborn little limber pine, they actually moved the railroad so as not to disturb it.' Even Cooper sounded vaguely impressed by the tree's pluckiness. 'Then, by the time the railroad moved and they wanted to put the interstate in, the tree was too famous to shift, so they made the road go around it.'

'Huh.' The tree in the road zoomed out of sight, and Dawn turned back in her seat, settling down again, thinking hard.

'Huh?' Cooper repeated. 'It's just a tree, Dawn.'

'No, it isn't.' She hadn't even got a decent look at the thing, but she already knew it was more than that. It was a parable. A promise. 'It's hope.'

'Hope?' Cooper's tone was even more derisory than normal, which Dawn hadn't been entirely sure was possible.

'Yeah. Hope.' The more she said it, the more sure she was. 'Think how many other seeds must have tried to grow into trees in that place and failed. All the saplings that didn't survive their first winter. Or seeds that landed on stone and just rotted. But not that one.'

'I guess.'

'That seed flourished, even though it shouldn't,' Dawn went on, warming to her theme. 'That tree grew in the most unlikely place, defying all the odds. And it was that defiance that kept it alive when the railways or the roads should have destroyed it. It was the hope it gave people— the promise of survival against impossible odds. It's basically American history in horticulture.'

Cooper laughed. 'Maybe you're right.'

'Of course I'm right.' And, if a tree could do it, why couldn't she? That little pine hadn't given up, so why should Dawn? 'Haven't you ever succeeded at something against all the odds, against all the people who told you that you couldn't?'

It was the wrong question, clearly. Cooper's face closed down instantly. 'Mostly I like to stack the odds in my favour first, to assure success. It's just good business.'

'Yeah, but there must have been something you stuck at, or went ahead with, even when it seemed hopeless?' She could tell there had been. If there hadn't been, Cooper wouldn't have reacted that way.

'Nothing that ended well,' he said darkly, and Dawn winced.

'Well, *I'm* going to be more like that tree,' she said firmly. Then she risked a cheeky smile in his direction. 'You can be more like the giant bronze head of Abraham Lincoln, if you like.'

He didn't dignify that with a response, and Dawn only just held in her laughter.

Cooper wasn't sure why he insisted on driving so far that day when they were both already so tired, but he suspected it had something to do with Dawn's musings on succeeding against the odds and perseverance.

The only time he'd ever done anything that smacked of defying conventional wisdom was when he'd fallen in love with Rachel. Hell, it hadn't been even just conventional wisdom he'd defied—it had been his own. He'd known better, and he'd fallen anyway.

He hadn't been in love with Melanie, back when he'd been twenty-one and his mother had asked him to show her around the company and teach her the ropes—but he knew he could have fallen, if she'd let him. She'd been a student on a summer placement, and he'd been showing off because she was beautiful and he wanted to impress her. She'd flirted, smiled and let him think that he mattered, that he was important. He'd been so full of himself he'd let all sorts of company secrets slip—and she'd turned around and given them to her boyfriend, who'd just happened to work for their biggest competitor.

Coming back from that, proving to his father and the board that he could be trusted again, had been one of the hardest things he'd ever had to do. But he'd done it by setting his own rules. By understanding that everyone wanted something from you, and you had to figure out the cost before you decided if it was worth paying.

Then his dad had died and he'd taken over the company, and for a long time work had been more important than anything else. And, when he'd finally had time to breathe again, he'd known who he was. He'd known what he had—money and power. He'd known what people wanted from him. And he'd made damn sure only to give it away on his own terms—until Rachel.

Rachel had broken past his walls, made him believe that she wanted something else, something no one had ever wanted from him before. Love.

He'd given it all to her—and it had nearly destroyed him.

Love, he'd decided, was the most illogical thing of all.

But he had a feeling that the damned tree in the rock had inspired Dawn to go and chase it again.

Just hopefully not with his brother.

They swapped seats after a swift late lunch in a roadside diner, Dawn sliding in behind Claudia's wheel as if she'd been driving her all her life. She cranked up the radio— still playing Elvis—and started singing along, mangling the words so badly that Cooper couldn't help but join in on the chorus.

She beamed at him as he sang, and he rolled his eyes and pretended he wasn't really singing, even though he obviously was.

Still, as the skies started to grow orange and red as the daylight faded, Dawn looked exhausted.

'Are we planning to stop soon?' she asked, the question truncated by a jaw-cracking yawn.

'Lexington,' he said shortly. 'About another hour.'

'Right.' Another yawn, and Claudia swerved slightly as Dawn took her hand off the wheel to cover her mouth again.

Cooper swore silently. She wasn't going to make it to Lexington. She'd hardly slept the night before, because she'd given him the bed. And, as much as his aching arms didn't want to drive any more today either, he would have to take over the wheel or risk them crashing.

Maybe Lexington *was* too far to aim for tonight. But he knew they had to make it, all the same. He had to get to Justin, to help his brother escape making the same mistake he had.

He glanced across at Dawn again, her eyes sleepy but her jaw set. He couldn't help but think she'd be a better match for any man than Rachel had been, but what did he know? His swift divorce was proof that he was no judge of women.

Maybe Dawn was just a better actress than his ex-wife.

Up ahead, Cooper saw lights and a familiar sign, and smiled.

'Pull over at the next turn-off,' he said. 'We'll swap over.'

Dawn frowned as she signalled. 'Here?'

'Yep,' Cooper replied as the giant likeness of Buffalo Bill came into view. 'Right here.'

* * *

It had been *years* since Cooper had been to Fort Cody, the replica frontier-redoubt that claimed to be Nebraska's largest souvenir and Western gift store. He struggled even to remember how they'd come across it, or why they'd even been travelling through Nebraska in the first place—it certainly wasn't the sort of place the Edwards family had frequented when he'd been growing up. But that was precisely why Cooper liked it so much.

'Fort Cody Trading Post,' Dawn read doubtfully. 'Western gifts?'

'It's a souvenir place, mostly.' Cooper unbuckled his seat belt. 'With a bit of frontier history thrown in. Come on.'

Dawn's uncertain expression started to fade as she took in the log stockade walls and the wooden lookout towers with the stars and stripes flying from them.

'So is this where the real Buffalo Bill came from?' she asked, reading the information board under the giant, thirty-foot-tall Bill Cody sign.

'Well, maybe not originally,' Cooper allowed. 'But he lived here for a while.'

'I suppose that counts.' Dawn flashed him a cheeky grin. 'I suppose when a country only has a few centuries of history you have to take what you can get.'

'Of course, even when a country is as vast and influential as the United States, it's still quite an achievement to have so much history everywhere you travel within it,' Cooper countered, and Dawn laughed.

'I'll let you have that one,' she said, linking her hand through his arm casually. He stiffened at her touch, then forced himself to relax. 'Come on, let's go in. I have a lot of family to buy souvenirs for.'

She didn't let go until they were well inside, when she

dashed off to study some Buffalo Bill keyrings, and suddenly Cooper felt a chill, despite the warmth of the evening.

Unsettled, he watched Dawn flit from stand to stand within the main shop, collecting tacky memorabilia in her arms as though it was precious jewels, holding it close against her chest. She looked like a child in a sweet shop, and Cooper tried to remember the last time he'd seen such sheer enjoyment in anyone.

He couldn't. But, if he could, he knew for a fact it wouldn't have been caused by a Buffalo Bill keyring.

The people in his life—work colleagues, family, a few acquaintances that had hung around after his divorce—weren't the sort of people to get excited by souvenirs and *faux* Western decoration. None of them. If he'd brought literally anyone else he knew to this place, they'd have rolled their eyes at the spectacle and told him they'd wait in the car.

Which led him to the very uncomfortable conclusion that Dawn wasn't like anyone else he knew.

Maybe that wasn't too bad in itself, but it was the thought it led to next that was causing him real problems.

'I just need to go pay for these, then we'll get some coffee, okay?' Dawn said, bouncing up next to him, her arms full.

Cooper just nodded and watched her bound away again towards the shop desk.

If Dawn wasn't like anyone he knew, she wasn't like Rachel. And spending the last few days in her company had led him to only one disturbing conclusion. One he knew in his gut was absolutely true, even if it made no sense at all.

Justin was wrong about her.

So what the hell did he do now?

CHAPTER NINE

THEY RAN INTO a traffic jam not far outside Lexington, stuck in a long line of stationary cars just a few miles from the hotel Cooper had booked while they'd been at Fort Cody, while the sky grew darker and night time fell. Dawn was relieved that Cooper was driving, not sure that she'd have been able to stay alert enough to deal with the stop-start traffic and the idiots trying to pull unsafe manoeuvres to get them home sooner.

But, as Cooper's jaw cracked with a huge yawn, she realised that she wasn't the only one who was tired, and it was her duty as a road-trip buddy to keep him awake and attentive.

Which meant it was time for the time-honoured tradition of car games. Starting with Fortunately/Unfortunately.

'Fortunately, we're not too far from our hotel,' she said with a perky smile.

Cooper narrowed his eyes at her. 'Unfortunately it could take us hours through all this traffic.'

'Fortunately, we're in the best car in the world!'

'What are we doing here?' Cooper asked, and Dawn clicked her tongue with disappointment.

'That's not the game!'

'We're playing a game?'

Dawn shook her head. 'Don't you know anything?

We're on a road trip, we're stuck in traffic. We have to play games.'

'Do I at least get to know the rules, then?' Cooper looked faintly amused at the prospect of car games, which Dawn decided was probably the best reaction she could expect from him.

'It's easy. I say something positive and optimistic—like, fortunately we're not far from our hotel—and you do what apparently comes totally naturally to you, since you didn't even realise we were playing, and say something negative, like—'

'Unfortunately it could take hours,' Cooper finished for her.

'Exactly!' She grinned at him. 'Ready now?'

'Hang on. Why can't I do the "fortunately" part?' Cooper asked.

Dawn blinked. 'Uh, I guess you could. If you liked.' And if he honestly thought he could come up with positive things to say for the next twenty minutes, or for however long they would be stuck in this traffic jam. 'I suppose it could be more of a challenge that way round.'

Because *she* was the positive one. The one always looking for a happy-ever-after. And he...well, wasn't.

'Fortunately, I like a challenge,' Cooper said. And just like that, the game was on.

'Unfortunately for you, I am a champion at this game.'

'Fortunately for me, I'm a quick learner,' Cooper countered.

'Unfortunately, you're an eternal pessimist.' Okay, that was a little harsh, but Dawn was playing to win.

'Fortunately, I've been taking lessons in optimism from you.'

'Unfortunately, my optimism is at an all-time low—

after being, you know, jilted on my wedding day—so I might not be such a great teacher.'

Cooper gave her a soft smile. 'Fortunately, I know it would take more than that to keep you down.'

Dawn felt a strange warmth filling her at his words. Was he right? She hoped so. 'Um… Unfortunately… Damn.' She couldn't think of anything.

'Want to switch to I Spy?' Cooper asked, and Dawn nodded. Much safer.

An hour or so later, Dawn sank down onto the hotel room bed, closed her eyes and smiled. Cooper had insisted on finding somewhere a little nicer to stay in Lexington, after the disaster at the motel the night before—adding that he'd cover it before she even had time to worry about the hit to her credit card—and she really hadn't been able to say no. The fluffy bathrobe, power shower and ridiculously comfortable mattress almost made her forget that she'd spent most of the last two days in a car. And possibly a significant portion of her remaining money on Buffalo Bill keyrings for her family.

'Are you sure you've got enough of those?' Cooper had asked, nodding at her heavy bag as she'd carried it in from the car after an epic game of I Spy.

She'd shrugged. 'I have a lot of family who flew a long way for a wedding that didn't happen. I figure the least I owe them is a keyring. I kind of wanted to get the moose's head for Dad, but that would be a nightmare to ship, so… keyrings all round.'

Cooper, she'd noticed, hadn't bought anything at all, despite how excited he'd looked at stopping there. She wondered if it had been some sort of childhood favourite, one that Justin had shared, although Justin had never mentioned it.

She'd half-thought that Cooper might have bought something for his brother, but he hadn't. She hadn't either, after some consideration. Showing up with gifts would smack a little too much of her coming after him to grovel, to beg him to come back. And the more distance she got from the wedding the more certain she was that she didn't want to do that.

And only a little bit of that reasoning was down to Cooper.

Dawn couldn't get a good read on him. One minute he was laughing and calling their car Claudia, stopping for ridiculously huge boxes of doughnuts for the journey, pulling over at stupidly fun roadside attractions or playing road-trip games. That Cooper she liked, could relax with and even enjoy his company.

It was the other Cooper who was causing her problems. The one who glared at her when she cracked a joke, who shifted the conversation away from any question she asked about his past or his personal life. The one who looked at her so hard sometimes she felt as though he were trying to see right through her skin, right to the heart of her.

She wondered what he saw there. She hadn't quite found the courage to ask yet.

A knock on the door pulled her from her reverie, and she groaned as she forced herself to her feet to answer it. Probably room service with the wrong room. Even nice hotels seemed to screw that up sometimes.

'I didn't order anything— Oh. Hi.'

Cooper stood outside her door, dark eyes warm in the dim lights of the hotel corridor. 'You left this in Claudia.' He held out her phone charger; it must have fallen out of her bag, she realised. She really needed to buy a proper bag to keep her stuff in, rather than relying on a ratty carrier bag. 'I figured you'd probably need it tonight.'

'I hadn't even noticed it was missing,' Dawn said, reaching out to take it from him. 'Thanks.'

He shrugged nonchalantly. 'No bother.'

'What were you doing back at the car anyway?' she asked.

Cooper's expression turned furtive. 'Nothing. Just… checking something.'

Had he been planning to leave? To abandon her here in the middle of nowhere, Nebraska? And, if so, what made him change his mind?

Her suspicions must have shown on her face, because Cooper sighed. 'Look, I wasn't making a run for it, I promise. I just needed to clear my head, so I went for a walk and found myself at the car. Your charger was sitting on the front seat. I didn't drive a yard.'

'You were sitting in the car imagining you were some fifties movie star, weren't you?' Dawn joked, mostly to distract herself from the overwhelming relief flooding through her. He *hadn't* been leaving her.

'Something like that.' Cooper gave her a small, lopsided smile. 'I guess I find Claudia calming.'

'You are the only person I know who, after spending basically a whole day sitting in a car, would voluntarily head back out there to sit in it some more even though you weren't getting anywhere.'

'Who said I wasn't getting anywhere?' Cooper asked.

Dawn frowned. 'You said you didn't drive anywhere.'

'No, but that's not always the same thing.' Leaning against the doorframe, Cooper looked at her—that deep-down, searching look she could never read properly—and Dawn tried not to flinch under his gaze. 'I had some thinking to do, was all.'

'About life, the universe and everything?' Dawn asked flippantly.

'About you.' By contrast, Cooper's tone was a hundred per cent serious.

'Me?' Dawn wasn't sure she liked the thought of that. What was there to think about, anyway? She liked to think she was a pretty open book.

'Yeah. You're a puzzle, Dawn Featherington.'

'I'm really not.' Somehow, as they talked, she'd leaned in closer to him, so she was halfway through the doorway herself. She just hoped no other guests happened on them. Their conversation must look far more intimate than it really was. Yet Dawn couldn't quite bring herself to pull away. 'What are you trying to figure out? Just ask me and I'll tell you.'

She would, Dawn realised. She'd answer any question he had, just to get him to stop looking at her as if he was seeking out all her secrets.

Or maybe to make sure he never stopped.

She wasn't entirely sure.

And *that,* right there, was a problem.

Dawn stepped back away from the doorframe, away from Cooper and his too-knowing eyes. He was her almost-brother-in-law, nothing else. The last thing she needed was to be sharing secrets and *moments* with this man.

Cooper looked as if he understood, because his smile turned sad. 'Ah, but where would be the fun in that?' he asked, and it took her a full minute to remember what she'd offered.

He pushed away from the doorframe and raised a hand in farewell. 'I'll see you in the morning, Dawn.'

'Eight in the lobby?' she guessed.

Cooper was already halfway down the hallway towards his own room a few doors down but he threw his answer back over his shoulder. 'Let's make it nine. We can get pancakes before we leave.'

It wasn't until she saw him disappear into his own room that Dawn shut the door, leaning against it and breathing deeply.

They'd talked about practically nothing. He'd returned her phone charger. They'd made plans for the morning, just like the last couple of nights.

So why did she feel suddenly as if everything had changed?

Cooper was already regretting the previous night's indulgence with the minibar by the time Dawn met him in the lobby. He'd known, after their conversation in her doorway, that he should just get some sleep. If sitting in Claudia examining his every interaction with Dawn so far hadn't given him a better understanding of whatever game she was playing—or the possibility that Justin had been mistaken—he definitely wasn't going to find any answers at the bottom of a miniature bottle of alcohol. Or even several miniature bottles.

But he'd tried anyway. And, by the time he'd dragged himself to bed and to sleep, he'd been drunk and clueless instead of just clueless. Perfect.

'Pancakes?' Dawn asked in greeting, her tone far too annoyingly cheerful for nine in the morning.

'We should get going,' he replied shortly, then cursed inwardly as her face fell. 'But there's probably time for pancakes,' he conceded, cursing himself even more.

What was it about this woman?

The problem, he'd decided last night, a couple of bottles in, was that he was starting from a place of incomplete information. Gut instinct aside, all he really knew was: A: Justin loved Dawn, but also believed her to be a gold-digger, and B: Dawn was willing to drive all the way across the country with him to win Justin back. Even if she denied it, it was pretty obvious to him.

Those two pieces of information alone should have been enough to compel him to keep his interactions with Dawn to a minimum, or at least keep his distance emotionally. He didn't need to know her secrets, didn't need to understand her motivations.

But apparently knowing that wasn't enough to make him stop trying.

Worst of all was the realisation that had driven him to drink the night before: as he'd stood in her hotel doorway, taking in her fluffy bathrobe and handing her the stupid phone charger she'd left behind *again*, he'd realised he wanted to kiss her.

And that was, put simply, the worst idea anyone had ever had. Ever.

He reminded himself of that several times over breakfast: every time she tried to start a conversation with him that hit too close to the personal, when she smiled and thanked their waiter so graciously, and especially when she licked syrup off her lip with more enthusiasm than Cooper felt was really necessary.

Although, they were damned good pancakes. Even his bad mood couldn't hide that.

They'd been on the road for almost two hours before Dawn tried talking to him again; apparently his grumpiness at breakfast had warned her off, as he'd intended. But a couple of hours of open road and Claudia purring through the landscape had improved his mindset, as he reminded himself he just had to take what he could from this experience and focus on helping his brother at the end of it. Everything else could go hang.

'You know, the world's biggest time capsule isn't far

from here, in Seward,' Dawn said, her tone tentative. 'I mean, if you fancied swapping drivers anyway…'

'You want to stop and see it?' Cooper asked. Time capsules weren't really his thing. Although the idea of locking up the past and forgetting about it appealed, the thought that he'd have to dig it up and re-examine it again one day was less enjoyable.

'Well, I just thought…it could be interesting, that's all.'

Cooper didn't answer. But, when he saw the turn-off for Seward, he took it, all the same.

Dawn tilted her head as she stared at the large, white concrete pyramid set in the garden of a house in suburban Seward, Nebraska.

'The plaque says the original time capsule was buried in 1975, then the pyramid was added on top eight years later.' Cooper peered closer at the bronze plaque. 'Apparently there's even a couple of *cars* in there, for some reason.'

His tone held the same disinterest it had all morning, and Dawn wondered for the hundredth time what it was she'd done to force that distance between them. She told herself she only wanted to know so she could make sure to keep doing it—the last thing she needed was to give in to any fleeting attraction to Justin's brother.

But the truth was she wanted the camaraderie back. The way they'd been the second day or so of their trip, when everything had been new and exciting and she'd been focused on her goal.

Before she'd started staring at Cooper's lips when he talked.

Before she'd ever imagined what it might feel like to kiss him.

Did he know? Was that why he was pulling away?

Or did he really, truly have something against time capsules, since her suggestion to visit this one seemed to be what had set off this particular round of his hiding-behind-his-shades, don't-touch-me vibe.

Dawn really hoped it was the time capsule. Otherwise, it was going to be a very long few days to the Hamptons and Justin.

'What would you put in your capsule?' she asked, hoping to draw out any childhood traumas with time capsules that might be affecting him.

Cooper just shrugged. 'I don't know. What are you supposed to put in these things?'

'Items that represent your life right now, I suppose.' Dawn glanced at the plaque, hoping for guidance, but it was no help. It just told her that the thing wasn't to be opened until 2025.

Where would she be by then? Dawn had no idea, but it almost certainly wouldn't be Seward, Nebraska.

'Then probably the work file for the latest deal I'm working on,' Cooper said with a shrug.

Dawn turned away from the pyramid to stare at him instead. 'Seriously? That's the only thing you can think of? Nothing personal at all?'

Did he really have *no* personal life? She knew from Justin's few comments that Cooper was the ultimate workaholic, but surely even the most dedicated CEO had to have *some* friendships, hobbies or interests outside of the office?

'A pair of running shoes?' Cooper tried. Because *of course* he stayed in shape. Even she'd noticed that. Okay, so she'd noticed that quite a lot, since his new wardrobe of thin cotton tee shirts and jeans did rather more to show off his body than the suit and tuxedo she'd seen him in before.

'Let me guess, exercise is important because it helps you work longer hours, right?'

'And live longer,' Cooper added. 'Thus staving off retirement by a few more years.'

'Of course.' Dawn sighed. The man really *was* hopeless. 'So, no friendships or relationships you want to commemorate?'

Cooper's expression turned contemplative. 'I suppose I *could* throw in my wedding ring and a copy of my divorce decree, but I don't think that's the sort of upbeat, inspiring content you're looking for here.'

'I don't suppose it is,' Dawn said quietly. What had happened to make this man so bitter about people—especially love? He'd be amiable enough when they chatted about nothing in the car, or in the various diners they stopped in en route, but the moment she got close to anything personal he'd clam up. He liked to pretend that he cared for nothing and nobody outside the office, but here he was escorting her across the country to find his brother and her closure.

She didn't understand him.

But she really, really wanted to—even if she wasn't ready to admit why, yet, even to herself.

'What happened with your wife?' This was the closest Cooper had really got to talking about her since they'd met, and Dawn wasn't going to miss the chance to find out more—to obtain another piece of the complicated puzzle that was Cooper Edwards.

'Actually, it was rather like your parents' story. And yours and Justin's, to a point,' he said. 'Whirlwind romance, sudden wedding—except in my case it featured an even more sudden divorce.'

'At least you got to the actually married stage,' Dawn joked. Cooper didn't laugh.

She swallowed uncomfortably before asking, 'Where is she now?'

'Last I heard, she'd moved to Seattle with a wealthy

cosmetic surgeon and was planning another wedding.' Cooper didn't look at her as he spoke, and his words were completely devoid of emotion. Dawn felt sympathy welling up inside her.

'You must have loved her very much,' she said, trying to imagine Cooper ever feeling enough for anyone to propose—let alone falling desperately in love in just a few weeks. She couldn't.

'Rather more than she ever loved me, as it turned out.' He flashed her a bitter smile. 'I don't suppose that's quite what *you* were expecting from marriage.'

'Well, for starters I was expecting my groom to show up,' Dawn pointed out. 'But beyond that, yeah, I guess I was expecting true love. The "for ever" kind. Like my parents have.'

'I'm not sure mine ever did,' Cooper admitted. 'Even before Dad died, things were tense between them. And Mom…she knew what she married into with the Edwards family and she's always played the role perfectly. I guess I believed Rachel would do the same.'

'But she wasn't interested?' Dawn guessed.

Cooper's smile fell away. 'Not exactly. But enough about her. What about you? Would you be truly happy playing at being Mrs Edwards, matriarch and upholder of Edwards family values once Mom is gone?'

The question sounded too pointed to be just a casual one, and Dawn resisted her natural urge just to laugh at it. For some reason, this mattered to Cooper. He really wanted to know her answer. So the least she could do was consider it properly.

'I don't know,' she said slowly, surprised by her own admission. If anyone had asked her the night before her wedding, she was sure she'd have said yes in a heartbeat. As it was… 'I guess I never really imagined that far ahead.

I just thought about me and Justin being together, blissfully happy. Perhaps with a family—a couple of kids, a boy and a girl. I thought about summers together at the beach house, and Christmas together, one year in Britain the next over here. I thought about quiet moments, just the two of us. But I didn't think so much about the Edwards legacy or any of that.' She gave him a rueful smile. 'Maybe, in my mind, I sort of assumed that you'd get married again and your wife would take care of all that.'

'Well, that's never going to happen. So maybe it's for the best that Justin didn't show up at the altar.' Leaving her speechless, Cooper walked back towards Claudia, whose robin's-egg-blue paintwork was shining in the midday sun. Apparently the conversation was over.

Was that truly what bothered him about her—that she wasn't suitable enough to take on the Edwards legacy? That she wouldn't be able to step into his mother's shoes in the future?

Maybe he was right about that. But Dawn couldn't help but feel that there was something more to the story that she was missing.

Either way, his comments had cut deeper than she'd like, and she made a point of staying away from Claudia for longer than she otherwise would have, until she'd recovered her equilibrium. She tried to take in the details about the time capsule—the controversy about whether the large space underground that formed most of it really *was* the biggest in the world, which had resulted in the additional pyramid on top, and the fact that Guinness had actually dropped the category from their world records shortly after, so it didn't really even count.

But mostly she wondered if Cooper was right about one thing. Would she *really* have been happy as a corporate wife once Justin had stepped up and taken on a bigger role in the family business, as she knew he'd been planning to? Would she have been happy giving up her own job to support his, organising dinners and galas for him, sweet-talking potential business partners?

In truth, she was pretty sure she would have hated it.

Except that admission led her to the acknowledgement of another of Cooper's hard truths: maybe it *was* just as well Justin had jilted her.

'Are you coming?' Cooper called eventually from where he leant against Claudia's bonnet, his arms folded over his broad chest. 'I want to make Des Moines before we stop for dinner.'

Dawn absently waved a hand at him.

Des Moines could wait. She had a lot of stuff she needed to figure out first.

CHAPTER TEN

THERE WAS SOMETHING up with Dawn and, whatever it was, Cooper didn't like it.

She'd been quiet when she'd come back from the time capsule, and hadn't even objected to grabbing lunch from a drive-through to eat on the way to Des Moines. After they'd found a hotel that evening—which he'd put on his card without even thinking about it—he'd suggested dinner, but she'd declined, saying she needed some time to herself.

In Cooper's experience, that never boded well.

He'd spent the evening eating room service, avoiding the mini-bar and watching bad sci-fi movies, all while obsessing over exactly which part of what he'd said by that stupid pyramid had upset her. And, more pertinently, why he cared.

The thing was, he'd lashed out when it wasn't even her fault. He knew himself well enough to admit that talking about his ex-wife, and his abject failure of a marriage, put him in a lousy mood.

But what he couldn't tell was whether she'd been more upset at the suggestion that Justin jilting her at the altar was a good thing, or her realisation that he might be *right*.

Because he *was* right. He'd seen it in her eyes, however

fast she'd tried to look away, and as much as she'd been avoiding meeting his gaze ever since.

Justin needed a wife who could play the part, like their mother had all these years. But Dawn wasn't interested in any of that.

Which led him back to his initial question—why did Justin think Dawn had been after their money? Because, as far as Cooper could tell, she wanted the perfect, romantic, true-love marriage her parents had, whether it meant being poor for life or richer than she could imagine.

And that thought just made his head hurt even more than yesterday's hangover had.

He'd hoped that the weirdness of the time capsule, and their conversations the day before, would have passed by the morning. But when Dawn met him in the hotel lobby she was still quiet, and didn't even question his suggestion of doughnuts for breakfast again.

Yeah, he really didn't like this.

'I thought we'd stop for lunch around Walcott, Iowa,' he said, once they'd finished off the doughnuts. It was strange, he realised suddenly, how much of their day revolved around meals on this trip. Usually, he'd forget to eat at least one meal a day unless he was meeting with clients at a restaurant, or his assistant brought him something. Even then, he rarely really tasted them, distracted as he was by whatever he was working on while he ate. But on the road with Dawn he'd savoured pancakes, doughnuts, burgers, milkshakes, steaks and all sorts, and had enjoyed every mouthful.

Maybe it was the company.

No, he wasn't thinking that way. Even if he'd stayed up half the night, after the last movie had finished, with a sudden urge to put together a list of bizarre roadside attractions for them to stop off at during the rest of their journey. He'd told himself he was just being practical, but he couldn't deny that a large part of his motivation was the smile he knew Dawn would give him when they pulled off the interstate to check them out.

Oh, boy, he was in trouble.

'That sounds fine,' Dawn said, still staring out of the window. Cooper eyed her as closely as he could while still keeping his attention on the road, but didn't spot any sign that the name Walcott meant anything to her. So far, her discovery of roadside attractions had mostly seemed serendipitous, or discovered online while they'd been driving. Since she hadn't even taken her phone out of her pocket this morning, the chances were she hadn't even checked out their route for the day yet.

Good. He quite liked the idea of surprising her for a change.

He smiled to himself for the first time that morning as Claudia sped along the interstate—at least, until his mind caught up with him and started asking a whole bevy of new questions.

If Dawn was pulling away from him, it could be for two reasons, as he saw it. One, she was realising he was right and giving up any hope of a future with Justin. Which, on the off-chance that Justin *was* right about her motives, could only be a good thing. And actually, even if he wasn't, it probably wasn't exactly a *bad* one. Cooper knew his brother, and he was getting to know Dawn. They might have had the whirlwind romance but surely he was proof enough that those didn't always work out?

Of course the second reason was more troublesome. Because there was an even chance that Dawn was determined to prove him wrong instead. That she was pulling away so she could prepare herself for winning Justin back to silence the doubts that Cooper had raised.

And if that was the case he knew he couldn't let her drift too far. He had to keep her focussed on the truth—that she and Justin weren't meant to be. Not because, as his restless mind taunted him at night, the idea of watching her with his brother made his guts knot up with something he refused to call jealousy, but because it was the only way he could think of to spare Justin a messy divorce further down the line.

He never wanted his brother to have to go through the sort of heartbreak he had, whatever the cause. Dawn might not be a gold-digger—and he still wasn't one hundred per cent certain if he could trust his gut on that—but she wasn't the right wife for Justin either. The ending would be the same, bitter one, either way.

Except that Justin loved her. Which meant, if he knew that she *wasn't* after his money, he'd want her back. So it was entirely possible Cooper was driving Dawn to a reconciliation with Justin that he was almost certain was a bad idea.

But what else could he do at this point? Apart from anything else, he wasn't willing to give up a few more days on this journey with Dawn.

Not even for his brother.

Cooper's head hurt from all the permutations and possibilities. Maybe he'd just focus on their next stop and forget all about their ultimate destination for a change.

At least, until they stopped in Chicago that night. Because then they were well over halfway to the Hamptons, and Cooper knew he had to accept that they definitely weren't turning back then. Which meant he wouldn't be able to put off a certain task any longer. Justin might have been able to ignore the text messages and emails Cooper had sent him from the road but that couldn't go on for ever.

Tonight, it was time to call his brother and warn him they were coming.

* * *

'What is it with you guys needing to be the biggest and the best?' Dawn asked as she clocked the sign at the turn-off: Walcott, Iowa, home of the World's Biggest Truck Stop. She'd known it sounded familiar when Cooper had mentioned it that morning, but she'd been too preoccupied with her own jumbled thoughts to figure out why.

'By "you guys" do you mean Americans, men or just American men?' Cooper accompanied his request for clarity with a raised eyebrow.

'A bit of all three, probably. You have to admit, it's kind of an obsession.'

'Says the woman who insisted on eating hotdogs with the world's biggest dead polar bear.' Cooper shut off the engine and opened Claudia's door. 'At least this place has a museum. About trucks.'

'A museum and all the testosterone you can handle,' Dawn murmured as she followed him out of the car.

Cooper pointed at her across Claudia's bonnet. 'Just for that, you're driving the next leg to Chicago.'

Dawn rolled her eyes. 'I *always* drive after lunch. Because you're too grouchy to surrender the keys in the mornings—that, or you want to make sure we have the least healthy breakfast possible.' At least, that had been their routine for the past four days. Was that how long they'd been travelling together? Somehow, it seemed much longer. Wasn't time supposed to fly when you were having fun?

Because, whether she liked to admit it or not—and she didn't—Dawn *was* having fun with Cooper. Which had seemed an absolute impossibility at the start of the trip. Somehow, he was a different person out on the road.

Maybe it was Claudia's influence.

Or maybe it was hers.

Dawn shook the thought away and followed Cooper

into the truck stop in search of lunch. She had a feeling they'd be trawling around every inch of the truck museum afterwards, so she wanted to be well fortified. Bypassing the chain restaurants in the food court, she headed to the Iowa 80 Kitchen, her mouth salivating at the menu. It might not be a British fish-and-chip shop, but she'd take anything that wasn't caked in sugar at the moment. One of the many things Justin had never mentioned about his brother was his sweet tooth.

As she tucked into her creamy chicken pasta *al fredo* a short while later, Dawn reflected that, while it might not be the healthiest meal ever, at least it included vegetables. She'd never before been so glad of some broccoli and mushrooms.

She surveyed Cooper over his giant burger—his third in a week, on top of the doughnuts, the pancakes, the room service and the breakfast muffins. He ate like a teenage boy, but had the body of an athletic, thirty-year-old health nut. It really wasn't fair.

'How does a workaholic like you stay in such great shape living on this sort of food?' she asked.

Cooper took an enormous bite, chewing for a long moment as he wiped ketchup from his fingers.

'I know you said you exercise,' Dawn went on, impatient at waiting for him to finish eating. 'But seriously, you'd need to be cross training for hours and hours every day to work off this stuff, and I know for a fact you'd never leave your office for that long. According to Justin, anyway.' She frowned. 'Then again, I haven't seen you working much this week either. Are you spending all night dealing with your emails?'

Cooper finally swallowed before her babbling got too much further out of hand, for which she was thankful.

'I don't normally eat like this,' he admitted, dipping

one of his French fries in the sauce. 'And I haven't been working. I'm on *vacation*.'

Dawn blinked. 'Justin always said you didn't take holidays. Ever.'

'Well, then, this is my first one. My first since— Well, since my honeymoon.'

'Ah.' Wincing, Dawn looked back down at her pasta. Then across at his fries. Possibly the appeal of vegetables was wearing off.

Rolling his eyes, Cooper pushed his plate a little way across the table so she could help herself to the fries. She smiled her thanks before digging in.

'So this is your idea of a holiday, then—travelling across the country with me?' Dawn asked. 'I'd have pegged you for more of a "luxury private island in the Maldives" kind of guy.'

'That *was* my honeymoon,' Cooper admitted. 'Not something I'm particularly looking to relive.'

'I suppose I can understand that.' Although, given the chance, Dawn had to admit that the island sounded pretty damned good regardless. Except she'd probably get bored. She never had been very good at sunbathing holidays. 'Besides, there's lots more to see this way. Plenty to keep us entertained.'

'Absolutely.' The amused smile he gave her as she stole another chip suggested that *she* might be one of the more entertaining things on their trip. Well, whatever kept him paying for the hotel rooms was fine by her. They'd be sleeping in Claudia if they had to rely on her credit card for much longer.

'I was checking ahead on the route, actually,' Cooper went on. 'There's a lighthouse we could stop at tomorrow. And maybe a ghost town the next day? They're both a bit of a detour, but not too much...'

'Sounds good,' Dawn said, surprised. At the start of the trip, he'd been so desperate to get there as quickly as possible. Now he was suggesting detours? 'So, not hurrying to the Hamptons quite so much any more?'

Cooper shrugged and took another bite of his burger. 'Insert your cliché about enjoying the journey here,' he said between chews. Then he swallowed. 'Besides, if this is the only vacation I'm likely to get for a while, I might as well make the most of it, right?'

'I guess so.' Dawn smiled. 'In which case, we should totally hit the gift shop before the museum!'

That earned her a groan, but somehow Dawn sensed he wasn't quite as annoyed as he would have been four days ago.

Who would have thought it? She seemed to be growing on Cooper Edwards after all.

The truck museum, as Cooper had predicted, was wonderfully full of vintage trucks dating back to the start of the twentieth century. But, after checking them into the hotel in Chicago that night and heading to his room, he had to admit that his favourite part of their stop at Iowa 80 was watching Dawn steal his fries as they'd talked over lunch. Okay, it might also have been the very tight, bright-pink 'World's Largest Truck Stop' tee shirt she bought and insisted on wearing while she'd driven the rest of the way to Chicago.

But talking with Dawn…just talking, about vacations and lifestyle choices…reminded him how rarely he did that. Until this week.

He and Dawn had been chatting about everything and nothing since they'd made the pact to drive Claudia across the country together. But today it felt different. The conversation hadn't been as intense as the one at the time capsule, and for once she hadn't pressed with any difficult questions about his marriage or his personal life.

They'd just talked. Like friends. Like people who cared about each other.

How long had it been since he'd had someone like that in his life? Someone just to…talk to?

He shook his head as he stared down at the hotel keycard in his hand. *Too* long, that was how long.

'Cooper?' Dawn called.

He looked up along the hotel corridor and saw her standing outside her own door, just as he was outside his room. Her gaze was concerned as she watched him.

'Everything okay?' she asked.

He nodded automatically. 'Fine. I'll see you downstairs in an hour? We'll go find some dinner.'

'Sure,' Dawn said, but she still sounded uncertain. 'I'll see you there.'

Before she could ask anything else, Cooper pushed the key card into the slot and pulled it out again, the light thankfully turning green first time. Shoulder against the door, he made his way into the room, carrying his bag at his side.

It wasn't as light as it had been, he realised as he hefted it onto the bed. The bare essentials he'd bought in Sacramento four days earlier had been added to at every city and truck stop they'd broken their journey at, it seemed—as had Dawn's, he knew. In fact, her belongings were now in a cheap Des Moines-branded holdall, while his were stored in a brown leather bag he'd picked up in Salt Lake City. There hadn't seemed to be much time for shopping, but still he had a couple more outfits than he'd started with, a new book or two to read when he wasn't driving—something that annoyed Dawn a lot, since she got car sick when she tried to read in the car—and a new warm top that doubled as a dressing gown when the hotels were over-zealous with the air-con.

Basically, he'd started building up his belongings from zero again. And, while he had the funds to buy anything he chose without thinking about cost, he'd found himself choosing more carefully than he was used to. In fact, usually he just got his assistant to send out for clothes, shoes and so on from tailors and high-end stores he liked. On the road, his choices were more limited—yet he felt more satisfaction in choosing them himself than he ever had in the suit bags that arrived at his apartment from time to time.

Looking up from the bag on the bed, he was startled by his reflection in the mirror over the desk.

He barely looked like himself. His hair was unstyled, his stubble longer than he usually kept it and the tee shirt and jeans he wore unfamiliar compared to his usual suit and tie. But it was more than that...

Cooper moved closer, peering into his own eyes in the mirror. Somehow, despite the long hours in the car, the stress of the wedding that wasn't and his ongoing uncertainty about Dawn and her motivations, he looked more relaxed than he had in years.

In fact, he might even go as far as to say he looked... happy.

He blinked, breaking the mirror's spell, and spun away. This road trip was only temporary—a week out of his real life. He couldn't afford to read too much into it, not when he had responsibilities to get back to and obligations to uphold.

Starting with his brother.

Cooper tugged his phone from his jeans pocket and hit his brother's name from his call log. He'd tried a couple of times on the wedding day but had got no answer. Since then, he'd sent a few text messages and emails asking Justin how he was, but there'd been no reply to those either.

And, for some reason, he'd never quite got round to telling his brother that he was on his way to see him. With Dawn.

Probably that was the sort of thing it would be polite to mention before they just showed up on the beach-house porch.

The phone on the other end rang and rang, and Cooper raised it to his ear just as the voicemail kicked in.

'Hi, you've reached Justin Edwards. Leave a message and I'll get back to you.'

Except Cooper knew he wouldn't. If Justin wanted to talk to him, he'd have responded to one of his messages already.

Cooper pressed the end-call button. His brother was avoiding him every bit as much as he was avoiding Dawn. Which meant that leaving a message telling him they were coming was a sure-fire way to send him running off somewhere else. Somewhere Claudia might not be able to follow. Cooper—and especially Dawn—couldn't risk that. They both needed to see Justin.

Which meant they were just going to have to surprise him.

CHAPTER ELEVEN

DAWN STARED AT her reflection in the mirror. Cooper had said they'd go somewhere nice for dinner, but the problem was she didn't really have anything in the way of nice 'going out for dinner' clothes in the meagre wardrobe she'd managed to put together over the last few days.

Sighing, she gave up pretending that the denim skirt and white tee shirt she was wearing would ever be anything approaching a slinky cocktail dress and dropped to sit down on the bed. Honestly, those people who wrote articles about the joy of capsule wardrobes had clearly never tried to look good in the same skirt for a full week, while travelling in a vintage convertible whose seats creased *everything*.

Not that it seemed to bother Cooper, who looked perfectly pressed every minute of the day regardless. And he didn't seem to care about her limited wardrobe, either. She'd assumed he just hadn't even registered her clothes— most guys she knew wouldn't have. But then she'd seen his expression when she'd put on her new 'World's Biggest Truck Stop' tee shirt…

Justin had only ever looked at her like that when she'd worn designer dresses. Cooper appeared to have tastes that were rather easier to please.

Not that she was going to read anything into it. The top

had been *slightly* tighter than she'd thought it would be, that was all. Most men would have stared, right? It didn't mean anything.

Just like him letting her share his chips didn't mean anything.

Or the fact that he'd finally opened up a little bit about his wife.

All any of it meant was that they'd been spending a lot of time together and were getting to know each other. Which seemed a bit of a waste of time, now she wasn't going to marry his brother.

But somehow that didn't stop her wanting to know him even better. Or wishing she had a slinky dress to wear for dinner with him tonight.

Dawn sighed. At some point, she was going to have to acknowledge that she might have developed a tiny bit of a crush on her ex-fiancé's brother. She was just hoping it could wait until after this road trip was over. Admitting to anything now could only make the rest of the trip excruciatingly awkward.

Either Cooper would be horrified that she was thinking about him that way when she was technically still engaged to his brother—she hadn't returned the ring yet, so she guessed it still stood—or he'd admit to feeling the same, and then what? They'd kiss, avoid each other's eyes for the next few days, she'd go and talk to his brother about their failed relationship and then she and Cooper would part ways and never see each other again.

It would have to be some kiss to make that kind of awkwardness worthwhile.

Still. Her limited wardrobe choices and ridiculous crush aside, that didn't mean she couldn't make a *bit* of an effort. It wasn't as if she got asked out to dinner in Chicago every day. Or ever before, actually.

There wasn't much she could do about her clothes, but she did dig out the gauzy, hot-pink scarf she'd picked up from the bargain bin at a convenience store attached to the diner where they'd bought doughnuts one morning. Wrapped around her neck twice, with the ends hanging loose, it at least made her boring outfit look a little more interesting.

Taking her hair down from its ponytail, she brushed it out over her shoulders, fluffing it a bit so it fell in gentle waves. With the addition of some simple make-up and the bright-pink lipstick she'd bought on a whim in Sacramento— because a girl never knew when she might need a confidence-boosting lipstick—she *almost* looked as though she might have come prepared for a night on the town.

Cooper knocked on the door moments later, and Dawn steeled herself before opening it. What had it come to that she had to prepare herself for seeing him, knowing that if he looked too good he'd take her breath away? She felt like a teenager with a first crush, rather than a woman who'd been through the relationship mill too many times to count.

Maybe that was the appeal. She knew anything with Cooper could never be a relationship—he hated the idea of marriage and she'd already been engaged to his brother, for heaven's sake—and that made him safe. She could lust from afar, flirt over chips, have fancy dinners out and never worry about it meaning a thing.

She grinned to herself as she pulled open the door. Maybe she'd do exactly that.

'Wow,' Cooper said, eyebrows raised. 'You look…'

'Exactly like I've done every other day of this trip?' Dawn finished for him. 'Because I still haven't got round to buying a second skirt.'

'I was going to say great. Or beautiful. Or something

better than that.' Cooper's gaze seemed to be fixed on her lips.

Score one for the lipstick.

But her moment of triumph faded as she took in his appearance. He hadn't dressed up much either, for the same obvious reason, but still the jeans that moulded so perfectly to his legs, the collared tee-shirt that highlighted his throat and those broad, broad shoulders, the stubble that made him look just that little bit more devil-may-care than she'd ever imagined he could…all added up to a truly delectable picture.

One that really made her want to smudge her lipstick.

But, no. Flirting. Dinner. Fun. That was all.

Anything else could never end well.

She just had to keep reminding herself of that.

'Shall we go?' she asked, smiling brightly. And hoping against hope that she could hold off kissing her fiancé's brother until they hit the Hamptons.

Dinner was a hit. As he'd predicted, Dawn loved the steak place he'd picked for them to eat at, happily trying everything he suggested, as well as everything he'd ordered for himself.

'I spent too long eating boring food,' she explained after moaning around a mouthful of steak and sauce béarnaise. 'I'm making up for it.'

Simply watching her eat, those bright-pink lips closing around her fork, was making Cooper hungry. Just not for food.

He was hungry for her company, her conversation—the easy way they tossed thoughts and comments back and forth without needing to read too much into them.

Although he had to admit he might have missed some of what she was saying because he was too busy staring at her lips. Imagining how it would feel to kiss them. To be fair, though, Dawn had trailed off a few times mid-sentence too. Which only made things worse, because he was almost certain she was imagining the same things he was.

Which meant he was in really big trouble.

He wanted her.

He wanted his little brother's fiancée in a way he hadn't wanted anyone since the ex-wife who'd broken his heart and taken half his fortune.

And he knew the only reason Justin had called things off was because he thought Dawn was a gold-digger—something Cooper was almost certain wasn't the case. In which case…he had to take Dawn back to his brother. Give them another chance at happiness together.

Except they were wrong for each other, damn it! Having spent four days talking to her, and a lifetime knowing Justin, he could tell that instantly. She wouldn't be happy with him, and he'd want her to be things she wasn't. Or at least, things that didn't come naturally to her.

Justin was a caviar-and-champagne guy. He always had to have the most expensive of everything, just because it cost more.

Dawn, he'd established, appreciated the *best* things, whatever the cost.

No, Cooper was absolutely convinced that Dawn and Justin together would be a mistake.

The only problem with that was that he was hugely, ridiculously biased, and he knew it.

What if he only saw these problems because he wanted them to be true? Because he wanted Dawn for himself? He'd only seen them together as a couple for twenty-four hours before Justin had run out. What did he know about their life together? Maybe Justin was a different guy with Dawn.

Cooper sure as hell was.

After he'd paid the bill, they'd walked the few blocks back to the hotel, talking about nothing at all. And it wasn't until they reached her room that Cooper admitted to himself quite how much he didn't want the night to end.

'So, we'll meet in the lobby as normal?' Dawn asked, leaning against her door as she smiled up at him.

'Yeah. Say, nine?' Cooper hoped he managed to sound normal and unaffected by her presence. He definitely didn't feel it.

It wasn't her clothes, or her hair, make-up or even the soft scent of whatever products she'd been using that filled his lungs and made him want. It wasn't even the conversation. It was her smile—the easy, happy, optimistic smile that told him that she didn't want to be anywhere else, that she didn't need anything from him, that she was just happy to be there.

That was the part that was going to ruin him.

'Goodnight, Dawn.' Leaning down, he brushed a swift kiss against her cheek, then turned away, heading back to his own room.

He needed sleep. And he needed to move past this strange connection he'd forged with his brother's fiancée.

Even if he had no idea how to do that.

And even if he knew he would spend all night dreaming about pink lipstick—and *wanting*.

'So, tell me about this lighthouse of yours,' Dawn said as Chicago faded away into the background through Claudia's back window.

Cooper had beaten her down to the lobby that morning for the first time all week, and had been waiting for her with warm and gooey cheese and ham croissants—

always the sign of an excellent day, in her book. Following on from a great evening the night before, as it happened.

Dawn was glad she had picked out her bright-pink 'truck stop' tee shirt to wear again that morning. From the way Cooper's eyes roamed over the logo on it, she figured it was basically a thank-you in clothing form for the croissant.

'I wouldn't call it *my* lighthouse,' Cooper said with the nonchalance of a man who might actually own a lighthouse somewhere. His family certainly had the money, and Dawn had never been able to keep all their property straight in her head.

'You were the one who wanted to stop there,' she pointed out. 'So what's so great about it?'

Cooper shrugged, glancing away from the road to look at her. 'I just saw a picture on the Internet and figured you might like it, was all.'

A warm feeling flowed through her at his casual words. However bad an idea her crush was, at least after the last day or so she was almost certain that Cooper returned it. Maybe they'd never be able to act on it, but just knowing that he'd picked out a place to visit because he thought she'd like it went a long way to making her feel a little better about the whole situation.

'It's still a good four hours' drive, though,' Cooper added. 'If you wanted to get some sleep?'

'Are you saying I look tired?' she asked, eyebrows raised. Admittedly, her night's rest had been punctuated by more dreams of him than she was willing to admit to, but Dawn didn't think it was anything her concealer hadn't hid. But, as she looked at him, she realised that *Cooper* looked exhausted. As if he hadn't slept all night.

As if he'd been as disturbed by dreams and imaginings as she had.

Huh.

'You look full of the joys of summer, as always,' Cooper said with a mocking smile that suddenly didn't seem so mocking.

'Do you want me to drive?' she asked bluntly. 'I mean, if you need to sleep, I can drive to the lighthouse. You can take over afterwards.'

She could see common sense warring with pride in his expression. Clearly he was too exhausted to drive safely, but he was also equally unwilling to admit it.

So Dawn made the decision for him. 'Pull over.'

'I don't need you to—'

'And I don't plan to die in a car accident before making it to the Hamptons, thanks. So pull over and we can swap seats.' She stared at him until he did as she asked.

Dawn climbed out of Claudia's passenger side first, moving swiftly around to the other side to open Cooper's door for him. As he got out, he held her arm gently to stop her sliding into his vacated seat.

'Thanks,' he said softly, his mouth so close to her cheek she could feel his breath. 'I...didn't sleep much last night.'

'Bad dreams?' She stared up into his eyes as she asked and watched his pupils grow wide and black.

'Quite the opposite, actually.' Cooper's voice, rough, low and dark, rang through her body until she felt as though every cell of it was vibrating at the sound.

God, she wanted him. And it looked as though he wanted her every bit as much.

She swallowed and looked away, fumbling for the steering wheel as she climbed into her seat.

'We should get going,' she said.

Cooper nodded, making his way round to the passenger seat. 'Long way to the lighthouse,' he agreed.

And an even longer way to the Hamptons. And her ex-fiancé.

When Cooper awoke again, Dawn was singing along to Elvis on the radio—it seemed to be the only music Claudia would consent to play—and they were just passing a sign for Marblehead Lighthouse State Park. Dawn's phone was set to the sat nav app, and calling out periodic directions.

'How long was I out?' He straightened up in his seat, rubbing at the back of his neck to try and ease the ache there.

'Felt like for ever,' Dawn quipped as she turned onto a smaller road. 'Any more dreams?'

The look she gave him told him that she had a pretty good idea what his dreams had been about. Hardly surprising, given the heat that had radiated between them when he'd told her the reason he hadn't slept.

Thankfully, he'd been too exhausted to dream during his car nap, because otherwise things could have got very awkward, very fast.

'Totally dreamless,' he said with relief.

'Glad to hear it,' Dawn replied, although her tone said something different.

Did she *want* him to dream about her? Had she been dreaming about him?

Cooper stared out of the window and bit back a curse. Apparently, ignoring the attraction between them wasn't working any longer—if it ever had.

Which meant they were going to have to talk about it. *Damn.*

Dawn parked and together they made their way into the

state park, both stretching as they walked to work out the kinks that four-plus hours in a car gave a person.

On the shores of Lake Erie, the park was strangely peaceful, even in the summer high season. As they followed the trail towards the shore, the red-tipped lighthouse, white except for its cap and the red railings lower down, stood proudly against the water. He'd read something about tours, Cooper thought vaguely, and about climbing the steps to the top of the lighthouse and looking out. But he was content just to look at it from the outside. To soak up the atmosphere and the calm of the lake and park.

To relax, for once.

At least, until Dawn said, 'So, are we going to talk about it?'

It was just like pulling off a sticking plaster, Dawn reasoned. Obviously there was something between them—something distracting, awkward and potentially difficult. The sooner they talked about it, the sooner they could move on.

Even if her heart was pounding in her chest as she asked.

'Talk about what?' Cooper asked, his expression blank. Then he sighed. 'Never mind. I know what.'

He sank down to sit on a nearby bench, the summer sun glinting off his dark hair, and his legs stretched out in front of him as he stared down at his hands.

Dawn perched beside him, her own hands clasped too tightly in her lap as she tried to figure out what she wanted to say.

Cooper beat her to it. 'Here's the thing—I don't have friends. I never really noticed until this week, but I don't. I have colleagues and business contacts, maybe even a few acquaintances I know well enough to meet for a drink if I'm in town. But not friends. Not until this week.'

'You think we're friends?' Dawn asked, surprised.

'I think we could be.' Cooper looked up at last, meeting her eyes, and she almost gasped at the sincerity in them. 'I think that spending this week with you in that stupid car, stopping at ridiculous roadside attractions and eating junk food for every meal, has been the most fun I've had in years.'

'You need to get out more. Meet more people,' Dawn joked, but Cooper didn't laugh.

'Maybe you're right. Maybe it is time to get back out there. Meet people.' And by 'people' Dawn assumed he meant women.

In fact, he sounded as if the thought was a revelation. As if he'd just realised a universal truth—probably the same one men had been realising all through her life.

Dawn's spirits took a nose dive. Talk about backsliding. Her last relationship had made it all the way to the altar, even if it hadn't got any further. This one—if you could even call it a relationship—hadn't even made it to the first kiss.

'The thing is, I don't think it's *people*,' Cooper said. 'I think it's you.'

Dawn jerked her head up to stare at him. 'Me?' It was never *her*. That was the point.

Cooper nodded. 'Because I meet people every day, Dawn. And I don't let them in. I don't want to let them in. I didn't want to let *you* in.'

'I kind of got that.'

'But you got there anyway. And maybe that's just forced proximity in Claudia.'

'You're making this sound like a sort of Stockholm Syndrome friendship here,' Dawn pointed out.

'Or maybe it's just you,' Cooper finished as if she hadn't spoken. 'But the thing is, Dawn, I'm a different person with you. And I like him a lot more than the person I've been since Rachel left me.'

Rachel. So that was his ex-wife's name.

'So…me and this new you,' Dawn said cautiously. 'We're…friends?'

'Yes,' Cooper said, but there was something in his voice. A note of uncertainty, maybe. Something she couldn't quite place until he added, 'Except I keep dreaming about your pink lipstick.'

Score two for Flamingo Shimmer.

'My lipstick?'

When had he got so close? One moment they were sitting beside each other on the bench, a perfectly respectable distance between them, and now…now she could almost feel the warmth of his skin in the sunshine as his arm brushed close to hers and his lips moved closer.

'Uh huh. I keep imagining how it would feel to kiss you. Dreaming of it, in fact.'

'Just…kissing?' Dawn asked, because apparently she didn't know when just to go with a good thing.

'No,' Cooper admitted. 'Not just kissing.'

And then, before she could even process that thought, Cooper leant in that extra inch and suddenly his lips were on hers, warm and soft and perfect, just as she'd imagined.

Until they were gone again, far too soon.

'I shouldn't have done that.' Cooper pushed away against the floor until he was sat at the far end of the bench.

'I beg to differ.' Dawn said, her lips still tingling.

'You're engaged to my brother.'

'He left me at the altar,' Dawn pointed out. 'I think that's a pretty clear sign that it's over.'

'Then why are we chasing him across the country?' Cooper raised his eyebrows as he waited for an answer.

Dawn stared at him in amazement. 'Oh, my God. You think I'm going to beg Justin to take me back!'

'Well, aren't you?'

'No!' Dawn said, but honesty compelled her to add, 'Maybe I might have wanted to, at first. Just a bit. But that's not why we're on this road trip. It's not what you think.'

'Then explain it to me. Please.'

It wasn't a story that Dawn really wanted to tell, but the brief flare of hope that shone in Cooper's eyes told her she needed to.

'Okay. But not here. Come on, we need to get Claudia back on the road if we want to stop in Cleveland tonight.'

She stood and held out a hand to Cooper. After a moment, he took it. And somehow, as they walked to the car, he never quite let go.

CHAPTER TWELVE

'Do you know what my sisters call me?' Dawn asked as Claudia pulled out of the Marblehead Lighthouse State Park.

Cooper glanced across at her in surprise. Given their previous conversation, this was not where he'd imagined their talk going next.

'Dawn, I'd assume,' he said flippantly.

'They call me the Dry Run.' There was pain in Dawn's voice—pain he wanted to kiss away, if only he hadn't been driving. But, for the life of him, he couldn't figure out what the nickname meant.

'I don't get it.'

'Every guy I've ever dated—and I do mean every single one,' she clarified, leaving him wondering exactly how many there had been. 'Every guy I've ever been out with has left me then gone on to meet the love of his life and marry them within the next two years.'

Cooper blinked. Suddenly the number seemed more relevant than just calming his sudden jealous spurt. If it had been one or two guys, that might be put down to co-incidence. But more...

'How many boyfriends are we talking here? For statistical reasons only, I promise,' he added, when she started to object.

'Five,' Dawn answered. 'Six if you count Billy Nolan, which I suppose we could.'

'Billy Nolan?'

'We were ten, so the marriage part took a little longer. But the next month a new girl moved to town and they were sweethearts all through secondary school and university, and got married the day after graduation.'

'Six men. Six different men seriously passed you up to marry someone else?' The words were out before he could think about their implication, but the pink tinge on Dawn's cheeks told him she didn't much mind.

'I'm the girl guys date for years, knowing it's not everything they ever dreamed of but thinking it might be enough—until they find the real thing and they realise I could never compare.'

Okay, now he understood that pain. The bitter ache he heard in her words. The crushing feeling of never being enough, of not measuring up. Of being a fool for ever thinking you could. He knew *exactly* how that felt, and he hated that Dawn had ever had to experience it once, let alone six times. It made him wonder how she could possibly keep picking herself back up and trying again. How she could keep that unflagging optimism.

But the one thing he couldn't help but notice she *hadn't* said was that she didn't want Justin back. She might not plan to beg, but that wasn't the same as not wanting.

He wouldn't press her. But he wouldn't ignore it either. And he knew he couldn't kiss her again, not as he had by the lighthouse anyway, without knowing her intentions towards his brother. Knowing if she still loved him.

Which meant they were on hold. But they were still friends, and suddenly he wanted to give some of that friendship back to her.

'Rachel cheated on me on our honeymoon,' he said,

without really knowing why. Maybe he just wanted to offer her something of his own pain to balance things out.

He saw Dawn wince out of the corner of his eye, and kept talking just to stop himself having to hear her inevitable sympathy and pity.

'In fairness, she'd been cheating on me all through our engagement too,' he said. 'And I didn't actually find out until we'd been married a month or so. Turns out that the whole fidelity part of marriage had passed her by entirely.'

Dawn shook her head. 'I don't understand. Why would she do that? How could she?'

Because all she wanted me for was my name, my lifestyle and, most of all, my money.

But that truth still hurt too much to share, to know that his entire worth could be numbered in dollars and still be found lacking.

'We had different expectations from marriage, I guess,' he said instead. 'She wanted someone who would pay for the lifestyle she wanted—who would get her into the parties and places she thought she belonged in. Someone who could give her prestige and position and the money to do anything she wanted. And I could give her all of that, of course. In return, I just wanted her love, but apparently that part wasn't for sale.'

'I'm so sorry.'

'It was years ago now,' Cooper said, trying to brush her pity aside. He didn't need it. 'And at least she taught me an important lesson about people.'

'Which is?'

'You can never know another person fully. Not really.' Cooper's realised his knuckles were white where he gripped the steering wheel, and tried to loosen his hold. 'The best you can try and do is know yourself.'

'And do you?' Dawn asked. 'Know yourself, I mean?'

Cooper looked across at her. 'I always thought I did,' he said, softly. 'Until I met you.'

'We still need to talk about that kiss,' Dawn reminded Cooper as they stopped outside their adjoining motel rooms in Cleveland that night. She'd had a text from her credit card provider with the news that her limit increase had been approved, so she'd insisted on paying again. Of course, that meant they were in a cheap motel on the edge of the city with doors that faced out onto the car park and a cheap porch covering overhead—because the increase wasn't *that* much—but she still felt better for being able to pay her way.

Even if the walls were so thin she'd probably be able to hear Cooper snoring that night. Or if he called out anything in his sleep.

Like maybe her name…

'We do.' Cooper sounded exhausted and he leant against the wooden doorframe as he spoke. The second part of the day's driving—which should have only taken another hour or so—had ended up taking three, thanks to a pile-up on the interstate. They'd stopped and eaten a silent, exhausted dinner on the way into town so they wouldn't have to leave the motel again once they were checked in.

He looked absolutely ready to drop, and here she was asking him to have a deep and meaningful conversation about their feelings.

No wonder men left her.

'It'll keep,' she said, with a smile she didn't feel. 'We can talk tomorrow.'

'That might be best.' Cooper's answering smile had more than a little relief in it. 'I have a feeling it's not the sort of conversation you'd thank me for falling asleep during.'

'Probably not.' She slipped her key into the door and opened it, turning back to say, 'Goodnight, Cooper.'

To her surprise, he leant forward and pressed another soft kiss to her lips. 'Goodnight, Dawn. Sweet dreams.' Then he was gone into his room, the door shutting firmly behind him.

Dawn stood staring after him all the same. Somehow, she had a feeling that her dreams that night would be anything but sweet.

Especially when she opened her own door and found a naked stranger in the middle of the room.

Ten minutes later, Dawn had established three things. One: that the new app they were using to book hotels since the disaster with the one in Salt Lake City also sucked, since it had let her book two rooms in a motel where there was apparently only one free room. Two: the girl running the reception desk at this motel didn't much care for her problems. And three: she was far too tired even to think about finding anywhere else to stay that night.

Her eyes itching with tiredness, Dawn leant outside Cooper's bedroom door and tried to work up the courage to knock. What was the worst he could do? Send her to sleep in Claudia instead?

Even that sounded preferable to being awake for another moment. And it might even be more comfortable than the couch in Salt Lake City.

Raising her hand, she knocked lightly on the door, hoping she wouldn't wake him.

'Dawn?' Cooper answered it wearing just a pair of shorts, his dark hair even messier than normal and his eyes barely open. 'What's going on? Are you okay?'

'I think we're actually cursed,' she said. 'I can't believe it happened again.'

'What happened again?' Cooper frowned, and she saw the moment he got it. 'Oh.'

'Yeah. The stupid motel overbooked,' she explained. 'My room is already occupied by an alarmingly naked old guy, and there aren't any others free. Can I crash in here with you tonight? I'll even take the couch again.'

Cooper's eyes widened at that, and Dawn was suddenly all too aware that this wasn't like last time. Last time, he hadn't kissed her just that afternoon. Last time, she hadn't even imagined that she could want him to do it again.

And it suddenly occurred to her that this could look like something it wasn't.

'I swear this isn't a play, Cooper. There really aren't any other rooms. And to be honest, I don't think either of us has the energy to make this into anything tonight anyway.' If they couldn't even stay awake long enough to *talk* about the kiss, what were the chances of it happening again before either of them got any sleep?

Cooper didn't answer, so Dawn reached down to pick up her bag again and stepped back. 'Never mind. I'll sleep in the car.'

'No!' His hand shot out at that, grabbing her wrist and tugging her towards him. 'Sorry. I'm just half-asleep. Of course you can stay here. And you don't have to take the couch. Not least because there isn't one.'

He let her go, running a hand through his hair as he stepped aside to let her into the room.

There wasn't much of it, she realised. What with the naked guy next door, she hadn't taken in much of the room she'd originally been assigned, but it was clear now that they'd got what she'd paid for: not much. A double bed, barely more than a single, a small table with a kettle and mug on it, with some instant coffee sachets, a TV on the wall and presumably a bathroom through the other door on the far side.

Absolute basic, minimum-requirement motel room.

'We could go find somewhere else to stay,' she suggested, looking back at the very small bed. 'If you'd rather.'

Cooper covered his mouth as he gave a jaw-cracking yawn. 'Dawn, it's late. We're both exhausted. We can share. Come on. Let's go to bed.'

She nodded, hoping this wasn't the worst idea she'd ever had. Although it wasn't as if it didn't have some stiff competition.

It was strange, getting ready for bed in the bathroom, knowing that Cooper was just in the next room, already under the covers. The covers they needed to share. God, what if he was a blanket hog?

And she still hadn't bought any pyjamas. Damn. It hadn't been such a problem last time, when she could wrap a blanket round herself for full coverage.

Pulling out the longest of her collection of tee shirts, she pulled it on, leaving her knickers on with it and hoping for the best. Like he'd said, they were both too tired to think, let alone have inappropriate thoughts about each other. This would be fine. Two friends sharing a bed. That was all.

No problem.

She tried to smile at herself in the mirror, but even her reflection seemed to know that she was lying.

Well, no point putting it off. Dawn finished cleaning her teeth then turned off the bathroom light, heading back into the bedroom.

Cooper lay on the far side of the bed, his back turned towards her, the covers pulled up to his waist and his torso bare. Dawn gave herself precisely fifteen seconds to enjoy the view before she slipped into the bed beside him, her back to his, and pulled up the sheets to cover her. Reaching out, she switched off the light and lay, eyes open, in the darkness.

'Goodnight, Dawn,' Cooper murmured without moving.

'Goodnight.' The bed wasn't particularly soft, but it was better than Claudia's back seat. And the blankets might be scratchy, but they were keeping her from touching Cooper's skin and losing her mind.

All she had to do now was remember how to sleep, when Cooper was lying next to her half-naked.

Yep. Absolutely no problem at all.

Cooper hadn't expected to sleep from the moment Dawn had showed up at his door, room-less and bed-less for the night. Just the idea of trying to pass out while she was curled up beside him seemed impossible.

But it turned out that complete and utter exhaustion had its benefits.

The only problem was, he slept *too* well, and woke up fully rested at six the next morning.

Wrapped around Dawn's sleeping body.

Cooper froze as he came suddenly and completely awake. Okay, this was bad. They still hadn't talked about that kiss, he still didn't know if she still loved Justin, he still hadn't figured out if he should even tell her about his brother's suspicions...and here he was, every inch of his body pressed against hers. And damn him if he didn't want to get even closer.

No. Not like this.

It took all his willpower to carefully unravel their closeness, his jaw set and tense as he eased his way out of the bed without waking her.

He needed to figure out all kinds of things before he could be that close to Dawn again, and he wasn't sure his resolve would last if she woke up and blinked those big eyes at him. If she smiled. If she kissed him again…

Damn it. He needed to stop.

With a shuddering breath, and one last look at the woman asleep in his bed, Cooper went to find a very cold shower. And hopefully some more willpower.

Dawn woke alone, and had showered away the vague sense of regret about that and managed to get dressed before Cooper returned to the room fully clothed and with breakfast in his hand.

'We should get going,' he said, not looking at her directly.

So. It was going to be like that.

'I'm ready when you are,' she said as she brushed past him towards where they'd parked Claudia the night before.

And she meant it. Sooner or later, they'd have to talk.

Although apparently, if Cooper had his way, it would be later. Much, much later.

Usually, their conversation was sparse in the mornings as Cooper slowly worked his way out of the bad mood he always seemed to wake up in. But today, he was full of things to say—keeping her distracted from the conversation they weren't having by instigating all sorts of other ones instead.

Dawn played along. For now.

By the time Cooper pulled into a roadside diner for lunch, she had learned all sorts of new things about her road-trip companion. His favourite colours, favourite Elvis song, his most annoying habits—which his assistant had alphabetised—least favourite airports…and many more. But nothing on the one subject she was interested in.

That kiss.

She didn't think he was regretting it, exactly, but he was pulling away all the same. Filling the distance between them with minutiae and top-ten lists.

Well, he wasn't going to get away with that for ever.

Caroline's Diner was just like any of the others they'd stopped in over the last five days or so: red seats and white tables, jukebox in the corner, burgers on the menu. But this lunch didn't feel anything like the same.

'So, what are your favourite burger toppings?' Cooper asked, already hidden behind the menu, and Dawn knew it was time to call him out.

'Cooper. Stop.'

'Stop what?' His dark-brown eyes appeared over the top of the menu, trying too hard to look innocent.

Dawn sighed. 'Look, if you're regretting the kiss, or even last night… If you want to forget that it ever happened—'

'No! I don't. Really.' Dropping the menu to the table, he reached out and placed his hand over hers. 'Really, Dawn.'

'Then what's with the constant games of twenty questions, when none of the questions are anything either of us actually care about?'

Cooper pulled a face. 'I guess I don't… I don't know how to do this.' He gestured between them.

'What, hold an actual conversation?'

'About our feelings? Basically.'

She laughed. Of course he didn't. The man didn't have any friends.

'I figured if I just kept talking, eventually I'd say the right things just by sheer probability theory.' He shrugged. 'Of course, there was the chance I'd say all the wrong ones first.'

'Not wrong. Just irrelevant.'

'Is it, though?' Cooper tilted his head as he stared

across the table at her. 'I mean, we agreed we were friends. Friends know this stuff about each other, right?'

'I suppose so,' Dawn allowed. 'But is friends what we're still going for here?' Because those kisses had said otherwise. As had her rather spicy dreams the night before. In fact she was almost certain she'd woken in the middle of the night to feel his arms wrapped around her before she'd drifted off again…

Cooper looked away. 'Dawn, you're still engaged to my brother. And I know he left you, but he had reasons, and I can't get between the two of you until you sort things out.'

Of course. It all came back to Justin. How was he still screwing her over even *after* he'd jilted her?

'Your brother left me at the altar,' she pointed out. 'Trust me when I tell you that even I, Miss Dry Run herself, has more self-respect than to chase after a man who has made it so abundantly clear he doesn't want to marry me.'

Cooper raised his eyebrows at her and gestured to Claudia. 'Then care to explain to me what the last five days have been about?'

She supposed he had a point. It did look rather a lot like they were chasing Justin across the country.

Dawn took a deep breath. 'I'm not going to talk to Justin to win him back.'

'Or to reclaim your passport or belongings, I assume, since he could have easily have arranged to courier them back to you by now.'

She winced as she remembered the lame excuses she'd made that first night. She should have known he'd see through them.

'No. Although I do want them back.' Dawn tried to find the right words to explain, and settled on the one Ruby had used that first night. 'I'm not chasing Justin. I'm chasing closure.'

'Closure?'

'Yeah.' He wasn't getting it, she could see. 'This time, I need to know why. I need to know what it is about me that isn't good enough for anyone to want "forever" with me. I need to understand what I did wrong.'

'What *you* did wrong?' Cooper asked. 'Sweetheart, you remember that *he* was the one who stood you up on your wedding day, right?'

Dawn sighed, searching for a way to make him understand. 'When you found out that Rachel was cheating, did you ask her why?'

'No.' Cooper shifted in his seat as he said the word, looking uncomfortable.

'Well, maybe you should have done. It might have helped you move on sooner if you understood her reasons.' Although, to be honest, Dawn could only assume insanity. Had the woman even *seen* Cooper? Who the hell had she thought she was going to find who was better than Cooper Edwards madly in love with her?

'Her reasons were that she was an untrustworthy, lying, cheating—'

'Those aren't *her* reasons,' Dawn interrupted. 'They're your interpretations. Like me saying that Justin is a twisted, cruel man for jilting me.'

'Dawn, I know my brother isn't perfect, but he's not cruel. Usually.'

'I know,' Dawn said simply. 'And that's why I need to see him. To understand what made him act that way.'

'I suppose that makes sense,' Cooper allowed. 'But what happens next? When you have your closure?'

'I move on.' Just the thought of it made her smile. 'I start the rest of my life. But first, I need to exorcise all my ghosts about every guy who ever left me and went off to find his true love. I need to let it all go.'

Cooper smirked. 'In that case, you're going to love our next stop. Come on. I'm driving.'

CHAPTER THIRTEEN

COOPER WASN'T ENTIRELY sure what he'd been expecting from a ghost town, but it hadn't been this.

The highway petered out as they approached, the road becoming cracked and uneven. Grass grew between bits of tarmac, and he thought he could even see a strange wisp of steam rising from between one of the cracks.

Uneasy, he pulled Claudia over to the side of the road and cut the engine. He had a feeling the car wouldn't enjoy exploring the town ahead.

'It says on this website that there's been a fire raging underground here for over fifty years,' Dawn whispered, staring at the road ahead rather than the phone in her hand. 'The fumes are toxic, so I guess we'd better not get too close to those cracks.'

Cooper reached for Claudia's keys again. 'Okay, maybe this wasn't such a good idea. We can just exorcise our ghosts the way normal people do—with alcohol and bad choices.'

But Dawn was already climbing out of the car. 'No. I want to see it. I want to do this.'

Well. It wasn't as though he could let her go alone, so…

Locking Claudia behind them, Cooper followed her along the road into what remained of the town of Centralia.

'It used to be a mining community,' Dawn told him as

they walked. He smiled to himself. It might have been his idea to come here but, as usual, it was Dawn who'd read up on all the details and memorised them. 'There were fifteen hundred people living here once.'

'So what happened?' He'd already read the website himself, but somehow it felt more real when Dawn told him the story.

'They think the fire started in a rubbish dump over a coal seam,' she said. 'Firefighters tried to put it out, but the fire clung to the coal and went underground. It's been burning up the earth under the town ever since, making everything unstable. Including Graffiti Highway.'

She gestured to the road in front of them, and Cooper saw instantly what she meant. The whole road was covered in street art spray-painted on the crumbling road, a riot of colours and designs.

'Graffiti artists come from all over to paint here, even though they know it could collapse at any time.' Dawn sounded bemused by the idea.

'I guess some people like living on the edge. Taking chances.' He couldn't help but stare at her as he said it, though, instead of the road.

'Do you?' she asked, looking up to meet his gaze.

'I never thought I did,' he answered honestly. 'But this week… A little risk-taking doesn't seem like the worst thing in the world.'

Her smile told him she knew he wasn't only talking about exploring a volatile ghost town.

Cooper reached for her hand as they wandered up the highway to a small graveyard—one of three in the town, according to Dawn's research. Cooper let her words wash over him as she told him about the residents who wouldn't leave, and how the town had been shut down in pieces. It was interesting, of course, but none of it seemed to matter as much as being there with *her*.

She wasn't trying to win Justin back. She was ready to move on. She hadn't told him she wasn't still in love with Justin, of course, but it was a start. No, it was more than that. It was something he hadn't felt in a long time. Hope.

Maybe all he'd take away from this road trip in the end was memories of the person he'd been. But maybe, just maybe, he could keep something more.

Dawn.

'Are you ready to go back to the car?' she asked as they looked out over the small graveyard. The eerie stillness of the place sent a shiver down his back but, even though every inch of him was itching to get away, he made himself stand there a moment longer.

'That depends. Have you exorcised those ghosts?' he asked.

Dawn tilted her head to the side. 'I think so. This town…it's desolate. Everyone—or almost everyone—has abandoned it and left it. But it's still beautiful, in its own way. And one day, maybe that fire will stop burning. Maybe life can return here.'

Was she describing the place or herself? He hoped it was the former. Although, he had to admit, he felt a sense of kinship with Centralia as she described it. As if he were the town, and the fire burning the place up from the inside was Rachel's and Melanie's betrayals, and everything that had ever made him feel like he couldn't trust the world.

Maybe it was time to put that fire out at last.

Time to feel something again.

Maybe even love.

'Then let's go.' Cooper tugged on Dawn's hand and led her back towards Claudia. He hoped her ghosts were gone.

But he knew for certain he was leaving his own behind in this ghost town.

* * *

Dawn shuddered a little as she pulled Claudia away from Centralia and back towards the interstate. The town had been interesting, if creepy, but the most fascinating part to her had been how Cooper had reacted to the place.

She didn't mind that he clearly hadn't been listening too attentively as she'd given him her best tour-guide impression, because he'd obviously been lost in thought. He'd taken her hand again, and kept hold of it as they walked, as if that were just normal for them, now. Better still, she'd actually been able to see his expression turning lighter, his shoulders relaxing.

Odd as it sounded, something about that eerie, toxic, abandoned town had let Cooper release something. She hoped it might be his past.

'We should make it to New York tonight,' Cooper said as the more familiar landscape of the I-80 surrounded them once more. 'What do you want to do then?'

'What are my options?' she asked.

'Well, we could carry on, arrive at the beach house late tonight and bring this whole road trip to a close.' He left that hanging there, obviously waiting to see how she liked it.

Dawn's nose wrinkled up. She didn't like it very much at all, as it happened. 'Or?'

'Or we could stay in New York and have a night on the town before we go get you your closure.'

'I suppose it would be better to arrive in the morning than late at night,' she said, giving him a small smile.

He returned it. 'Closure does work better when you're well rested, I've heard.'

'Plus it would just be rude to arrive so late,' Dawn went on.

'Exactly.' Cooper grinned. 'I guess I'd better find us somewhere to stay, then.'

He pulled up the familiar hotel app on his phone, and Dawn bit her bottom lip, forcing herself to keep her eyes on the road and not on his phone screen.

Not even to check if he was booking two hotel rooms or just one.

They switched driving again when they stopped for coffee in New Jersey, and as night started to fall Cooper drove them through the Holland tunnel and into the bright lights of New York City.

'Where are we staying?' she asked as they stuttered through the stop-start city traffic.

'You'll see,' was all Cooper would say.

She assumed he'd have booked one of the more famous hotels, mostly because she knew he liked quality. Which was why she was surprised when he pulled into a small, private parking garage right next to Central Park.

'Where are we?' she asked as he cut the engine.

He flashed her a smile. 'Home sweet home.'

'You have an apartment in New York.' Of course he did. How had she not remembered that before?

'I do.' He reached out across the seats and took her hand. 'Care to stay here with me tonight? I can book you a hotel, if you'd rather. I did look, but given the luck we've had with that booking app lately… I figured, if we had to share a bed, I'd rather it be mine.'

She saw the real question in his eyes and swallowed hard. This wouldn't be like last night—awkward distances and pretending to sleep until her body overcame her mind and she passed out. This wouldn't be two friends sharing a bed out of necessity.

This would be them. Together.

Tomorrow they'd be with Justin. She'd find her closure and be ready to move on—to go and find her own future.

And Cooper… Well, he was ready to find love again, she was certain. But it couldn't be with her.

'Just for tonight?' She met his gaze and saw understanding there.

This couldn't be anything more. They both still had healing to do to move on from their past relationships. Not to mention the fact that family gatherings would be *beyond* awkward. And hadn't he been the one to point out that she'd never be happy living the life of the corporate wife he—and Justin—both needed?

For once, Dawn was stepping into something without thinking about forever. Tonight wouldn't lead to a white dress and a happily ever after. When it was over, she'd still be the same Dawn she'd always been, the Dry Run. And Cooper… He'd do what men always did after they left her—find the love of his life.

She could give him that.

She'd take one night of pleasure in his arms then set him free to find his happy ending.

And maybe, just maybe, she'd find hers one day too.

But until then she was going to enjoy the moment, for a change.

'Just for tonight,' Cooper murmured back to her, the air thick between them.

Dawn smiled. 'Then lead the way.'

'I can still take you out for that fancy night on the town, if you like?' Cooper offered as he pushed open his front door. How long had it been since he'd been back to his New York place? It couldn't have been more than a month or so, before the Europe trip and the wedding that wasn't. But somehow it felt much longer, as though he was a different person, now he was here again.

Or maybe it was just that he wasn't used to being here with company.

He dropped Claudia's keys and his own into the bowl on the kitchen counter, and ignored the stack of mail sitting next to it. His housekeeping staff in the building kept the place in good shape while he was away, and he knew anything of importance would already have been forwarded to the office.

'Maybe…it might be nice to actually spend a quiet night in, for once,' Dawn said, a soft, promising smile on her face.

Did she know what that look in her eyes did to him? The one that told him that whatever she had in mind for him wouldn't be all that quiet?

Probably not, which might actually be why he found it so damn appealing.

He could see how Justin had fallen for her all too easily. What he still couldn't understand was how his brother had come to the conclusion that Dawn was a gold-digger. Everything he'd learned about her over the last week had showed him a different person altogether.

A woman he'd fallen for, even when he'd thought his heart was dead. Even when he'd believed the worst about her, he'd wanted her.

And now, finally, he might get to have her.

He wasn't thinking about tomorrow, wasn't going to imagine what might happen when she saw Justin again or when Justin realised the truth about her. She said she was over him, but she didn't know the whole truth yet.

And, as much as Cooper knew that he should tell her, he couldn't. Not when it might take away this one small chance he had with her.

Tomorrow, all their truths would come out. But until then he was more than happy to keep living the lie.

'A quiet night in sounds perfect to me too.' Leaving his bag beside the counter, he moved closer, towards where she stood by the front door. 'So, would you like the full tour?'

'Sounds great,' she said. Her tongue darted out across her bottom lip, and Cooper bit back a groan.

The woman was trying to kill him.

Worse, she was killing him and she wasn't even *trying*.

Another step and the space between them disappeared. Dawn dropped her own bag by her feet and leant in when he raised his hands to her waist, resting against another of her mesmerising, brightly coloured tee shirts. The ones he'd been dreaming of stripping off her for almost a week.

Would tonight finally be his chance?

He bent his neck, his lips achingly close to hers. But he couldn't kiss her. Not without being sure.

'Dawn…'

Her eyes were dark when her gaze met his, holding it firm until he couldn't have looked away if he'd tried.

Not that he wanted to try.

'I want this, Cooper,' she said, her voice low and dark. 'I want you. Just once. Just for tonight.'

Just for tonight. That was the deal. Tomorrow belonged to Justin. But tonight…

Tonight Dawn was his.

'Let's start our tour in the bedroom,' he said, and his blood burned as she smiled her agreement.

Okay, so maybe the 'being well rested before seeing Justin again' part of the plan wasn't happening, but Dawn had to admit she felt more relaxed and content than she had in years—even if she might need a nap later to make up for all the lost sleep.

Cooper's apartment faced east and, since they hadn't

bothered to close the blinds the night before, sunlight filtered in over them the next morning. Dawn stretched against the expensive cotton sheets, feeling all the kinks and knots in her muscles from the long days in the car giving way under the force of her bone-deep satisfaction.

If all she ever got was one night in Cooper Edwards' arms, at least she'd made the most of every moment of it.

The man himself slumbered on beside her, and she smiled as she watched him sleep. She liked to think he'd remember the night fondly too. Maybe even their whole week together.

He was right, she realised as she sat up, wrapping the top sheet around her naked body. Their trip had felt like a week out of time. Like they were living another life.

But in a few hours they'd be in the Hamptons, where Justin was waiting.

And then her real life started up again. The life in which she'd been abandoned at the altar by yet another man who'd decided she wasn't good enough for him.

Except…she wasn't that Dawn any more. Life on the road might not have been real life, but that didn't mean it hadn't changed her—every bit as much as Cooper said it had changed him. Or maybe…maybe it hadn't. Maybe it had just given her the opportunity to be *herself* again. She'd spent so long trying to be what someone else expected—Justin, her family, every other guy before Justin—that she'd almost forgotten who Dawn was.

But a week on the road with Cooper Edwards had helped her find *her* again.

She knew now that she was more than just the Dry Run sister. She was more than 'poor Dawn, let down again'. She was worth more than all the sympathy and the pity.

And she knew that she never wanted to wait at the end

of another aisle for some guy, or to sit at a romantic restaurant breathlessly waiting for him to get down on one knee.

She wasn't married. So what? She could go out and chase a hundred other dreams—like driving Claudia from coast to coast with the hottest guy she'd ever seen naked—and have a hell of a better time than she ever had waiting to get married.

Yes, she still wanted love. Still wanted someone to love her unconditionally, just the way she was. But she knew now, without a doubt, that Justin wasn't that man.

She liked the Dawn she'd been on her road trip with Justin's best man—but she knew that Justin wouldn't have. He'd have hated the cheap tee shirts with tacky logos, would never have sung along to Elvis on the radio. He'd have wanted consommé in diners that only served waffles, and complained about the beer on tap. And he'd have *hated* Claudia after the first twenty miles. He'd have loved people seeing him driving such a cool car, but Dawn knew without a doubt that they'd have ditched it for something state-of-the-art with Bluetooth within the first twelve hours.

And, for all that Cooper was supposed to be the workaholic of the two of them, Dawn suspected that Justin wouldn't have been able to stay away from his emails and deals the way Cooper had that week.

Not to mention—although it made her guilty to even think it—the fact that Justin had *never* made her body sing the way Cooper had last night.

Beside her, Cooper stirred, turning under the covers to wrap an arm around her waist and pull her back down against him.

'Good morning, beautiful.' His voice was rough and heavy with sleep, and it made her blood hum with anticipation.

Yes, they had to face Justin today.

But maybe not just yet.

'Good morning,' Dawn said, and kissed him.

CHAPTER FOURTEEN

'GOT EVERYTHING?' COOPER leant against Claudia as Dawn approached with her bag. She'd eventually kicked him out of his own apartment to fetch them breakfast for the road, and so that she could 'actually stand a chance of keeping some clothes on'.

'Think so.' She handed him her holdall and he stowed it in the boot, an action so familiar it was impossible to imagine that this might be the last time he ever did it.

'What about that lacy pink bra I last saw hanging from my bed frame?' It had been a delightful discovery that her lingerie matched the candy colours of her tee shirts.

Dawn's cheeks were tinged with pink. 'Yep, got that.'

'Shame.'

He pulled her in for a kiss before opening the car door for her, enjoying every last second he could keep her in his arms. He might be resolved to give her up at the end of the day, but that didn't mean he wasn't going to make the most of the time he had.

They hadn't spoken about what might happen next but, as he pulled out of the parking garage and into the sluggish New York traffic, he knew that it was on her mind as much as his. He could feel it in the way the silence filled the car. There was no Elvis on the radio, no ridiculous roadside attractions to aim for, no twenty questions, I Spy or even much in the way of conversation at all.

Instead, there was just the two of them staring out at the road ahead, his hand resting on her leg and a sense of encroaching dread.

Normally, once Cooper was out of the city, he started to breathe more easily, the open road along the coast to the beach house automatically relaxing him. Today, however, the sight of the ocean only made him feel even tenser.

He'd avoided thinking about this for as long as he could, but now the moment was here he couldn't put it off any longer.

Dawn had to know the truth—that Justin had left her because he believed a lie. Whether that would change her feelings, he couldn't predict. But he was fairly sure that Cooper's assurances that Dawn wasn't after the money would go a long way to convincing Justin that it was okay to love her—to marry her, even.

If she still wanted to.

God, what if he'd screwed up his own brother's chance of happiness? How could Justin ever forgive him?

How could Dawn?

No. He might be a despicable human being, but he knew Dawn now. He knew that she had wanted him every bit as much as he had needed her, and if she'd truly loved his brother that couldn't be the case, right?

Maybe, one day, they'd all look back and say that this was all for the best. Somehow. Even if it was impossible to imagine right now.

'Are you okay?' Dawn asked as they approached the familiar road that led to the Edwards family beach house. Had she even been here before? He couldn't remember. Not that it mattered, he supposed.

Nothing much did now.

'I'm fine,' he lied. Then he spotted something on the side of the road he didn't remember from his last visit and forced a smile. 'Hey, one last stop? For old times' sake?'

He gestured to the new ice-cream parlour, promising the best frozen desserts this side of the Atlantic, and Dawn nodded.

'You and your sweet tooth,' she said fondly. 'I don't know how you're going to go back to salads and vegetable juices after this.'

'Neither do I.' But he wasn't talking about his diet. He meant all of it.

How could he go back to that office and stare at a screen, or play internal politics with the board of directors, when he'd spent a week staring at the open road and the ever-changing landscape of his country? How could he be interested in contracts and deals after he'd had giant polar bears, time capsules and ghost towns?

But most of all how could he go home alone every night, when he'd grown used to having Dawn with him every moment of the day? Just two nights of sleeping in the same bed, and already he couldn't imagine her not being in his arms when he woke up. Just one night of them being together, as close as it was possible to be, and he already couldn't bear to think about never feeling her, touching her that way again.

He should have known that one week, one road trip, with Dawn would never be enough.

He wanted it all. And instead he had to give her back to his brother because that was the honourable thing to do.

And because, however much he wanted it—wanted her in his life forever—he knew that wasn't how it worked for him.

He'd sworn he'd never fall in love that way again, that

he'd protect his heart at all costs. And he couldn't break that vow. Not even for Dawn.

Could he?

'Mint choc-chip?' Dawn asked, and Cooper realised he'd been staring at the flavours board for minutes without even seeing them. 'Or do you want to get a couple and share?'

'You pick,' he said, stepping back. 'Get a few for us both to try. I'll…find us a seat.'

He left her debating the merits of honeycomb over rocky road and collapsed into the nearest booth, the smooth plastic seat hard against his back.

He couldn't love her. It had been less than a week! And, okay, he couldn't remember the last time he'd spent so much time with *anyone*, but this was *Dawn*. His brother's fiancée. The woman who, until a very short time ago, he'd been convinced was only after Justin's money.

But it didn't matter. He knew he'd give her everything he had if it meant she'd stay with him. If she'd help him be the person he'd discovered, out there on the road. The version of himself he liked so much more than the one he had to go back to.

For the first time in his life, he didn't care about the money, about success or family obligations.

He cared about her.

Cared about a woman who loved kooky roadside attractions and hated sugar for breakfast, who couldn't narrow down an ice-cream choice to less than four, it seemed, and who wore cheerful tee shirts and short skirts and had the best legs he'd ever seen. Cared for a woman who listened when he talked of heartbreaks he'd thought he only wanted to ignore, to pack away and never deal with again. Who sang along with Elvis on the radio even when she didn't know the words. Who kissed him as though she was giving him her whole heart and everything she was.

He loved Dawn the same way that she loved life—with hope, even while expecting to be let down. The way she hoped for happy endings, even after so many romantic disasters.

The way she'd given herself to him, even though she knew it was only for one night.

He loved her.

And he was so far beyond screwed now.

The ice-cream place was nice, but Dawn couldn't help but suspect that Cooper had an ulterior motive for stopping there, so close to the beach house, especially since he hardly even seemed to taste the ice-cream he'd been so desperate to try.

'Which was your favourite?' she asked as they climbed back into Claudia.

'Um, the honeycomb?' he said uncertainly.

'Right.' She hadn't ordered any honeycomb.

So, yes. There was definitely something going on with Cooper. Several times between there and the beach house he opened his mouth, as if about to tell her something, or ask a question, then shut it again without a word.

It was enough to make a girl very nervous indeed. Just in case the idea of facing up to the guy who'd left her at the altar wasn't nerve-racking enough.

Eventually, and just before Dawn's stomach ended up *entirely* in knots, Cooper took one last turn and, suddenly, there it was. The fabled beach house Justin had told her so much about, had shown her photos of, but never actually taken her to.

The white timber fronting glowed in the sunshine, the black shutters framing large windows and matching the gable roofs and the roof of the porch. Out the back, she knew, was a large private pool, and inside would be decorated in perfect beach-house style by whoever Cooper and Justin's mother had paid lavishly to do the job.

It was perfect, and beautiful...and Dawn would far rather have stayed in Claudia than ever go in, if that was okay with everyone.

Except it wasn't.

Cooper stopped the car at the front, then turned to her. 'You ready?'

'No.'

He gave her a small smile. 'You mean we drove thousands of miles and now you don't even want to go in?'

Put that way, it seemed a little ridiculous. She sighed. 'I suppose I need to get my passport back.'

'Attagirl. Come on. I'll be your wingman.'

The house seemed quiet as they approached, but as Cooper let them in with his key they heard Justin's familiar laugh from the back porch.

Frowning, Cooper moved ahead, dropping Claudia's keys onto a sidetable. Dawn followed, oblivious to the house itself, focused only on that laugh. How could something so familiar sound so alien all of a sudden?

Cooper opened the sliding doors that led out to the pool, then froze. 'Dawn. Maybe you should go back to the car.'

Oh, that wasn't good. Suddenly, the heavy feeling in the pit of her stomach that had plagued her all morning made sense. Whatever this was, it was going to be bad.

But she had to live through it anyway.

Pushing past Cooper, she stepped out onto the porch, feeling the warmth of the day against her skin as she looked out over the pool. There was Justin, his arms wrapped around a slender redhead, his lips on hers, looking happier and more relaxed than she had ever seen him in their months together.

'It's happened again,' she whispered, and Cooper was at her side in an instant. 'He left me and he found true love.'

'He'd better hope it happened that way round.' She glanced up at the thread of fury in Cooper's voice and saw his expression was thunderous. In fact, for someone who'd slept with his brother's fiancée the night before, he looked surprisingly self-righteous, she thought.

But that wasn't the most surprising thing. The part that shocked her most was how angry she *wasn't*.

'Justin!' Cooper yelled, his voice echoing out over the water.

The couple in the pool sprang apart. Justin stared up at them, his eyes wide with shock.

'Cooper? Dawn? Oh, God, Dawn.'

Suddenly, she didn't want to do this. She didn't want to know why she wasn't as good as the woman in his arms. She didn't want to hear that a person couldn't help who they fell in love with, or that everything happens for a reason, or any of the other clichés they all used.

She didn't want to hear any of it.

Turning, she walked back into the beach house. But not before she heard Cooper say, 'Get dried off and get in here *now*, brother. We have things to discuss.'

He shut the screen door behind him and moved across to where she stood, looking at a photo of the two brothers when they'd been much younger, both wearing wetsuits and emerging from the sea. They must have been close once. Dawn wondered what had come between them.

Cooper's hand at her waist made her turn.

'Are you okay?'

'I think so.' She did a quick check for the usual despair

and misery that came around this point. Maybe she'd got it all out of her system on the wedding night that wasn't.

Or maybe it just felt different this time because she knew it was for the best.

She sighed. 'I'm not quite sure what I feel. I mean, I'd accepted that Justin had seen the cracks in our relationship before I had—that he'd realised what a mistake it would have been for us to get married. It took me a whole week in a car with you for me to figure it out.' She gave him a crooked grin, but he didn't return it.

'When did you? Figure it out, I mean?'

'I guess it came a bit at a time.' There hadn't been one moment, had there? Just a growing feeling that life as Mrs Justin Edwards might not have suited her as well as she'd assumed, that she'd been jumping into it all too fast. And then the acknowledgment of all the warning signs she'd missed—how she'd had to dress like someone else for Justin, had had to change her habits, her hobbies, what drink she ordered in a restaurant. How she'd never quite fitted in or measured up, never been quite enough.

But, most all, never been truly herself.

Because she'd forgotten who that even was until Cooper had driven across the whole of America with her and helped her figure it out.

She looked up into Cooper's eyes, saw the concern there and knew he was waiting for her to say something more.

'He never saw the real me,' she said slowly. 'Maybe that's why it doesn't hurt so much. He wasn't leaving *me,* but the person I thought he wanted me to be.'

And it wasn't just him, she realised suddenly. It had been all of them.

With Trevor, it had been pretending to like modern art. With Richard, long walks in the countryside where she hadn't even got a pub lunch afterwards. With Harry, she'd had to pretend to love his family the way he did, even though they were vile to her. For Patrick, she'd embraced a love of horse racing she *really* hadn't felt. Even Ewan had wanted her to be more like the ex-girlfriend who'd left him.

Every one of them had wanted her to be someone else.

'I see you.'

Everyone except Cooper.

She'd never bothered to put on an act with him, because she'd never expected anything from him. And somehow he'd given her everything, anyway.

'Dawn, I need to tell you something.' Cooper's words were hurried, his eyes frantic. 'Before Justin gets here. The reason he left—'

But then the screen door opened and Justin walked in, dressed in chinos and a tee shirt, still rubbing a towel over his wet hair.

'Okay, I'm decent, and Cynthia has gone up to get showered and dressed. Maybe you can tell me what the hell you're both doing here?'

Cooper spun round, anger coursing through his body. 'You want *us* to answer questions? Brother, you're the one who failed to show up for his own wedding, who left me that note saying—well, you know what it said. And now you're here—'

'I don't know what it said.' Dawn's words cut him off as she came to stand beside him, looking between Cooper and her ex-fiancé. 'All he said to me was that he had to give us both our best chance of happiness. I assume, in your case, that meant Cynthia?' Justin at least had the good grace to look a little guilty at that. 'But that's not what he told you, Cooper. Is it? Did you know? Did you know what you were bringing me here to see?'

'No!' God, she thought he'd known Justin had been

cheating. He grabbed her arms gently, forcing her to look into his eyes, to see the truth there. 'I swear to you, if I'd known he'd left you for someone else, I'd have told you. After Rachel... You believe that, don't you?'

Dawn gave a slow nod. 'I do. But if it wasn't that...what reason did he give you for leaving?'

And there was the rub. 'He told me he thought you were only marrying him for his money. And...' Hell, but this hurt. 'He knew that would work—that I'd support him and take care of everything—because that's what Rachel did to me.'

'And I told you so before you even married her,' Justin pointed out. 'You didn't listen.'

Cooper ignored him, keeping his gaze fixed on Dawn's, waiting to see the moment she accepted he was telling the truth.

'That's why you hated me so much to start with,' she said. 'You thought I was like your ex-wife.'

'You're nothing like her,' he said fiercely.

'But when did you figure that out?' she asked, her voice dangerously calm. 'Before or after you kissed me?'

Behind them, Justin barked out a laugh. 'Wait! You two are here to berate me for falling for another woman when you've been carrying on together for a whole week behind my back?'

'No.' Dawn turned towards Justin and Cooper could see the fury in every step she took closer to him. Good. She *should* be angry. She *deserved* to be angry.

Maybe this was the closure she really needed.

'I came here for two reasons, Justin. Firstly, because you left with my passport, you utter idiot, so I couldn't go anywhere else. And, secondly, because I needed to know why—why I wasn't good enough for you, why you left me there at the altar. But that one doesn't matter now. Cooper helped me figure it out when he agreed to drive three thousand miles across the country with me.

'It wasn't me that wasn't good enough. *You* weren't deserving enough to see the real me. You wanted me to be a person I'm not, and neither of us would ever have been happy that way in the end. So I'm *glad* you left me at that altar. Because it didn't break me, the way I thought it would. It made me stronger. And, quite frankly, it's none of your damn business what I got up to after that point.'

'None of my business? You're still wearing my ring, Dawn. And you're trying the same tricks on my brother you tried on me!' Justin turned to Cooper. 'I don't know what she's told you, how she's convinced you, but she's just like all the others, Coop. Just like Rachel. She'd do anything to get in with our crowd—do you know, I found a credit card statement just before the wedding? She'd near enough maxed out her cards buying designer clothes, spending cash in fancy bars, all trying to fit in. To be good enough.'

Cooper froze at Justin's words. *Just like Rachel.* But he'd been so sure that Dawn was different. His instincts had screamed at him that she wasn't like the others.

But his instincts had been very, very wrong before.

'That's not how it was!' Dawn protested, but Cooper knew his brother. He knew when he was lying.

And, right now, Justin was telling the truth. And it broke his heart.

'She'd have done anything to marry me,' Justin went on. 'And now she's doing the same thing to you. Being the person she thinks you want her to be so you'll fall for her act. After all, she needs someone else to pick up the tab on those credit cards now, doesn't she?'

Dawn looked up at him, her green eyes wide and panicked, and suddenly he knew for certain that it was all true. Every bit of it.

Of course it was. Because that was all he was to women, wasn't it? A bank account. Why on earth had he let himself believe that Dawn—happy, free and joyful Dawn—would have any interest in a man who barely left the office most days?

He'd been an idiot to think that the last week was anything more than a holiday from reality. Tomorrow, life would go back to normal, and he already knew that Dawn had no interest in living that with him. Hadn't she said just one night?

Would she have pretended to want more, if he'd given her the chance, now that she knew there was no way for her to win Justin back? Maybe. He could almost see it—her sudden change of heart after a night in his bed, needing his comfort after everything with Justin. Suddenly they'd have been talking about living together to save her paying rent, and then it would have been diamond rings, wedding venues and…

And he'd already lived that once. He didn't want it again.

But then Dawn said, 'You know me, Cooper,' her voice low and hard. 'You don't have to listen to him. You know me.'

'I thought I did,' he replied, and watched as the hope in her eyes died.

This. This was the one that was going to break her heart.

'I didn't believe my brother last time, Dawn, and look where that got me.' Divorced, she supposed. And heartbroken. So heartbroken, he wouldn't even risk it again.

Especially not for her. Why would he, when no one else ever had?

'*I* believed your brother, when he told me he loved me, and it got me jilted at the altar,' she pointed out. 'You're going to need a better reason than that.'

He'd told her he saw her. He *knew* her, not whichever act she was putting on today, trying to be the girlfriend or fiancée she though a man wanted her to be.

If Cooper walked away from her, it would be because the *real* her wasn't enough.

And that might ruin her.

'Tell me it's not true.' There was a hint of pleading in his voice, and that surprised her. Cooper Edwards would never beg for anything—she knew that. But here he was anyway, wanting to believe her. 'Tell me you don't have credit cards that need paying off, that you didn't spend money you didn't have trying to fit in with Justin's world, knowing he'd pay it off when you were married.'

Dawn froze. If he'd asked her outright, was she with Justin for his money, the answer would have been easy— no. But that wasn't what he'd asked her.

'I can't,' she admitted. Because that part, at least, was all true. And she'd done it all not to win Justin's money but to win his heart.

And she'd been left with neither.

'Then how does that make you any different from Rachel?' Cooper's voice was flat, the pleading, the hope, all gone.

Dawn shook her head. 'It *is* different. I didn't do those things because I wanted to get my hands on the Edwards family money. But you're never going to believe that, are you?' The realisation chilled her heart. 'It doesn't matter what I say, because you've convinced yourself that the only reason anyone could ever want you is for your money.'

Cooper flinched. 'This isn't about me.'

But it was. She could see it now.

Not caring that Justin was still watching them, Dawn moved closer to Cooper, resting one hand against his chest as she looked up at him, wanting him to look at her the way he had in the beginning. When he'd stared so deep into her soul she thought he might come up again holding all her secrets.

She wanted him to this time. She wanted him to see the heart of her.

She wanted him to understand what she only knew for sure in that moment: she was in love with him.

'It *is* about you,' she whispered. 'About us. You know I don't care about money, and you know, deep down, that the only reason I'd do those things was to find what really mattered to me—true love. I wasn't winning Justin's money, I was winning his heart. But I couldn't, because it wasn't meant for me. He's not my happy ending. I was trying to be the person he needed, the true love he was looking for, but that wasn't me. The Dawn you know... that's the real me. The me that fell in love with you, somewhere in the middle of nowhere on the I-80, when I was least expecting it. When I wasn't trying to be anyone but myself.'

'You can't love me.' His words were a statement, not a question.

'I can't do anything but,' Dawn replied with a sad smile. 'But I know it's not going to make any difference. Not until you believe that you're worth loving for more than your bank account, or your family name.'

Her heart breaking, she stepped away. 'Justin? Courier my stuff to me at the office, okay?' She slipped her engagement ring from her finger and placed it on the table by the photo of the brothers, picking up the keys Cooper had left there. 'Goodbye, boys.'

And with that she walked out of the Edwards' beach house, climbed into Claudia, her heart aching, and drove away, knowing that this time Cooper wouldn't do a thing to stop her.

CHAPTER FIFTEEN

COOPER WATCHED DAWN walk out of the door and knew in that instant she'd taken his heart with her.

Well, it wasn't as if he'd be using it, anyway. He'd probably hardly notice it was gone, once he got back to work.

'Is she right?' Justin asked, sounding oddly anxious.

Turning to face his brother, Cooper raised his eyebrows. 'Right about what?'

Justin shifted from one foot to the other, looking from the ring on the side table to his brother. 'Do you really think no one could love you for anything but your money?'

'Don't you?' Cooper asked bluntly.

Because that was how it worked. People used love, sex and even friendship to get what they wanted out of the world. And what people wanted most, in Cooper's experience, was exactly what he had: money and power.

Why would anyone want anything else from him?

'I think I might have just made a huge mistake,' Justin said.

Blood pounded in Cooper's ears. 'You want Dawn back.' Hadn't he known it would come to this?

But Justin laughed. 'No, you idiot. And, even if I did, she wouldn't have me.'

'You've got as much money as I have. Why wouldn't she?'

'Because she's in love with you.'

Cooper shook his head and threw himself onto the pale-blue couch his mother thought was calming, but had the most uncomfortable cushions in the world. 'So *now* you believe her motives are pure.'

'I think I might have misunderstood them.' Justin dropped to perch on the coffee table in front of Cooper, his expression sincere. 'I met Cynthia at work, two weeks before the wedding. I told myself that I was imagining the connection between us, that it was just lust or something. Dawn was everything I'd ever wanted in a wife, so what reason did I have to look elsewhere, right? But I couldn't deny the way I felt when I was with Cynthia, and I couldn't avoid her, because we had to work together. And, with every moment that passed, I became more and more certain that she was perfect for me.'

'Why didn't you say something? Call things off earlier?' Cooper asked.

'Because I'm a coward. And I didn't want it to be my fault.'

Cooper huffed a small laugh. That made sense. Justin never had liked taking the blame for anything.

'When I found that credit card statement, I thought about everything you went through with Rachel and I thought…what if this is the same? And maybe I convinced myself it could be, so I had an excuse to not show up at the altar that day.' Justin looked up, his gaze locking with his brother's. 'I don't regret not marrying Dawn. It wasn't meant to be, not the way I'm meant to be with Cynthia.'

They all find their true love and get married within two years.

Dawn's voice echoed in Cooper's head. She was right; it had happened again.

But it wouldn't for him. He was sure of that.

'So, you don't think she's a gold-digger?' Cooper asked.

Justin shook his head. 'And neither do you. Do you?'

'No.' Cooper sighed. 'I've known she couldn't be since almost the day we set out on this road trip, although I tried to convince myself otherwise. I wanted to believe you, brother. And I needed a reason to—' He broke off.

'To keep your hands off her?' Justin guessed.

'Something like that.'

'But the point is, Coop, if she's not after your money, you must have something else she wants.'

'Like?' Because, for the life of him, Cooper couldn't imagine what else he had that was worth a damn.

'Like your heart,' Justin said gently.

But Cooper didn't have that to give. Dawn had already taken it.

And suddenly he wasn't at all so sure he could live without it. Not without holding hers in return.

He jumped to his feet. 'I have to go.'

Laughing, Justin tossed him a set of car keys. 'Her passport's in the glove box. Save me a courier fee.'

'You can spend the savings on our wedding present,' Cooper called back over his shoulder.

Dawn drove and drove. Focussing on the road ahead of her meant that she didn't have to think about everything she'd just walked out on. And, when the thoughts crowded in anyway, she turned Elvis up louder on the radio and let him block out her own pain with songs of his heartache.

Eventually, though, she needed to stop. Even Claudia, the best ride in the country, got a little uncomfortable after a while—and besides, she needed coffee if she was going to do this drive alone.

A familiar sign flashed on the roadside up ahead, and without thinking Dawn turned towards it, parking Claudia alongside Caroline's Diner and trying to forget the man with whom she'd stopped here last.

Inside, everything was just as it had been the day before, as if her whole world hadn't shifted and quaked since then.

The same waitress who'd served them yesterday brought Dawn a coffee without even being asked, and Dawn sat and sipped it while staring at the menu without reading the words.

Justin had been cheating on her. He'd honestly believed she'd only wanted his money.

And now he'd convinced Cooper of the same.

And Cooper, idiot, believed him. Not because he didn't know Dawn, but because he didn't know *himself.*

Oh, he probably thought he did, but he had no idea. She could sympathise, though. She'd spent long enough being someone she wasn't for other people. She just wished she could have taught Cooper how to break away from that too.

She'd wondered, all through their trip, how to reconcile the Cooper she was getting to know with the one she'd heard stories about. The serious, boring workaholic who was too busy for family, or friends, or love. The business shark who always got the best deal, who protected the family finances and business interests. The protective older brother who didn't approve of Dawn.

None of those people were the Cooper *she* knew. The one he'd been on their road trip.

She wished she could show him the man she'd fallen in love with.

She wished he could see him too.

The bell over the door to the diner rang, but Dawn didn't turn around. There was no one coming for her.

But then the jukebox kicked in and Elvis started playing.

She frowned. Coincidence. It was just that sort of diner.

Then Cooper slid into the seat opposite her, and hope flared in her heart again.

'You were right,' he said.

Dawn sipped her cold coffee. 'About what?'

'Let's say everything, just to be on the safe side.'

'Probably a good idea.'

Cooper sighed. 'I'm sorry. I'm so sorry, Dawn. You know I—'

'I know.' At least, she thought she did. 'You know I'm not after your money.'

'I do. I just… I struggle to see what else you could want.'

'Why?' When it was so blindingly obvious to her, how much more he had to offer.

Running a hand through his hair, Cooper stared across the table at her. 'I told you about Rachel.'

'Just because one woman only wanted you for nefarious reasons, doesn't mean they all will, you know.'

'It wasn't just one.' Cooper looked away out of the window and Dawn felt her heart sink.

'Tell me.' Reaching across, she took his hand in hers and listened.

'When I was twenty-one, and just starting out at the company, my mother brought in this student-placement candidate called Melanie and asked me to show her around. She was gorgeous, and funny, and I played the big guy on campus, showing off for her.'

'So far, so normal. Who wouldn't?'

'Yeah, well. What I didn't know was that she was taking all the company secrets I let slip in an attempt to impress her and passing them on to her boyfriend, who just so happened to work for our competitor.'

Dawn winced. 'Ouch.'

'That's why I should have known better, when Rachel

came along. Why I should have listened to Justin when he tried to tell me what she was really like.'

'And why you listened to him this time,' Dawn guessed.

'Exactly.'

She sighed. It wasn't as if she didn't understand his position. Wasn't as though she didn't have fears of her own—that Cooper would turn out to be like every other guy, running off to find his true love the moment he was done with her.

She couldn't know it wouldn't happen. She just had to have faith.

And so did he.

'You told me you don't know what else I could want from you,' she said slowly. 'And I get that in the past people have wanted your money, or your business, or whatever. But to me? That's the least interesting thing about you.'

'Then what is it that *you* want?' Cooper asked.

Dawn smiled. That one was easy. 'I want the man I went on this road trip with. The man who explored weird road-side attractions with me and sang Elvis too loudly with the top down.' Was that so much to ask?

Apparently so. 'The thing is, Dawn…that man doesn't exist. He's…he's like you with Justin. He's me pretending to be someone else, just for a little while. Just for the escape.'

Dawn tilted her head as she looked at him. 'I think you're wrong.'

'You think you know me better than myself?' Cooper asked, eyebrows raised.

How presumptive would she have to be to say yes?

Except she *did*. And he was still wrong.

She took a breath and let it out fast. 'Yes. I'm pretty certain I do.'

'Go on, then. Tell me about myself.' Cooper leaned back in his seat and waited.

The words came without her even having to plan them. A truth she was so sure of she didn't even have to think. She just believed. 'I think, this last week, you were being the person you wanted to be. Free from work and everything else, you got to be yourself, maybe for the first time in years. And I think you liked it.'

'Doesn't change the fact that I have to go back to normal on Monday morning,' Cooper pointed out.

'It *could*.' He looked at her with confusion, and Dawn sighed. 'I spent months trying to be the woman I thought Justin wanted, right? I was playing a part. But, with you, I was myself. And I think you're looking at it the wrong way round. The person you're going back to when you walk into the office on Monday…that's the act. That's you being who you think you need to be. But you don't. You could be *my* Cooper, all the time.'

'Yours, huh?' Cooper gave her a small smirk.

Dawn stood her ground. This wasn't a joke. This was their future. Possibly. 'If you wanted.'

And he *did* want. She could see it in his eyes. The only question was whether he'd let himself have it. 'And if I do? What happens now?'

Wasn't that the million-dollar question? Dawn sighed, swirling the last of her coffee around in her cup while she considered her answer.

Love had always been easy for her. It was making it last she'd struggled with. And this, she knew, was her best chance. She had to do this right, and she had to do it her way. As herself.

'I have to go back to California,' she said eventually. 'I have a job to get back to. I have to check on my family, distribute Buffalo Bill keyrings before they all fly home. I have to sort out my life, my*self.* Figure out how to live as me again, before I can do anything else.'

'And us?' Cooper asked. 'What happens there?'

She looked up at him, smiling sadly. 'I think you need to do the same thing. I think you need to go figure out the Cooper you want to be, in the real world, not just on the road. And then...'

'And then we can try,' Cooper finished for her. 'See who we are *together.*'

'Exactly,' Dawn said, relieved that he seemed to get it.

She didn't want to leave him. But she needed to know that she'd be able to stay—and so would he. Needed to know who she was on her own, before she let anyone else in again. And just in case, once she was gone, Cooper did what everyone else had done and found what he was really looking for—and that it wasn't her.

It was a risk, but one she knew she had to take.

Maybe she wouldn't find her happy-ever-after with Cooper. But she wanted to give it her best shot. As herself.

Cooper lifted her hand from the table. 'I've got your passport in the car. I'll drive you to the airport in Claudia. Justin can get a ride out here and pick up his car himself.'

'Eager to get rid of me?' she asked.

'Eager to get you back again.' He frowned. 'Should we set a date? A place?'

Dawn considered. 'Three months.' If she couldn't get things together in that amount of time, she probably never would. 'You can pick the place.'

Cooper's smile made her feel a little nervous. 'I'll let you know,' he promised.

Dawn smiled back, already knowing that these were going to be the hardest and longest three months of her life.

Three months later

Kansas in November was cooler than Cooper had imagined it would be. Still, if everything went to plan, things should be warming up any time now.

As long as Dawn showed up.

It had been a long three months. Sure, they'd texted most days, and called from time to time, but the process of extracting themselves from the lives they'd been living for others, and finding the ones they wanted to live for themselves, had taken time and energy.

Cooper had started small. Listening to Elvis in his office. Eating a burger for lunch now and then. Finding the quirkiest and weirdest New York attractions and visiting them. He'd started choosing his own clothes—ones he liked, rather than ones that matched what everyone else wore at the office.

Next, he'd upped his game by actually taking weekends. Of course, he'd struggled to fill them alone, but it turned out that some of his colleagues could actually become friends, if he gave them the chance, so he'd tagged along on nights out, trips to sports events and even a birthday party or two.

It all felt a little empty without Dawn, but even then he was happier than he'd been in years—except that week on the road with her.

His biggest step, though, had been with the board of directors. It had taken some convincing, but between Justin and him they'd managed it—and, suddenly, Cooper's whole life opened up with possibilities. Which was what led him here, to Kansas, in November.

Standing beside the world's biggest ball of twine with a diamond ring in his pocket.

'That is one *big* ball of twine.'

Cooper spun at the sound of her voice, moving towards her even before he saw her. When he did, he stopped and just drank in the image.

She had her hair up, bouncing in a high ponytail that hit between her shoulder blades. Her bright pink lipstick matched her woollen coat, and her smile lit up his heart.

'You came,' he said, still amazed at how beautiful she was.

'You think I'd miss the world's biggest ball of twine? Never.' Stepping closer, she braced a hand on his chest and stood on tiptoes to press a kiss to his mouth. 'Besides, I missed *you* too much.'

'I missed you too,' he murmured back. 'So much.'

'So, I have news,' Dawn said.

'So do I.' News he really, really hoped she'd like.

'I quit my job,' Dawn said. 'Only, not really.'

'That makes no sense.'

She grinned. 'I know. The thing is, I loved doing the marketing and promo side of my work, but working with the same products all the time…it got a little dull. So I decided to go freelance, and my company hired me on the spot to keep doing what I'm doing, only for more money. Plus I get to take on other clients, too, and I can work from anywhere I want in the world.'

'That sounds…perfect.' And it happened to fit in perfectly with his plans too.

'What's your news?'

'Justin and I decided to change the structure of the business,' Cooper said, remembering his brother's smile when he'd suggested it. 'He's taking over a lot of the stuff I used to do—which, since Cynthia wanted to move to New York anyway, is pretty much perfect for them.'

'So what will you be doing?' Dawn asked, a small frown in the middle of her forehead.

'Basically? Whatever the hell I want.'

She laughed. 'You don't take half-measures when it comes to designing your ideal life, do you?'

'Why should I?' Cooper asked. 'The deal is that the business will utilise me in a consultant capacity—using my knowledge of the business and the market to trouble-shoot wherever I'm needed. It means more time travelling, visiting different sites, different places.'

'Sounds like you'll be on the road a lot.'

'Which is why I bought Claudia,' he admitted. 'And this.' He pulled the ring from his pocket and held his breath.

'You bought Claudia?' Dawn asked, still caught up on the first part of his sentence. 'The most impractical car in existence who only plays Elvis?'

'You love that car. I'm also rather hoping you might like the ring.'

Her eyes widened as she finally focussed on the diamond in his hand. 'You want to marry me?'

'I want to spend my life with you,' he corrected. 'On the road, at home, everywhere. I want to be with you. Everything else is negotiable.'

'Except for Claudia.'

'Hell, yes, we're definitely keeping Claudia.'

'I can live with that.' Dawn finally raised her gaze from the ring to his eyes, and his breath caught at the hope and love he saw there.

'You haven't said yes yet,' he pointed out.

She smiled. 'You already know my answer.'

'I'd still like to hear it.'

Carefully, Dawn took the ring from his hand and placed it on her ring finger. 'Yes, Cooper Edwards. I'll go any-where and everywhere with you. For ever.'

'That's all I'll ever need,' Cooper said. 'Well, that and doughnuts for breakfast.'

Dawn laughed, and he kissed her, knowing their adventure together was only just beginning.

* * * * *

THE MAVERICK'S
BRIDAL BARGAIN

CHRISTY JEFFRIES

To Stephanie Uribe Roman Phillips,
my college (and beyond) roommate,
my partner in crime, my wingwoman,
my dance floor equal, my V&T co-conspirator,
my maid of honor, my sister in mommyhood,
my therapist, my mainstay,
my very best of best friends.
And that's just the first 25 years.

❤C

Chapter One

While Vivienne Shuster no longer made assumptions about whose marriages would last, she could say with certainty that the bride and groom sitting across the conference-room table from her didn't appear to be the type who would maliciously smash cake in each other's faces.

Not that being a Junior Wedding Planner—yes, her boss had actually put that title on Vivienne's business cards—in Kalispell, Montana, gave Vivienne any sort of sneak peek into the future, but it did give her an inside track as to how a couple navigated one of the most stressful events of their relationship. Because if they couldn't deal well with simple decisions like color schemes and invite lists, the pair was doomed when it came to handling the more important realities of life after the wedding glow burned out.

Listening intently, Vivienne nodded as she scribbled notes inside the brand-new binder she'd started when Lydia Grant and Zach Dalton came into her office fifteen minutes ago. So far, Lydia was the ideal bride in that she was already eager to leave most of the details to Vivienne and seemed to be more excited over the prospect of getting married than the actual reception. In fact, the groom was the one who'd scheduled the initial consultation in an effort to take some of the pressure of planning off his soon-to-be wife.

Zach and Lydia were clearly enamored with each other and, so far, the meeting was going smoothly, with everyone on the same page. Vivienne wasn't surprised to find herself back on Team Romance—which was what she secretly called this euphoric mood that made her believe long-lasting love might actually be possible. It was times like these when she absolutely adored her job.

Unfortunately, in her chosen profession, the good moments were starting to become a lot less frequent than the headache-inducing ones.

Glancing at her slim smartwatch, she realized that she had only another hour before her boss showed up. Vivienne had purposely scheduled this appointment for seven in the morning, well before normal business hours, because she knew that her boss would be salivating once she found out that the couple wanted to have their wedding in Rust Creek Falls. The owner of Estelle's Events weighed all of ninety pounds—not counting her makeup and false eyelashes, which added at least another five—and had been smoking a pack a day for the past fifty years. If Estelle got her acrylic claws into this easygoing bride, then the small town of Rust Creek Falls, Montana, would never know what hit it.

"So we've got three bridesmaids," Vivienne confirmed with Lydia, before turning to Zach. "What about groomsmen?"

"Now, that may be a problem." Even without his Stetson, Zach was good-looking. But when the guy hitched up one side of his mouth into an aw-shucks grin, he became a double threat—gorgeous *and* charming. "I have four brothers."

"Four?" Vivienne gulped, blinking a few times to keep her eyes from bugging out. There was more than one handsome cowboy like this out there somewhere?

Zach pulled a picture from his wallet and handed it across the desk as though to prove it. She attempted to study the photo with as much professionalism as she could muster. There were two pairs of cowboys sitting on the top slat of a wooden corral, bookending a fifth cowboy who was standing in the middle. Zach was probably one of the sitters, but, honestly, Vivienne barely gave those guys a passing glance. She quickly narrowed in on the one in the center, though only because his central position and straight posture drew all of her attention. It had nothing to do with his sexy smirk or alert blue eyes. And it certainly wasn't because of the way his jeans fit perfectly on his—

"Is it a problem if we're uneven?" Lydia asked, yanking Vivienne out of her inappropriate thoughts. The bride-to-be was wearing jeans, a retro T-shirt advertising the band Lynyrd Skynyrd, and had a mess of brown curls piled into a ponytail. She definitely didn't strike Vivienne as the type to be bothered by unconventional appearances.

"No problem at all," she assured Lydia, smiling as she clung to the picture she wasn't quite ready to return. "It's your big day. There is no right way or wrong way to do things."

She snuck another peek at her watch, knowing the uproar Estelle would make if she overheard Vivienne saying that to a client. As a Junior Wedding Planner, Vivienne's so-called office actually doubled as the conference room and was currently open to the reception area so she could pull double duty as the receptionist. It also meant Vivienne could easily be overheard whenever she was talking to her clients, which was why she always tried to conduct these initial appointments when her boss wasn't around.

"So, with that many brothers, are you willing to pick just one to be the best man?" Vivienne asked, needing to move this meeting along but not wanting to rush Zach with what could be an important decision.

Judging by the happily casual way they were all posing in the picture, it was easy to make the assumption that the Dalton brothers were close. But as an only child, her experience in dealing with sibling rivalry had been limited to what she'd witnessed during prior weddings. She'd had her share of brides who didn't want a prettier sister upstaging them on their big day. There'd even once been an usher who decided that the start of his brother's ceremony would be the perfect time to propose to his own girlfriend. In short, nobody liked having their thunder stolen.

Zach held his cowboy hat in his lap, tapping the brim as he considered his options. Vivienne cleared her throat. "Or you could pick a friend or a cousin or even skip having a best man altogether."

He looked at Lydia, who simply shrugged. "It's up to you."

"I should go with Booker because he's the oldest," the groom began. "But Cole can have a bit of a hero complex and will think he's the only one—"

The front door creaked open, interrupting Zach and forcing all three of their heads to swivel down the short hall in that direction. Vivienne held her breath, praying it was only a delivery person and that Estelle hadn't decided to come in early.

But before she could stand up and intercept whoever it was, the middle cowboy from the picture strode across the reception area toward them, his boot heels clicking on the hardwood floor, his jeans well-worn and snug on his long, muscular legs. An electrical current shot through Vivienne and it took a few attempts for her to get her wobbly legs steady enough to rise to her feet.

How was it possible that the man was even better looking in person?

"Speak of the devil," Zach said to her and then also stood up and turned to the newcomer. "What are you doing here, Cole?"

"Did you even look at your left rear tire before driving all the way to Kalispell this morning?" the newcomer said to Zach. Then, as if suddenly realizing that his brother wasn't the only one in the room, the man removed his off-white cowboy hat and addressed his soon-to-be sister-in-law. "Hey, Lydia."

"Hi, Cole. This is our wedding planner, Vivienne Shuster," Lydia responded. "Vivienne, this is Cole Dalton, one of Zach's brothers."

Thankfully, Vivienne had braced one hand on the edge of the table when she leaned across it to shake his, because the warmth of Cole's palm enveloped her and she would've found herself moving in closer to him if there hadn't been three feet of heavily polished antique walnut separating them.

"Sorry to barge in on you like this, ma'am." His words drew her in even closer until her hips pressed against the table.

Growing up in Montana, despite having lived only in the bigger cities, Vivienne was accustomed to the occasional cowboy calling her *ma'am*. But there was something about Cole's voice that was both honey filled yet crisp at the same time. She cleared her throat and replied, "It's no problem."

"What's wrong with my left rear tire?" Zach's words penetrated Vivienne's improper fascination and, thankfully, reminded her to pull her hand back.

Her cheeks stung with heat as she looked down to straighten her still-empty binder, then took a swig of her iced coffee nearby. The last thing her overactive imagination needed was caffeine, but there were only so many things she could focus on besides the good-looking man with the sexy voice and mesmerizing handshake.

"When I went out to the stables this morning, I noticed the pressure was low," Cole told his brother, and Vivienne sank slowly into her chair, relieved that nobody else in the room was paying any attention to how her body had just responded to a complete stranger. "I was going to get the compressor out of the shed and fill it up for you after I got done changing the poultice on Zorro's foreleg. But you'd hightailed it out of there before I got back. Aunt Rita told me about your appointment, and the whole way here I had to keep my eyes peeled to make sure you weren't stranded on the side of the road with a flat."

Zach looked over his shoulder and mouthed the words *hero complex* to Vivienne and Lydia before turning back to his brother. "Why didn't you just call?"

"I did. You didn't answer. I also called the bridal shop here, but all I got was an answering service."

Vivienne was about to explain that they weren't just a bridal shop as well as the fact that, technically, they weren't open yet. But the concern on Cole's face seemed genuine, and his indignation about his brother's safety made the guy even more attractive, if that was possible.

Zach rolled his eyes, pulling his cell from his pocket. "Sorry, man. I must've accidentally set it on sleep mode."

"You know the family rule about phones." Cole crossed his arms over his broad chest, and his brother's expression turned from playful annoyance to humble remorse.

"You're right." Zach reached out and squeezed Cole's shoulder. "Why don't we go outside and look at my tire?"

The men excused themselves and the front door had

just clicked shut behind them when Vivienne asked Lydia, "What's the family rule about cell phones?"

She wanted to kick herself for asking a client such a personal question that was absolutely none of her business. But Lydia was an assistant manager and sort of reporter-at-large for a small-town newspaper and would, hopefully, understand Vivienne's blatant curiosity.

"Do you remember hearing about that horrible wild-fire in Hardin last year?" At Vivienne's nod, Lydia continued. "Well, their ranch and the family house caught fire."

The woman looked up at the ceiling as though she was weighing whether or not to continue the story. When she lowered her head, Vivienne realized Lydia's eyes had grown damp. Reaching into her go bag, where she always kept an emergency stash of anything a bride might need on her big day, Vivienne grabbed a package of tissues and slid them across the table to Lydia. "That must've been a horrible loss."

"It was beyond horrible. Their mom was also in the house at the time and nobody had been able to warn her about the blaze because she'd left her cell phone in her car outside."

Vivienne's chest felt hollow and she pressed her lips together to keep from asking the obvious question. But judging by the way Lydia released a ragged breath, the answer was pretty clear. Her heart broke for Zach and Cole and, really, for all of the Dalton brothers. Especially since the loss of their mother was so recent.

She reached back into her go bag and replaced the tissues with a king-size bag of M&M's. Vivienne was no stranger to delicate situations, but some wedding dynamics called for a little more finesse and a lot more chocolate.

Cole Dalton didn't waste any time reading his brother the riot act as soon as their boots hit the parking lot. "Zach, it's one thing if you insist on driving around town on four bald tires when it's just you in the rig, but now that you're shackling yourself with a wife, you'll be responsible for someone else's safety and happiness."

"Shackling?" Zach lifted one of his eyebrows. "You make it sound like a prison sentence."

Cole sighed. "It's not that I think marriage is a prison sentence. After all, our parents were in love and probably would've been married for another thirty-five years…" He let his voice trail off. Nobody liked thinking about what could have been, and the men of the Dalton family especially weren't eager to talk about it. "Anyway, I'm sure you won't mess things up too badly with Lydia."

"Yeah, right. When you can commit to a woman for longer than a slow dance at the Ace in the Hole on a Saturday night, then you can give me relationship advice, big brother."

"Commit? Oh, please. I've got my hands so full looking out for you and the rest of our oversize family, I barely have time to schedule an appointment at the barbershop, let alone take a woman out on a proper date."

"Is that a fact?" Zach asked, and Cole took off his Stetson to show his brother how long it'd been since his last military-regulation haircut. Okay, so it had been only a few weeks, but when Cole had been on active duty in the Marine Corps, he was used to getting a high and tight every ten days. Zach whistled and replied, "It sure seemed like you had all the time in the world when you wouldn't let go of that pretty wedding planner's hand a few minutes ago."

Cole folded his arms over his chest, knowing his brother was just trying to rile him up. All the Dalton boys enjoyed going back and forth with each other like that. But the defensive stance also helped hide the way he was flexing his right hand, which still tingled from the softness of Vivienne's palm fitting so perfectly inside it.

Cole nodded toward the building's entrance. "I was just caught off guard by all the froufrou decorations in that war zone they call an office."

"War zone?" his brother repeated, his brow arched. "Froufrou?"

"It looked like someone crashed a Humvee full of roses into a lace factory. I mean, how many pictures of fancy white dresses and champagne glasses do they need in that place? It's like a single man's kryptonite inside of there, sucking out all masculine logic and rationale. You're lucky I was able to break you out when I did."

"I can't disagree with you on that, although I was surprised you were able to notice anything else in the room besides Vivienne." Zach grinned, then held up a hand when Cole began to argue. "As much as I'd love to stand out here in the parking lot and listen to you try to deny it, I need to go back inside, since I promised Lydia I wouldn't make her do all of this wedding planning alone."

"Fine. I'll take your truck over to the gas station up

the street and fill the tires while you finish." Cole held out his palm and waited for Zach to toss him the keys.

"Thanks, man."

A few seconds later, Cole yelled across the parking lot to his brother's retreating back. "I'll leave them under the floor mat when I'm done."

Because he sure as hell wasn't going back inside that bridal shop and dealing with his unexpected attraction to some fancy—but totally unnecessary—wedding planner. Cole shook his head as he hopped into the cab of Zach's truck and started the engine. Some sappy love song blasted out of the speakers and his finger dived toward the radio to switch off the country music station.

Yet he couldn't get the image of the blonde woman out of his mind. Her hair had been pulled back into some kind of loose ponytail, but he could tell it was long and wavy and soft. Her white button-up shirt was all business, and even her navy blue pin-striped skirt was relatively professional, except for the fact that when she'd stood up to greet him, she'd had to tug the hem down. But not before he'd caught a glimpse of a dark brown freckle on the inside of her thigh.

Her lips were soft and pink and her eyes were a fascinating shade of green. She was on the taller side, maybe five-nine. He hadn't seen if she was wearing high heels or not, but cool and classy ladies like that usually wore fancy, useless shoes. However, all of those details were slow to register with him because when he'd been shaking her hand, Cole hadn't been able to think of anything but that sexy little freckle.

He turned into the gas station and pulled the truck

up to the air hose before squeezing his eyes shut and trying to clear his head. It wasn't like Vivienne Shuster was the first good-looking woman Cole had ever met. He'd been in the Marines, stationed all over the United States, as well as a few bases overseas, and had always known where he could find a date on the few times he'd gone looking for a fun time.

So then why had his muscles gone all soft and his brain turned to mush when he'd met her?

Unlike his brother Zach, who'd actually placed an ad in the newspaper looking for a wife, relationships weren't exactly on Cole's radar at this juncture. Hell, they weren't even in his atmosphere.

Sure, once upon a time, he'd pictured himself moving back to Montana eventually and settling down with a wife and possibly having some kids of his own. But ever since his mom passed away, Cole had realized there were no absolutes in life. There was no point in planning that far into the future. Right now, his dad needed him. The property they'd been interested in buying fell through and, while they weren't exactly wearing out their welcome at the Circle D with his aunt and uncle, they still had to help their dad find a new ranch and get it running. Phil Dalton deserved to have a working place of his own, a place he could share with his sons. Yet Cole also owed it to his family to keep things as normal as possible, to prevent them from realizing how much responsibility he was shouldering.

So, yeah, he let his relatives think that he was in the market for the occasional date. He'd even gone out with a few women back when his cousin was filming that reality TV show in town. But Cole was always sure to flirt only with the ladies who didn't take him seriously. He certainly didn't react to them the way he'd responded to Vivienne.

But that was just a one-off. Surrounded by all that happily-ever-after propaganda and poster-sized images of wedded bliss back in her office—even for the few minutes he was exposed to it—who wouldn't have gotten overwhelmed and panicked? He'd been all fired up when he'd walked into her bridal shop, his worry and annoyance with Zach having snowballed during the twenty-minute drive there from Rust Creek Falls. Then, when he got inside, he was so out of his comfort zone he'd felt like one of those green plastic army toys thrown into a frilly, decked-out dollhouse. He'd had to do a complete one-eighty and rein himself in.

Cursing under his breath at his ridiculous reaction to the whole situation, Cole made quick work of the tires, using a pressure gauge he'd brought along with him to ensure that he didn't overinflate them. The sooner he returned the truck to the parking lot, the sooner he could get back to his aunt and uncle's ranch and let some much-needed manual labor push these fanciful notions from his mind.

Unfortunately, when he pulled into the parking lot of the tiny strip mall that housed Estelle's Events, his brother and Lydia were standing outside waiting for him.

Along with the wedding planner.

When Cole exited the truck, his eyes had a mind of their own and kept returning to that spot on Vivienne's skirt, hoping for another glimpse of her hidden freckle.

Since he couldn't very well pitch his brother's keys over the hood and beat a hasty retreat to his own truck, he was stuck with having to walk over to the trio. The smug grin on Zach's face reminded Cole of the time he'd lost a hay-bale-stacking race with his younger brother and had to volunteer to be on the prom committee at their small, rural high school. Although, the joke ended up being on Zach when Rondalee Franks—a senior on the cheerleading team who'd been in charge of decorating the gymnasium—asked Cole, a mere sophomore, to be her date. It wasn't his fault that the ladies loved a man who was always willing to help out.

The professional wedding planner, whose back was ramrod straight despite the uncomfortable-looking four-inch-high heels on her feet, had a death grip on a thick three-ring binder and didn't appear to be the type who needed assistance from anyone, let alone a former Marine-turned-rancher like him.

Cole knew that he should offer to shake Vivienne's hand goodbye, if only to prove to his brother—and himself—that his initial physical response to her was nothing out of the ordinary. Instead, he came only close enough to toss the keys to Zach. When a late-model purple Cadillac sedan pulled into the parking lot, he tipped his hat and simply said, "Ma'am."

Then he climbed into his own truck and refused to look back.

Chapter Two

Vivienne's skin was still tingling from the sound of Cole Dalton's sexy drawl as she waved off Zach and Lydia before her boss got out of her car. Luckily, Estelle was still on the phone with one of their flower vendors when their newest clients drove away, saving Vivienne from an awkward introduction. Unfortunately, she hadn't been able to save them—or anyone else within a block radius—from hearing exactly what Estelle thought of having centerpieces set in burlap-covered mason jars, because the Cadillac's speaker volume was always set to Ridiculous.

Behind the windshield, Estelle's red acrylic fingernail jabbed toward Vivienne, the gesture clearly telling her that her boss wanted her to wait right where she was. After several minutes of threats to never refer another bride to them again, Estelle finally disconnected the call and exited the boatlike sedan like a ninety-pound bleached-blonde tornado, ready to blow through anything that stood in her way.

"Who was that leaving?" Estelle asked, not bothering to take off the giant tortoiseshell-framed sunglasses that hid more than half of her face, as well as the healing scars from her most recent visit to the plastic surgeon.

"Those are our new clients," Vivienne replied, her shoulders straighter than they had been for the past three months, when Estelle had first started pressuring her to bring in more bookings.

"Gah. More cowboy weddings," Estelle complained, before lighting up a cigarette. "I hope you told them that flannel isn't a bridesmaid dress option. We can't have people thinking we're running a rodeo over here."

"They're from Rust Creek Falls," Vivienne explained, waiting for the significance to sink in. Surely, the woman would be impressed now that their company was officially branching out into the small town that was becoming well-known for so many recent marriages.

"You got the full deposit from them, right?" The woman was happy only when money was exchanged. At Vivienne's nod, Estelle continued. "Good. Who was the other cowpoke with them?"

Despite the older woman's insulting tone, Vivienne's tummy did a somersault at the mention of Cole. "That's one of the groom's four brothers."

"Four?" Estelle pushed the supersize sunglasses on top of her teased platinum curls. Even the heavy mascara loaded onto her fake lashes couldn't conceal the gleam in her eye. "Are they all single?"

Vivienne flashed back to an earlier glimpse she'd had of Cole's strong, tanned fingers and reminded herself that the lack of a wedding ring didn't mean he wasn't in a serious relationship. "You know, I didn't think to ask."

"Well, find out if they are," Estelle told her, before reaching into the back seat. "Girl, in this business, you always need to be thinking one step ahead. If the other three are as good-looking as those two, there are bound to be some more weddings in the works. And I want *you* to book them."

A feeling of incompetence raced through her. They'd been having a similar conversation for the past year. She knew she was supposed to be bringing in more business, but there was something icky about force selling happily-ever-after. Vivienne was of the opinion that her work should speak for itself and happy couples would be more likely to refer their family and friends her way. But before she could argue as much, Estelle passed her a small plastic cage holding a shivering black-and-white guinea pig.

Their company had done weddings with everything from songbirds to butterfly releases to dogs as flower girls. But they'd never done one with rodents. Vivienne crinkled her nose. "What's this for?"

"When I went in for my post-op last week, the doctor told me my blood pressure has been through the roof lately. But with my high cholesterol and thyroid problems, I'm on so much stinkin' medication right now, the last thing I want to do is shove more pills

down my throat. Apparently, there've been recent stud-
ies about pets helping to ease people's stress levels, so
I thought I'd give it a try." Estelle used the remainder
of her cigarette to light up a new one before crushing
the butt under her size-four stiletto. Cutting back a
pack a day and not constantly yelling at wedding vendors would probably be more beneficial, but Vivienne
knew better than to suggest as much. "Since I'm al-
lergic to cats and I can't stand the stench of dogs, my
only choices at the pet shop were this little guy or a
turtle. And I don't do moldy tanks."

Vivienne held the cage up to eye level and peered
inside. There was something achingly familiar about
the startled fear reflected in the poor animal's eyes. "So
why did you bring him to the office?"

"The stupid thing is defective. It was up all night long
making this weird wheezing sound." Estelle grabbed
two binders off her back seat and hooked her trademark
purple tote bag over her bony shoulder. The ash from
her cigarette was almost an inch long and hanging on
precariously as she headed toward the office door. "I
need you to take him back to the pet store. Maybe you
can get me the turtle instead."

Vivienne was pretty sure the guinea pig wasn't defective; it was just overwhelmed. After all, Estelle's
nose and lungs had had decades to build up a tolerance
to her heavy-handed application of dime-store perfume
and her chain-smoking. Usually, Estelle never smoked
in front of clients, but since those had been scarcer
lately, her boss was lighting up at an alarming rate.

Vivienne remained outside in the parking lot, setting

the cheap plastic cage on the hood of Estelle's car. She wanted to unlatch the metal door, but she was afraid the thing would run away.

"What am I going to do with you?" she asked. The guinea pig twitched its nose in response, the whiskers on either side of its face quivering.

Vivienne wasn't much of an animal person. Growing up, she'd had only one pet, and that had been short-lived. When her parents divorced the first time, not only had they fought for custody of Vivienne, they'd also fought for custody of Filmore, a fluffy Pomeranian who didn't understand the concept of every-other-week visitation. Vivienne was at school one day when Filmore snuck out of her dad's sparsely furnished apartment and tried to make his way back to the house he was used to—the split-level home her mom got in the divorce. He never made it.

Her mother accused her father of giving the dog to one of his girlfriends, and her father accused her mother of leaving a trail of bacon the entire two miles between his apartment and her house. At first, Vivienne was heartbroken over her lost pet, but a week later, she was getting off the school bus a block away from her mom's place and saw Filmore in the window of the Petersons' house. She knew the Peterson girls from school. They were younger, and their parents never screamed at each other on the front lawn like hers did. So Vivienne decided not to say anything, because at least Filmore would get to live with a happy family even if she couldn't. Every once in a while, she would go over to their house and pretend she was interested in having make-believe tea parties and playing with their babyish pink palace dream house just so that she could visit her dog.

When her mom and dad eventually got back together, Vivienne asked if they could go over to the Petersons' and get Filmore. However, her parents were so caught up in each other and making up for lost time that they didn't want the burden of a pet again.

Vivienne bit her lower lip as she studied the helpless guinea pig. Maybe she should take him back to her apartment for now. She should also call the pet store and tell them that under no circumstances were they to sell that poor turtle to Estelle. But, first, she had a wedding to put together. Balancing her binder in one arm, she carried the cage into the office.

The peanut M&M's were long gone, so she broke off a piece of the granola bar she'd thrown in her purse this morning when she realized she wouldn't have time for breakfast, then pushed it through one of the slots toward her new friend. The guinea pig cautiously moved forward and sniffed the food before using its tiny paws to shove the whole thing into its cheek. Then Vivienne settled into her chair and got to work.

She opened the binder to see that a photo had gotten stuck inside one of the divider pockets. And not just any photo. *The* photo. All five of the Dalton brothers were handsome. And after hearing about the tragedy of losing their mother, Vivienne was fascinated to find out more about them. She told herself she was interested in learning all their stories, but it was really Cole she stared at, Cole's story she wanted to hear.

Something inside of her ached. Maybe it was all the romance novels and bridal magazines pulling at her heartstrings. She'd read her fair share of both, and every once in a while she could forget about the bridezillas and the uninterested grooms and the wedding marketing ploys and wonder if there was such a thing as love at first sight.

Not for her, of course. Having witnessed the whirlwind of her parents' marriage, Vivienne was smart enough to want to get to know her future husband for at least a few years before she decided if they were compatible.

She was also smart enough not to get all worked up by a pair of well-worn jeans and a sexy smirk and a honeyed voice calling her *ma'am*.

A week later at the Circle D, Cole was in one of the corrals exercising his uncle's injured horse when a Jetta zipped down the driveway toward the ranch house. As the car approached, he recognized Vivienne behind the wheel and his pulse sped up. Paying attention to the driver instead of where he was going, Cole kept walking straight as the horse rounded the turn. Zorro's front hoof grazed the side of his boot, causing them both to stumble.

"Easy, boy," he said more to himself than to the stallion.

She was wearing some sort of silky floral dress that wrapped around her curves like a second skin, and her high heels had no business navigating the dirt driveway, which was still fairly muddy after a recent spring rain. Balancing that big binder on her hip, Vivienne used her free hand to carry a tall vase. A strong wind caused the side of her dress to flip open and his lungs froze as he was treated to a full view of her shapely thighs. When she tried to pull her dress back into place, she dropped the binder, its contents spilling out everywhere.

Quickly, Cole secured the lead rope to the mechanical arm of the hot-walker, then hopped over the fence, mentally kicking himself for initially staring at her like a lovesick calf instead of immediately rushing to her aid. On his way, he picked up scattered papers and pictures of cakes and flowers. The dainty images and carefully handwritten lists made his work-roughened hands look big and coarse, and he quickly shoved the stack at her.

"Thank you," she said, not noticing that the notebook she'd just pulled to her chest was covered with mud. "I'm supposed to meet Zach and Lydia here at the ranch and then drive over to check out Maverick Manor as an option for a wedding venue. But I'm running a little early."

"You're getting dirt all over your…" He pointed at the mud now covering the neckline of her dress, then slammed his fingers into his front pockets when he realized he was gesturing toward her breasts. When she pulled the binder closer as if she could shield his inappropriate gaze, he felt his cheeks flame.

"Do you want to wait for them on the porch?" he asked. He had no idea when Zach and Lydia would get here, and while Cole could rescue windblown papers, he wasn't much for entertaining guests or making small talk. Racking his brain, he asked himself what his aunt Rita would do if she were home. "Can I get you a drink?"

Vivienne rotated her slender wrist to glance at her watch. "Actually, if you wouldn't mind me using the restroom, I could try to clean myself up a little before they get here."

"No problem," he said, taking the tall vase from her. "Follow me."

He slowed his pace so that she could better follow him without getting one of her heels stuck in the driveway. His uncle and aunt's sprawling log ranch house was pretty big, but with Cole's dad and brothers living there temporarily, he couldn't vouch for the cleanliness of anyone else's bathroom but his own.

He said as much as he led her down the hallway toward the girls' wing. Then, because he didn't want her getting the wrong idea about where he was taking her, he added, "We have to walk through here to get to the Jack-and-Jill-style bathroom."

"This is *your* bedroom?" she asked, her gaze focused on the fierce pink sign on the door ordering all boys to keep out.

"Originally, the two rooms on this side of the house belonged to my cousins Kristen and Kayla before they got married. So I can't take credit for the decor. All the frills and ruffles and throw pillows were here when I moved in."

"That's good to know." Vivienne's playful smile sent an electrical current through his gut. "I had you pegged for more of a roses-and-chintz type of guy, so the daisy quilt and eyelet curtains threw me off for a second."

"Roses? Me? And here I thought I was sending out a strong tulip vibe." He grinned back at her and then continued on toward the bathroom.

"I think it's sweet that your masculinity isn't threatened by a few pastels and floral prints."

"Listen, I slept in much worse conditions when I was deployed in the Marine Corps."

She didn't respond, so he turned back to see if she was still following him. Vivienne had paused right outside the bathroom door, her head tilted. "You were in the Marines?"

"You seem surprised," Cole replied.

"In my line of work, I try to never be too surprised about anyone." She crossed over the threshold and set her muddy binder down on the tile counter. "Although, I had assumed that you were just a cowboy."

"*Just* a cowboy?"

"I didn't mean it like that. I meant like a full-time job. Your brother Zach mentioned that he's been so busy working here with your uncle and helping your father find a new ranch. I saw the picture of you with your brothers dressed up in—" she gestured toward his daily uniform of boots, jeans and a flannel shirt "—all that cowboy gear and I figured that you guys all worked together."

"Some of us work harder than others," he said as he winked. Then he wanted to kick himself for flirting when nobody was even around to witness it. Well, nobody except Vivienne, who seemed way too serious and professional to engage in harmless bantering. Still, she had made the first joke, so maybe he'd read her wrong. "If it's any consolation, you were right and I'm now a full-time cowboy."

"So then you're not a Marine anymore?"

"Well, you know what they say. Once a Marine, always a Marine." He saw the confusion creasing the smooth skin of her forehead. "I put in my time and was honorably discharged."

"Oh. How long did you serve?" Vivienne focused on him when almost any woman he knew would've already directed her full attention to her own reflection in the nearby mirror, worrying how she would get all that dirt off her pretty dress.

Cole was surprised by how natural it would've felt to hitch his hip up onto the countertop and shoot the breeze with her. Five minutes ago, he'd been dreading talking to her about anything more substantial than whether she preferred ice in her sweet tea. Yet the lady who had at first appeared to be all business now seemed completely at ease making small talk in such close and personal quarters.

Unfortunately, his departure from the Corps and the circumstances surrounding it brought back the painful memory he would never be comfortable talking about with anyone, let alone a stranger—no matter how attractive she was.

Instead, he did what he always did when he wanted to avoid something. He winked and made a wisecrack. "You'd need to have security clearance to get that type of information out of me."

Vivienne's hand rested casually on the edge of the sink as she faced him and wiggled her eyebrows. "As the wedding planner, you'd be amazed at some of the insider intel I can access."

His glance dipped down to the V of her dress as he considered how far she might go in her fact-finding mission. A throbbing of awareness below his belt buckle yanked him back to reality. When he dragged his eyes up to meet hers, she was staring at him in a way that made him feel completely exposed.

Cole purposely broke eye contact by reaching for a couple of pink washcloths in the cabinet before handing one to her. "Why's that?"

"In addition to organizing everything, my job is to be part psychologist, part coach, part fortune teller and a full-time mediator. I have to get all the data I can about not only the couple, but also their friends and their families, to prepare for a multitude of possibilities."

"But it's just a wedding. What could possibly go wrong?" he asked as he began cleaning the binder in one of the bathroom sinks.

She used a washcloth at the other sink to wipe the spot of mud on her dress, looking in the mirror as she spoke. "I need to know which uncle—or aunt—is likely to have too much to drink. I have to make sure that there aren't any bickering cousins sitting together at the head table or any exes coming as someone else's plus-one. It helps to find out in advance if the father of the bride has any food allergies and what the mother of the groom's favorite song is for the…" Regret dawned in her eyes and, thankfully, she caught herself just before saying the words *mother and son dance.*

But the image was already out there for Cole.

His mom.

The woman who'd dreamed of being a dancer on Broadway before she'd fallen in love with a rancher from Montana. The woman who'd taught them all how to do a basic waltz and an electric slide before they were in sixth grade. The woman who used to stop whatever she was doing when the perfect two-stepping beat came on the radio, grab whichever boy was nearest to her and then laugh and sing as she twirled a kid around the house.

Diana Dalton would never get to dance at any of her sons' weddings. The thought was like a punch to Cole's gut.

"I am so sorry," Vivienne began, but he held up a palm. Hearing her pity would only make the guilt twist deeper inside of him.

"Don't worry about it." He forced his tense lips into a casual smile, but his reflection revealed that it was more of an uncomfortable grimace. They were looking at each other through the mirror, and even though it wasn't direct eye contact, it was still too much. He grabbed a towel off the rack behind him, buying himself a few seconds to regain his composure before he turned back.

Vivienne's own hands had stilled under the stream, so he shut off the water and passed her the clean binder. His voice sounded normal enough when he said, "Here. Good as new."

Then he reached for another brightly colored hand towel and held it out to her. She opened her mouth, but before she could apologize, he cut her off. "Don't tell my brothers this, but when we moved to the Circle D, I purposely drew the short straw because I've always been partial to the color pink anyway."

Then, as if to prove that everything was fine, he gave her another wink in the mirror before walking out.

Chapter Three

Vivienne lingered in the bathroom a few more minutes, mentally berating herself for slipping like that and bringing up Cole's mother. Bracing her hands on the counter, she bent her head and tried to reason that she hadn't technically been referring to *his* mother. Still, the angst that had flashed across his face was due to a freshly painful subject that she'd brought up.

She pinched her eyes shut. Vivienne was usually much more sensitive in her dealings with clients, even if they looked like ruggedly tough cowboys who were quick to tease. But she hadn't been herself since the moment she'd driven up. When she'd gotten out of her car earlier, she'd been surprised to see Cole outside, his shirtsleeves rolled up and working with that horse like a hero out of some Western novel. Something had stirred inside of her and she'd tried to distract herself with the task of getting too many things out of her trunk at once.

Then she'd accidentally flashed him when her wrap-around skirt had blown apart, and she'd dropped everything she'd brought, including her pride. She'd been speechless and muddy and completely vulnerable, which must've been the reason she'd willingly followed the man into his bedroom of all places.

It had taken every last bit of nerve she possessed to look Cole in the eye and make small talk with him as though having conversations with strange men in the tight confines of their bathrooms was the most normal thing in the world. Vivienne had been forced to focus on his face so that her eyes wouldn't dart off and stare at the shower just behind where he'd been standing. She had done her best to maintain an ounce of professionalism while simultaneously imagining what he would look like all damp and steamy, wrapped in nothing but the small towel hanging on the hook beside the beveled-glass-door shower stall.

They had been inches apart at side-by-side sinks for goodness' sakes! Was there ever a more intimate environment to be in with a man? How would she know? The few relationships she'd had in college were with guys who lived in different dorms, and she'd never seen a need to sleep over. After graduation, she'd made her job her top priority and had gone on only a handful of dates since then—none of which required the sharing of a bathroom.

Vivienne looked back at the boy-band poster taped to the wall behind her. Okay, so maybe this particular bathroom wasn't *that* intimate of an environment. But Cole had been wearing those jeans and doing that lazy smirk, and her brain had gone all cloudy. Obviously, she hadn't been in her right mind or else she never would have mentioned mothers at all.

Sure, he'd bounced back from her inept comment fairly quickly, graciously acting like nothing was wrong. He'd even delivered a saucy wink that was so believable she'd all but dropped her stupid binder a second time on the ivory-and-pink rag rug.

Vivienne frowned at the binder. She preferred to keep most of her work on an electronic tablet, but Estelle insisted on having hard copies of everything. The three-ring notebook made her feel as though she was back in middle school, a trusty Trapper Keeper in her arms the only thing separating her from the cute boy who had the locker right next to hers.

It also made her feel as though she was constantly lugging her boss around with her, a not-so-subtle reminder that she was supposed to be booking more clients. Not only did she need to be professional and do her job, she needed to do it well enough that others would be willing to hire her, as well. And flirting with the groom's brother in the bathroom was not the way to accomplish her career goals.

Standing up straighter, she decided that she'd already hidden out in Cole's bathroom long enough. Plus, she was pretty sure she heard voices coming from somewhere outside, so it was time to get to work.

Vivienne wished she had paid more attention to the house layout when she'd followed Cole back here. Instead, she'd kept staring at his jeans-clad rear end, and now she was stuck navigating her way back to the main area of the house. She made only one wrong turn, telling herself that every framed family photo on the wall was merely insight to better understanding her clients.

Relief flooded through her when she spotted Lydia and Zach in the front room. Thankfully, there was no sign of Cole.

"Sorry we're late," Lydia said.

Vivienne waved her off. "No, I was early."

The three of them stood there for a few awkward moments until Vivienne finally asked, "Should we sit down somewhere?"

"Sorry," Zach said, somewhat sheepishly. "I may be living here, but I'm not used to playing host. Why don't we head over to the kitchen table?"

Vivienne followed the couple into the large, sunny kitchen and came up short when she saw Cole standing in front of the refrigerator with a big plate covered in foil. "Don't mind me," he told them. "I worked through lunch and wanted to grab a quick snack."

"Does Aunt Rita have any of that lemon icebox pie left over from last night?" Zach asked his brother.

"She did," Cole replied, before hiding the plate behind his back. "Finders keepers."

Zach responded with a noise that sounded suspiciously like an oink, then lunged at his brother's elbow, trying to pull his arm forward.

"I'm the pig?" Cole used his shoulder to deliver a powerful block. "Don't you have a fancy tuxedo you're gonna need to fit into?"

"Do I have to wear a tux?" Zach turned toward her and Lydia, causing Vivienne to let out the breath she'd been holding when she thought the two brothers were going to come to blows over a piece of dessert.

Lydia looked at her for the answer. Vivienne cleared her throat. "Not if you don't want to. You can dress as formally or as casually as you like. But since we're talking about outfits, have you guys thought about a color scheme?"

Vivienne opened the binder on the table and pulled out several pictures she'd printed after the first meeting with the couple. They spoke about suits and lace and blush pink and everything Vivienne easily discussed on any given day. However, her mind was completely elsewhere, and she found herself constantly losing her train of thought.

Cole opened cupboard doors and shuffled things around inside the fridge as though he were scavenging for more food. Yet he didn't eat another bite. His mouth was too busy sputtering anytime Vivienne answered a question or made a suggestion. It was obvious he was not only listening to every word they were saying, but that he also had a completely differing set of opinions.

After Cole had snorted for at least the seventh time, Zach finally said, "Please ignore my brother. He thinks he's an expert on everything, including event planning, apparently."

"Pfshh. I'm an expert on not wanting to go to lame events."

"Lame?" Zach repeated. "Back in high school, his idea of a party was to invite all of his junior lifeguarding buddies from the community pool over to our house for a refresher course in CPR."

Cole's eyes narrowed as his lips eased into another one of those slow smirks. "Maybe we just wanted an excuse to practice mouth-to-mouth resuscitation on some pretty teenage girls."

"Yeah, right." Zach chuckled before cupping his hand around his mouth to stage-whisper, "Shawn and I were spying on them and the only exchanging of saliva came when Rondalee Franks double-dipped her carrots in the ranch dressing. And even that was limited, since Cole launched himself at the dip bowl like it was a live grenade."

"What can I say?" Cole shrugged. "I saved everyone from a potential outbreak of mononucleosis."

"That's right." Zach pointed a finger at his brother. "Wasn't she the girl who was absent from school for a couple of months?"

"Yes. And you're welcome." Cole made an exaggerated bow and Zach threw the crumpled-up piece of foil from the pie plate at him.

"If you really wanted to be useful, you could whip up a plate of brownies or at least set out some cheese and crackers for our guests."

"For Lydia and Vivienne, I might be willing to rustle up something," Cole said as he pulled a bag of potato chips out of the pantry. "But you should probably lay off the carbs if you plan to hire a professional photographer. I hear the camera adds ten pounds."

Both Dalton men were six feet tall, with similar lean, muscular builds. While Vivienne was more appreciative of the way Cole filled out his jeans, neither one was at risk of needing to watch his calories. But that didn't stop them from arguing over who was entitled to which snack.

Someone needed to pass Vivienne something to eat soon, because she couldn't keep up this charade for long. Stress made her hungry, and while this was one of the easiest couples to work with, Cole's constant presence wasn't exactly relaxing, despite her comfortable seat at the long pine table. If the awkward moment in the bathroom hadn't happened, she might be able to enjoy this family's teasing camaraderie. But that wasn't what she was getting paid to do.

"All this talk about food brings up another thing we need to be thinking about before we go look at venues," Vivienne said in an effort to smoothly transition the conversation back to the purpose of their meeting. "Do you guys have a preference for a buffet, or would you rather serve a formal plated meal?"

"Hmm. I guess we have to feed our guests, don't we?" Lydia put her elbow on the table and propped her chin on her hand.

"Not necessarily." Vivienne gave a discreet cough, attempting to block out Estelle's voice in her head drilling her to always upsell. "Some couples prefer to save money by having only light refreshments and cake."

Luckily, this particular bride and groom had already laid out their budget at the initial meeting, and she doubted that Zach and Lydia would be the type to skimp on their guests' comfort. Still, she felt the need to always give people their options.

"Seems to me like you guys should just drive over to the courthouse, say the I do's and be done with the whole thing." Cole gestured at the binder. "That paper you guys sign is going to be the same whether you throw away all your money on this nonsense or not."

Nonsense? Did the man realize that he was indirectly implying that Vivienne and her job were completely useless, as well? Her spine straightened at the insult but soon lost some of its steel resolve when she couldn't really argue the point. More often than not, she felt that weddings and even marriages were just a big waste of effort and time. But she wasn't about to admit as much in front of her clients. She was supposed to be drumming up more business, not losing it.

Thankfully, Lydia jumped in. "Cole, this wedding isn't just about me and Zach. It's about our families and our friends and our journey to finding each other. It may be nonsense to you, but to me, it's an opportunity to celebrate everything and everyone who is important in our relationship."

Zach opened his mouth—probably to defend his bride, who was clearly capable of speaking up for herself—but his cell phone went off at the exact same time Cole pulled his own vibrating phone from his pocket.

"It's a group text from Dad," Cole said first.

"I know," Zach replied, not looking up from his cell. "I'm part of the group."

It seemed like a race to see which brother could read the message first. Not that she had a view of anyone's screens from her seat on the opposite side of the table, but curiosity had Vivienne scooting closer to the edge of her chair.

Cole's fingers were already flying across the electronic keyboard, likely because he wanted to be the first to respond. She was sensing a competitive edge to the middle Dalton son.

Luckily, Zach didn't appear to have the same sense of urgency to reply, because he announced, "Looks like Dad just made an offer on some property a few miles away."

"That's fantastic," Lydia said. "Where is it?"

"He said Sawmill Station," Zach replied. "I know we're still pretty new to Rust Creek and I've heard of Sawmill Road. But I've never heard of a ranch by that name."

Lydia tilted her head. "That's because Sawmill Station isn't a ranch. It's an old abandoned train depot."

"Why would Dad make an offer on an abandoned train depot?" Cole asked as he continued typing.

Zach's phone made another ping. "I'd ask him, but I can't dial out when my phone keeps buzzing with incoming texts from you."

"I just told him that I'm here at the Circle D with you and we can swing by to check it out."

"I know," Zach told his brother, holding up his phone. "I can read."

Lydia looked at her watch. "We have another hour before our appointment at Maverick Manor in town. Since Sawmill Station is on the way, we could swing by and check it out. Would you mind, Vivienne?"

She leaned back slowly in her chair to prevent herself from sliding under the table to get away from Cole's penetrating stare. Anticipation hummed through the kitchen and it was obvious that buying this property was a monumental occasion for the Dalton family. Normally, she liked to meet with her clients at their homes or workplaces because seeing them in their natural surroundings gave her a better sense of their personalities, which translated to a fuller picture of how they envisioned their big day. However, tagging along on a private family outing was surely beyond the boundaries of her job description.

Yet all three of them looked so eager she couldn't very well deny them their side trip. And they could just as easily discuss bouquets and music playlists in the car. Besides, this was her last appointment of the day. The only thing waiting for her at home was a to-go box containing half of a three-day-old club sandwich, and an unsocial guinea pig who refused to come out of its cage.

Vivienne managed a weak smile and said, "Sure. Why not?"

Cole should've just driven his own truck, but GPS navigational systems were still spotty this far out and Lydia was the only person who knew exactly where they were going. They could've gone caravan style, but Cole had never been the type to blindly follow while one of his brothers took the lead. Riding together seemed like the most logical solution.

Of course, that was before he realized that he'd be crammed into the back seat of the crew cab next to the hoity-toity wedding planner who kept her body so stiff there wasn't a bump or pothole along the way that would dislodge her from her seat-belted perch.

Fortunately, the soft fabric of her overlapping skirt wasn't as rigid and would gape open a little wider every time his brother navigated a curve on the winding, narrow road that led to the new property. Cole had just gotten a peek of the freckle on Vivienne's thigh when the truck made a sharp right at a faded yellow sign that might've once read Sawmill Station.

"I thought Dad was going to buy an actual ranch," Zach commented as he slowed the vehicle in front of a run-down brick building that was way too enormous to be a barn or a stable.

"It's certainly a far cry from the Circle D," Cole agreed. "But Dad said he was buying it for the acreage. I guess we're supposed to envision it once we get those old structures torn down and some pastures mapped out."

Lydia's yelp from the front seat was more like a squeak. "You can't just tear down those buildings. They're historical landmarks."

Cole waited for Zach to put the truck in Park before unbuckling his seat belt. As he hopped out, he asked, "Are we going to run a ranch or a museum?"

He walked around to the passenger side of the truck, where Vivienne was tentatively placing one high-heeled foot on the running board in order to climb down. Cole reached out instinctively and cupped her elbow as she descended onto the mud-caked asphalt. Feeling a tug low in his belly at her nearness, he had to force himself to let go when she began to straighten her skirt.

"I recently helped out on an article about all the

abandoned railway lines in Montana," Lydia said with some awe as the four of them stood in a row in the weed-infested gravel driveway. "A hundred or so years ago, this property used to be a feed mill and ran adjacent to a logging camp. Back then, the best way for businesses to distribute their products throughout the West was by freight car. The original owners laid some tracks and opened a small depot, naming the place Sawmill Station. Their vision was shortsighted, though, because, as you know, the logging industry never stayed in one place very long, so the camp moved on. Then as more ranchers came out west, the feed mill's business boomed. Unfortunately, this location was pretty remote, and with the invention of eighteen-wheelers and interstates, using trains way out here fell by the wayside. The company had to change with the times and eventually relocated to Kalispell."

Cole had always thought himself to be too practical for nostalgia, but the acreage was vast and grassy if he looked past the buildings. Plus, it was kind of cool to own a place with a little bit of history, a place that someone else had once sunk their own blood and sweat into. Maybe it was all those years living in barracks on military bases, but he was itching to replant some roots and this neglected-looking property needed him. It felt good to be needed again.

The possibility of a challenge flared up inside of him and he wondered out loud, "So maybe instead of bulldozing everything to the ground, we can repurpose some of these buildings. If only we knew what was what."

"Down at the *Gazette* offices, I think we have an old photo of this place in its heyday," Lydia explained, walking toward a smaller structure. "I believe that this peeling white building up front is the actual depot, but because nobody in town came this far out, it never saw too many passengers. That huge brick monstrosity back there is a freight house, where they'd store the loaded cars."

"Looks like they left one behind when they closed down operations." Vivienne pointed to an abandoned railcar sitting at a crooked angle, the lower half almost hidden by overgrown grass and the inside probably home to several different species of critters. Cole watched the wedding planner as she studied their surroundings. He'd half expected her to jump back into the truck at the first sight of a prairie dog. But she surprised him when she said, "There's something alluring and fascinating about it all, isn't there? I mean, all that rustic brick is totally back in style right now. And the tiny depot is adorable. Can't you just picture what it would look like with a fresh coat of white paint and some flower boxes planted around the platform?"

"What *used* to be the platform, you mean." Cole squinted at the collapsed, rotted-out planks.

"Let's go check out the freight house," Vivienne suggested, surprising him again by leading the way. Her legs trembled slightly as she trudged through the path in her high heels, and Cole found himself appreciating her determination and curiosity.

When they got to the wooden plank doors of the large brick structure, he saw that the padlock was relatively new, but the hasp was so rusted that it all but fell at Zach's feet when his brother gave it a slight tug.

"Whoa," Cole said, taking a step back. "Isn't that breaking and entering?"

"Not if you guys own the property," Vivienne replied, before being the first to walk inside. Cole almost asked if prowling and trespassing were included in her wedding-planner fees, or if she charged extra for that service.

"We don't own it yet," Cole called out when Zach and Lydia followed her lead. Super. Now they were all committing a crime. He stepped in after them. "Technically, Dad never mentioned whether or not the offer was accepted."

"Relax, Sergeant Save-the-Day," Zach said, using the hated nickname from childhood. "The lock is probably just to keep out the bears and the teenagers looking for a hangout. It's not like they're storing any valuables in here."

Okay, so maybe his brother had a point. Aside from some spiderwebs and a few broken wooden crates in one corner, the place was empty.

"Wow." Vivienne did a complete circle as she looked up at the row of dormer windows lining each side of the roofline. "Look at all the natural light coming in here. An open floor plan like this would be the perfect place to host some sort of housewarming party."

Cole squeezed his eyelids shut for a few seconds, then opened them, wondering if the woman was seeing the same run-down barren building he was. Who in their right mind would throw a party here? Or maybe the fee calculator in her mind was ka-chinging like a cash register, and Vivienne was hoping to make a killing on his family with her suggestions for additional parties they didn't need.

"I'm afraid your vision is completely lost on me," he said, crossing his arms in front of his chest.

"Look." She pulled a small electronic tablet out of her purse and made her way toward him as she tapped on the screen. She held up a picture of what looked to be some fancy hall decorated to look like an old barn. Or maybe it was an old barn cleaned up to look like a fancy hall. "People actually pay thousands of dollars to rent out aged buildings just like these for private events."

"Yeah, but how much work would it take to make this—" Cole gestured to the brick walls and windows caked with years of grime before pointing at her device "—look like *that*?"

"I guess it would depend on how motivated you were. I bet a cleaning crew could have this place scrubbed down in a couple of days. The roof might need some repairing, just in case it rains during the event, and you'll probably need a new shed door. I'm not an expert at refurbishing old buildings, but you'd only need to make it structurally sound, not livable. Part of the charm is in keeping the thing as rustic as possible. Then you bring in your own tables and chairs, or you get them from a party rental company, call up a caterer and go from there."

"Can I see that picture?" Lydia asked as she and Zach huddled together on one side of Vivienne. Cole found himself practically pressed up against her other side so that he could still see the screen as she swiped through similar images. But instead of focusing on the photos, his eyes kept straying toward the V-neck of her dress. Again.

Lydia's gasp caused his head to jerk up, an innocent expression pasted all over his guilty face. But instead of accusing him of ogling the wedding planner, his soon-to-be sister-in-law said excitedly, "You know what would be perfect? We should have our reception here. Just think! It would serve a dual purpose of celebrating our wedding and formally welcoming the Daltons to Rust Creek Falls."

"I love it," Vivienne gushed, before looking down at a text that popped up on her tablet. Unlike Zach and Lydia, who had stepped back and were too busy making googly eyes at each other and the derelict building, Cole was still right by Vivienne's side and could easily see the message.

You better be getting more bookings while you're there, or else. Her finger quickly swiped to hide the notification, but as soon as it was gone, a second one popped up. This time, there were no words. Just a row of dollar signs.

Luckily, he was able to look away right before she turned her head in his direction, probably hoping he hadn't seen her boss's directive. Even though his instincts had now been confirmed, there was something about the threat at the end that evoked just the smallest pang of sympathy.

Once, he'd had an old blowhard of a first sergeant who'd gotten in his face and cussed him up one side and down the other when he caught Cole helping another recruit clean the latrine. The dressing-down took place in front of the entire platoon, who all did their best to pretend nothing out of the ordinary was happening. So he was familiar with being embarrassed by high-handed bosses who never appreciated a job well-done. If only Estelle of Estelle's Events could see that her employee was currently reeling in her clients hook, line and sinker.

Still. Someone had to look out for his brother and make sure nobody was taking advantage of the lovestruck groom. Cole couldn't tamp down the need to remind the couple of the more practical side of things.

"I know you guys are thinking with your hearts right now, but maybe you should be thinking with your checking accounts." Honestly, Cole had no idea what their budget was, but every time Vivienne had made a suggestion during the car ride over here, he'd been reminded of one of those bar-code scanning machines in the grocery store, each beep signaling a rising total.

"Like I said, I'm not sure how much it would cost to get the building fixed up, but if you're not tearing it down, you'd likely be investing that much money into the place anyway to use it as a barn or a shed-thing or… whatever you would use it for on a ranch." Vivienne was definitely a city girl, all right. Yet she didn't let her lack of knowledge about cattle operations keep her from continuing on. "The table and chair rental will depend on what your final guest count is, but I have a vendor who includes linens and delivery and setup in the cost. Using a caterer is going to give you more flexibility with the menu than you might have at a restaurant or hotel. The flowers, the music, the cake and the photographer are all separate businesses you'd be hiring out anyway, so the location wouldn't matter. If you give me a day or so, I can draw up a new budget for you with some projected prices, but based on my experience, it'll be at least a few thousand dollars cheaper to have the reception here rather than using a formal venue."

Wait. Did Vivienne just say *cheaper*? As in she was trying to *save* Zach and Lydia money? And the woman was smiling as if she was actually happy to take a cut on her commission. Assuming she was working off a commission. Cole had no idea how people were paid in her line of work or why anyone would ever need to hire a wedding planner in the first place. It wasn't like it was a real job that required much effort.

His head spun at the whirlwind of conflicting thoughts and he tried to make sense of it all.

But when he saw his brother and Lydia walking around the space, eagerly talking about where they could put a dance floor and whether they should forgo a church ceremony and say their vows under the canopy of aspen trees outside, the weight of determination settled in Cole's chest. The Daltons, or at least their branch of the family, hadn't had anything to celebrate in a long time. So if having the party here gave Zach even a glimmer of happiness, then Cole was going to make sure the bride and groom had the biggest and best wedding the town of Rust Creek Falls had ever seen.

Chapter Four

Estelle was going to have a fit about their company doing a "cowboy" wedding, Vivienne thought to herself as she drove toward Rust Creek Falls on a Sunday morning three weeks later. But ever since she'd seen that beautiful brick freight house, her brain had been buzzing with all kinds of ideas and she hadn't felt this motivated at work in a long time.

When Cole had made that comment about checking accounts and the cost of the Grant-Dalton wedding, Vivienne was certain that he'd seen Estelle's text to her about locking in more wedding contracts while she was in Rust Creek Falls. Then, out of nowhere, he'd all of a sudden switched gears and was promising that they could have the buildings on the family's new property ready within a month after closing.

The guy was a complete mystery to her. One minute, he was all stoic, chastising his brother for not having his cell phone on. The next minute, he was winking at her and calling her *ma'am* in that sexy drawl of his. Then he was suggesting that weddings were a waste of money right before volunteering to remodel the old washroom in the back of the freight house and turn it into a ladies' restroom.

Vivienne was used to unexpected changes and rolling with the flow. Both her childhood and her job had trained her well. But it'd sure be nice if Cole would pick a lane.

When she made a right onto the long driveway for Sawmill Station, she immediately noticed that there was a lush green lawn in place of the overgrown fields and there was freshly laid gravel preventing her compact car from landing in a pothole. But the biggest surprise of all was the crisp white paint on the clapboards of the train depot.

Vivienne's fingers froze on the gearshift as she put it in Park. No, the biggest surprise was seeing the sexy and unpredictable Cole Dalton on the roof of the depot, hammering in new shingles. He turned to look in her direction, and she took a few steadying breaths as he pulled a small, blue square of fabric from his back jeans pocket and wiped his forehead.

She thought about grabbing her phone or tablet and pretending she was busy on a call or returning emails, but Cole had obviously already caught her staring at him, because he was now descending the ladder propped up against the side of the building. Vivienne's mouth went dry. The tool belt slung low across his hips caused her gaze to focus on that area of his body and she reached up to make sure her sunglasses were still covering her eyes.

Reminding herself that she was a professional, Vivienne sucked in one last gulp of air and climbed out of her car. Instead of the straw cowboy hat she'd seen on him before, he was wearing a bright green ball cap, and judging by the dampness of his thin white tee, he'd ditched his usual flannel work shirt long ago. Just below the edge of his short sleeve, a tattoo peeked out with the letters *USMC*.

She swallowed as he walked toward her, wiping his hands on the back of his jeans. Vivienne told her muscles to unclench and tried for a casual greeting. "I can't believe how far along you guys are."

"Thanks. My brothers and I have been working around the clock to get the place in shape for the wedding. Personally, I don't see why Zach and Lydia are so hell-bent on rushing things along, but I figure the sooner we get them off on their honeymoon, the sooner the rest of us can get to work on actually building the main house and setting up for the cattle."

"Well, three more weeks and I'll be out of your hair for good." Vivienne's smile hardly slipped out of place. She'd planned weddings in shorter amounts of time, so it wasn't like this was much of a challenge for her. But she'd also never had Estelle breathing down her neck about bringing in more business while simultaneously having to fight her attraction to one of her client's brothers.

Confusion marred his brow for a brief moment before he jerked his chin toward her empty arms and asked, "Where's your trusty binder?"

"Oh. It's in the back. I'm supposed to meet Lydia here at noon, but I wanted to come early and set up a few decoration samples for her to decide on so I can place orders. Do you know if the electrical stuff is finished inside the freight house? I brought some strings of lights I wanted to test out."

"That was one of the first things we got sorted out." He tapped on the cordless drill holstered inside his tool belt. "You know men and their power tools."

Actually, what Vivienne knew about handyman cowboys wouldn't even fill a shot glass. And with how dry her mouth had grown in the last sixty seconds, she could sure use a shot of something right now.

They were facing each other over the hood of her Jetta and, since Cole didn't seem to be in any hurry to return to work, she stammered, "So, uh, I'll just head on over to the freight house and let you get back to your roof."

He tipped his cap but didn't turn away.

"Okay, then." Vivienne gave an awkward nod and pivoted toward the rear of her car, using her remote to pop open the trunk. She'd just go about her business and, hopefully, Cole would get the hint that he should go about his.

Instead, the sound of crunching gravel followed her, and she felt the heat of his nearby presence as she stared at the cardboard box of mason jars and stacks of table runners. "Here, let me help you carry this stuff."

Before she could refuse his offer, he'd already stepped in front of her and hefted out a roll of burlap and a spool of twinkling lights. "You don't have to do that. I can get it…"

Her protest died as he walked off, balancing his loads under each rounded bicep. As she watched his backside, her heart skipped several beats before she grabbed a centerpiece in each hand and rushed to catch up. Thank goodness she'd learned her lesson about wearing heels out here in the country. Today she'd thrown on her favorite pair of Chuck Taylors after choosing an outfit that she didn't mind getting dirty.

Fortunately, the freight house was no longer dirty at all. In fact, the windows had been thoroughly scrubbed—with several broken ones replaced—and the floors had been swept out. The cobwebs were long gone and the place was no longer littered with rodent droppings. "Wow. This is even better than I'd expected."

Cole set his load down in a corner before taking the flowers out of her hands. "Are you serious? It looks like an empty old warehouse in here."

"I know! That's the look we're going for."

Doubt flashed in his cool blue eyes, but his only response was a slight shake of his head. "I guess you're the wedding expert."

"Trust me." This time *she* gave *him* the saucy wink, then spun around and hurried back to the car before he could see the heat staining her cheeks.

They didn't speak again until they'd brought everything inside, which took only two more trips, since the man could carry more than half his body weight in tea-light candles. Vivienne did a mental inventory to make sure she hadn't forgotten anything, then stopped short.

"Hey, Cole, Zach picked up a banquet and sixty-inch round from the office a few days ago. Do you know where he put them?"

He took off his cap and ran his hand through his short black hair. "I have no idea what you just said."

"They're tables." Vivienne extended her arms as far as they'd go. "One's sixty inches in diameter. The other is a long rectangle for banquet seating."

"Right. I don't speak wedding." He just spoke power tools. And probably trucks and cattle and semper fi. "We stored them inside the depot when we sealed the concrete floor in here. I'll grab them for you."

"I can help." She might not have broad shoulders or sinewy forearms or six-pack abs like him, however, she'd certainly carried her fair share of folding tables. Okay, so maybe she wasn't exactly sure about his abs, but his shirt was thin and tight enough to suggest that there might be a few ridges underneath.

Vivienne quickly caught up alongside him so that she wouldn't be forced to examine his body as they made their way to the depot. He opened the blue door, which had been painted to match the large sliding shed-style doors on the freight house, and extended his arm, indicating she should enter first. A shiver shot down her spine as she wondered if he was now going to be the one studying her from behind.

The depot was a one-room building, only about nine hundred square feet, with a long, dusty counter dividing the majority of the space from the back wall. She pointed to a small enamel basin affixed to a corner with some broken pieces of wood framing out a square around it. "Does that sink work?"

"It might have at one point, since we found some pipes running from that corner to the main water line. Our best guess is that someone had started building an indoor restroom for the public to use, but then business tanked and the thing never got finished."

Vivienne tapped her chin with two fingers, looking between the fixture and the counter. "How hard would it be to install a bigger sink? Only temporarily?"

"Why would someone only need a temporary sink?"

"I was thinking that the caterers could work out of here."

"You want us to build you a kitchen?"

"Not for me. For the caterers. And not an actual kitchen. That would be terribly expensive and would probably require building permits. With only three weeks to go, nobody has time for that. But with the counter already here and a bigger sink, the caterers could do some of the food prep and staging here, which would save time and cut down on costs."

"I suppose we could do that."

She swiveled in his direction, her palms held up. "Unless you guys had another plan on how to use this building."

"Well, since we can't bulldoze it because it's a landmark and it's too small for a stable, I have absolutely no idea how to put it to good use on a ranch. I'll ask around and find you a bigger sink."

For the first time all morning, Vivienne's smile wasn't forced when she looked at him. "Thank you."

"I'm glad to help." His eyes lowered to her lips and a rush of warmth swirled in her tummy. She told herself to take a step back, but her feet stayed planted where they were. Instead, her gaze dropped to his mouth and when the corner tilted up into a knowing smirk, Vivienne gasped.

The short intake of air startled her back to reality and she recovered by clearing her throat. "I should probably head outside to get away from all this dust."

Whipping around to the door, she took several purposeful strides, praying that he wouldn't notice how shaky her legs had suddenly become. Cole's voice stopped her when she got to the threshold. "Aren't you forgetting something?"

"Like what?" she asked, making a pretense of searching her surroundings for forgotten items, without actually turning around and facing him again. She'd definitely left her pride behind somewhere, but she bit back that response.

"The banquet and sixty-inch round?"

She narrowed her eyes before realization dawned. The tables. The whole reason for coming in here with him in the first place. "Of course."

Luckily she needed to take only a couple steps back before she could cut a diagonal path to the front wall where they were propped. She started to roll the bigger one, then froze when his hand covered hers. "I didn't mean for you to take them with you. I planned to carry them. I just needed you to tell me where they go."

"I can help," she said, rotating inward to slip her hand out from under his warm, strong fingers. But the maneuver was a mistake, because she hadn't anticipated how close he was behind her and she ended up two inches away from the wall of his chest. And he still hadn't released her hand, preventing her from moving too far. She inhaled deeply, catching his scent of fabric softener and hardworking male.

"Let me do it for you," he replied, his voice low and his breath a soft caress against her forehead.

Tilting her face back, she melted under the intensity of his eyes and couldn't look away. Vivienne no longer knew what he wanted to do for her, but she parted her mouth, about to allow him full access.

Cole moved in closer, his head dipping down toward hers. But before his lips could make contact, a horn blasted outside.

Cole couldn't believe he'd been right about to kiss the wedding planner before the boisterous caravan of his extended family honked their arrival. He'd known his aunt Rita and uncle Charles had told all of his cousins that everyone was going to pitch in today to help get things finished in time. Just like an old-fashioned barn raising. Minus the barn.

But he hadn't expected them all so soon. Of course, he also hadn't expected to get distracted by pretty Vivienne Shuster.

They'd both jumped apart so quickly when that first horn sounded, the table they'd been fighting for control over almost went crashing down to the floor. Then her face had turned a charming shade of crimson, and she'd blinked several times before whirling toward the door and leaving him holding the sixty-inch round.

Now, two hours later, Cole watched her from his perch on top of the rafters in the freight house, where he'd been hanging all these ridiculous twinkly lights. Uncle Charles had volunteered to string the things up, but Cole couldn't very well let his father's older brother risk breaking his neck by climbing up and down the ladder so many times.

Plus, it gave Cole an excuse to stay inside where Vivienne was busy working. She was fifteen feet below him, standing with Lydia and Aunt Rita as they surveyed the different table settings she'd arranged. From up here, all the plates and flowers and different-colored tablecloths looked like a bunch of fuss. But judging by the way the other women were oohing and aahing over Vivienne's displays, it was evident that she must be fairly good at her job. Not that he was any clearer on what exactly her job was.

But she certainly knew how to orchestrate all his relatives to do her bidding. And she was so subtle and diplomatic about it, doing that chin-tapping thing, tilting her pretty little head and wondering out loud about a possibility; half of them hadn't even noticed that she was adding to their workload. In fact, right this second, his baby brother Shawn and his cousins Eli and Derek were at the lumberyard in town buying up a truck bed full of wood because Vivienne had suggested that a gazebo would be perfect between the two aspen trees outside.

Booker, his oldest brother, and Zach were proving

their lack of plumbing skills by installing a new sink and vanity in the old freight office, which was currently undergoing renovations to be turned into a restroom for guests.

Wherever there was a broken-down mess, or even just a plain, empty space, Vivienne Shuster had an idea of how to improve upon it—usually in the most simple and inexpensive way. More important, she had an uncanny knack of relaying her vision with so much enthusiasm that everyone was eager to see it to fruition.

Hell, even he'd offered to build her a kitchen inside a hundred-year-old shack that had been nothing but an eyesore only a month ago. Still. Annoyance had prickled at his skin every time one of his single male relatives jumped at the opportunity to impress her. Not that he was jealous or anything. It wasn't like he *wanted* to be attracted to her. He certainly had no intention of acting on that attraction, despite how close he'd come to doing just that inside the train depot. It was simply that he didn't want anyone else helping her carry tables.

Hooking the staple gun onto his belt, Cole surveyed the final strand of lights and called out, "Okay, Dad, plug them in."

But the bulbs stayed unlit.

"Dad?" Cole braced his hands on the wooden beam so he could lean over and search for the older man.

"Phil's outside with Garrett," Uncle Charles offered as he navigated a huge box strapped to a dolly. "They're looking at the old train tracks, trying to figure out how to make them safe so that nobody trips over them."

Lord, all his family needed was to have one of the

partygoers indulge in too much of Homer Gilmore's spiked punch—which had been rumored to be responsible for many Rust Creek Falls weddings not too long ago—and risk twisting their ankles or doing a faceplant on the Dalton property.

As he climbed down the ladder rungs, Cole made a mental note to look into whether they might need an extra insurance policy. He shook his head. "And Dad thinks *Garrett* is the best one to come up with a safe solution?"

Uncle Charles shrugged and replied, "He's pretty mechanical. Besides, everyone else was already working on something."

"This is an accident waiting to happen," Cole muttered to himself, and since he was striding past the women as he said it, three sets of eyes turned to look at him.

Vivienne handed a mason jar full of flowers over to Lydia and said, "You guys talk over which option you like best. We can always use the burlap for the chair sashes if you'd rather have the linen runners on the tables."

Cole continued past them, but before he knew it, Vivienne was matching his pace and gave his arm a gentle tug. Her soft touch caused him to almost lose all sense of direction and he slowed down.

"What's wrong?" she asked, her voice hushed as her concerned eyes darted back toward Lydia. While Cole appreciated the fact that Vivienne didn't want to worry his soon-to-be sister-in-law, this new development was a pretty big deal.

"Oh, nothing. Except for the fact that we have half a mile of broken-down railroad tracks all over our property, and someone thought it would be a good idea to get a bunch of people wearing high heels and slick cowboy boots together at night, serve gallons of rum punch and then send them out to walk around in the dark."

"But Garrett said he could fix it."

"Clearly you don't know my brother."

When they got to the door, he looked at Vivienne in time to see her eyes widen and her throat constrict as she swallowed. "Enlighten me."

"Garrett would just as soon build a roller coaster on those tracks rather than pull them up. Wait." He stopped when they got outside and planted himself in front of her. "Can we even pull the things up? Are they part of the landmark preservation thing my dad agreed to?"

Her only response was to bite her lower lip, again reminding him of the fact that he'd almost kissed her earlier today. What had he been thinking? What had any of them been thinking?

He groaned and continued walking. "Man, I can't believe we didn't do something about this sooner."

"Cole," she said, catching up to him again. "There's always a workable solution."

He kept walking. "Did they teach you that in wedding-planner college?"

"No. Life taught me that. And just for the record, my degree is in business administration. Wedding planning is only my fallback career."

Cole drew up short, immediately feeling like a jerk for making the snide remark. Especially because he knew what it was like to have a fallback career. If it were up to him, he'd still be in the Marine Corps. He'd also still have his mom here, but he couldn't go back in time and fix the past. He could only solve today's problems.

Guilt washed through him. "Sorry. That was a crappy thing to say. I didn't mean to insult your profession."

"Listen, you're not the first family member I've dealt with who thought hiring an event company was a waste of money." Her smile would've been more reassuring if it matched her eyes.

"I know I acted that way at first, but you've really taken a lot of the pressure off my brother and Lydia. I know they're both overwhelmed with throwing this thing, and you're so good with Lydia, giving her ideas and suggestions without bullying her into what *you* think she should have."

"Thank you," she said, this time looking as though she meant it. "Now, let me do my job."

Vivienne walked toward the platform of the depot, where Garrett was lying down on his belly next to the side of the track and using one open eye and an extended hand to measure something off in the distance. His dad was resting his hands on top of a shovel handle, his forehead planted on his stacked fingers as he shook his head at whatever Garrett was saying.

"Hey there, gentlemen," she said sweetly as they drew near. "Have you guys come up with any clever solutions so far?"

Garrett jumped to his feet and dusted the dirt and gravel off his belly. "Well, I was thinking we could find a couple of those old mining carts and use them to ferry the guests back and forth from the parking area to the freight house."

A vein throbbed in Cole's temple and he squeezed his lids shut.

"Hmm." Vivienne nodded, as if she was seriously contemplating his brother's asinine suggestion. "You mean like one of those handcar things with the crank that people pump up and down to make it move?"

"Actually, I meant one of those huge carts with the sides about so high." Garrett gestured toward his chest. "The ones that miners used to fill up with coal and supplies and stuff. Then we could harness it to one of the horses and pull people inside, kind of like an old-fashioned buggy ride—except on the rails so they can haul butt. To be honest, though, your idea of the hand-cart sounds way more fun."

"I think they both sound fun," Vivienne stated, and Cole rolled his eyes, ready to interject. "However, you could probably only operate one or two at a time, and at last count the guest list was pushing two hundred. That's a lot of shuttle trips back and forth and people won't want to wait. Would it be difficult to turn the tracks into some sort of walkway? Maybe use cement or dirt or something to pack between the two rails so that the metal part is still showing, keeping the old-fashioned charm, but making it more of an outline of a modern sidewalk?"

His father's face slowly lifted and Garrett's eyes lit up. In fact, Cole's own head tilted as he considered that possibility.

Vivienne continued. "But all of you have already done so much work in such a short amount of time and I don't want you to do anything to your property that you're not comfortable with."

"I know I don't want to tiptoe around these tracks and risk falling down and breaking my old neck," Phil Dalton said. "Sounds like a good enough plan to me."

"But if we turn it into a sidewalk, we won't be able to use any handcarts on the tracks. Don't you think it'd be kinda cool to have races and stuff with them?" Garrett was enthusiastically bobbing his head up and down and Cole opened his mouth to tell his brother that he shouldn't leave the house without a helmet.

Fortunately, Vivienne spoke before him. "There's still the track on the back side of the freight house. You can set up your handcarts over there. After the reception is over, obviously."

"Obviously," their dad repeated, his eyes drilled in Garrett's direction, as if to drive home the implication that there weren't going to be any carts or any racing at any time during the wedding.

Cole had to admit it—the woman really was brilliant at solving problems without making others feel as though she was steering them in a direction they didn't want to go. And before he knew it, she was steering him back toward the freight house. "Let's go plug in those lights."

Cole tossed a smug smile in his brother's direction before eagerly following along.

Chapter Five

"Where did those come from?" Vivienne asked the oldest Dalton brother as he rolled two old-fashioned barrels on either side of him through the freight house. What was his name again? Booker? She needed a chart to keep track of all the relatives.

"They were stacked in a storage room built behind the office. After we moved them, we found a trapdoor hidden in the floor and Lydia thinks that the former owners might've operated a still down there during Prohibition. The Dumpster is already full, so I'm going to load them in my truck and find somewhere to get rid of them."

"No, they're perfect. Can I have them?"

"For what?" Cole asked her. He'd already had her all flustered after that near kiss in the depot. While she worked, she didn't need him following her around second-guessing everything she was doing.

She was saved from responding by the sound of another car horn outside. Was that a Rust Creek Falls thing? Why did everyone who drove up have to honk their arrival?

"Food's here!" Charles slapped his palms together as he came out of the freight office area. "After we eat, you guys should go check out the moonshine room."

An idea flickered, but Rita Dalton was waving everyone outside, barking orders to her sons and nephews to help set up the tables. Vivienne would have to give this so-called moonshine room a little more thought.

"Uncle Ben and Aunt Mary are right behind us," the newly arrived driver said. Two more women she thought might be Rita's daughters carried boxes advertising Buffalo Bart's Wings-To-Go, and Vivienne found herself standing in the center of the gravel lot as Dalton after Dalton sped by her, unloading wooden benches and two picnic tables and dozens of assorted containers of what looked to be homemade side dishes.

It felt odd not to be the one giving direction as the whirlwind of activity happened around her. She was used to crowds at other weddings or parties, but this was different. It was all one family. And they were huge. And overwhelming. And loud. But in a good way.

She startled when Cole's hand touched her lower back. He leaned to whisper, "You better get in line before all the chicken is gone."

Vivienne's stomach rumbled. She had a healthy appetite and could put away a fair amount of food. But looking at the heaping platters and salad-filled bowls, she calculated that it would take even this brood at least three days to consume all of it.

"C'mon, Vivienne," Rita called, holding out a paper plate.

Feeling everyone's eyes on her, Vivienne carefully scooped out small amounts of potato salad, coleslaw, green beans and sliced watermelon. The chicken looked incredible, but she limited herself to three boneless strips. Then she saw the pan of corn bread and her tummy told her that she would feel so much more at ease if she topped off her plate with a hunk the size of her fist. By the time she got to the end of the table, all the other women had filed in behind her, following her lead.

She took her food toward one of the benches set up under the shade of the aspen trees, balancing her full plate on her knees, since many of the guys were lounging around the other picnic table waiting for their turn in line. Rita and Lydia came next, and the rest of the ladies joined them on nearby benches. Cole and Booker were the last ones to get their food and most of the seats were taken by that point, with some of the men standing up to eat.

There was about a foot of space left next to her, and Booker made his way toward it, as though he intended to squeeze in beside her. But right before he could sit down, Cole appeared with his elbows outstretched and rammed his body between Vivienne and Booker, causing his brother to drop his plate as Cole slammed himself onto the bench hard enough to jostle the opposite end.

"Darn it, Cole," Rita said, recovering from the

bounce and wiping her mouth on a paper napkin. "This isn't a teeter-totter."

Cole was pressed up so close against Vivienne's arm that her own paper plate was in danger of folding in on itself. But instead of an apology, he looked smugly at his big brother while the rest of the Dalton men hooted and laughed.

"Gotta be quicker than that, Booker," Garrett catcalled.

"Hey, Lydia," Zach, who was standing with the other men, hollered to his fiancé. "Why don't we play musical chairs at the reception? If we put our money on Cole, we could probably win enough bets to pay for the whole wedding."

"Nah," Shawn Dalton said. "Cole'll only compete if there's a pretty wedding planner in the open seat."

Heat flooded Vivienne's face and Cole threw a buttermilk biscuit at Shawn, who was too busy doubling over with laughter to duck.

"You boys mind your manners," Rita said in a firm, authoritative voice. Then she turned to Vivienne as the guffaws were smothered into mere snickers and smirks. "Honey, don't pay them any mind."

Cole's shoulder remained pressed against hers, and each time he took a bite, she felt his movement. There was no way he could be comfortable sitting so close to her on such a small area of wood. But the man didn't budge. It was almost as if he needed to prove to his relatives that he wasn't the least bit affected by their teasing. Or maybe he truly wasn't bothered by it. Which meant Vivienne shouldn't be bothered by the comments, either, especially the one about him wanting the seat by the wedding planner.

Surely, the only reason he was sitting here was because it was the last spot left, and he'd been working long before everyone else got there, so he was probably exhausted. Or perhaps he was only sitting here because he had an inherent need to compete and beat one of his brothers out of something. That had to be it. With his straight spine and cocky expression, Cole resembled a bridesmaid who'd just beat out every other single woman trying to catch the bride's bouquet.

Which reminded Vivienne to get back to business. "Lydia, did your maid of honor pick up her dress yet?"

"Yes, and Joanna says hers fits perfectly," Lydia said, referring to her childhood friend. "Jolene tried hers on at the *Gazette* office and has been talking about matching accessories at work nonstop. And Eva dropped hers off with the tailor yesterday."

Vivienne clenched her jaw at the mention of Eva-Rose Armstrong's name but tried not to show her concern. Most brides didn't ask one of their groom's prior dates to be part of the wedding party, and Vivienne could only hope that Lydia was right and that the woman Zach once went out with had happily moved on with the new man in her life.

"How are you going to wear your hair, dear?" Aunt Mary asked Lydia, who gave a helpless shrug.

"I don't know. What do you think, Vivienne?"

Out of all the women here, most of them their own age, Lydia had asked her. Pride blossomed in Vivienne's chest, knowing it was the ultimate vote of confidence when a bride valued her opinion. Sitting up straighter, she accidentally rammed her elbow into Cole's steely bicep. He didn't even flinch.

"It depends on how formal you want to look," Vivienne said, knowing that Lydia rarely wore makeup and preferred to keep her brown curls loose and casual.

"I want it to look natural, but I also want it to be special."

"Well, I have mobile beauticians and makeup artists on speed dial if you want to go that route. Or we can keep business local and use Bee's Beauty Parlor in town. In either event, we should probably pull up some styles that you'd prefer and ask around." Vivienne tapped her chin before continuing on. "Actually, I was kind of toying with the idea of a little theme and I think it would work well with your dress."

Lydia's face brightened. "I love a theme. What is it?"

"Well, you guys found what might've been an old still and with the hundred-year-old train depot and your work at the newspaper, we could do sort of a Prohibition era 1920s revival thing. I'm not thinking of a full-on speakeasy and flappers doing the Charleston. But maybe some subtle touches to complement the property's history."

"It's like you know exactly what I want before I could possibly even think of it," Lydia gushed, making Vivienne's chest fill with satisfaction.

But the satisfaction was short-lived as everyone else began chiming in with their own ideas. Some of them were good; however, some of them had Lydia crinkling her nose.

One of the female Dalton cousins clapped her hands.

"Ooh, we could dress the ring bearers up like little newsies with tweed derby hats. They could pass out programs and yell, 'Extra, extra, read all about it.' How adorable would that be?"

"What about the groomsmen?" Garrett asked, his eyes bright and energized. "Can we get zoot suits and tommy guns?"

Vivienne tried to tamp down the panic wedging in her throat. She should've waited to talk to Lydia and Zach alone about a decision this size. Once again, it was time to rein things in.

Leaning forward to look around Cole, who was still squished up beside her and shoveling food into his mouth, Vivienne asked Zach, "Didn't you already decide what color tuxes you wanted? If you're using that rental company I suggested, we're going to need to get everyone fitted as soon as possible."

"Whoa." Shawn held up his plastic fork like a stop sign. "I'm not wearing a tux."

Cole's upper arm brushed against hers as he swiveled in his seat and planted both boots on either side of the edge of the bench to face his brother. "Who says you even get to be in the wedding?"

"I say," Shawn replied. "As long as I don't have to put on a monkey suit or slow dance with any of the bridesmaids."

"Yeah, entertaining the ladies isn't exactly in your wheelhouse, Shawn. I believe that's *my* specialty." Garrett might've been the one speaking, but the wall of Cole's back pressed up against her side prevented Vivienne from seeing much of the playful banter going on in that direction. "In fact, that's why Zach wants *me* to be the best man."

"I do?" Zach asked.

Vivienne's pulse sped up and she turned questioning eyes toward Lydia. *Please say you've already decided this.* But the woman looked as clueless as Vivienne felt.

"I doubt it, Garrett," Cole argued. "You're the most likely to lose the ring."

Shawn laughed. "That's right. Dad, remember when Garrett forgot me at the county fair that one year? You put him in charge of buying me a corn dog, but then he ditched me to go on the Scream Xtreme with Rondalee… What's her name? You know, the girl who had the big—" Shawn cupped his hands to his chest and Phil interrupted him with a severe shake of his head. "I was going to say tomatoes, Dad. She won the blue ribbon in gardening that year."

"I didn't *lose* you," Garrett defended. "You wandered off and Cole found you in one of the 4-H pens trying to feed cotton candy to the goats."

"That's right." Cole stood up abruptly and Vivienne almost toppled over. "*I* was the one who found you. And then *I* called the vet for those poor goats. Lydia, trust me, you don't want these two ensuring things go right on your big day."

"If you ask me, it's simple." Booker looked up from the table where he was getting a third helping of food— well, only a second helping if one didn't count the plate Cole had made him drop. "I'm the oldest, so I get to be the best man."

Vivienne saw the muscles in Cole's chest expand as

he drew in a gulp of air. He exhaled on a sigh. "Zach, do you recall Booker's valedictorian speech in high school? We spent years trying to get the teachers to forget we were related to him. Would you really want him giving the best man toast?"

Zach's only response was to laugh. Phil Dalton hitched up his belt and said, "Well, sons, there's only one way to settle this."

Someone whooped and one of the cousins produced a bucket of metal horseshoes. Vivienne leaned toward Rita to ask, "What are they doing?"

"They're going to play a game of horseshoes to decide." The older woman shook her head. "Just be glad they haven't moved any of the steers or horses out here yet. The last thing this wedding needs is someone showing up with a broken leg after a bronc-riding contest."

When someone hammered a metal stake into the ground, Lydia stood up and Vivienne asked, "Is this really happening?"

Lydia smiled. "Welcome to Rust Creek Falls."

"Let me go grab my tape measure," Cole said when Zach tried to count out the distance between the two stakes. Garrett had upended one of the wooden benches to use as a backstop, before his aunt Mary told him to put it back and find a scrap of wood somewhere else.

When Cole returned, he had his tool belt slung over one shoulder and Vivienne's tote bag in his hand. "Your purse was ringing in the freight house, so I thought you might need it."

She looked at the missed-call log and saw Estelle's name listed several times. And, apparently, so had Cole, who was still standing right next to her. She offered him a weak smile and said, "It's no big deal. I can call her back."

Cole gave her a terse nod before joining his brothers. She was glad one of the Dalton cousins outlined the rules, because Vivienne had no idea how the game was played. Lydia reminded everyone that they still had a building they needed to get ready for a wedding, so it was decided they'd do only one round with two pitches each. The brother with the best score would win.

Setting her tote bag on the abandoned bench, Vivienne joined the rest of the spectators at the makeshift horseshoe pit. She watched intently as each Dalton took his turn, with Phil and Charles measuring who came closest.

She found herself holding her breath when Cole opted to pitch last. His first horseshoe easily spun around the stake and his second landed less than an inch away. Excitement bubbled through her when Zach announced that Cole was the winner and she was surprised to realize that she'd been secretly rooting for him all along.

Instead of pumping his fist in the air or making macho whooping sounds like other guys might do when they won, the newly designated best man simply spun on his boot and looked directly at her. She finally recognized the look that had been on his face earlier when he'd beaten his older brother to the spot on the bench.

It was triumph.

"We want a rematch!" Booker and Garrett shouted at the same time.

Shawn took a more subtle approach by directing his

appeal toward Lydia. "I hope you know you're making a big mistake by reinforcing Sergeant Save-the-Day's ego."

In all of the weddings she'd planned, none of them had needed an athletic competition to decide who was going to head up the wedding party. Maybe Estelle had been right to warn her about doing cowboy weddings.

And speaking of Estelle, Vivienne's phone chimed with the distinctive ring tone she'd chosen for her boss—the whistle from the Hunger Games movie series—and she reached into her bag to switch the thing to vibrate. But not before Cole looked at her and saw what she was doing. She was tempted to turn it off completely, but she remembered the Daltons' rule about phone accessibility and didn't want to inadvertently offend anyone again.

Vivienne slid the cell into the side compartment of her bag just as Cole walked toward her. "Is everything okay?"

"Yep. We should probably start cleaning up over here and get back to work," Vivienne told him, but it was difficult to keep a neutral expression when her bag began vibrating.

Cole tilted his head. "Maybe you should take that."

She bit back a retort that maybe he should mind his own business. After all, even she had to concede that it would appear beyond unprofessional to blatantly ignore her boss. "Excuse me," she murmured to him before turning her back and sliding her finger across the screen to accept the call.

"Hello?"

"Have you scored us any more bookings out there in the backwoods?" Estelle's gravelly voice was louder than ever, and Vivienne frantically searched for the button to turn down the volume on her earpiece before anyone could overhear.

"Oh, hey there, Estelle. I'm, um, on-site for the Grant-Dalton wedding. Can I give you a call back later this afternoon?" Vivienne hoped the subtle statement would be enough to remind her boss that she wasn't in a position to be talking about drumming up more business.

But Estelle launched into her without regard for who was nearby. "You promised me you'd deliver another client by now, but instead you're avoiding my calls and building barns on my dime. This is what happens when you don't use one of our prearranged venues and decide to get creative."

"It's an old train station, not a barn," Vivienne said through a semi-clenched jaw. The depot was the closest building, so she headed in that direction for some quick privacy.

"Is it a new client, though, or is it the same cattle rustlers you brought to the office last month?"

"Estelle, you know that I'm doing my best—"

"I know nothing of the sort. You're over there in the latest marriage capital of Montana and you still can't bring me another viable customer? I took a chance on you when you were a fresh-faced kid out of business school and I expected great things from you. I poured a lot of energy into training you, going out of my way to introduce you to vendors, putting my own reputation on the line every time you came up with some harebrained plan to do things different and trendy. At minimum, I would like a return on my investment."

Vivienne reached the front door of the depot right as the tears threatened to fill her eyes. "I assure you that I am working on several leads and—"

"Leads aren't good enough," Estelle snapped. "I need results."

"And I'll have results. Just give me another week."

"You have twenty-four hours to get another booking or you're fired."

Cole was probably the biggest jerk of all for following Vivienne inside when she so clearly was trying to avoid having anyone overhear her phone call. But she'd looked so concerned and nervous, which was completely opposite to the controlled and capable image she usually projected. As the newly appointed best man, his primary job was to ensure that this wedding went off without a hitch. And if that meant seeing to the wedding planner, then so be it.

"You okay?" Cole asked her when she bit her cheeks, her eyes looking up, as though she was trying to decide how much to tell him.

"I'm fine. I was just startled to see you in here, that's all."

"Is that really all?" He cocked his head.

She leaned against the old countertop and gave a nervous chuckle that caught in her throat. "So you heard all that, huh?"

He nodded and she blew out a breath, causing one of the blond wavy locks that had escaped her ponytail to dance along her temple. "It sounded like you were in trouble with your boss."

"Trouble is an understatement. But it's nothing for anyone else to worry about."

"Could this affect Zach and Lydia's wedding?"

Vivienne's shoulders sagged and a look of defeat crossed her face. "I wish I could say it won't, but I'm pretty sure I'm about to be fired. Which doesn't necessarily mean that Lydia and Zach will be left in the lurch only three weeks before their wedding. Of course, they'll still have their contract with the company and my boss will honor it. But then they will have to work directly with Estelle and I doubt that will be a smooth transition."

Cole searched her face for some sort of indication that would tell him whether or not the woman was fishy or dishonest or unethical. He doubted it, but if she was, it was better she hop in her little Jetta now and drive away. "You said *about* to be fired? Did you do something illegal or break some wedding etiquette rule or something?"

"No!" Her hand flew to her chest, and a blush stole up her cheeks. "Nothing like that. It's just that my boss wants me to book another client."

"Is that all?" Cole's tension eased. "Then let's go out and talk to my cousins. Every time I turn around, somebody in this town is getting married. I'm sure they'll know someone else who might need a wedding planner."

Vivienne sighed. "I wish it were that easy."

"Seems simple enough to me."

"Weddings are very personal and special things,

and a couple should be comfortable with whoever they choose to be involved. Estelle wants a contract signed tomorrow and, in good conscience, I couldn't have someone rush into making that kind of commitment just to save my own job."

Cole studied her, one half of his brain telling him to keep his mouth shut before he said something stupid, the other half telling him that he was the only person who could fix this.

"So just to clarify... You only need to book *one* client?"

"For now, at least."

"For *one* wedding that can happen whenever?"

Her eyes narrowed with suspicion. "Correct."

"Then plan mine."

Chapter Six

Vivienne felt the flurry of emotions cross her face, the most prominent one being disgust because all she could think of was how he'd almost kissed her before the rest of his family had shown up. Vivienne had to flatten her palm against the worn countertop to keep from curling it into a fist. "You're engaged?"

"Of course I'm not engaged." Cole visibly shuddered. "I'm not even boyfriend material, let alone husband material."

Confusion quickly replaced her anger and Vivienne could only stutter, "Wh-why?"

"I guess because I have more important things going on in my life right now than to cozy up to some female I'm not interested in and pretend like I give a damn about all this commitment crap."

"No, I mean why would you need to plan a wedding if you're not getting married?"

"You said you need to book another client." He rocked onto the heels of his boots. "Well, I'm your next client."

Vivienne shook her head as if she could jiggle all the scattered pieces of this puzzle into place. "A client who has no intention of getting married?"

"Yes. But it's not like your boss would know the difference."

"She might figure it out when no actual marriage takes place. If you're not boyfriend material, then does that mean you don't have a girlfriend? I mean, who would we say you're marrying?"

Okay, so that first question Vivienne threw in for her own clarification. Even though they hadn't exactly kissed, she needed reassurance that she wasn't lusting over some guy who was off-limits.

"Nope, no need for a girlfriend," he said, and she felt some of her apprehension drain. But then he took a couple of steps closer. "We can make something up, but why would it even need to get that far? Look, you just need to buy yourself some time to bring in more business. So you sign me up or whatever you need to do to get your boss off your back, and then after you bring in some more customers—legitimate ones—my fake fiancée will have cold feet and we'll call it off."

If her eyes squinted any more, they'd be squeezed shut. And then she'd miss his normal teasing smirk telling her that he was only kidding. But his jaw was locked into place and the set of his straight mouth looked dead serious.

"It would never work." She waved her hand at him, deciding one of them should try to write this whole conversation off as a joke.

"Why can't it?"

"Estelle requires a contract. Like the kind that's legally binding in a court of law."

"So I come into your office and sign the contract. There's got to be a cancellation clause in there somewhere. You can't tell me you guys have never had someone cancel their wedding before."

"There is. Which is why she demands a security deposit up front."

"What are we talking about? A hundred bucks? Two hundred? How do you get paid, anyway?"

"Fifteen hundred," Vivienne replied, then almost smiled as Cole's eyes went round.

"And only the bride and groom pay that?" he asked. "You don't get any kickbacks from the florist or the minister or everyone?"

"First of all, clergy members are only offered a small honorarium that they oftentimes donate to their house of worship. Second of all, do you think I'd take money from a minister?" She quickly put her hand up. "No. Don't answer that. It's not like I work off commission. We get paid for the amount of hours we spend working on your wedding. So if it's going to be a big event, plan to pay for at least eighty hours of my time. Even if you and your pretend fiancée require the smaller, twenty-hour package, it's still a hefty chunk of change."

"Right." The man shrugged as if the pickup truck he drove wasn't at least twenty years old. "I have some money saved up from when I was in the Marines. My dad didn't want me dipping into my personal savings to invest in the ranch, since it's supposed to be a family operation. It's not like I have anything else I need to spend it on."

They stood there staring at each other across the counter. Vivienne racked her brain for another flaw to his ridiculous suggestion. But she felt completely empty—drained of all emotion and rational thought. And with his determined stance and squared shoulders, Cole didn't seem to be the kind of man who backed down from anything.

"Why would you do something for someone you barely know?"

"I could give you a hundred reasons, from the fact that you haven't once tried to sell my brother something he doesn't need, to the fact that you're hardworking and not afraid to jump in and get your hands dirty. But the bottom line is that this wedding is important to Zach and Lydia. I need it to go smoothly and I'm convinced that you're the best person for the job."

Then why did Vivienne feel as if she was a complete fraud?

What Cole didn't tell Vivienne was that it almost tore his heart out to see her hiding inside the train depot, fighting back those tears. So maybe he'd been a little impulsive when he'd made his offer yesterday. But once he'd put it out there, he knew there was no turning back. No backing down.

Still, when he pulled up to her office the following morning, it took him a solid five minutes to convince himself that he could put on a courageous face and brave the feminine confines of Vivienne's office again. It might've been a slight exaggeration when Cole had told his brother that the place reminded him of a war zone; however, he definitely felt like he was going into a battle he didn't know how to fight.

Before he got out of his truck, he looked at his reflection in the rearview mirror. He'd done the right thing, hadn't he? A voice told him that if he was so convinced about what he was about to do, he would've mentioned something to his dad yesterday. Or even to Zach or Lydia. Yet he'd remained silent the remainder of the day, keeping to himself as the rest of his family followed Vivienne's advice on everything from landscaping to repurposing old wood. Cole had been sure to avoid her, because he knew that if he allowed her to dwell on his plan, she'd try to talk him out of it.

But what was he supposed to do? Let the woman get fired from her job? He grabbed his checkbook as he finally exited his truck. He wasn't protecting her, he reminded himself for the hundredth time. He was doing this to help his brother and Lydia.

Cole must've lingered in the parking lot too long, because before he could get to the entrance, Vivienne came sailing out the front door. "I was going to call you this morning to tell you not to come in. But then I realized I didn't have your number."

"Is this morning a bad time?" he asked, looking around at the quiet storefront.

"I talked it over with Lord Nibbles last night and we both decided that I couldn't let you do this. It's too much."

"Who?"

"My guinea pig. The sound of my voice makes him less anxious, so we had a big discussion and I ran everything by him. When I told him I wasn't going to go through with it, he finally relaxed enough to eat the pretzel I was offering him."

"You fed your guinea pig human food? Didn't you hear the story yesterday about the 4-H goat and the cotton candy?"

"It was just one little treat." There was a crease between Vivienne's brows. "You don't think he'll get sick, do you? He looked fine this morning."

Cole tightened his grip on the checkbook. Maybe it was a bad idea to go into business with a woman who took job advice from a rodent. But then again, it wasn't really as if she was actually going to be working for him. The money was just to keep her doing what she was already doing for his brother and Lydia.

Yet before either one of them could persuade the other, a late-model Cadillac sedan pulled diagonally into the two parking spots to the right of his. The older woman's caked-on lipstick was clamped tightly around a cigarette and the rest of her makeup and teased blond hair appeared to have been plastered into place the decade before. Her petite frame and lavender business suit did nothing to detract from her assertiveness as she swung her heavy door open, narrowly missing banging his passenger side.

"Are you that cowboy who was here a few days ago picking up some tables?" The woman's voice sounded just as loud and abrasive as it had when she'd been laying into Vivienne over the phone yesterday.

"I believe that was my brother, ma'am. I'm Cole Dalton." He tipped the brim of his more formal black felt Stetson—after all, nobody could say he hadn't come dressed to take this appointment seriously.

She studied him from under lids weighted down with eye shadow before dropping her cigarette onto the asphalt and stepping on it with a white high-top sneaker that contradicted the rest of her outfit. "I'm guessing you brought the tables back, then?"

"No, Estelle, he's not—" Vivienne started, but Cole cut her off.

He held up his checkbook. "I'm here to book a wedding planner."

The woman's expression went from doubt to dollar signs as she reached out her bony, age-spotted fingers. "Then glad to meet you. Come on inside and Vivienne will get you all squared away with the paperwork."

Estelle didn't release his hand and Cole was forced to follow her as she dragged him past Vivienne and through the door. He pretended not to see the warning look the younger woman directed his way. After five minutes in her boss's company, he knew he made the right choice to offer his help.

The owner of Estelle's Events had the disposition of a yappy Chihuahua and the tenacity of a pit bull.

"But how do you know your fiancée wouldn't go for a hot-air balloon ceremony? If she were here, I would tell her that they're all the rage right now." That was the eighth time Estelle had made a reference to the fact that the so-called bride-to-be wasn't here.

"She's afraid of heights," Cole said, rubbing the bridge of his nose to make sure it wasn't growing.

"Uh-huh," Estelle replied as she slid a colorful brochure across the conference table toward him. "Have her look this over. Just in case."

Cole smiled stiffly as he tucked the folded paper into his front shirt pocket. He looked at Vivienne, who was sitting across from him, hiding behind her laptop screen, her fingers not making any sort of clicking sound on the keyboard.

"How's that contract going?" her boss asked her.

"Um, all I…uh…need is the bride's name." Her eyes pleaded with him to forget this whole thing.

But Estelle looked at him expectantly and Cole knew what would happen if he walked out and Vivienne didn't secure her booking. He said the first name that popped into his mind.

"Susie Starlight." Then, because it sounded way too far-fetched saying it out loud like that, he quickly added, "Roper. Her last name's Roper."

"You've got to be kidding me." Vivienne's face flew up from where she'd been ducking for cover. Her boss made a sound as though she was trying to clear her throat, which ended up triggering a lung-rattling smoker's cough.

"Or Susan, if you want to be formal," Cole said with a purposeful shrug of his shoulders to make his slip seem more plausible. "But everyone calls her by her nickname. Can I get you some water, Estelle?"

The older woman waved him off as she walked back to her office, her wheeze barely subsiding.

"I am not writing that name on a legally binding contract," Vivienne whispered.

"Why does it have to be on there at all? Clearly, I'm the only one who is here to sign the document anyway."

Vivienne studied him across the table. "Estelle probably won't make too much of a fuss about it as long as she gets her deposit."

She tapped the keys a few times and gave the mouse a click, and the printer in the corner whirred to life just as her boss walked back in, sucking on a lollipop. "I've been trying to cut back on the nicotine," Estelle said around the white stick. "Viv got me these to help take the edge off."

"Sounds like Viv here is quite the asset," Cole suggested, but the asset in question made a subtle sweeping gesture across her neck. Yeah, maybe he was laying it on too thick. Already uncomfortable with the false details he was making up to just keep this big lie believable, he shifted in his seat and said, "Who do I make the check out to?"

Estelle eagerly took the twenty-five percent down payment of the company's fee, her sneakers squeaking across the hardwood floor as she hotfooted it back to her office—probably to make out the bank deposit slip. He wouldn't be surprised if the ol' gal didn't have one of those apps on her phone that snapped a picture of the check to transfer the funds before he changed his mind.

Cole looked over the paperwork, then lowered his voice. "I hope you stipulated in here that I'd be working primarily with you."

"Don't worry. Estelle doesn't bother leaving the office much these days. Besides the occasional phone call, I'm almost always the one who works with the clients." Vivienne handed him a contact information form to fill out. "But she will want the bride's email address to register her for a subscription service from various wedding vendors. I suggest you give her yours unless you want them kicked back as invalid."

Cole wrote down his contact information, wishing he had thought this whole plan out a little better. Or at least wishing he hadn't underestimated Vivienne's boss.

"Here's your detail organizer, Mr. Dalton," Estelle said as she brought a large three-ring binder into the room. He recognized it as the same type Vivienne brought to all her meetings with Lydia and Zach. The company must buy them in bulk. "Why don't you and Vivienne get started on filling it in with ideas?"

"Actually, I'm starved." Cole leaned back and patted his stomach. It was a bit early for lunch, but trying to outmaneuver a crafty businesswoman had certainly worked up an appetite. Plus, he couldn't take sitting in this office a second longer. "Vivienne, is there someplace nearby where we can grab a bite and go over this stuff?"

"Of course there is," Estelle responded on Vivienne's behalf, making a shooing gesture at them. "Go on now, Viv. Give the client what they want. That's our motto here."

Vivienne's mouth opened as if to object, probably because her boss had just spent the entire meeting trying to convince Cole of things he absolutely did *not* want.

Ever.

In fact, right this second, the only things he wanted were a good meal and the satisfaction from doing a good deed. He was about to get both.

"Susie Starlight?" was the first thing out of Vivienne's mouth when they sat down at Matilda's Diner and Pie Shop. The only reason she'd agreed to join him for lunch was because she'd been eager to get out from under Estelle's watchful eye and remind Cole that what they were doing was a horrible idea. She certainly hadn't intended to bring up his fictitious fiancée.

"That was the name of my first love." Cole didn't bother looking up as he casually read his menu. Not that this was a date or anything, but their newly formed business arrangement didn't lessen the stab of jealousy Vivienne experienced. Or maybe it was irritation that she was out in public with a man who was still pining over another woman.

"Was she a showgirl?"

"No. She was my horse. I hardly think someone who refers to their guinea pig as Lord Nibbles should talk."

"Well, he didn't start out as *mine*," Vivienne said before thanking the server who delivered two iced waters.

"I've gotta hear this," Cole said, raising one dark eyebrow as if he was actually interested in talking about her pet.

Vivienne sighed and sat back against the leather booth. As long as she didn't have to talk about her boss or getting fired from her job, the man could lead the conversation in any direction he wanted. "He was Estelle's. I don't know what she was thinking when she up and bought him a few weeks ago. I was supposed to return him to the pet store, but I kept finding reasons not to."

"Such as…?"

"Such as he's absolutely adorable whenever I feed him and he daintily starts nibbling on his morsels, as though he is at a proper dinner party."

"Okay, so that explains the 'Nibbles' part of the name," Cole replied, then stood up to retrieve a red crayon that had rolled off the table next to them. He handed it to the toddler in the high chair before sliding back into their booth and not missing a beat of their conversation. "But why 'Lord'?"

"Because he's very proper, like a British peer. And he has this black fur with a funny patch of white on his chest that makes him look like he's wearing a waistcoat."

Vivienne pretended to look for the waitress so she wouldn't have to see Cole laughing at her. Clearly she'd been reading too many Regency romance novels lately.

The restaurant was busy, but the server was quick to return to their table. Cole ordered the grilled chicken club and was polite enough not to say anything when Vivienne requested a hot pastrami sandwich, loaded tater tots and a slice of cookies-and-cream pie.

"I eat when I'm stressed," she said by way of explanation.

"Why are you stressed?" he asked. "You got your booking and Estelle got her check. You're off the hook, aren't you?"

"Ha. You don't know Estelle if you think she's ever going to be appeased." Vivienne pulled the brand-new three-ring binder out of her tote bag and set it down on the table between them. "She'll get suspicious if I bring this thing back empty. The real work is about to start."

Chapter Seven

Cole fingered the indexed tabs of the binder, handling it as though it was a live explosive. "Do you seriously fill one of these things up with info on every single wedding?"

"Usually it's just for ideas. And I prefer to keep things organized on my tablet. But Estelle is still wrestling with the age of technology and likes to be able to monitor my work. Plus, you never know when you're going to be out of Wi-Fi reception or lose power." Vivienne didn't point out that she'd had low signals on both when she'd been working on their property in Rust Creek Falls.

"So how much is my pretend wedding going to cost?" He stared at the list on the first page and did a double take when his eyes landed on the suggested budget. "Whoa. Do people seriously pay this much for a party?"

Vivienne gave her shoulder a slight lift. "Some people do."

"Would you?" The question caught her off guard. People always asked her opinion on what *they* should do. But they never asked her what *she* would do. The truth was she didn't know.

"Probably not. But I'm not your normal bride."

"Do you want to be one someday?"

"I'm not going to say that I haven't thought about it. But I've also thought about whether or not to cut my hair short."

"Don't. I like it long."

A shiver raced down her spine, and she kept her hands clamped together in her lap so she wouldn't be tempted to self-consciously tug on her loose ponytail. "I, uh, was just making a comparison on how it's one of those things that crosses your mind, but you don't actively consider it because, deep down, you don't really have any intention of making any changes."

He studied her so intently she wondered if she'd spoken a different language. Then he said, "Usually when a good idea crosses my mind, I make it happen."

"As is evident by you showing up at my office this morning," she murmured. Then she spoke louder, "Do you always rush into things like this?"

"You mean into helping people when they need me? Of course."

One of Zach's comments the first day they'd met

kept coming back to Vivienne. What was it? Something about being a hero?

"So what did your family say about you rushing into this?" Vivienne tapped lightly on the binder. He was temporarily saved from responding by the appearance of their lunch.

The server had plates arranged up her extended arm as she set food down in front of them. Way too much food. Even stressed, Vivienne didn't think she could eat this much.

"Here's the thing," Cole said after blowing on one of his French fries. "I didn't say anything to them yet. Do you think your boss will tell my brother and Lydia what we're up to?"

"We?" She had tried to talk Cole out of this stupid farce, but at this point the ball was already rolling with no way to stop it. Making her just as culpable. She took a sip of her soda before continuing. "Most likely not. Up until now, I've kept Estelle out of the loop with their wedding by scheduling appointments either in Rust Creek Falls or when she's out of the office. Which I would've had you do as well, if you hadn't just shown up out of the blue like that this morning."

"It wasn't out of the blue. I told you I was coming. Are you going to eat all those tater tots?"

Vivienne put the side dish in the middle of the table, right on top of the binder, so he could reach them. "Yeah, but I'd figured you'd change your mind when you realized that it was a stupid idea. I was up half the night thinking of ways to talk you out of it."

"Well, apparently my idea worked, so it wasn't that

stupid. Estelle bought it. Which means you still have a job and my brother still has a wedding planner."

"For now. But if I go back to the office without your ideas on guest counts, indoor venues and favorite cake flavors, she's going to know something's up. I'm telling you, the woman is ruthless."

"Come on." Cole took a long gulp of his iced tea, the smooth muscles of his neck flexing as he swallowed. "I was a Marine. I think I can handle a little old lady in a purple suit."

Famous last words.

Cole hadn't expected Estelle of Estelle's Events to blow up his email inbox with so many links to bridal services. Hell, he didn't even know there were this many bridal services out there. But since they'd gotten along pretty well at lunch and he'd been able to control himself from kissing her, he pulled out Vivienne's business card that evening and sent her a one-word text message: Help.

As soon as he'd pressed the send button, he'd wanted to call it back. Cole wasn't the one usually asking for assistance. He was the one delivering it. But it was well after business hours and he was afraid that if he didn't send something requiring an instant response, he'd spend the rest of the evening wondering if she was avoiding him.

He had to wait only half a minute before she replied: What's wrong?

Cole leaned against the pillows on his bed—which was really his cousin Kayla's old bed—and typed.

I keep getting these emails about laser hair removal and spray-on tans that won't stain my white dress. Am I supposed to respond to Estelle every time she sends me one of these?

Please don't. It will only encourage her.

Then she sent a separate message with just a smiley face.

He chuckled, then tapped his screen. Did she like my answers to the questionnaire?

There'd been an initial interview form Vivienne had gone over with him at lunch. She'd cautioned him about his tongue-in-cheek responses, but he'd made her laugh with a few of them and he was pleased to see that the woman had a great sense of humor.

Suffice it to say she wasn't a fan of the hay bale racing idea or your preference for the groomsmen to wear cow-printed vests.

A second bubble popped up.

She also said she hopes Susie Starlight Roper has more sense than you. I told her not to hold her breath.

A pang of nostalgia shot through Cole at the reminder of his childhood mare. What he'd said earlier today was true. Old Susie had been his first love, but he had no idea why he'd come up with her name when asked about his fake bride. Maybe because all the wedding business and planning for the new ranch had him constantly thinking about their old home in Hardin, as well as his mother and the life he no longer had.

Another alert popped up on the blue envelope app, which he normally never used, since he mostly worked with horses and cows and they never sent him emails. He clicked on the link, only to get the annoying little red alert symbol to disappear. Cole groaned at the subject line and then sent Vivienne another text.

Do you know they have stores where you can go online and pick out which gifts you want people to give you for a wedding present?

They're called wedding registries. But don't worry. You and Susie won't need to start one until right before you send out your invitations.

Ol' Susie would've been happy registering for a new saddle blanket and a bag of carrots.

That means 2 of your guests will be buying a gift. What should the other 498 people related to you bring?

Cole smiled to himself as he reread her joke about his large family. He wanted to write back something clever, but everything he could think of might come across as too flirtatious.

Nothing. I still can't believe people waste their money on this junk.

I know. You should've seen this one client we had today. That sucker paid us money up front to plan a fake wedding for him.

Cole was still laughing when he set his phone down and switched off the pink lamp on the bedside table.

But he wasn't laughing two days later when, after a hot, backbreaking day of digging around railroad ties and laying cement for Vivienne's walkway, he made the mistake of looking at his inbox right before bed. The advertisement about bridal lingerie had him tossing and turning all night, thinking about Vivienne dressed in nothing but a white, lacy bustier…and his desire to get her out of it as fast as possible!

Vivienne was having some fantasies of her own, and they weren't all about resurrecting her career. It didn't help that, in order to keep up pretenses, she'd had to call several times this week to ask Cole things like his preference for a DJ over a band and whether his "fiancée" would be interested in a special promotion the bowling alley in Kalispell was having for bridal showers and bachelorette parties.

Estelle wasn't letting up, despite the fact that Vivienne had a consultation scheduled for the anniversary party of a former client's parents, as well as several leads on more events.

Then, the following Monday, Cole sent her a text jokingly asking where he should go on his honeymoon. She was on the home stretch on the Grant-Dalton wedding while trying to convince her boss that she was still working on more bookings, and all she could think about was Cole walking on a beach on the French Riviera, dripping water off his rippling muscles and—

Whoa. She really should not be going there.

Thankfully, Estelle's late arrival was a welcome distraction from Vivienne's inappropriate thoughts. The older woman hustled through the front door of the office with more agility than an Olympic runner.

"Where are we with the Roper-Dalton wedding?"

Okay, maybe that wasn't quite the distraction Vivienne had been hoping for. "We're right where we need to be on it."

"Have they set a date yet?"

"Last I heard, the groom wanted to focus on his brother's event before starting the planning of his own."

"That's odd, if you ask me." Estelle dropped her purple handbag on the reception desk, where it would probably remain until Vivienne moved it.

"I think it's pretty normal that someone wouldn't want to upstage their sibling on their big day."

Estelle shooed a hand at her. "Not that. I mean, it's odd that we're still only dealing with the groom. What kind of bride doesn't take an active role in the planning of her own wedding?"

"It's still early. I'm sure Su—" Vivienne couldn't bring herself to finish the fake name. "I'm sure the bride will make an appearance soon."

Vivienne realized the odd choice of words when Estelle paused halfway down the hall toward her office. Oh, no. Her boss turned around. "Actually, why don't you call her and ask when she's coming into the office to sign the contract?"

Yeah, she'd been wrong about Estelle not wanting both of their clients' signatures. Why have only one person on the hook for a cancellation fee when she could have two? Vivienne should've never second-guessed the woman's dogged tenacity when it involved the risk of forfeited deposits.

"No problem." What could she do but paste a smile on her face as if there was nothing she'd enjoy more than making a pretend phone call to a pretend bride. Vivienne's veins felt as if they were pumping ice water, and she looked at the thermostat on the wall to see if the air-conditioning had been switched on. She tried to keep her teeth from chattering when she offered a weak excuse. "Except I only have the number for the groom."

"Then call him," Estelle said, pulling out one of the heavy chairs across the conference table and settling her tiny frame in the middle of it, a queen on her throne.

Vivienne opened the binder and flipped to the client information sheet. After all, she didn't need her boss to know she already had Cole's number programmed in her contact list or that they'd been talking to each other all week. When she pulled out her cell phone to dial, Estelle tapped a long, purple fingernail on the black landline, indicating she wanted the call on speaker.

Each drawn-out ring echoed in the conference room and grated on Vivienne's tightly wound nerves. Just when she thought the call was about to go to voice mail, Cole's sexy drawl answered.

"Hi, Cole, this is Vivienne Shuster from Estelle's Events."

"Oh, hey. Why are you calling me from a different—"

"I'm here with Estelle and we have you on speaker."

Cole cleared his throat. "What can I do for you ladies?"

"This is Estelle speaking." Her boss's voice was deeper and raspier, and since she was yelling directly into the desk phone, it was also louder than Vivienne's. She rolled her eyes at the unnecessary introduction, but Estelle continued. "I wanted to know when your fiancée is going to be coming into the office to sign the contract."

There was a long pause on the other end of the line before Cole finally spoke up. "Well, you see, ma'am, my fiancée lives in Billings and she doesn't get much time off from her job."

"What does she do again for work?" Estelle asked, leading him down a path that might prove to be too slippery.

"She's a model."

"In Billings?" Her boss looked doubtful.

"Yep. Definitely in Billings. There's a big demand over there for ads with feed companies and horse shows. You know, that sort of thing." The lies rolled off the man's tongue so easily, Vivienne began to wonder if he'd carefully prepared his answers or if he actually believed everything he was saying.

"Billings, you say?" Or maybe Estelle wasn't all there mentally, because the man had said the city's name twice already. Then Vivienne saw the gleam in her boss's eye and her blood went from cold to frozen when Estelle covered the speaker and whispered, "She might have more model friends. That's a much bigger market for us to get into."

Vivienne wanted to yank the phone cord from the wall. She wanted to scream out a warning to Cole. But there was no stopping Estelle, who removed her hand from the speaker and kept talking.

"What a coincidence. There's a bridal expo going on in Billings and I was going to send Vivienne," the woman said, causing Vivienne's head to jerk up because this was news to her. "Cole, why don't you drive on over there, as well? Viv can take you and Susie to the event. We have lots of contacts out that way and you might even find a venue more suitable for someone in the modeling industry."

Vivienne reached into her go bag for her emergency stash of chocolate.

"I…uh…" Cole started, but he was having a difficult time coming up with a diplomatic way to tell the older woman what he was really thinking.

"That wouldn't be a problem for you, would it?" Estelle's raspy voice taunted.

In for a penny, in for a pound, his mom used to always tell her sons when they committed to something. While Cole doubted that his mother would've approved of his less-than-honest methods, she would've been glad that he was doing this for Zach. "I think I can swing that."

Cole made up an excuse about a cow getting loose from the herd—even though he was currently in his truck in the parking lot at the hardware store in the middle of Rust Creek Falls, where there wasn't a heifer to be found—and quickly disconnected. He needed to get his breathing under control and rethink his moral downfall before the owner of Estelle's Events roped him into any more ridiculous lies.

Less than an hour later, just when he'd thought of a legitimate reason he couldn't go on the trip to Billings, his phone rang again. This time, Vivienne's cell was the number that popped up on his screen. Still, he answered tentatively just in case he was on speaker again.

"Why did Susie Starlight have to be a model living in Billings?" she asked by way of greeting, indicating that nobody else was within listening distance.

"Because I was trying to stick to the truth as much as possible. When I was eleven, my mom had a photographer friend who needed a white horse in Billings to do some photo shoots for a grain company there. I didn't get to go because I couldn't miss school. I missed her like crazy."

"You know that you're not actually planning a wedding with your childhood horse, right?"

"I'm not supposed to be planning a wedding with anyone. But here we are."

Vivienne groaned. "Estelle's already registered me for the expo and ordered new company brochures and business cards for me to pass out while we're there. Thank goodness she finally left for her hair appointment, but not before she warned me that Rich LaRue is also going to be there. God forbid the man gets to one of our potential clients first."

"Who?"

"He owns another event planning company called A LaVish Affair. He's Estelle's biggest competitor and her sworn nemesis. I'm not sure, but I think there might be a court order somewhere directing Estelle not to get within five hundred feet of him, which is why she obviously can't go herself."

"You should look on the bright side, then. At least you'll get a free trip to Billings and a weekend away from your nightmare of a boss."

"Ugh. I don't have an extra weekend like this to waste. Do you have any idea how much I still need to do for Zach and Lydia's wedding? Wait, did you just say *you*?"

"Uh…" Cole had no idea where the woman was going with this rant. "What?"

"You did. You said *you*. As in *I'll* get a free trip to Billings. *I'll* be going alone."

Cole tossed his hat onto the bench seat of the truck so he could scratch his forehead. "I'm confused. Are you not going?"

"Oh, I'm going all right. But you're the one who decided to have a fiancée over there. So if I have to go to Billings, you're coming with me."

Chapter Eight

The sun had yet to rise on Saturday morning when Vivienne gave Lord Nibbles an extra scoop of food and a handful of grapes. "This should hold you over until tomorrow. Be good while I'm gone."

Her one-bedroom apartment had come furnished, and despite her love of fashion and decorating and entertaining, Vivienne had never done much to spruce the place up. When she'd been growing up, one of her parents had moved out so often that personal effects had become a symbol of petty property disputes, such as who got to take the brand-new comforter set and who had to make do with the odd-shaped quilt her great-aunt Shelly had sewn for their wedding gift. Neither her mom nor her dad had wanted either; they just wanted to argue over the items.

The last thing she wanted was for Cole to see her lackluster homemaking skills and get the impression that she wasn't up to the task of beautifying his family's property in time for the wedding. It would be better to simply meet him outside.

She was loading her small carry-on suitcase into the trunk of the Jetta just as Cole's truck pulled into her apartment lot. Billings was almost a seven-hour drive, so there was no point in them taking separate cars. Besides, the man had offered to do most of the driving, which would free Vivienne up to make last-minute phone calls to vendors and to track down a railway handcart, which she'd promised to Garrett.

It also freed her up from having to wonder if Cole would be staring at her, because the man couldn't possibly pay attention to her if he had to keep his eyes on the road. Hopefully.

"What time are we supposed to be there?" he asked, stifling a yawn.

"Not until one. Luckily, Estelle was too late to register for a booth, so we're going to be free to walk around and check out everyone else's exhibits."

"And pass out brochures to get you more customers." Cole took the keys from her hand. "I mean, that's why you're going in the first place, right?"

"Something like that," she replied, before thanking him for holding open the passenger door for her. When he scrunched his six-foot frame into the driver's seat without complaint, she realized that they both needed to make the most of this awkward situation. "I know I'm supposed to be networking and finding more business, but it just doesn't feel very organic to walk up to strangers out of the blue and hand them my business card."

"That makes sense." He started the car and said, "When we get there, give me a stack and I'll help. The sooner we hand them out, the sooner we can get out of that place. I had nightmares the past two nights about some overeager bride mistaking me for her groom and tricking me into exchanging vows with her."

"You know it doesn't work like that, right?" she asked as Cole pulled out of the parking lot. Even though the road was deserted this early in the morning, he used his turn indicator and kept under the speed limit. This guy drove the same way he handled any other responsibility, like it was the most important task he'd ever been assigned.

"How does it work?"

"You have to get an actual marriage license at a county courthouse. You go there in person, show your ID and sign for it. *Then* you get mistaken for a willing groom and tricked into a ceremony. Since it's Saturday and all the county offices are likely closed, you shouldn't be able to get yourself into too much trouble."

"That's a relief."

"But I think it's cute that you're under the impression women you don't know are going to be falling over themselves trying to trick you into marriage."

"I didn't say falling over themselves, but some women find me—"

The ringing of her cell phone interrupted what he was going to say and Vivienne found herself suddenly curious about what some women found. Her bubble of curiosity popped, though, when she saw who was calling her at this hour.

"Hi, Mom. Is everything okay?"

"I'm leaving him," came Bonnie Shuster's reply. "I thought things would be different this time, but your father will never change."

"You always think it will be different," Vivienne said. She covered up the mouthpiece and whispered to Cole, "Excuse me for a minute."

"Do you know where he is right this second?" her mother asked, but the question was clearly rhetorical. Anyone who'd had a front row seat to the dysfunctional relationship of Bonnie and Richard Shuster could easily guess where her father was.

"At his apartment?" Vivienne asked at the same time her mother announced, "At his apartment."

"Probably with one of his honeys," Bonnie added.

As her mom launched into her version of their recent separation, Vivienne gave the required uh-huhs and murmurs of sympathy. After all, she was an expert at providing them to her parents. A tone for call-waiting beeped and she rolled her eyes, knowing exactly who it was without needing to check the screen.

"Mom, I'm on the road and the reception isn't great. Call me when Dad comes home."

"Mark my words, he is *not* coming home this time," she started, but Vivienne clicked over.

"Hi, Dad."

"Did your mother tell you what she did?" her father asked, before delivering his side of the story, which, as usual, involved a horrible argument over a forgotten anniversary—although, in his defense, who could remember which one to celebrate this year—followed by her mother's accusations of imagined infidelities. Again, she gave the required responses as she only partially listened, trying to get the call over with as quickly as possible.

By the time she disconnected, the sun was lighting up the sky. "Sorry about that."

"Should we turn around?" Cole asked.

"Why?"

"I…uh…couldn't help overhearing, but it sounds like your parents are splitting up."

"They're fine. By this time next week, they'll probably be back together," she said. At his questioning look, she continued. "I know it seems odd. But it's just what they do. Every few months they have some sort of major breakup and declare things are over. Twice, they've even filed for divorce. But then they make up and get back together. They've been married three times. To each other. Not counting all the vow renewals in between."

"That sounds…" Cole didn't finish his thought and she couldn't blame him.

"I know. It's crazy. But, on the bright side, it's also how I landed this job. My parents hired Estelle for one of their vow renewals a few years ago. I was fresh out of college and needed to work somewhere and I was already an expert at planning their so-called celebrations of commitment by that time. So it's been a good fit."

"Yeah, but after growing up that way, how can you

still believe in any of it? I would think you'd be pretty jaded by now." His tone echoed her own skepticism.

"Sometimes I am. But then I'll meet a couple like your brother and Lydia, and they're the kind of people who make it all worth it."

"But there have got to be times when you're planning someone's wedding and you just know for sure that it's never going to last. How do you deal with it?"

Vivienne reached for her sunglasses and slid them onto her eyes, carefully slipping back into professional mode. "I tell myself that I'm giving people what they want."

"Which is a bad marriage?"

"Which is a fairy-tale day. That, I can always deliver. What comes after that day is up to them."

Cole pulled into a McDonald's off the highway so they could use the restrooms and pick up some breakfast sandwiches for the rest of the drive. When they got back on the road, Vivienne asked, "What about you?"

"What about me?"

"What are your thoughts on marriage?" Vivienne's question caught him off guard and he accidentally swallowed a bite of hash brown without chewing it. After he recovered from a coughing fit, she clarified, "I meant, since we're going to a bridal expo, it seems only fitting that as your hired wedding planner, I steer you in the right direction while we're there."

Cole's thoughts on weddings were completely different than his thoughts on marriage. His parents had had a great union, so he knew they were possible. With a lot of work. They were also extremely risky when someone allowed himself to love too much. He took a sip of his coffee before purposely giving a vague response. "I think we all know how I feel about weddings."

"Yep." She powered up her iPad on her lap and began tapping. "But don't worry. There will likely be at least a couple other reluctant guys like you at the convention center in Billings who think everyone else there is nuts."

Several hours and a few hundred miles later, as much as Cole thought he was going to hate the bridal expo, he was actually having a lot of fun. Of course, it helped that when they arrived, the people at the welcome desk didn't have Vivienne's registration as a professional planner on file because of the late registration and they'd had to buy regular passes for the event, complete with name-badge stickers that read Bride and Groom.

Vivienne began to protest, but he'd peeled the thing from its backing and planted it on the neckline of her dress, right above the area that he really wished he could touch. Then he yanked his hand back and cleared his head before sticking on his own.

"Just go with it," he'd told her, and they'd spent the first hour pretending to be an actual couple planning their own wedding. At least it had started out as a good-humored game of pretense, but his palm was still tingling from where he'd touched her under the name tag.

When they were standing in front of samples of wedding cake, he asked, "Did you try the red velvet yet?"

"We've already eaten one from every tray," she whispered back to him. "If you take any more, the baker is going to ask us for a security deposit."

To get her to stop worrying, he took a small square of

cream-cheese-frosted cake and shoved it in her mouth. But instead of the playful act he'd intended it to be, her tongue darted out and touched his fingers and Vivienne closed her eyes, releasing a soft moan.

His pulse spiked to life and a sudden need hummed through him. Swing music blasted from a DJ's speakers nearby, filtering through his thoughts and reminding him that this was not the time or the place to be getting aroused.

"Oh, look," he said, making her lashes flutter open. He stepped behind her and placed his hands on either side of her waist, steering her toward a booth across the way. "They have one of those wheels we can spin to get a prize."

The posters hanging from the freestanding dividers behind the wheel advertised a luxury spa near Bozeman.

"Those things aren't real prizes, you know," she said. "They're just gimmicks to get you over to their resort so that you'll book your reception there."

"You're such a cynic. Just give it a whirl."

Vivienne gave him a doubting look as she took a turn spinning the wheel. But when she won a box of fancy chocolate truffles, she jumped up and down as though she'd just won a free supply of steaks for a year. Her enthusiasm was infectious and he found himself wrapping his arms around her waist when she bounced a little too close to him.

She responded by throwing her own arms around his neck and planting a kiss on his cheek before saying, "I've never won anything before!"

He was quick to release her, but the damage was already done. His skin was on fire and it felt as if her lips had left a brand above his jawline. Vivienne, thankfully, didn't notice because she was clapping her hands as they showed her the two-pound box of chocolate. Cole was still rubbing the affected spot on the side of his face when she grabbed his arm and pushed him toward the wheel. "Now you try."

"Honey," he said loud enough for the representative to hear. "I'm sure they only give out one prize per couple."

His use of the endearment had the desired effect, even if he kicked himself for causing her smile to slip. But the man behind the wheel waved him off and said, "Go ahead, give it a spin."

Not wanting to disappoint his so-called bride, Cole channeled all of his building attraction and tension and spun the wheel so hard it almost flew off the stand. Watching the bright colors go round in such a fast circle made him dizzy and he had to look away, but not before Vivienne grabbed onto his hand and squeezed it in excitement. He didn't look back until the clicking sound slowed, and even then all he could think about were their clasped fingers. Vivienne bounced in triumph again but stilled as soon as the representative asked, "Now, when would you two like to book your free couples massages?"

A free *what*?

The air thickened and his boots felt as if they were squeezing his feet into action. Cole had never had a professional massage, but judging by the photo on the glossy brochure, it involved candles, rose petals and getting naked under a sheet.

Vivienne's cheeks were stained crimson, and when Cole took the clipboard to fill out his contact information, he noticed the blush had spread down her neck and below the V-neck of her dress. His fingers shook slightly as he wrote down his name and number, but luckily Vivienne didn't see because she was too busy walking toward the next booth, her box of chocolates tucked under her arm.

Cole handed the clipboard back to the spa employee, who promised to be in contact. Crap. Why hadn't he given them a bogus email address? The last thing he needed was to be reminded of the awkward fantasy of getting Vivienne on a massage table.

Unfortunately, the next vendor booth was for a travel company, and as Cole approached his "bride," an eager middle-aged woman was midpitch about all the fabulous honeymoon destinations they offered. The agent turned toward him and gestured toward Vivienne. "If you could spend the most romantic week of your life with this lovely lady, where would it be?"

His throat muscles flexed and he had to remind himself how to gulp in more oxygen. At this exact second, the answer to that question was the nearest motel room. But Cole was saved from stuttering out an answer when he spotted a man down the aisle using a wobbly ladder to secure a fallen banner.

"I'll be right back," he said before rushing off. When he got to the man, the first thing Cole did was hold the ladder steady. "Can I give you a hand?"

"Thank you, young man." The gentleman's shiny bald head was a shade of dark mahogany and the silver of his thin mustache suggested his advanced years. He was dressed impeccably in a gray, pin-striped suit with a bright pink handkerchief square poking out his breast pocket. Instead of descending the ladder, though, he finished yanking a zip tie through one of the grommets.

Cole would've preferred the elderly man come down and let him climb the rickety ladder instead. But he didn't want to insult the man's pride. When the hot-pink sign, which matched the man's handkerchief, was finally in place, it read A LaVish Affair and Cole racked his brain for where he'd heard of that name before.

Stepping to the side as the man came down the last few rungs, Cole was surprised to see Vivienne nearby.

"If it isn't Vivienne Shuster." The dapper gentleman beamed a bright white smile before looking over each shoulder. "I don't feel any fire breathing down my neck, so I'm assuming that dragon of a boss of yours isn't with you."

Vivienne wagged a finger before stepping forward and giving the man a kiss on his cheek. She turned to Cole. "May I introduce the famous Rich LaRue of A LaVish Affair."

Cole extended his hand to Rich. He'd known he'd heard the name somewhere. Vivienne was certainly chummy with the guy who was supposedly her company's biggest competitor. "Nice to meet you."

Rich returned the handshake, his rich brown eyes darting between Vivienne's and Cole's name tags. "Looks like congratulations are in order."

"No, no, no!" Vivienne's hand slapped against her chest, covering up her sticker. "You know me, Rich. Always the wedding planner, never the bride."

The man's silver eyebrows lifted.

"Estelle wanted me to attend, but it was a last-minute thing and she was too late to get vendor status, so my *friend* Cole volunteered to come with me and the people at the door just assumed we were a couple and, well..." While Vivienne's explanation trailed off, Rich's forehead remained creased. And a knot formed in Cole's stomach at her emphasis of the word *friend*.

"The only part of that story that makes any sense is Estelle doing something last minute. Darling," Rich called over to an older woman in a frothy pink dress, also color coordinated with their booth. "Vivienne Shuster is here, and I'm pretty sure she's working as an undercover bride to get a different view of the industry. Brilliant strategy. Just brilliant."

"Hi, Glory," Vivienne smiled and waved at the lady who must be Rich's wife. "I'm not really undercover."

Rich leaned in toward Cole. "I've been telling her for years that she's wasting her talents working for Estelle."

Cole had only seen her in action with one wedding—not counting his own—and had already deduced that for himself.

Vivienne chuckled and patted Rich's hand. "You flatter me when you have potential clients you should be flattering instead."

"Time to get back to work." Rich straightened his lapels, then winked at Vivienne before stage-whispering, "And, don't worry. I won't blow your cover."

As they walked away, Cole tried to stick by Vivienne's side as she navigated them through a herd of ladies decked out in bridal gowns. A veil whipped at his face, catching him in the eye, and he lost sight of her for a second. But then her warm, strong hand clamped onto his and he held on for dear life as she pulled him to safety.

"Don't worry," she said as they moved into a booth occupied by an empty dentist chair and a sign advertising that Dr. Smile was the leading orthodontist in Billings. Vivienne squeezed his arm. "Your nightmare isn't coming true. You're not in danger of being forced to marry one of them."

Cole grinned at the reference, and not just because he wanted Dr. Smile to see that he didn't need braces before his upcoming wedding. This morning, when he'd told her about that, he'd said the word *nightmare*, but it really had been just a dream. It had even been a pleasant one where he was standing at the altar, excited to see an unknown bride walking down the aisle toward him. He'd startled awake before he'd figured out her identity, and the uncertainty of what the dream might mean had prevented him from going back to sleep. He nodded toward the mass of women moving toward the rear of the convention center like a cluster of fluffy white clouds. "Why are they in costume?"

"Because the fashion show is getting ready to start."

He couldn't stop from cringing. "Please tell me we can skip that part of the expo."

"Why? They're also going to be showing tons of bridesmaid dresses and all the latest flower-girl accessories."

Cole forced a chuckle, hoping she would join in. When she didn't, he said, "You know, you do a really good job of keeping a straight face when you're teasing."

"Who says I'm teasing?"

Chapter Nine

Most of the vendors were taking down their booths by the time Vivienne passed out only her fifth business card of the day. And it was to a florist out of Whitefish, not even a potential client. But the expo hadn't been a total waste. She'd gotten plenty of ideas and had actually enjoyed getting to play the bride for a change. A cosmetician providing complimentary makeup consultations even applied a set of fake lashes when Vivienne had a beauty makeover.

"I'm starving," Cole said as he hoisted a free canvas tote higher on his shoulder. They had been plied with swag bags and giveaway items every time they'd turned around. "Let's go grab some dinner."

"I don't see how you can be so hungry. I'm pretty sure you hit every catering booth in this place, filling up on samples," Vivienne teased, trying not to bat her long false eyelashes at him.

"C'mon. That wasn't real food. Just little bites here and there. I haven't had anything substantial since breakfast."

As they exited the convention center, Vivienne was relieved to see the sun was barely starting to set. She hadn't intended to stay so long, yet they'd practically closed the place down. Now that the pretense of being a carefree bride was fading away, her appetite was returning. Or, at least, the stress of spending more alone time with Cole was returning.

What she should do was check into the hotel, take a long shower, order some room service and open up the complimentary bottle of wine she'd gotten from a local vineyard that doubled as a wedding venue. Instead, she let Cole and the scent of herbs and sizzling meat guide her to the steakhouse across the street.

Neon lights curved around the arched entrance, and, when Cole opened the door for her, Vivienne didn't know if she was going into a restaurant or a honky-tonk. It soon became obvious that not only was it an eating establishment, it was one in high demand. When the hostess told them that there was a thirty-minute wait for a party of two, Vivienne shrugged and expected Cole to suggest a burger place down the road. He surprised her by saying, "Let's go grab a drink in the bar."

A flush of panic raced through her and she wondered what Cole meant by grabbing a drink. Having dinner with a client, even a pretend one, might arguably count as a business meeting and she could convince herself that she was still well within the bounds of professional behavior. However, sitting in a bar with a single man on a Saturday night had to cross some sort of ethical line.

Before she could think of which line that was, a server passed by with a tray weighted down by plates of prime rib au jus, mashed potatoes and creamed corn. Vivienne's mouth watered and her nose twitched as she followed the food into the depths of the restaurant. Cole caught up to her, and she felt his hand on her lower back steering her toward the lounge instead of the dining area.

The bar was equally crowded, but a high table opened up when another couple stood, hoisting a blinking pager overhead like they'd just won a trophy. Vivienne's stomach growled as she took a seat and Cole handed her a cocktail menu.

"Do you want to split an appetizer?" he asked, right as a woman wearing a motorcycle club vest and a tiara studded with plastic jewels spelling out Fifty and Nifty stood up to take a picture with the rest of the female bikers at the table nearby.

Unfortunately, the woman stumbled and got herself tangled up in a nest of birthday balloons tied to her chair. There was a loud pop, followed by a clinking sound before something thudded, and glass shattered on the ground. Several of the woman's friends—who wore similar leather vests and matching black T-shirts emblazoned with Judy's 50th Birthday Ride—shrieked, and Cole jumped off his high-backed stool and sprang into action. Within seconds, he had Judy untangled and was already kneeling down, picking up shards of a martini glass before the restaurant staff could respond.

A waiter used a damp washcloth to wipe up the spilled drink and Cole went to the bar, returning with a fresh neon-blue cocktail for the embarrassed birthday woman. He even offered to take a picture of the group using her phone.

The women gathered back into position for the photo and Cole counted to three.

"Here." One of Judy's friends handed a camera to the waiter. "Will you get one of us with the sexy cowboy?"

It was hard to tell with the dim interior lighting, but Cole's cheeks had turned a shade pinker. Still, what did the guy expect when he went around town in a cowboy hat and scuffed boots, dressed like a rodeo hunk? Vivienne bit back her laughter when the oldest member of the group patted Cole's rear end as he walked away.

When he returned to their table, Vivienne was still smiling. "Now I know why your family calls you Sergeant Save-the-Day."

Cole's blush actually deepened and he cleared his throat. "Well, then maybe you can explain it, because I have no idea why they do that."

"Really? No idea?" Vivienne made a *pfshh* sound. At Cole's blank look, she continued. "Let's see. Since we only have thirty minutes to kill, I'll limit my examples to today's rescues alone. First there was the mother fussing with her stroller in the registration line. You got the baby blanket unstuck from the wheel for her. Then there were the two girls who were fighting over the flower-girl wands at that florist's booth.

That took some smooth talking, but you bought them both their own crowns. And what about the older guy using a cane and tiring out quickly? You got him one of those motorized scooters available at the entrance and came riding to his rescue, like a cowboy on his trusty, battery-powered steed."

"They needed help."

"Have you ever noticed that you're always in the right place at the right time?"

A frown marred Cole's face for the briefest of moments, but then the harried server who'd just finished cleaning up the mess at the nearby table approached with two electric-blue cocktails in martini glasses. The waiter tilted his head toward the female biker group. "The ladies bought your first round."

Cole's lips turned down and his nose wrinkled at the fruity drinks. But he was too polite to send them back. Instead, he placed both in front of Vivienne and asked the server, "What kind of craft beer do you have on tap?"

After hearing several choices, Cole selected the pale ale. The waiter was in full retreat when Cole said, "Crap, we forgot to order the appetizer."

He handed her the bar menu and asked again if she wanted to split something. "Don't change the subject." She wagged a finger at him. "You were about to tell me why you're always the first one to respond to a crisis."

He groaned, or at least it sounded like a groan. It was becoming more crowded in there and Vivienne had to lean in closer to hear him.

"What was that?"

He scooted his chair up to hers. "I said I was just doing what anyone else would have done."

"No, you weren't. Don't try to be modest." Vivienne took a sip of the blue drink and winced at its sweetness. "You earned that nickname fair and square. And I want to know how."

Another blush spotted his cheeks, right under the shadow of his beard, and since his beer hadn't arrived, he helped himself to the other cocktail. He shuddered, then flicked his tongue out to capture the sugary crystals the rim of his glass had left on his upper lip. Vivienne's own mouth went dry and she took another gulp. But she wasn't going to let her attraction to him distract her. "I'm waiting."

"Fine," he finally relented. "It started the summer I was eight years old. It was a hot one and our parents took us camping at Flathead Lake. When we got there, my dad was busy showing The Bigs how to set up their tents."

"Wait," Vivienne interrupted. "Who are The Bigs?"

"Booker and Garrett. They're the oldest. Anyway, my mom was trying to unload the truck but kept having to chase after The Smalls—that's Zach and Shawn."

"So your family had The Bigs and The Smalls. Which group did you fall into?"

"Neither. I was in the middle, the overlooked kid who didn't really fit into either category. So I was given the boring task of lining rocks around the fire pit, which really was just a stupid chore my parents made up to keep me out of the way. But it also meant that I was the only one paying attention when ten-year-old Garrett was lured away from the campsite by the promise of the cool lake water."

The waiter returned just then with Cole's beer, along with an ice bucket containing a bottle of champagne. Again the server nodded toward the women at the birthday party table, which was getting a bit louder and had been increased with the arrival of four older gentlemen who Vivienne could've sworn had been seated at the bar when they'd arrived. "The ladies also wanted to wish you congratulations."

Cole's brows slammed together and Vivienne would've laughed at his response if she hadn't been equally confused.

"Hey, you two," Judy, in her birthday tiara, yelled across the room. "Good luck on your marriage. Hope it lasts longer than mine did."

The rest of the women cheered and cackled as Vivienne looked down at Cole's chest. Whoops. They were still wearing their Bride and Groom name tags. She managed a guilty smile as she used one hand to give a polite wave and the other hand to discreetly peel the sticker off her dress.

Cole unclenched his jaw long enough to down the rest of the martini. "Whoa, that was sweet," he said before taking a gulp of beer, probably to wash away the sugary taste.

The waiter had already removed the champagne cork, so it wasn't like they could send the bottle back. He brought over two flutes, and Vivienne quickly swallowed the rest of her cocktail so the server could clear the empty glasses and their table didn't resemble a fraternity house the morning after a homecoming party.

"So Garrett wandered off to the lake?"

Cole nodded. "He did. And I followed him, even though we'd all been told repeatedly to stay away from the water. But before I could make it down the embankment, he already had his shoes off and was wading in. I told him he was going to be in big trouble. But did he listen to me? Nope. When it comes to Garrett, everything's got to be faster and more dangerous." Cole finished off his beer. "Jeez, what was in that first drink? Pineapple? I can still taste it."

Vivienne filled both the champagne flutes, just in case he needed something else to drink. The waiter and bartender were being overrun with customers and there was no way they'd get some iced water before they sat down to eat. "So what happened to Garrett?"

"The knucklehead accidentally stepped on a rusted-out fishing hook and sliced open the bottom of his foot."

"Oh, no," Vivienne gasped. She looked at Cole's forearm and wondered how her hand had gotten there. However, her muscles felt too relaxed to pull it away.

"Oh, yes. So he's crying like a baby while I'm shoving his foot into the water trying to clean the wound. I found his discarded sock and tied it around the gash to stop the bleeding, then I carried him almost a quarter of a mile back to camp."

"You carried him? But wasn't he bigger than you?"

"By ten pounds, at least. Afterward, my parents were telling me how proud they were of me—before they yelled at both of us for wandering off. The campground host said I was the bravest boy who'd ever stayed there and the doctor at the urgent-care office praised my quick thinking, right before he gave Garrett a tetanus shot. Suddenly I went from being the forgotten middle child to the kid who saved the day."

"Hence the nickname?" she asked.

"Well, technically it started out as Ranger Rescue, but when I enrolled in ROTC in high school, it got switched to the military-themed version."

The pager lit up and vibrated against her champagne glass. Thank goodness their table was finally ready, because Vivienne's head was feeling lighter and she was having a difficult time backing away from Cole. She needed to get some food in her to soak up the alcohol she'd drunk too quickly. Or else she was bound to do something reckless.

Cole followed behind, his hand again at the small of Vivienne's back as he guided her to the hostess stand. Maybe it was the warming effects of the booze in his bloodstream, but the fabric of her wraparound dress was so thin her heated skin underneath left an imprint on his palm long after they were handed their heavy leather-bound menus.

"I see we already have drinks taken care of," a waitress said before setting down the ice bucket Cole had purposely left behind in the bar area. Usually he wasn't a big drinker, and he definitely didn't mix his alcohol. But since when had any part of this day been normal?

The young woman introduced herself as Heather and rattled off several specials. He'd seen the way Vivienne had been staring at the prime rib earlier and was willing to place a wager on what she'd order. Of course, he'd also seen the way she'd been staring at him, and he wondered how he'd make it through dinner if she leaned in and touched his arm again.

He was already exhausted from the long drive here, plus all the bridal expo nonsense, which was like nothing he'd ever experienced. Overstimulation had the potential to wreak havoc on his common sense when he was sober, so it was no surprise that the liquor was now doing the thinking for him, telling him that the soft knit dress hugging Vivienne's curves couldn't possibly be as smooth as—

"Let's start off with the sampler platter," Vivienne told Heather, snapping him back to reality. "I'd also like the wedge salad with blue cheese dressing and extra bacon bits. And the French onion soup. Oh, and if we could get some bread while we look over the rest of the menu, that'd be great."

"I thought you said we couldn't possibly be hungry after all those samples today," Cole reminded her when the server walked away.

"I know. But now I'm starving. What do you think is better here? The porterhouse or the prime rib?"

He recalled her joke about eating whenever she was stressed and he wondered if that was the case now. But they'd had fun for the most part and she'd been in her element, surrounded by brides and bouquets and beauty products. What could she possibly be stressed about?

Four courses and a bottle of champagne later, Vivienne ordered a slice of chocolate lava cake to go and

Cole slipped his credit card to the waitress. There was a brief argument about who should pay, since it was a business dinner. Yet Cole insisted. "Remember the company motto? I'm the customer, which means I'm always right."

"You're a client, not a customer," Vivienne replied.

"Do you normally polish off a bottle of champagne with your clients?"

"Oh, my gosh, I can't believe we finished the whole thing." She let out a little giggle, then covered her mouth and attempted a serious expression. "But the answer to that is no, I don't."

"I figured as much." Cole stood up and pulled her chair out. He tried not to stare at her rear end as he followed her toward the exit. But he couldn't keep his eyes off her tonight. Hell, who was he kidding? He hadn't been able to keep his eyes off Vivienne Shuster since the day he met her. Walking behind her, watching her hips sway and not being able to put his hands on either side of them and pull her to him was excruciating.

When they finally got outside, she said, "I'm so full you're going to have to roll me over to the hotel."

Cole stopped in the middle of the sidewalk. He'd been overheated in the restaurant and hadn't expected such a temperature drop in the cool evening air. Or perhaps he was frozen at the suggestion of a hotel, which implied they'd be staying here overnight. Together. "What hotel?"

"The one by the convention center."

His heart thumped frantically behind his rib cage. "You...uh...want to get a room?"

"I already have one. Or a reservation at least. I still have to check in, though. As do you."

A pang of disappointment slowed his racing pulse. So she hadn't meant that they'd be sharing a room. Or a bed. But he was still foggy on the part about having a reservation. "I didn't realize we were staying here tonight. But I guess neither one of us is in any shape to drive the seven hours home."

While they weren't falling-down drunk, either, Cole was usually much more prudent about driving after even one beer, let alone two, plus a blue fruity cocktail and half a bottle of champagne. But being with Vivienne made him do things he never would've imagined doing if he had his wits about him. Like attending a bridal expo or pretending to be engaged to get free samples.

He had begun to walk with Vivienne toward the crosswalk when she suddenly stopped at the red light and grabbed his arm. "Wait. If you weren't planning to stay the night, does that mean you didn't book a room?"

"Was I supposed to?"

Her response was to stare at him, her false lashes making her eyes appear wider and more startled.

His response was to tuck in his chin and draw in a long breath. "I'm guessing you didn't make two reservations?"

"Actually, I didn't make any. Estelle did. She was really determined to get me to Billings and get that contract signed." Vivienne tapped her chin. "But she only emailed me one hotel confirmation. I had assumed she'd emailed yours directly to you."

"Nope. But she'd emailed me every other offer or service I have no use for."

"Maybe she thought you'd be staying with Susie Starlight. But don't worry." Vivienne looked like a woman on a mission as she dashed across the street when the light changed, calling over her shoulder, "I'm sure they'll have extra rooms."

Stepping off the curb to follow her, he had to wait for a group of Harleys making a right turn before catching up to her determined stride right as she crossed into the lobby's entrance. Cole liked being the one to take charge, the one to fix things. But before he could open his mouth to address the clerk behind the registration desk, Vivienne was already speaking.

"Hi, there—" her eyes flickered down to the employee's name tag "—Dave. We have one reservation, but my friend here is also going to need a room."

Friend? That was the second time today she'd called him that and Cole didn't like it any better than the first.

Dave made a whistling sound through his teeth. "We're pretty booked, but I'll see what I can do."

After a few seconds of tapping at his keyboard, Dave shook his head. "Sorry. Even our sister property a few blocks down is sold out. Apparently, there's some sort of wedding convention in town and the Babes on Bikes Rally starts tomorrow, so most of the hotels in the area are at full capacity."

"What do you want to do?" Vivienne, always diplomatic when solving problems, asked Cole. "We might be able to find a single vacancy at a different hotel, but there's not much chance we can get two rooms at the same place."

"It's fine." Cole shrugged to reassure her. "I can sleep in the car."

"Don't be ridiculous," Vivienne replied. "I'm the wedding planner. I should've planned better. If anyone should stay in the car, it should be me."

Before Cole could argue that there was no way he was about to allow her to spend the night crammed into her back seat out in the parking lot, Dave cleared his throat. "If I may point out, the room does have two beds."

"See? You can sleep in the extra bed in my room."

"Are you sure?" Cole whispered to her after Dave passed them each a key card. They'd been doing a great job playing make-believe with each other all day. It shouldn't be a problem for him to keep pretending that he wasn't dying to see her in those Just Married panties she'd gotten in her bride's goody bag.

"Oh, no, we forgot all the swag and totes at the restaurant," she said, making Cole wonder if she could read his mind.

"I'll go get them," he replied, his boot heels already clicking along the marble floor of the lobby as he tore out of the hotel. He needed time to come up with a strategy on how he wasn't going to let his attraction for her make things more awkward. But it took less than thirty seconds to get across the street and the forgotten bags were already waiting for him at the hostess stand.

Not ready to face Vivienne yet, he stopped off at the sundries shop near the hotel elevators. He was going to need a toothbrush and a cold shower if he had any chance of falling asleep so close to her tonight.

But stopping to pick up overnight essentials turned out to be a pointless delay because when he finally knocked on the hotel room door, there was no answer.

Chapter Ten

Vivienne's speeding thoughts shot into overdrive as she'd ridden in the elevator alone, her pulse hammering with every step she took as she made her way down the empty, carpeted corridor to her room.

Their room.

Steeling herself, she took a deep breath and slid in her key card. As she dragged her suitcase on wheels behind her, the handle caught on the interior doorknob, knocking the do-not-disturb sign to the floor. She quickly scooped it up, a mortified giggle bubbling inside her throat at the thought of how unnecessary that placard would be tonight.

Light spilled out from under the crack of the closed bathroom door and Vivienne tried not to think about what the sound of running water meant. Staring at the two queen-size beds, she scolded herself for overthinking the situation.

The bags containing all their freebies from the day were lined up on the fluffy white coverlet of the first bed, so Vivienne lifted her suitcase and set it on the second one. Looking at the television, she decided that having on a sports or a news channel, even if it was only background noise, would make things feel less intimate. She grabbed the remote control and hit the power button but only got as far as the hotel's main channel displaying a welcome screen and classical music.

When she heard the bathroom door click open, she stood motionless.

"Hey, you're back," Cole said, relief evident in his tone. "I figured if you weren't here when I got out of the shower, I'd have to launch a search party."

"I went to the parking garage to get my suitcase." Her fingers trembled as she fought to stare at the remote control so that she wouldn't look at him. But the smell of lemon soap drifted closer and Cole's nearby voice forced her to raise her eyes.

"Is the TV not working?"

Vivienne's gaze slammed into him and she couldn't blink. He was wearing the same jeans he'd had on today—minus the belt—and not much else. His hair was scarcely towel dried and his bare torso was still damp from his shower.

Desire coiled in her belly and she would've opened another bottle of champagne if she thought it would alleviate her sudden thirst. Vivienne licked her lips, knowing that imbibing in too much sparkling wine was what had gotten her into this situation in the first place. Instructing herself to look anywhere but at the muscular ridges of his chest, she glanced down.

"You have nice feet."

He wiggled his toes in the plush carpet. "What?"

"Your feet. They're nice. I've never noticed them before because I've only seen you in boots."

Several seconds passed before she felt Cole's finger on her chin, lifting her head up to look into his face. "You're going to give me a complex about them if you keep staring."

"Sorry." She straightened her shoulders despite the quivering sensation making its way down her spine, but she didn't pull her head away. Vivienne searched the smoothness of his forehead, the lack of lines implying that he wasn't as confused about their situation as she was. She took in the nearly straight angle of his nose, the tiny bump on the bridge implying he wasn't afraid to fight for what he wanted. She scanned the fullness of his soft lips, the slight parting implying that he was breathing just a little heavier than normal. She landed back on the fringed black lashes of his blue eyes, his dilated pupils implying that he was just as aroused as she was.

His finger grazed along her chin until his palm was cupping her jaw. It could've been the champagne she'd had earlier, or maybe it was the realization that she had the same effect on him that he had on her, but her courage spiked and she suddenly felt the need to make something clear.

"I've never shared a room with a client before."

"Funny thing, I haven't really felt like your client all day." His words were whispery soft, his minty breath a soft caress on her face.

"So then if you aren't my client, I wouldn't be crossing any professional boundaries if I did this."

Even with him in his bare feet, Vivienne still had to rise up onto her tiptoes to kiss him.

The second Vivienne's lips touched Cole's, he exploded. One arm shot around her waist and the other hand dug into the loose hair at the back of her scalp, pulling her in closer. Her body pressed against him, fitting him perfectly. Her mouth slanted over his and he took the invitation to invade. Using his tongue, he sampled and tasted her welcoming warmth.

This was more than kissing. More than weeks of pent-up sexual attraction. More than pretending to be a groom who needed to hire her to plan a fictional wedding. This was real and it was powerful and it was raw.

Vivienne's palms flattened against his chest before sliding up to his shoulders and then down his biceps, as if she was frantically searching for something she'd been missing. Something they'd both been missing. Cole had never felt such an overpowering need for a woman, and the sudden realization of his own defenselessness scared him enough to make him take a step back. Her eyes were slightly dazed, clouded with passion, and her lips were swollen.

Cole was supposed to be the one who always kept a level head. Who always did the right thing. Who always made the safe choices. But if they went any further, he couldn't promise that he wouldn't lose all rational thought and spin completely out of control. Seeing his chest rising and falling under her fingertips, he waited until he could drag in a few ragged breaths before he spoke. "Are you sure?"

Her response was to step back and untie the sash above her hip. Cole had been fantasizing about the feel of the silky, soft fabric of her dresses for the past few weeks and he was almost disappointed that Vivienne was taking it off before he'd had the chance to unwrap it himself.

Almost.

It was like a curtain parting to reveal the hidden view all at once. Watching the entire side of her dress spread open filled him with a raging heat, and all he could do was stand there and let the flames engulf him as she exposed the pink lace of her matching panties and bra. As the material slipped off her shoulders, Cole groaned and reached for her.

Vivienne's mouth matched his, responding with an equal fervor as he walked her back toward the bed. His hands went to her rib cage, sliding behind her until he felt delicate lace underneath his fingers as he unhooked her bra. She moaned as he peeled the fabric forward, cupping her warm, full breasts as they spilled out.

Vivienne's head fell back, allowing him access to her slender neck as he rained kisses down to her collarbone. But the part he wanted to kiss the most was just out of reach. Cole placed his hands on either side of her waist and she squeaked as he lifted her up, standing her on the edge of the bed.

He took a dusky-pink nipple into his mouth and Vivienne's nails dug into his shoulders as she held on to him. He lavished equal attention on the other breast, and when he moved toward the flat plane of her stomach, she gasped.

"Cole," she said, her voice low, coming from the back of her throat, "I still have my shoes on."

He smiled up at her, feeling like the hero he'd always wanted to be when he slid his hand down her thigh, over her knee and lifted her calf. Unstrapping the high-heeled sandals wasn't as easy as he'd anticipated, especially since he got distracted by the sight of the freckle on her upper leg. That was what he'd been waiting for. His tongue flicked out to touch it just as her ankle strap fell from his hands.

Vivienne sighed before hooking her knee around his rib cage and pulling him with her as she lowered them onto the bed. She slipped her hands into his denim waistband, pausing briefly as she fumbled over the button of his fly. It took superhuman strength to push himself off her and rise to his shaky feet.

"I'll be right back," he said as he strode to the bathroom, tugging off his jeans as he returned to the bed. She was lounging against the pillows, her skin looking smoother than the sheets underneath, her panties long gone.

"You came prepared?" She nodded toward the box in his hand.

"I had to buy a toothbrush downstairs and, at the last minute, thought it would be a good idea to have these. Just in case."

"Always thinking about safety and protection," she said before smiling at him. Not wanting to hear any jokes about his nickname, he came down beside her, their bodies eagerly resuming where they'd left off.

Vivienne knew exactly where to touch Cole and how to angle her body to bring him in closer. As their kisses grew more intense, she opened her thighs and his hips settled against her as she rocked up to meet him. She was so warm, so slick with desire, it would have been easy to slide his length inside of her. But he pulled back at the last second to reach for a foil packet on the bedside table.

Cole's fingers quivered as he tore open the package, but instead of taking it from him, her palms covered the backs of his hands as they rolled the condom into place. Together.

When he positioned himself at her entrance again, Vivienne looked up at his face, her eyes wide and trusting, her lips open and delicious. She gave him a nod and that was all it took.

He moved inside of her slowly, carefully balancing his weight on his forearms as he eased them together. But Vivienne's arms locked around his shoulders, her breasts pressing against his chest, and he could no longer hold himself back.

Their speed intensified, their moans matching in frequency until Vivienne shuddered around him and called out his name. A groan tore from his throat as he found his own release.

Vivienne could honestly say that she'd never intended to make love with Cole, but she couldn't say that she hadn't thought about it. It was one thing to have fantasies; it was quite another to be courageous—or reckless—enough to act upon them. Fortunately, her fantasy had exceeded her expectations.

She watched him as he lay on the bed beside her, one arm thrown over his forehead, the other cushioning her neck as he intertwined his fingers with hers. The lights were still on, as was the television with the hotel channel flashing pictures on the screen, and Vivienne chewed on her swollen lip, wondering what people normally did in situations like these.

This was her first one-night stand. Or was it something else? Did Cole intend for there to be more nights than just this one? He'd made his thoughts about marriage abundantly clear when he'd hired her, but did that mean he wasn't a believer in any sort of committed relationship? And was now really the best time to ask him about it?

"I'm going to go take a shower," Vivienne whispered, carefully sitting up so she wouldn't dislodge the tan, sinewy arm covering his eyes. The effects of the champagne were wearing off and the insecurity was setting in. If her dress—or even a towel—had been nearby, she would've dived for it. But she had no idea when she'd last seen either of those things. Cole was sprawled on top of the covers, preventing her from yanking off a sheet and wrapping it around her body. And it would look pretty silly for her to use a pillow to shield her nudity after he'd already seen everything.

Calculating the distance from the bed to the bathroom, she considered making a run for it. But Cole's fingers trailing down her vertebrae to her tailbone made her pause.

"I'll join you," he said, his voice weak. "As soon as the tingling in my body dies down."

She'd made him tingle? Her tummy fluttered and a grin spread across her face, and she suddenly became a lot less self-conscious.

Twelve hours later, though, her confidence slipped again.

On the return trip, while the ride had started out playfully teasing and reliving their thoughts and experiences of the day before, the farther they got from Billings, the quieter the interior of the Jetta became. Vivienne didn't want to read too much into the growing silence, but it was difficult not to. Cole had done all of the driving up until this point and neither one of them had gotten much sleep last night, so maybe that was why there was less talking.

"Why don't we switch and I can drive for a while?" she offered.

"I'm okay," he said, then lost all credibility by covering his mouth for a deep yawn.

"Cole, I phrased it as a question, but it was more of a strong suggestion." When he hesitated in replying, Vivienne continued. "It's okay to let someone take care of *you* once in a while."

He wiggled his eyebrows at her. "I believe those were the same words you used this morning when you were waking me up by using your mouth to—"

"Oh, look." She pointed to the upcoming off-ramp, keeping her face averted so he couldn't see the flush of heat spreading across her cheeks. "A gas station. Let's stop and get some snacks at the convenience store."

Cole chuckled before flicking on the turn signal and pulling off the highway. While he filled the tank, she went inside to use the facilities and splash some cold water on her face. Looking in the mirror, she gave herself a silent pep talk.

Don't get all embarrassed and awkward now. If he's comfortable enough to tease about your lovemaking sessions, he's clearly not letting things get weird. Just keep things light and pleasant.

However, keeping her growing nerves at bay was easier said than done. On her way to the cashier, she grabbed some Pringles, then a couple of candy bars. The cheddar-flavored popcorn looked good as well, so she pulled a bag off the shelf. Vivienne scanned the wall of refrigerated cases. It wouldn't be a bad idea to have something to drink, either. Balancing all the snacks in one arm, she pulled open the glass door and reached inside for a Dr Pepper, then chose a bottle of sweet tea for Cole. Maybe the caffeinated beverages would perk them both up.

Thinking about caffeine reminded her of the French toast he'd ordered off the room-service menu this morning and his comment about how he would've been happy to make do with a donut and a coffee. She added a package of powdered donuts to her stack, then went back for the chocolate ones just in case.

By the time she was walking out of the convenience store, she had two plastic bags full of drinks and junk food. Cole had moved the Jetta to a parking spot away from the pump and was standing outside, that smirk of his making her forget all about the pep talk she'd just given herself in the bathroom.

"We could've stopped for a late lunch if you were that hungry." He jutted his chin toward her loaded hands. "There's a burger place right next door."

"Actually, a burger sounds pretty good right about now." What was she saying? Less than four hours ago, she'd plowed through a Denver omelet with hash browns and toast and one of Cole's triangle slices of French toast. There was no possible way she was actually hungry. Which meant she was letting her unfounded worries take hold of her. "But I really need to get back to Lord Nibbles."

"That's right. The infamous Lord Nibbles. How long can a guinea pig go without food and water?"

"He has plenty to eat and I left him with an extra bottle of water. But he's still new and this was my first time away. I'm concerned that he might have undiagnosed separation anxiety."

Cole came around to the front of the car. "Is that what you're concerned about?"

"Mmm-hmm," Vivienne murmured as he leaned in closer.

His lips were only inches from hers. "And here I thought you were regretting things and trying to figure out ways to ditch me once we got back to Kalispell."

Her knees buckled and her tummy turned inside out. She'd thought she'd gotten Cole out of her system last night. And then again this morning. But her body's reaction to his nearness suggested that it wasn't done with him yet. This had the potential to get very complicated if she let it.

"I'd never ditch one of my clients," she said, then planted a very unbusinesslike kiss on his surprised lips. She used the distraction to snatch the keys out of his hand before passing by him and saying, "My turn to drive."

They ended up using the drive-through at the burger place, and Cole dozed off in the passenger seat without finishing his French fries. Vivienne snacked on those and then systematically polished off both packages of donuts, the chips and a soda. By the time they were approaching Flathead Lake, she'd already rehearsed in her mind what she was going to say when they parted.

It was fun and I enjoyed myself. But we both know where this is headed, so we don't have to pretend otherwise. This week is going to be so busy...

That last bit still needed work. Vivienne wanted to make it clear that she didn't expect him to call her, and that they could go back to how things had been before they'd spent the night together.

But when they pulled up to her apartment complex and he unfolded himself from her front seat, lifting his arms up over his head to stretch, everything she'd planned to say floated out of her brain. Instead, she offered, "Do you want to come inside?"

Chapter Eleven

"This has been the most challenging wedding rehearsal I've ever had to pull off," Vivienne whispered to Cole as everyone was loading up into their cars to drive from his family's new property into Rust Creek Falls for dinner at the Gold Rush Diner—the first place Zach and Lydia had ever shared a meal together.

The comment took him aback because he'd been watching her direct and orchestrate and explain things for the past hour and she hadn't even broken a sweat. It was like she'd done this a hundred times. In her sleep.

"Really?" Cole asked. "I thought it went pretty smoothly. In fact, too smoothly. But don't worry, I'm ready in case something goes wrong tomorrow."

"There's always something that will go wrong. The

trick is to make the couple and the guests think that everything worked out perfectly."

Was that what she had done to him last weekend? Made him think that he'd experienced the most passionate, carefree night—actually two nights if one counted Sunday, when he didn't leave her house until the wee hours of the morning—in his life, and then politely redirected him at every turn this week when he'd tried to call her.

Vivienne had explained that the final days leading up to the wedding would be chaotic for her and, while she hadn't come right out and said that she didn't want to see him again, Cole got the impression that she was trying to convince him that it was his idea to cool things down between them.

Deep down, he knew that her strategy was for the best. As soon as the wedding was over, he and his brothers would be hitting the ground running, trying to get this land ready for a viable ranching operation. His dad needed him to be focused and not playing an ill-advised game of "chase the wedding planner."

Cole rocked back on his heels. "Are you coming to the rehearsal dinner?"

"Nope." Vivienne shook her head. "I have some last-minute stuff to finish here at the freight house."

"Do you need a hand?" he asked, wanting to cringe at the neediness in his voice.

"I got it," she said, smiling up from her tablet. "You should go and enjoy your family."

He knew he should let her get to work, but he hated

the thought of her staying out here at the property all alone. "How long are you going to be here?"

"Just another hour or two. Why?"

"I don't think you should be here alone after dark."

"Don't worry, Sergeant Save-the-Day." She patted his arm and his lips tightened at her condescending tone. "I'll be fine."

He opened his mouth to tell her about the dangers of being this far away from town, all alone in the Montana wilderness, but one of Lydia's bridesmaids chose that second to walk up.

"Hey, Vivienne, do you have a quick second?" Eva asked. "I know that tomorrow is going to be crazy and I wanted to catch you when you had a second of downtime."

"Of course," Vivienne said brightly, tucking the iPad under her arm.

"I wanted to tell you that I loved the invitations you came up with for Lydia and Zach. How cute was that to make them look like an old-time newspaper? And the way they were addressed? That typeset-style font on the envelopes was absolutely perfect."

"Thanks." Vivienne beamed. "But that wasn't a computer font. I actually found an antique typewriter from the 1920s and did those by hand. My fingertips were numb by the time I finished, but it's those small details that make all the difference. I'm glad you liked them."

"I adored them! Listen, Luke and I are getting married soon and my mom has been bugging me to hire a wedding planner. She's already talked to someone at a company out of Helena called A LaVish Affair, but I kinda thought we should try to go with someone more local."

"Oh, they're fabulous. Having someone local can be convenient, but LaVish works weddings all over Montana."

Eva nodded, but her expression suggested she was slightly confused. "So you think I should hire them?"

"Well, you can't go wrong with Rich LaRue. I know parents can get really emotionally invested when it comes to planning weddings, and even if they have good intentions, they can steer you in directions you may not want to go. My advice would be to meet with Rich and consider whether or not he shares your same vision."

Cole's jaw nearly fell open. Seriously? Vivienne had the prime opportunity to sell herself and land another client and *that* was the advice she chose to give? But before he could stutter out an objection, Eva thanked her and called out, "See you tomorrow."

"Your dad and brother are waiting for you," Vivienne said to him as she discreetly pointed toward Cole's truck.

Garrett leaned over the front seat of the cab and honked the horn, then yelled out the open window, "Let's go, Sarge. The last one there buys the first round."

"My family makes absolutely no sense sometimes," Cole said only loud enough for Vivienne to hear. He pinched the bridge of his nose. "Like, they're all going to go thirsty as they sit there waiting for the last person to show up and pay for their drinks?"

Her chuckle seemed a little forced and she politely said, "Have fun."

It wasn't until he was in his truck that he realized

that Vivienne had never explained why tonight had been such a challenge for her.

With the exception of the awkward rehearsal last night, Vivienne hadn't seen much of Cole in the week leading up to the wedding. But that was by design because she was there to work and not get sidetracked. Her personal life, once again, needed to be placed on the back burner.

Yesterday should have been routine for her. Walk everyone through the ceremony, tell them where to stand and what to do. In fact, the minister was more than capable of doing it for her, but Vivienne had needed to direct her energies toward something that wasn't Cole Dalton.

Yet every time she'd turned around, there he was. Talking to the ring bearer about why he had to slow down and wait for the flower girl, busting out his tool belt when he thought the gazebo needed a few more nails to hold the railing in place, tracking down a wooden picnic bench for his aunt Rita and aunt Mary to sit on, since the rental chairs weren't coming until the following day.

Vivienne found herself constantly focusing on where he was and what he was doing rather than performing her job. If that wasn't bad enough, every time she'd given in to temptation and looked his way, he would tilt the corner of his mouth up and wink at her, completely oblivious to the fact that someone in his family would surely catch them staring at each other.

Then she'd had to make up an excuse about needing

to stay at the freight house to finish up some details. She was afraid that if she joined Lydia's friends and family and the rest of the Dalton clan at dinner, it would only serve to show her what she would be missing once she and Cole resumed their normal lives.

She didn't need Estelle telling her that getting too friendly with her clients was never a good idea. They were paying her to do a job, not to get cozy with the groom's brother. So when she arrived at Sawmill Station at eight o'clock the morning of the wedding, she was relieved nobody else was there.

She had a job to do.

Unlocking the freight house, she walked inside and closed her eyes, envisioning exactly how she wanted the space to look in the next seven hours. It was something she did before the start of every wedding day, like a military general surveying the battlefield before leading his troops to a victory. There were going to be tears and sweat and sacrifices today. But, hopefully, no bloodshed—as long as she remained confident and executed her plans quickly and efficiently.

The rumbling of a diesel truck outside was her call to arms and Vivienne squared her shoulders, marching outside to meet the cavalry. Or rather, the first vendor of the day. She instructed the rental company on how to line the seats for the ceremony, a V-shaped formation with an aisle down the center. Tables were set inside the freight house and, thankfully, Zach and Lydia didn't mind sparing the extra expense of renting double the amount of chairs so that Vivienne wouldn't have to enlist the catering staff or some other unfortunate volunteer to transfer two hundred chairs from the ceremony area outside to the reception inside.

The florist showed up next and stayed to help put out tablecloths and runners. When the caterers got there, Vivienne was able to set them up in the recently remodeled depot so they could use it as a temporary kitchen. Luckily, they'd also brought their own waitstaff, so boxes of dishes and silverware were soon unloaded. After she showed them how she wanted the place settings, she had to remind herself to use the restroom, eat a protein bar and down a bottle of water.

She was using twine to hang mason jars filled with white hydrangeas and sweet peas from long, freestanding iron hooks lining the aisle when Lydia arrived with Jolene, Joanna and Eva. The bride's hands were clasped under her chin and her smile was infectious. "It's looking better than I ever could have imagined!"

"We're not done yet," Vivienne said. "Do you need help carrying stuff inside?"

"That would be great," Lydia replied. "I had a heck of a time getting my dress laid out onto the back seat. I'm afraid it's going to be a wrinkled mess."

Vivienne followed the women to one of their cars, which was loaded down with garment bags and shoe boxes. "Here, take the veil and show your bridesmaids to the bridal suite. I'll get the dress."

"Okay," Jolene snickered as they were walking away, "whose idea was it for us to get ready in an old railcar?"

"That would be Garrett," Cole said, making Vivienne hit her head on the roof of the car as she shot up in surprise. Where'd he come from? They were way too early.

"Where's Zach?" she asked, rubbing the top of her head as she searched the gravel lot for more trucks. "He's not supposed to see Lydia before the wedding."

"He's riding here with Booker and Shawn. I was already set to go and didn't want to wait for them. What can I do to help?"

Vivienne's throat constricted and her palms went damp at the vision of Cole Dalton in his tailored outfit. There'd been a heated discussion regarding the men wearing jeans and matching vests versus tuxedos, but in the end, Vivienne was glad they'd gone with the less formal dove-gray suits. Zach had a penchant for bolo ties, and the cowboy boots were obviously a given. Vivienne had even helped select matching felt Stetsons in a soft shade of granite as groomsmen gifts.

But none of them would look half as good today as Cole did.

She swallowed, then shook her head. "You can't help. I don't want you messing up your fancy duds."

"I don't think carrying some clothes is going to dirty me up," he said, brushing by her to reach inside for the covered gown. "You know, I recently learned that the dress needs to hang outside of the garment bag so it doesn't lose its shape before the bride wears it."

She looked around in alarm. "Did you tell your family about where you attained this newfound knowledge?"

"Nope. And I don't plan to." He winked, cradling the bridal gown in his arms as he walked toward the repurposed railcar.

It was a good thing, too, because if he'd looked at

her a moment longer, he would've seen her suck in her cheeks in frustration. No matter how many blatant winks he risked sending her way, Cole had no intention of telling his relatives that he'd spent the weekend with Vivienne. Which meant that their relationship, for the short forty-eight hours that it had lasted, was a secret.

Thank goodness the world wasn't about to stop and allow her to dwell on it. The hairdresser and makeup artist pulled into the parking area, and from that point forward, Vivienne was in constant motion.

Several more Daltons arrived, and then she had to get Zach into the freight house so that he wouldn't see Lydia. The bartender asked her for a cart to transport bottles of liquor from his truck to the makeshift bar she'd created using the abandoned barrels and some planks of wood. It turned out Uncle Charles had an old wheelbarrow in the back of his truck and Vivienne grabbed some flowers and a hand-lettered sign to incorporate the thing into part of the decorations.

The photographer needed the groom and groomsmen for pictures. The band needed to know where to set up. The minister needed to know who had the marriage certificate.

Buttons broke, missing tea lights were located and last-minute seating arrangements were swapped. Lydia's mother, Rhoda, who was walking her daughter down the aisle to give her away, had forgotten her dress shoes at home and someone had to be dispatched to pick those up.

By the time the first guests began to arrive, Vivienne had already changed from her work clothes into a nondescript dress that would help her blend in with the background. It was her standard operating procedure.

However, every time she saw Cole greet another relative or escort someone to their seat, she was reminded that she would remain in the background. Which had always been okay with her, she thought as she watched Lydia walk down the aisle toward Zach.

Until now.

Cole stuck to his father like glue leading up to the ceremony and immediately afterward, when it was time to pose for all the family photos. That was when Cole, his dad and—he assumed—the rest of his brothers felt his mother's absence the most. No matter how the photographer staged them, there always seemed to be a void where his mother should've been.

While Phil Dalton was happy for his son, as they all were, Cole was probably the only one who noticed how quiet his dad was being. The only one who recognized the lost look in the older man's eyes, as if he wasn't quite sure where to stand or who to talk to next. And when his father didn't look confused, he looked deep in thought, staring off in the distance. There wasn't sadness, exactly, like there had been at his mom's funeral. Yet it didn't feel right to leave his dad on his own so that Cole could take off and celebrate the night away with the other guests.

Vivienne's prior comments about wedding days being fairy tales swirled together with his own painful reminders that love didn't always last. Not everybody got their happily-ever-after.

Sitting at the head table beside his father, he watched Zach and Lydia dance to their first song together. If anyone deserved forever, it was the two of them. Still, that kind of unconditional love wasn't a risk Cole was willing to take for himself.

And just like that, his thoughts of risk had him seeking out Vivienne for the millionth time today. In fact, her whereabouts were never really far from his mind. She hovered near the cake table, speaking with one of the hired servers and arranging the heirloom serving knife set Aunt Mary had insisted they use.

Since Lydia's father hadn't been in her life since she was five years old, Cole's sister-in-law had only one parent there as well, which meant that Mrs. Grant was happy to forgo the traditional father-daughter and mother-son dances. The cutting of the cake was the next item on the agenda. Cole's best man toast would follow, and after that the dancing would commence.

Thirty minutes later, someone clinked a glass and others joined in. The band's lead singer handed Cole a microphone, but his skin felt clammy, his heart felt heavy. It would've been too emotional to say what he was really feeling, so in the end, Cole did what he always did and tried to make light with his toast.

Afterward, he realized that going out of his way to pretend that everything was normal—to pretend that he was *not* the serious, responsible brother—took more out of him than just accepting his mantle of constant dependability. Cole wished he could really be that carefree, that he could just sit back and enjoy the evening, but his nerves remained on edge.

He would've begged Zach to refrain from the traditional garter toss, but Cole knew that begging in the Dalton family signaled a weakness to be mercilessly teased and exploited. And in Rust Creek Falls, home of the infamous wedding punch incident and *The Great Roundup* reality show, determining who was going to get married next was becoming a spectator sport. So when all the single women gathered on the dance floor behind Lydia, Cole knew that was his cue to go outside and get some fresh air.

The June evening was brisk, helping relieve some of the stuffiness of the formal suit Cole had been forced to endure. He was leaning against the east side wall of the freight house, out of sight from the caterers running back and forth between the bigger building and the smaller train depot. Which was why he was surprised to see Vivienne turn the corner.

"Did they send you to round up all the bachelors for the next event?" he asked. Her head tilted in confusion, so he explained. "The garter toss. Are you looking for willing victims?"

"Victims? Oh, I get it. No, actually, that's a tradition I could do without."

"Really? I'd think that'd be a target-rich environment for you to book more clients."

Vivienne let out a deep breath, stretching her arms behind her back. "As you've probably figured out, that's one area of my job that could use some improvement."

"Well, you certainly excel at everything else," he said, unable to look away from the way her stretch caused her breasts to jut forward. She dropped her arms and made a snort. "No, seriously. Don't roll your eyes. This wedding was amazing, and Lydia and Zach are so happy. I even heard a few of my cousins' friends talking about getting some tips from you."

"Trust me, if every job could be like this, this would be the ideal career for me."

"But...?" he prompted.

"But back in business school, nobody told me that the practical side of making money was a lot tougher than the theoretical side. I mean, deep down, I know that in order to be a successful wedding planner, I need to land the big clients, charge the bigger fees and direct them to the biggest vendors so that I can get more referrals, thereby starting the cycle all over again. I just didn't realize I'd have to be a saleswoman to do so. When a bride comes in wanting a simple garden wedding with only twenty guests, Estelle expects me to convince the woman that what she *really* wants is four hundred of her closest friends eating caviar and listening to a twelve-piece orchestra at the luxurious Thunder Canyon Resort."

Her honesty was refreshing. Not that he hadn't already seen the type of woman she was when she'd had plenty of opportunities to look out for her own interests. "Well, I think what you gave Zach and Lydia tonight was better than anything Estelle or Rich LaRue could've done."

His fingertips stroked along her temple, but before he could lean down and kiss her, her phone, which was clipped to the sash of yet another sexy wraparound dress, pinged.

"That's the bartender." Vivienne stood at attention,

as if she was ready to conquer the next battle. "We're running low on ice."

"You stay here and take a breather. I'll go get the ice."

"You're a guest. This is my job."

"Vivienne, you've been going nonstop since when? Ten? Eleven?"

"More like eight," she mumbled.

"See? You need a break. Hide out here and relax for a few more minutes." The music cued up, so Cole knew he was now at least safe from accidentally catching a garter or a bouquet. "Besides, it'll give me an excuse to miss the chicken dance."

He left her with a smile, knowing full well that she wasn't about to stay there lounging about. And he'd been right. By the time he'd delivered the ice and returned to his father's side, Vivienne was helping the waitstaff clear empty glasses and bottles from the abandoned tables. All the people his age were on the dance floor, but Cole didn't feel like kicking up his heels.

He was just ready for this night to be over. He was ready to have Vivienne all to himself again. Cole squeezed his eyelids tightly, squelching the thought that had come out of nowhere. Vivienne wasn't really his, and he knew that. But she had a way of taking his mind off things, and he was simply wishing himself to be anywhere but here.

Everyone finally gathered outside for the big send-off, and when Zach and Lydia pulled away in the rumble seat of the 1930s roadster driven by one of their old friends from Hardin, Cole anxiously turned to his father. "You ready to take off?"

"Truth be told, I'm exhausted. But this is our property now." His father paused, letting the significance of his words sink in. "We're the hosts, so we can't go until everyone else is gone."

"Look, Dad. People are already starting to leave. Booker and Shawn can stay to close up," Cole suggested. "Hell, even Garrett can shut things down, if he ever puts down his beer and gets off that railcar Vivienne set up out back."

"Speaking of Vivienne, I should probably find her and thank her for doing such a good job on everything. She made it real fancy, but it also felt simple and down-home. Not too showy. I only wish your—" Phil's voice cracked, then he sniffed and carried on. "It's too bad your mama couldn't have been here to see how perfectly it all came together. She always did love a wedding."

As his father turned to head back toward the freight house, Cole's boots remained rooted to the grass near the gravel parking area. The guilt he'd been holding back all evening raced through him, and he looked up to the darkening sky, which was still streaked in a haze of orange and pink from the late-setting sun. His fist clenched as he crossed his arms in front of his chest, and his throat clogged when he whispered, "Sorry you couldn't be here, Mama. Sorry for letting you down."

Chapter Twelve

"I'm gonna catch a ride back to the ranch with your aunt and uncle," Cole's father told him when he finally made his way back to the freight house. They were coming outside as Cole was walking inside, Uncle Charles yawning and Aunt Rita carrying one of the centerpieces. Most of the guests were already gone and the tables had been cleared of dishes. "I couldn't find that pretty wedding planner, but I know she's still hopping around here somewhere. That gal's got energy to spare and she's too quick for me."

Cole waved off his old man. "Get on home, Dad. I'll find Vivienne and thank her for us."

"You do that." His dad squeezed his shoulder. Was it his imagination, or was there a little twinkle in Phil Dalton's tired eyes?

Cole was a cowboy, a former Marine. He was used to being on his feet all day. But his dressy ostrich boots were still relatively new and had been pinching him all night. Still, that didn't stop him from helping the band haul their equipment outside or carrying the last load of stainless-steel trays to the caterer's van.

"Cole, you don't have to help," Vivienne said as she folded the last tablecloth. "I told you I'd lock up when everyone left."

"I know." He shrugged, not having the emotional energy to argue. Instead, he asked, "What are we doing with all the tables and chairs?"

"The rental people are coming tomorrow morning to get those, so just leave them where they are."

By the time he clicked the padlock into place on the sliding doors of the freight house, the only two cars remaining in the gravel lot were his truck and Vivienne's Jetta. She was standing on the platform in front of the train depot, a cardboard box in one arm and her trusty tote bag hooked on the other.

He met her at the steps. "These country roads get pretty dark at night. Why don't I drive you back to Kalispell?"

"Cole, I'd tell you that I'm more than capable of driving on a two-lane highway and there's no need for you to go out of your way like that, but then you'd insist. I'd say that I don't want to leave my car here for someone to see and then you'd counter that you could leave your truck here instead. To be honest, I'm way too exhausted to go through all that arguing."

"Good, give me your keys."

"Then how will you get back?"

He looked over at his truck. Did it really matter how he got back? He was well aware that driving Vivienne home was just an excuse to spend more time together. But, like her, he was too tired to rationalize it. He just wanted to be with her. "I'll follow you, then. Make sure you get home safely."

The drive took almost thirty minutes and all that time alone in the dark cab of his truck gave him too much time to think. To feel. To let his emotions get the better of him. So when he met her in the parking lot of her apartment complex, he was filled with a raging need and a determination that he'd never experienced before. She hadn't even gotten her purse out of the back seat when he spun her to him, pressed her back against her car and planted his lips on hers.

With all the emotion throbbing through him today, the kiss consumed him, filling him with more passion than anything he'd ever experienced. Nothing mattered but sinking into her embrace, into her depths. He didn't care about anything but the fact that her mouth was welcoming him eagerly and that she was clinging to him with equal desperation.

If someone had asked him what was going through his mind, he couldn't even put into words what this sensation was and he definitely wasn't ready to describe it, let alone think it. All he knew was that being with Vivienne at this exact second felt right. It felt perfect.

Vivienne had been well aware that Cole was just doing his hero thing, offering to follow her home. Yet something about the way they'd come together last night had been different, more intense than it had been when they'd first made love. As she stretched out on her bed beside him the following morning, she was careful to not wake him up. She was also careful to not let her thoughts stray too far. After attending a successful wedding, it was easy for people to slip into the kind of romantic afterglow that made them think their hearts were ready to conquer the world.

Not that Cole had been waxing poetic. In fact, she'd noticed how stoic he'd been throughout the ceremony and how he'd purposely avoided most of the customary wedding festivities. And neither one of them had been doing much talking after he kissed her in the parking lot, so it should've been easy to replay in her mind his previous jokes about matrimony.

The problem was, as much as she'd given up on marriage lately, Vivienne hadn't given up on falling in love. Maybe it was just the aftereffects of witnessing such a beautifully poignant ceremony and successful reception last night, but she had a pretty good idea that what she was currently feeling for Cole would cause the self-professed eternal bachelor to run for the hills.

She blew out her breath in frustration, dislodging a loose curl on her forehead. How could she have let herself get so caught up? She was smarter than this.

Cole groaned beside her, keeping his eyes shut as he flexed his arm and pulled her closer. His warm body surrounded her and erased every rational argument she'd just outlined in her head.

Lord Nibbles's exercise wheel squeaked to life from

the living room, where Vivienne had moved his cage after the first night she had him and realized that he was a nocturnal animal. She looked at the watch she'd been in too much of a hurry to take off last night.

Hmm—6:08 a.m. It was unusual for him to be up at this time. It was also unusual for him to use the noisy exercise wheel. He'd done the same thing last week when she'd left him overnight to go to Billings.

Did guinea pigs hold grudges?

She slipped out of bed and padded across the cheap, thin carpet of her apartment to give him some attention. But the prim and proper chap ignored her finger extending into the unhinged door, his little wiggly nose lifted into the air. Vivienne went to the cupboard and pulled out a Nutter Butter cookie. There was no way he'd ignore that.

"Are you supposed to be feeding him peanut butter?" Cole asked from the doorway. He was wearing nothing but a pair of boxer briefs, riding low on his hips, and Vivienne's heart spun like the exercise wheel inside the cage.

"It might be a little fattening, but Lord Nibbles isn't watching his waistline."

Cole's eyes darted down to the hem of Vivienne's tank top. "Speaking of waistlines, I enjoyed watching yours last night when you were straddling—"

"Can I make you some eggs?" she interrupted, making an about-face toward the minuscule kitchen and popping a cookie into her own mouth. She continued between bites, slurring her words, "Maybe shum coffee?"

Cole's chuckle was low and deep. "So what does a

wedding planner do after the wedding? Are you now off duty until the next one?"

She'd barely swallowed before shoving another cookie in, reminding herself of Estelle, who would use the dying end of a cigarette to light a fresh one. "What nexsht one?"

"Well, you're still planning mine, right?"

Vivienne turned around to switch on her coffee-maker. Not necessarily because she needed the caf-feine, but because she didn't want to face him for this conversation. "I, uh, figured that now that Zach's wed-ding is over and I'm not at risk of getting fired before-hand, you and Susie Starlight would be calling yours off this week."

"Hmm," he said, coming up behind her, sliding his warm hands over her hips. He whispered against her hairline behind her ear, "I wouldn't mind having a few more consultations with my planner."

Consultations. Her brain tried to concentrate on that one word, but it was quickly overridden by the tighten-ing of her thighs and the ticklish pricking of the stubble from his jaw rubbing against her neck.

"I thought you had a family ranch you needed to get running."

Cole sighed as he straightened up, leaving a cool breeze along her shoulder where his warm breath had just been. "You're right. We're putting up fence all this week. And my dad has an architect coming tomorrow to show him the blueprints for the new house and barn. Hey, is that my binder?"

Vivienne looked across the open kitchen to the white

plastic binder on her coffee table. Besides forging Susie's signature on the contract, she hadn't touched it since they'd returned from Billings.

She was saved from answering as he walked the few steps to retrieve it. "It looks way thinner than the one you had for Zach and Lydia."

Grabbing another cookie, Vivienne followed him to the living room. "That's because most couples—you know, the ones who actually have real plans to get married—tend to provide me with lots of ideas to fill up the pages."

"Well, I'm fresh out of ideas." He spread his hands out wide. "Besides, you outdid yourself yesterday. There's no way I could come up with something better than that."

His tone was playful, but something nagged at Vivienne.

"Really? Because I got the impression that you weren't really enjoying yourself last night."

Tension flickered across his face before he shrugged. "It wasn't that. It's just none of that stuff is my thing, you know?"

What could she do but nod? Cole had made himself abundantly clear in that regard. At the same time, he'd also made it pretty clear that he wasn't planning on stopping whatever this was that they had between them. It wasn't that Vivienne was opposed to having a casual relationship, as long as both of them knew that things weren't headed in a different direction. One thing she'd learned from her parents' marriage was that she didn't want to go back and forth. She didn't want this emotional tug-of-war raging inside of her.

As she was the kind of person who thrived on organization and communication, compulsion forced her to lay it all out on the table.

"Look, Cole. I think we both have a lot of things going on in our lives right now. You've got the ranch and Lord knows I need to focus on my career, or else I'm not going to have one. Which means Lord Nibbles and I can kiss this glamorous apartment—" she gestured toward the nondescript rental furniture "—goodbye. Anyway, neither one of us probably has time for anything more than some casual fun. Do you agree?"

Initially, when she'd started talking, his face had been like stone, hard and unreadable. His eyes had been steady but not panicked. That was a good thing, right? Twisting her bottom lip between her teeth, she waited for his response. And tried not to stare at the muscular ridges of his abdomen, because if she glanced down, she would surely lose her nerve to continue this conversation and wind up pushing him back onto the beige tweed sofa to have her way with him.

After several seconds of uncomfortable silence, his face finally relaxed and his smirk suggested that he was relieved that she wasn't asking him for any sort of commitment. "I'm definitely a fan of the fun part—"

His phone let out a shrill ring from the bedroom, and he cut off whatever else he'd been about to say as he strode to the bedside table.

"What's wrong, Garrett?" he said by way of answer. Vivienne couldn't hear the other side of the conversation, but Cole was quick to reply. "Because you never call me after a night of drinking unless there's something wrong."

He ran a hand through his short, dark hair, then balanced the cell phone between his ear and his shoulder as he pulled on his gray slacks from the night before. "Uh-huh," he said, then paused a few more beats. "You've got to be kidding me!"

Filled with a sudden sense of worry, Vivienne walked to the side of the bed so she could be there to lend whatever support Cole needed.

"Fine. Text me the address and I'll come pick you up." He yanked on the white button-down shirt she'd practically torn off him last night, then made a grunting sound. "And you guys all told me the Share My Location app was overkill. I'll meet you outside in a minute."

Cole disconnected the call and tossed the phone onto the bed as he tugged on his boots.

"What happened?" Vivienne asked.

"Well, speaking of fun and casual," he said, not looking up, "Garrett had a bit too much to drink last night and went home with one of the waitresses from the catering company. Unfortunately, he woke up in the waitress's roommate's bed instead and isn't sure how that happened. He snuck out a few minutes ago and is outside in the parking lot."

"Here? In *my* parking lot?"

"Yep. He was going to call Shawn to come pick him up, but I installed this app on their phones so that— Never mind. Anyway, he got an alert that my phone was only a few blocks away and, wanting to get out of

Dodge before the waitress or her roommate woke up, he did the walk of shame over here."

Cole put his phone and wallet in his pocket, grabbed his keys and was almost to the bedroom doorway before he turned around and pulled Vivienne into his arms. "Sorry my brother is a dumbass. I'll call you later."

His parting kiss was short but thorough and left little doubt that he would in fact be calling her soon. He scooped something off the coffee table on his way out the door. Sergeant Save-the-Day was off on his next mission.

It wasn't until she lowered her fingers from her swollen lips that she realized he'd taken the white binder with him.

It was later that night before Cole allowed himself to text Vivienne.

She couldn't have been clearer that she wanted to keep their relationship as status quo, which was fine with him. Especially since he'd expected her to call things off altogether. When she'd begun her speech about them both having busy lives, he'd had to work to keep his face from showing any disappointment, because even though he didn't want anything serious, he also wasn't quite ready to stop seeing her.

That was why he kept his message simple. Drove by Sawmill Station. The rental company picked up the tables and chairs. Thought you might want to know.

Sitting in his cousin's former bedroom, he stared at the pink ruffle along the edge of the curtain as he waited for what felt like an hour but was probably only a couple of minutes. Finally his phone vibrated in his hand with her reply. Thanks. How's your brother?

He let out a breath. They were still good.

Stupid and hungover, Cole typed, then debated whether or not he should text her *Talk to you soon* or *Can't wait to see you again.* But he didn't want to sound too needy. He ended up going with a simple Good night.

The week after the wedding was busier than the week leading up to it. It was time for the real work on the ranch to begin, and Cole was up before dawn and dragging his tired body home well after dark every night. He tried to find reasons to text Vivienne, but most of them were asinine questions about the wedding emails Estelle had him subscribed to. What he really wanted to ask was if he could see her this weekend. He remembered that she was working on a big sixtieth birthday party for some wealthy Kalispell socialite, but he couldn't remember the exact date.

On Thursday, he was on an all-terrain vehicle they'd borrowed from Uncle Charles, digging holes for fence posts, when his cell phone vibrated on his hip. So far, the ground had been hard and the midday sun had been unforgiving, but seeing Vivienne's name on his screen made him grin.

"Hello?" he said, putting the phone to his ear.

"Uh, hi, Cole. It's Vivienne Shuster over at Estelle's Events." Her tone was hesitant yet professional, and there was only one reason she'd feel the need to give her last name and place of employment to the guy she'd slept with just a few days ago. Estelle was listening.

"Miss Shuster," he replied, suddenly annoyed by

their formal pretense. At one time, it had seemed amusing and slightly wicked to trick her boss. Now Cole wished everything was out in the open, that they didn't need a reason to call each other or to see each other. "I almost didn't recognize your voice."

There was a brief pause and Cole mentally kicked himself for the sarcastic comment. But then Vivienne continued. "The reason I'm calling is that Estelle would like me to come get the planning binder from you."

"The what?"

"The planning binder. You know, the one you took last weekend when your *fiancée* was in town for your brother's wedding? You guys were going to try to fill out some more of it, maybe add some pictures of ideas you wanted to incorporate for your own big day?" Her emphasis implied that she was hoping he'd go along with whatever excuse she'd told her boss, but it took him a second to realize why she was asking about the binder.

That's right, he'd taken the thing from her apartment on Sunday. At the time, it had been a split-second decision, almost a subconscious last resort to ensure that he still had a reason to talk to her despite all her hemming and hawing about the status of their relationship. "How soon do you need it?"

"No rush," she started, then there was a muffled sound as if she'd covered the mouthpiece of her phone. "Actually, if I could pick it up tomorrow, that'd be great."

"Tomorrow works," he said eagerly, before realizing that his dad and the three of his brothers who weren't on their honeymoon would be out here working with him. He didn't want them asking why he needed to meet with Zach's wedding planner. Cole was about to suggest meeting her in Rust Creek Falls, but then someone in town might ask the same question. Instead, he said, "Actually, I have to come to Kalispell to pick up some supplies for the corrals we're going to start next week. Why don't I meet you at Matilda's for lunch and I can give it to you then?"

His gut twisted while he waited for her reply. He'd been hoping to ask her out on a proper date, but suggesting a business lunch was the best he could come up with while still maintaining the charade for her boss.

"That would be great," she said, and Cole's stomach unclenched at the relief in her voice. "I have a new client coming in at one, so I'll need to be back to the office in time for that."

"I'll pick you up at eleven thirty, then."

"No need for that. I can meet you there. See you tomorrow." Vivienne disconnected first and Cole stared at her name vanishing from his screen.

Putting away his phone and picking up his shovel, he tried not to dwell on her rushed response or her refusal of his offer for a ride to the restaurant. All that mattered was that he would be seeing her tomorrow. He turned the volume up on his iPod and tried to figure out where he could find some pictures to shove into his pretend-wedding-planning binder.

Chapter Thirteen

"I'm so sorry I'm late," Vivienne told Cole, who slid out from the booth and stood up when she arrived for lunch. "Estelle wanted to reschedule her weekly hair appointment so that she could come with us and I had to convince her that I could handle it."

"No problem." His good manners didn't surprise her, but she was definitely taken aback by his kiss hello. She'd turned her face just in time to present him with her cheek instead, praying that nobody else in the diner had noticed. Kalispell wasn't as small a town as Rust Creek Falls, but people here still talked.

Especially Matilda, the owner, who had no problem asking her customers personal questions.

The woman appeared with an iced tea for Cole and a Dr Pepper for Vivienne, her plastic cat's-eye glasses not hiding her raised eyebrows. "So, Viv, I heard from this handsome stud that you did a great job on his brother's wedding out in Rust Creek."

Vivienne's tight smile remained firmly in place despite the heat rising all the way up to her hairline. She nodded, then put the straw to her mouth for a long, slow sip to avoid further conversation. Thankfully, the lunch rush hour was beginning, and Matilda had other customers to chat with.

"I hope you don't mind," Cole said, nodding toward her red plastic cup of soda. "I knew what you would want to drink, but I wasn't sure how stressed you'd be today, so I haven't ordered lunch yet."

Amazed, Vivienne sat back in the booth. Had anybody ever ordered for her before? At least correctly? Growing up, her mother had always monitored Vivienne's intake of food, suggesting lighter portions and insisting that boys didn't like girls who ate more than them. And Estelle, on the rare occasions she'd taken pity on Vivienne for having to work through breaks, would simply pick up two of whatever she was having. Vivienne was usually the one seeing to everyone else's preferences. Nobody had ever really paid attention to hers. "Thanks."

"I've been meaning to ask you," Cole said as he watched her slurp down half of her Dr Pepper. "What exactly does Estelle do? Because she wasn't at the wedding last Saturday and she didn't attend the bridal expo. As far as I can see, you do all the labor."

"She used to be much more active, back in the day. But times have changed and Estelle is of the opinion that if something ain't broke, don't fix it. When she hired me, I was fine with the distribution of duties because it let me do the part I loved and she took care of all the behind-the-scenes things, like drawing up contracts and paying the bills. But now that she's slowing down and becoming more pushy and cranky with the clients, we're not getting as much business as we used to. But the birthday party we're doing this weekend is for one of her friends, so she'll be more hands-on with that."

A different waitress approached and Vivienne ordered the Cobb salad, then changed her mind and got the chicken potpie lunch special, which came with a side salad. There was always too much gravy in Matilda's potpies, so she requested a side of mashed potatoes to help soak some up. "And I better order the blackberry cobbler now, since I have to leave in forty-five minutes."

"I'll do the Western bacon burger with onion rings, please," Cole said, handing the waitress their menus. He looked at Vivienne, one brow raised. "I hope it's your one-o'clock clients that are stressing you out, not me."

She forced a chuckle, but it was definitely not Dolores Stack's anniversary party next week that had Vivienne wanting to eat like a starved grizzly bear getting ready for hibernation. Dr. and Mrs. Stack had the same party at the same country club every single year and Vivienne could throw it blindfolded. But she didn't tell Cole that. Instead, she changed the subject. "So how's the ranch coming along?"

"Good. My dad and I met with the architect who is designing the new buildings. Now we need to figure out who is going to live where."

"What do you mean?" She finished off the rest of her soda and wished the diner served appetizers or something other than the basket of prepackaged crackers.

"Well, my dad will live in the main house, obviously, but he wants each of us to build our own place on the property, which is generous of him, but I don't like the idea of him being alone. Booker, Shawn and Garrett—especially Garrett—are all single, and while I don't see anything changing on that front anytime soon, they're already chomping at the bit to have their own space. Zach's the only one of us who would have any foreseeable need for a house, but he's going to be living in town with Lydia for a while. That leaves me to stay with my Dad and keep an eye on things."

Vivienne's heart swelled at his love for his father. Of course he planned to live with his dad. Cole was the family caretaker. But it was also further proof that he had no intention of ever having his own home, his own family. This was why she hadn't seen the man all week and she'd purposely tried to keep the limited messages between them casual. There was no long-term for them.

"So tell me about the design for the main house," Vivienne said. The topic of plan layouts and decorating were familiar enough that she could easily follow along, yet neutral enough that she wouldn't have to discuss her own future and lack of picket-fence expectations.

Cautioning herself not to shovel her food into her mouth so quickly, Vivienne listened to Cole talk about the layout, the number of bedrooms and a ridiculously large stone fireplace using some of the creek-bed rocks they'd salvaged after the fire at their ranch, Dalton's Gulch.

It was the perfect opportunity to ask him about his past. "Do you miss your old ranch?"

He paused, an onion ring halfway to his mouth. "Sometimes. It's weird. When I shipped off to boot camp, I was eighteen years old, a fresh-faced baby who wanted nothing more than to serve others and save lives. But I was so homesick, like physically sick to my stomach. At night, I was too exhausted to feel anything, but I used to lie in my bunk every morning, willing myself not to puke. We could send letters and that helped, but we didn't have access to phones or anything. Thirteen weeks later, my mom and dad came to my graduation at the recruit depot in San Diego, and it was like a miracle cure. It made me realize I wasn't missing my home, I was just missing my family. After that, it didn't matter where they stationed me. As long as I could talk to my parents every so often, I was fine. So I guess that's the long way of saying I don't really miss Dalton's Gulch, because my dad and brothers aren't there anymore. But I'll always miss my mom."

Vivienne reached across the table, laying her hand on his. "I'm so sorry, Cole."

She'd been around him enough to know that he liked fixing things, pretending that he was above being bothered by his own problems. So when she saw that his eyes were slightly glassy, as though a mist was covering them, she wasn't surprised that he immediately shrugged off her sympathy and looked up at the ceiling before giving her a little smirk. "It is what it is."

The man was too stubborn to succumb to something as human as tears. In fact, he'd flipped his hand over and was now using his fingers to stroke the inside of her wrist as he tried to change the subject. "What about your parents? Has your dad moved back home yet?"

"Ugh." Vivienne picked up a spoon and began digging into the vanilla ice cream melting over her cobbler. "He came home, but now my mom has moved into the apartment. She says it's *her* turn to live the bachelorette lifestyle this time."

"I can't believe they keep an apartment just for when they have fights."

"Technically, it's my apartment. Or it was. I was living there when they had one of their longer breaks. Unlike you, home is wherever my parents are *not*. So I sublet the unit to my dad and found the place where I'm living now. The rent is a bit more than I can afford, but I try to tell myself that I can't put a price on peace of mind, you know?"

Vivienne immediately regretted her words when the bill came and Cole's tanned, muscular forearm shot out to grab it.

"I'm not broke," she argued. Technically, it wasn't a lie because she wouldn't necessarily be broke unless she lost her job. "You don't always have to pay for me."

"I know." Cole gave her an indulgent smile, which made Vivienne feel even more like a charity case, as he stood up to retrieve his wallet, peeling two twenty-dollar bills out and throwing them on the bill. "I better get you back for your next client."

Annoyance at his constant attempts to take care of her was prickling at her.

"I can get back on my own," Vivienne said, a bit too

defensively. Then she amended, "You wouldn't want to risk having Estelle see you. We've had two calls this week from potential clients in Rust Creek Falls raving about the freight house, and she wants to talk to you about converting the place into a proper venue for more weddings."

"Lord save me from any more weddings or wedding talk," Cole replied, placing a hand on her back as they walked toward the exit. "Which reminds me. I need to grab that binder thingy out of my truck for you."

It turned out his truck was parallel parked a block away from the diner, which meant that they were only another block away from her office. Surely, he wouldn't insist on walking her the rest of the way. As much as she wanted to soak up every minute they had together, it was a bad idea to get too attached.

Cole used his key to unlock the passenger door. Looking back on it, Vivienne wished she would've stayed on the sidewalk near the tall cab of his truck instead of waiting for him by the back bumper. That way, when he pulled her into his arms for a long and thorough kiss goodbye, Estelle wouldn't have seen them as she was driving down the street.

"I trusted you" was the first thing out of Estelle's mouth when Vivienne walked up to the office. Actually, the first thing out of her mouth was the cigarette she'd just lit. But the nicotine apparently wasn't having a calming effect.

Her boss was standing outside the front door, her petite frame blocking the entrance, forcing the confrontation to happen where anyone could walk by and overhear them. "I trusted you with my clients, with my reputation, with my entire business, yet this is how you repay me? You start up an affair with one of our grooms?"

"It's not an affair." Vivienne was quick to defend herself before she clamped her jaw shut at the risk of further implicating herself. But it really wasn't an affair. At least, not the kind Estelle meant. Vivienne clung to the binder Cole had given her before he'd driven off, thankfully oblivious that Estelle had just busted them.

"You were kissing him in full daylight out on the street!" It appeared that steam was coming from Estelle's ears, but it could also have been smoke from the heavy cigarette puffing she was doing between sentences. "I bet Susie Starbright would beg to differ."

It was Starlight, and she was a horse. But it wasn't like Vivienne could tell her boss that. Or justify her behavior in any way. If she explained that there was no bride to begin with, no wedding to plan, then she'd be admitting that she'd lied to Estelle from the get-go. That she'd had Cole sign a contract and pay them a deposit under false pretenses. The liability for that would be far worse than having her boss think she would break up a marriage. As much as Vivienne hated having her character called into question, it was better to be thought a home wrecker than a disreputable fraud.

"I knew you were too good to be true," Estelle muttered, causing Vivienne to wonder what all that "I took a chance on you" attitude Estelle had projected less than a month ago had been about.

"Perhaps we should talk about this later," Vivienne

suggested calmly. "I have a new client coming in at one, remember?"

"Oh, no, you don't." Estelle pointed her finger, the long ash barely hanging on to the tip of her cigarette. "*I* have a client coming at one. You have some want ads in the paper you need to start looking through for your next job."

Want ads? The woman was so old-fashioned she didn't even know that people nowadays found jobs online. Wait. Panic washed through her. "Are…are you firing me?"

"You can't think I'd allow you to stay on my payroll and sleep with the next groom that walks in the door?"

The allegation was worse than a slap in the face. Not only was she accusing Vivienne of being a slut, she was accusing her of being a predatory one at that. Vivienne was frozen in place. How could she make Estelle understand?

"But I brought in more clients…" Okay, so Cole wasn't a legitimate client, but he was a paying one. And the one coming this afternoon was another Rust Creek Falls bride who'd called her after Lydia and Zach's wedding.

The big shoulder pads in Estelle's 1980s style suit jacket lifted in odd angles as she extended her arms across the front door of the office. "If you think I'm letting you step one foot inside my business, you better think again. There's no way I'm giving you another second of access to my clients and my vendors and all the contacts I've spent decades building."

Vivienne's mouth hung open in shock as her heart squeezed together on the inside. She'd put plenty of hours and sweat into building up this business as well, and now Estelle wasn't even going to let her collect her personal things?

"My laptop is in there," she said, her voice weak and pathetic. "My phone charger and…" Vivienne couldn't think of what else belonged to her.

A retired couple walked toward the entrance of the CPA's office next door and it became evident that standing out here and pleading with Estelle was causing even more of a scene. Thankfully, Estelle lowered her raspy voice and said, "I'll send a messenger with your final paycheck and all the things you left behind, including that stash of peanut butter pretzels and granola bars you keep in the credenza. If you leave quietly, I won't tell everyone we do business with that you broke up a marriage."

Vivienne flinched. It was one thing to be fired because her boss of over three years thought so poorly of her. It was another thing to become a pariah of the event-planning industry. If a rumor like that got out, she'd never get another job.

Her mouth opened and closed several more times, but the disgust coming out of Estelle's eyes was too intense, too hate filled. Vivienne had always prided herself on her diplomacy skills, on being the voice of reason in the most emotionally charged situations. Yet there was nothing she could say to save herself.

She couldn't even hold her head up as she turned and walked away, still clutching Cole's binder to her chest.

Chapter Fourteen

Four days later, Cole was looking down at his phone, wondering why Vivienne hadn't responded to any of his texts since their lunch on Friday. He'd known she was busy with an event over the weekend, but it wasn't like her to not respond at all. Unless she was trying to cool things down between them.

His palms itched and his mind immediately went to the worst-case scenario, the way it always did when he started worrying about a loved one.

The thought stopped him cold. A loved one? He didn't actually love Vivienne, did he? Because if he fell for her, that would put him at risk of losing her and getting hurt.

No, he told himself. He didn't love her. This feeling was nothing more than a powerful sense of responsibility. He'd experienced this with countless people. Squad mates, his cousins' friends, hell, even horses. As though to prove it to himself, Cole slipped his phone into his holder and went back to work on the never-ending fence line.

Even with the train depot and freight house, the acreage on this property was almost twice the size of their last ranch. And they were starting from scratch. He could've stayed back with his brothers, working on the new barn and stables. But he'd been in a bad mood since Monday, when he'd tried to call Vivienne and it had gone to voice mail. Garrett had asked if it was a woman who had him so twisted up and Cole reminded his brother that after the mess he'd gotten himself into the night of the wedding, he shouldn't be talking to anyone about problems with women.

The sound of the diesel engine of his dad's Dodge forced him to shove away all thoughts of Vivienne. Cole walked over to the dirt path where his father had parked and was now exiting the crew cab.

"You didn't come to the barn for lunch," Phil said, holding up a small blue cooler by the handle.

See, this was what his family did. They looked out for each other. Cole wasn't the only Dalton who had a tendency to be overprotective. "Thanks, Dad."

"You know, you *are* allowed to take a break occasionally," his old man said.

Cole responded with a slight shake of his head. There was too much to do and too much to think about. He took the insulated jug off the back of his all-terrain vehicle and used the spout to grab a quick drink before letting the cool water spray onto his face and then his forearms. Pulling a handkerchief out of his jeans pocket, he dried his hands before wiping off the back of his neck.

"Son," his father said, putting a leathery tan hand on Cole's shoulder. "I know you think you're the only one who can get this ranch up and running. But you're not going to be any use to the rest of us if you're out here until all hours dragging yourself till you're in the ground."

"I know my limitations."

"Do you?"

Cole didn't answer, because it was a well-disputed opinion in his family that he had a tendency to work himself ragged trying to do everything for everybody. His brothers called it a hero complex, but Cole called it serving a need.

"How's that pretty little wedding planner doing?"

"What?" Cole's damp head whipped around at his father's sudden change of direction.

"Vivienne. You know, the gal you had lunch with last week?"

Cole squinted. "How did you know I had lunch with her?"

"You think you're the only one who likes to keep tabs on where his family is?"

"Hmm. At least it's good to know everyone's finally using the locator app I installed on your smartphones."

"Pfshh." Phil waved him off. "Don't need that technology nonsense when I've got good old-fashioned small-town word of mouth."

"Since when did you become a gossipy old man?"

"There's a difference between speaking gossip and listening to it," his dad said, and Cole lifted a brow. "And I'm not about to reveal my sources, but some of the same people who shop at the hardware supply in Rust Creek Falls also occasionally go into Kalispell to get their pie fix. I mean, Eva-Rose's pies are mighty fine, but Matilda has a heavy hand with the whipped cream, you know. Ever since this person's wife got on him about his cholesterol, he's had to steer clear of Daisy's Donut Shop and sneak out of town whenever he wants a proper dessert."

"You'd think the mailman would be more careful talking about who he ran into in Kalispell if he didn't want his wife to find out."

Phil's eyes widened in surprise at Cole's accurate guess that Barney was his so-called source, but he quickly recovered. "Anyway, my point is that you've been spending a lot of time with Vivienne Shuster, and the way I heard it, the two of you were looking pretty cozy out on the sidewalk when you kissed her goodbye."

Cole's mouth tilted at the memory of that kiss. It had packed quite a punch, and at the time neither one of them had seemed to care who might see them. But now that Vivienne hadn't talked to Cole in a few days, maybe he'd misinterpreted things.

"So, you are dating her?" His dad must've noticed the mix of expressions that crossed Cole's face every time he thought of Vivienne.

"I guess you could say we were dating. But I don't exactly know what's going on between us right this second." Cole wasn't one to talk about his relationships with anyone, especially his family. But his father didn't appear to be in a hurry to take off anytime soon. In fact, the older man scooted his hip onto the supply bed of the ATV. Cole sighed. "I haven't heard from her in a few days."

"I bet that must be killing you." Phil Dalton didn't tease his boys often, but when he did, the resemblance between him and Garrett was uncanny. They had the same devilish grin. In fact, their mother used to say that all her sons had that playful smirk.

"Why do you say that?"

"Because God forbid someone doesn't ever return your call." As soon as the words were out of his dad's mouth, pain flashed in the older man's eyes and he sucked in his whiskered cheek before blowing out a breath. "I'm sorry, Cole. I didn't mean to bring that up. You're right to worry about that sort of thing. We all are."

Cole's lungs felt hollow, and he folded his arms across his chest as though he could keep his heart from sinking any further.

"I know you guys all make fun of me for being up-tight about phones, but I was the one who…" Cole couldn't bear to finish the last sentence.

"Do you think you're the only one who feels guilty for what happened to your mom? Hell, son, she was *my* wife and I wasn't able to protect her any more than you were."

None of the men liked talking about the circumstances surrounding Diana Dalton's death. However, while he was sure that all his brothers held on to a sense of guilt at not being able to save her, Cole was ultimately the one responsible.

When it happened, he'd just returned stateside after a deployment to Iraq, waiting for his commanding officer to approve his leave paperwork so he could hop a plane to Montana. At the same time, his father and brothers were hauling feed to a herd of cattle at the far end of their property when a fast-moving wildfire headed directly toward their ranch house. His mom had been home and probably didn't even see or smell the fire until it was too late. Her husband and sons had tried to call her from their cell phones, but the landline wires had already gone down in the blaze and she didn't answer her own cell—which was later found in the back of her burned car.

"Cole, saving people is what you do. I get that. You've always been in the right place at the right time, but this was one instance when you weren't. Even if you hadn't been thousands of miles away, you couldn't have saved her."

"No, but I could have prevented it."

"You think you could've prevented a massive wildfire that scorched tens of thousands of acres in under an hour?"

"No, Dad. But I was the last one she spoke to on her cell phone. Right before she set it down inside her trunk so she could carry in all the groceries." Cole's throat tightened as he pushed out the words. "The groceries she'd just gone to the store to get to cook my favorite homecoming meal for me."

It was hard to meet his father's eyes, but his dad's stare was too long and intense to escape. The older man spread his arms. "Get over here, son."

But Cole's feet felt heavy in his boots and he didn't take a step. After his mother's devastating death, he'd been the one to pull his dad into *his* arms. He'd been the one to offer the emotional support, all the while knowing that *he* had been the cause. It would have been so easy to return to the Corps, to go back to being a full-time Marine and not have to think about everyone hurting at home. But instead of reenlisting, Cole opted to hang up his dog tags and move back to Montana to help his father rebuild his life. It was what his family needed. What his mother would've wanted. He owed them all at least that much.

"I said come here." It had been a while since he'd heard Phil Dalton issue a command in his no-nonsense, authoritative voice, the one he used to unleash when he was bringing five unruly boys to heel.

And just like a reluctant eight-year-old, Cole hung his head, his feet dragging through the dirt as he stepped into his father's embrace. The older man's arms were still as big and almost as strong as they'd been when Cole was a little boy, and the shoulder he offered now was just as tough and comforting as it had always been.

"It wasn't your fault," his dad whispered as he squeezed his son tighter. "And I'll let you in on a little secret—it wasn't Booker's fault, or Zach's, or Shawn's, or Garrett's, neither. Like I said, every one of us has our own reasons for feeling like we were responsible. But at the end of the day, it was a terrible and tragic accident, and your mama would hate for us to be kicking ourselves over it this way."

Cole shuddered. The weight hadn't exactly been lifted from him, but hearing his father's words, feeling the old man's love wrapped around him, Cole knew that they shared the same burden. And his dad was right. Diana Dalton would never want them beating themselves up over it.

He clung to his father and they stood there like that for a few minutes, not needing any words to express their shared pain. Then a quick honk forced them to take a step back and look at the arriving vehicle.

"We brought out more fencing supplies," Booker said as he climbed from his own truck. "You guys having a party out here or what?"

"Nah," Garrett said as he exited out of the passenger side—after all, nobody was foolish enough to let his lead foot get behind the wheel. "I don't think Cole would throw a party without his personal party planner here to help him."

A bristling sensation made its way down Cole's spine. Garrett had been too hungover the morning after the wedding to ask why he'd been at an apartment complex in Kalispell. And even if his brother had asked, Cole certainly wouldn't have revealed that he'd spent the night with Vivienne. Nor was there any way he would've let it slip that he'd actually hired the woman to plan a fake wedding.

"What are you talking about, Garrett?" Cole asked, praying that his brother didn't *actually* tell them all what he was talking about. He walked to the back of Booker's truck and let down the tailgate.

"That pretty wedding planner? Vivienne?" Garrett grabbed some posts and followed behind Cole. "I heard you two were making out at some pie shop in Kalispell."

"You guys really need to stop getting your gossip from the mailman," Cole grunted as he rolled a huge spool of barbed wire toward his ATV.

"Nah," Garrett said. "I got mine from one of the waitresses at Matilda's. She also works for the caterer who did Zach's reception and she recognized both of you from the wedding."

Booker snickered, dropping another load of posts. "Is that the same waitress you went home with? Or her roommate?"

"Neither." Garrett looked at their dad and at least had the decency to turn an unmanly shade of pink. "Listen. Maybe I had a bit too much to drink that night and was pretty free on who I gave my number to. But we're not talking about me. We're talking about Cole and Vivienne. Should we get the freight house ready for another Dalton wedding?"

Absolutely not was the first thing that came to Cole's mind. But he gritted his teeth together before they could accuse him of protesting too much. The supplies had already been emptied from Booker's truck, making it impossible to avoid their curious stares.

"If you boys are so bored that you have time to be standing out here jawing and teasing each other, I'm sure I can find some manure for y'all to haul to the fertilizer plant," their dad suggested, a classic threat from their childhood.

So far, Garrett had been the only kid who'd ever been reckless enough to actually earn that punishment, and judging by his sly grin, he was about to earn it again. "Dad, we don't even have any cattle out here yet."

Booker grabbed their brother by the scruff of his neck. "Don't worry, Pop. I'll get this one back to the barn and find him some muck to shovel up."

The guys threw playful punches at each other, along with some light shoves as they made their way back to the truck. Dust was spitting up from the reversing tires when his dad turned to Cole. "So this wedding planner of yours…"

"She's not exactly *my* wedding planner." Cole hoped a thunderbolt didn't come from the heavens, striking him down for the borderline lie.

"Right. So this Vivienne of yours… You said you don't know what's going on with her right now. Does that mean you're hoping for something more?"

"Dad, since when do you ask us about our love lives?"

"Since I have to do the job of both parents." Phil's words hung in the air and there was no way Cole was going to go back to the emotional subject of his mother's death. He was better off answering his father's question about whether he wanted more with Vivienne.

"Maybe. All I know is that I was doing her a favor, and then it just kinda turned into something else."

Phil lifted a bushy gray eyebrow. "Something else?"

"I don't know, Dad. Yes, I like her, okay? I thought she liked me. But now that the favor is over and she has no need for my help, I haven't heard back from her. Part of me wants to check on her and make sure she's all right because...you know." Again Cole had accidentally circled around to the topic of his mother, and even *he* wasn't so oblivious that he couldn't see he might be overreacting about not hearing from her. "But the other part of me needs to learn to accept that not every unanswered phone call means someone has a problem. Sometimes, it just means that they're over it."

Vivienne hadn't returned Cole's calls right away because she was worried that she might slip and tell him that she'd lost her job. If he found out, there was no doubt he would hop in his truck and floor it all the way to Kalispell wanting to rescue her.

On the other hand, she didn't want to worry him by totally ignoring the messages and letting him think the worst. So on Tuesday afternoon, she sent him a simple text saying she was working on a few things and would call him soon.

It wasn't a complete lie. She *was* working on a few things, namely finding gainful employment. She'd looked at her checking account and, even if she only bought food for Lord Nibbles and limited her grocery-store spending to the bare minimum, she'd barely be able to afford two more months of rent.

Picking up her cell phone and making this call wasn't her first choice. In fact, it felt like an even bigger betrayal to Estelle than the one she'd been accused of. But Vivienne needed a job and it wasn't until she'd lost hers that she realized how much she would miss doing event planning. Sure, she wasn't necessarily any good at bringing in new business; however, she was confident in her abilities to give the clients what they wanted.

While Estelle had promised not to completely pulverize Vivienne's reputation, the woman also hadn't sent over a glowing letter of recommendation with her final paycheck and the personal belongings Vivienne had been forced to leave behind last Friday.

Which put her in a no-win situation.

Since most of the local vendors knew Estelle, they'd start asking questions the minute Vivienne sent out her first résumé. Some of them were familiar enough with her former boss's demanding nature that they might sympathize with Vivienne's less-than-honest approach, but not enough to hire someone they probably wouldn't trust. Nor could she blame them.

When Rich LaRue had left her a message this morning saying he'd heard that not only had Vivienne and her talents been noticeably absent from Valentina Souza's *quinceañera* on Sunday, but she also hadn't been answering calls at Estelle's Events, it reaffirmed her belief that the event-planning grapevine was ripe with juicy gossip about her already.

Watching Lord Nibbles pressed up against the corner of his glass cage—she'd traded out the cheap plastic one he'd come with—Vivienne took comfort in the fact that at least one of them was blissfully unaware and content that their next meal was only a nap away. Her guinea pig was finally overcoming his anxiety issues and she couldn't risk moving him into the apartment she'd dubbed Heartbreak Hotel the first time her dad had shown up asking for a place to stay.

Having no other choice but to see how bad the damage was going to be to her career, she dialed Rich's number and only listened to one full ring before he answered.

"Vivienne!" He didn't attempt to disguise the excitement in his voice. "Is it true? Have you finally told the old dragon that you weren't going to take her crap anymore?"

"Not exactly, Rich." She'd been debating how much she should tell him, but once she began talking, it only felt right to disclose the whole thing. Vivienne told him about her inability to land new clients. She told him about Cole's offer and how she never should have taken it. She even admitted that when she'd run into Rich at the bridal expo, she was there on Estelle's dime while allowing the woman to believe that she was there working. Okay, so, technically, she had been fulfilling part of her duties by doing research and networking. But she'd also been with Cole, which had made the whole trip feel more like a vacation. A reckless and inappropriate vacation that she never wanted to forget.

Rich tsked and made mmm-hmm sounds while she spoke. When Vivienne finished with the part of how Estelle saw them kissing and fired her there on the spot, he gasped and then let out an almost gleeful squeal. "So you're officially a free agent? Estelle can't accuse me of poaching you from her?"

Poaching Vivienne? How could anyone want her after the mess she'd made with Estelle?

"Rich, did you hear what I said? She fired me. And for good reason. She said nobody in town would ever trust me to work for them."

"Darling, do you think you're the first person who had to resort to a bit of trickery to get that she-tiger off their back? Denise over at Perfection Confection once faked an emergency gall bladder surgery rather than admit to Estelle that she couldn't do a wedding cake shaped like a grizzly bear for a couple whose alma mater was UM. Flora, the owner of Flora and Fauna, once told Estelle that red gladiolas were out of season because it was obvious that the bride had her heart set on a white bouquet. She had to hide two buckets full of flowers in the cooler for a month and then sneak them out to the Dumpster in the middle of the night so Estelle wouldn't see that she had them all along. Even Glory, my own sweet wife who is an absolute saint, lied to Estelle about moving to Florida to take care of her dying mother when she quit ten years ago to marry me. Of course, we all know what happened after *that* particular ruse came to light."

"But I lied about Cole being our client," Vivienne pointed out.

"I thought you said he paid her. And signed a contract?"

"He did…"

"Then he was a client," Rich argued. "Look, half the vendors in Kalispell only agree to do business with Estelle if they get a guarantee that they'll only have to work with you."

"So you don't think it will be too hard for me to find a new job?"

"You don't even need to look. I'm hiring you."

Vivienne's breath suspended mid-inhale. She had to remind herself to exhale before asking, "You want me to work for you?"

"I've been trying to get you to come work for me for ages. But here's the thing, Viv. LaVish is expanding and I've already rented out office space in Denver. I have someone for weddings, but I need an employee who could specialize in event planning."

"You mean move to Colorado?" Her mind was spinning.

"Yes. Unless you have something or *someone* keeping you in Montana." His emphasis could only imply that he was talking about Cole.

However, it wasn't like she and Cole were in an actual relationship. Or at least in a relationship that had any sort of potential. He'd agreed eagerly that they were just having fun and keeping things casual.

Growing up, one of the biggest complaints Vivienne would hear from her mother was that Bonnie had given up so many opportunities to be a wife, specifically Richard Shuster's wife. Was Vivienne willing to let an offer like this—which was perfect for her because she'd get to focus on parties, and not get weighed down with all the lovey-dovey romantic details of weddings— pass her by just for some casual fun?

Chapter Fifteen

"I can't believe Estelle fired you," Lydia said when Vivienne answered her apartment door the following afternoon. "Zach and I just got back from our honeymoon and I went by the office to drop this off. The woman told me she was surprised I would even want to see your face after what you pulled at my wedding."

Lydia held up a gift bag stuffed with tissue. She'd called Vivienne's cell phone a few minutes ago asking if they could meet and Vivienne had invited her over. Though, now that Lydia's eyes were studying the collapsed packing boxes stacked in the corner of her living room, Vivienne wished she had suggested meeting somewhere else.

"Are you moving?"

"I think so."

"You *think* so?" Lydia asked. "Wait. Back up. What does Estelle think you pulled at my wedding? Because as far as I'm concerned, you did an amazing job. I mean, you really went above and beyond."

Well, she had definitely gone above and beyond with the bride's new brother-in-law. Vivienne was suddenly hungry and wanted to ask Lydia to walk to the diner. But this really wasn't a conversation they should have in public. So she went to her small pantry and pulled out a bag of chips. "I don't have any salsa, but I have a nice bottle of chardonnay that Cole and I won at a bridal expo."

"I think I'm going to need a seat for this." Confusion crossed Lydia's face and the newlywed plopped onto the stiff beige sofa. "Cole went with you to a bridal expo?"

In her cupboard, Vivienne found a single wineglass decorated in pink puffy paint with the words *Michelle's Last Stand.* She'd brought it home in a bachelorette party gift bag when one of Michelle's cousins failed to show up for the festivities because she didn't like the fuchsia bridesmaid dress she was being forced to wear. There was some boycotting involved and sides were taken until Vivienne had finally gotten the bride to compromise on having a tailor remove the puffy sleeves.

Vivienne brought the wineglass over to the coffee table, along with a coffee mug bearing the logo of a company that had hired her to throw their corporate holiday party. Hmm. She'd never realized before now how sad it was that she didn't even have a set of matching glasses, let alone a single throw pillow, to pack in those moving boxes.

Handing Lydia the bag of corn chips, Vivienne went to work with the corkscrew. "Cole only went with me because he'd hired me to plan his wedding and we had to go to Billings to get his fiancée's signature for the contract."

Vivienne was glad she hadn't poured any wine yet because Lydia surely would've choked on hers had she taken a drink. "What?" she sputtered.

"Let me start at the beginning," Vivienne offered, then proceeded to come clean to the woman who'd once trusted her. She had to refill Lydia's wine during the telling, but her guest had yet to take a sip of the second glass.

"So, why does Estelle think you pulled something at my wedding?"

"I have no idea. Maybe she thinks that's when I started my affair with Cole."

"Is it?" Lydia asked, then took a hefty drink.

Vivienne didn't want to talk about the intimate details but admitted, "We, uh, had to share a hotel room when we went to Billings, so things had already turned physical before your wedding."

"Okay, but if you and Cole are in a relationship—which I totally approve of, by the way—what's with the moving boxes?" The woman worked for the local paper and really didn't miss a detail.

"I don't think we're in an actual relationship. I mean, we both agreed to keep things casual."

"Is that what you want?"

"I don't know."

"I'm guessing you haven't told him that you've been fired?"

"Are you kidding? If I did, he'd try to fix it. And that's what got us into this mess in the first place."

"You said 'mess.'" Lydia studied her. "If it's supposed to be casual, then how did it get messy?"

"I meant me losing my job. But I guess somewhere along the way, my feelings for him got a little complicated, too."

"Do you love him?"

"I think so. But if he doesn't love me, what's the point in staying?"

Lydia seemed to ponder this a moment before tilting her head. "You know, it's been my experience that the Dalton men don't always know what they want, even if it's right in front of them."

"But I've never been a pusher and love shouldn't have to be forced."

"Does he know you're moving?"

Vivienne bit her lower lip and slowly shook her head. "But I will tell him."

By the time Lydia left, Vivienne was already second-guessing her promise. Especially after she unwrapped the gift, which was a framed picture of Vivienne with Lydia and Zach on their wedding day. No other couple had ever thought to include her when commemorating their big day. She was supposed to stay in the background, to not get emotionally invested.

She knew that it was only right to tell Cole that she was leaving, but she wasn't sure of the best way to say it. The last thing she wanted was to come across as needing him to save her, because that's exactly what he would try to do.

The truth was, Vivienne wanted to be loved, not rescued.

"Just wanted to let you know that I got a job offer in Denver. I can never tell you how much you meant to... how much it meant that you helped me out with Estelle. Anyway, I wanted to thank you and wish you the best."

Her voice sounded upbeat at first, but then there had been a slight catch. Or maybe Cole was imagining it. He listened to Vivienne's message for the third time. Though, now he was far enough away from the sawing and hammering and loud voices of his brothers working inside the stables.

She was moving to Colorado? Out of the blue like that?

Why?

And why had she called to tell him? Especially when the last time they'd texted, she'd said she was very busy and he hadn't heard from her since. He wanted to convince himself that with her leaving like this, he was going to be better off. He was going to be able to get through a day of work without thinking about her a hundred times and worrying when it would all end for the two of them. Unfortunately, his confusion at her message and the timing of it didn't help to persuade him of the positives.

"Was that the pretty wedding planner?" his dad asked, surprising Cole by coming out of the stables.

"Yeah," Cole replied, still replaying her words in his mind.

"Are you going to see her soon?"

"I, uh, guess not. Sounds like she's moving to Colorado for a new job."

"Really? That's a surprise. You'd think she'd have all the work she could handle right here in Rust Creek alone."

"You'd think," Cole echoed, disappointment clawing at him.

"So you're not going to see her before she goes?"

"I guess not."

"Hmm…" his dad said, and Cole jerked his head up. "What's that?"

"I was just mumbling."

"No, you weren't. You said 'hmm,'" Cole accused. "The way you do whenever you're trying to get one of us to do something we don't want to do."

"So you're saying that you *don't* want to see her before she goes?"

"I didn't say that."

"Heck, Cole, you're blaming me for trying to get you to do something you don't want to do. All I want here is to figure out what exactly that is."

"Okay, so maybe I *do* want to see her. But maybe I also know I dodged a painful bullet later on down the road."

"Since when do you dodge bullets?"

"Since I found out that loving someone hurts."

"Of course it hurts, son. It's also what makes the pain worth it. I've seen the way you look at Vivienne.

It's the same way I used to look at your mama. I'm not such an old man that I don't recognize that look in my own sons." His father held up a palm when Cole began to respond. "Now, before you start on all that 'losing somebody doesn't make it worth the risk' nonsense, let me stop you right there. For thirty-five years, I loved your mother, okay? In fact, I loved that woman so dang much it tore me up inside when I lost her. But I'll tell you this much. I'd happily go through every single second of that grief all over again, even if I only got to love her for half as long."

Chapter Sixteen

After Lydia had left her apartment, Vivienne succumbed to a moment of weakness and went out to her car to retrieve the planning binder she'd purposely stashed in her trunk after the fateful afternoon when Estelle had fired her. She hadn't wanted any reminders of Cole to influence her decision about taking the job with A LaVish Affair.

That same night, though, she'd poured herself another glass of wine and opened the binder before staring at the pictures Cole had cut out from magazines or printed off the internet. None of the pictures had a single wedding detail in them. They were all of tropical beach destinations and shoved into the folder marked Honeymoon Ideas.

The man truly had no desire to get married and it

was suddenly clear that Vivienne needed to let him go and move on with her life. The following morning, she'd waited until she knew he'd be busy working at the ranch and called him, a calming relief settling over her when his voice mail picked up.

It had been three full days since Vivienne had left Cole that message about her leaving town. When he didn't respond, Vivienne had the bittersweet satisfaction of being right all along. The guy had never been looking for something serious in the first place. And since she'd been very careful in not mentioning anything about being fired, it proved her theory that he only came running when he thought she'd issued an SOS.

There was nothing left for her in Kalispell.

"I think you'll like Denver," she told Lord Nibbles as he rolled through the living room, exploring the apartment in his clear plastic exercise ball. When Vivienne began taping moving boxes together, the guinea pig had gotten restless in his cage, pacing back and forth and twitching his nose at lightning speed. She was determined to keep his anxiety about the upcoming move at a minimum, so she'd put him in his ball to allow him to expend some energy.

Now if she could only convince herself that everything was working out for the best. Standing in her kitchen, she opened a cupboard and, for the millionth time that week, stared at the hodgepodge of contents inside and debated whether or not she should even bother taking the mismatched glasses and plates with her.

She was starting a new job in a new state. Maybe it was time to buy herself a proper set of kitchenware for her new home. Rich had promised to increase her salary; however, she was still going to be on a tight budget for the first few months.

The knock on her door startled her out of her inner debate about needing more than a four-piece set of silverware and she almost tripped over Lord Nibbles as he ran in his ball toward the bedroom to get away from the unfamiliar sound.

Since Vivienne wasn't expecting anyone, she looked through the peephole, then flattened her forehead against the wood panel of the door, squeezing her eyes shut and only reopening one to take another peek. To make sure that her mind wasn't playing tricks on her.

Yep. That was Cole Dalton, all right. Standing on the tiny concrete stoop in front of her apartment, his cowboy hat firmly in place and his plaid sleeves rolled up on his forearms, as though he was about to get to work.

Maybe he was here to offer his expert packing services.

She took three deep breaths before finally unlatching the dead bolt and twisting open the knob. "Hey."

"Hi, there." He took off his hat and Vivienne's stomach dropped. Why did he have to be so handsome and charming? She leaned against the edge of the door for support, then realized she wasn't being very hospitable when he drawled, "May I come in?"

"Of course." She stepped back. "But watch out for Lord Nibbles. He's on a tear racing around this place in his exercise ball."

If her heart hadn't been falling apart at the sight of him, it would've been comical to watch Cole in his boots, carefully scanning the carpet and taking small steps to ensure he didn't accidentally kick her guinea pig.

"So you're really moving?" He jerked his chin toward the still-empty moving boxes lined up on her sofa.

"It's looking that way," she said, then clamped her jaw shut. No, it wasn't *looking* that way. It *was* that way. She was moving. Why couldn't she just come out and say it?

"That's too bad." His words were like a jump start to her heart and her pulse began pounding.

"Why's that?"

"Because I need to hire a wedding planner."

This again? Her shoulders dropped in defeat. "Unfortunately, I'm no longer in that line of work."

"You mean you're not moving for another wedding-planner job?"

"Technically, Rich is hiring me as an events planner. But I can refer you to Estelle's Events for all your wedding-planning needs."

"I don't want Estelle. I want you."

Vivienne looked up at her ceiling, trying to get her fluttering emotions in check. "Is it me you want or is it just another chance at rescuing me that brought you here?"

He stepped closer to her. "I want *you*."

"I thought you wanted to keep things casual."

"I thought that was what I wanted, too." His fingers swept along her jaw. "But then something changed."

"What if something changes again?" she asked, refusing to let her racing heart take over her rational head. "I don't want to be like my parents—in and out of love over and over again."

"I'm a Dalton." He slowly winked and her tense muscles went soft. "Once we fall in love, we're as good as gone. I can't help it."

She flattened her palms against his chest, but she didn't push him away. "What about marriage?"

"Are you proposing to me?"

"No. Not now," she said, and he raised an eyebrow. "I mean, we both made an awful lot of fun of the institution of marriage. But what if down the road one of us…" She trailed off.

"I never made fun of the institution of marriage. I made fun of weddings. Didn't you look at my binder? It was full of places where we could elope." He rested his hand on her waist. "I love you, Vivienne."

Her throat tightened, and all she could do was look at him.

His dad had said that loving someone was worth the risk of losing them. But when Cole finally admitted his love, she didn't reply. She just stood there, searching his face for something, but he had no idea what.

"Can you please say something?"

"You love me?" she asked, her voice barely louder than a whisper.

"How could I not? You're selfless and creative and smart and beautiful, and being with you always feels right."

"So you're not here to rescue me?"

"What would I need to rescue you from?"

"Estelle fired me."

Anger surged through him, making his skin tight

and his feet restless. Yet he wasn't able to release her. "Why in the world would she fire you? You're the best wedding planner in all of Montana. And trust me, I've been to the biggest wedding expo in the state, so I'm officially a reluctant expert on this subject."

"She saw us kissing last week after we met for lunch."

"So? You're not allowed to date a client?"

"Not an *engaged* client."

Realization sank in. She'd lost her job because of him. Pieces of the puzzle fell into place, and now he understood why she hadn't been quick to return his calls and texts. "Why didn't you tell me?"

"Because I was afraid you would drive over to Estelle's and tell her the truth and demand that she take me back."

"That's exactly what I would've done."

Vivienne's palms slid up his chest and toward his cheeks, holding his head in place. "I didn't want you to rescue me. I'd been unhappy working for her for a long time and I needed to rescue myself."

Her smooth hands felt so good on his skin he didn't want to shift his head. He caught a glimpse of the cardboard boxes out of the corner of his eye. "So that's why you took the job in Denver."

"I thought you wanted to keep things casual," she said, and his gut twisted, hoping she wasn't about to shoot him down. "There was nothing else for me here but heartbreak."

He clung to that last word. "I never want to break your heart."

"You can't save me all the time, Cole." Her warning whispered against his skin as she pulled his face closer.

"I know. When I came up with the idea of hiring you, I thought I was coming to your aid. But somewhere along the way, you ended up rescuing me."

Her lashes fluttered closed and a soft smile spread across her face. "I think I fell in love with you that day inside your cousin's pink bathroom."

Warmth flooded Cole, filling him with both relief and passion, and he closed the space between their lips. As he kissed her hungrily, all he could think was that this woman in his arms loved him. He would do everything in his power to keep her happy.

"Tell me again," he said.

"I love you, Cole Dalton." Vivienne traced a finger along his lower lip just as something crashed into his ankle and he looked down to see the little black-and-white guinea pig in its plastic ball.

It brought Cole back to the present situation and Vivienne's upcoming job. If they were going to make this a successful relationship, he couldn't be rushing in and fixing things for her all the time. "Listen, I don't want to stand between you and your career, but do you think we could do that whole eloping thing before we move to Colorado?"

"We?" Her eyes widened. "You'd move with me? What about helping your dad on the ranch?"

"I have four other brothers. It's time for one of them to take on the hero role for a change."

Vivienne chuckled, then grew serious. "Cole, I would never ask you to leave your family. They mean more to you than any job ever will to me. Besides, if what you say about all you Daltons falling in love is true, there are going to be plenty of upcoming weddings and baby showers to plan in Rust Creek Falls."

For the first time in his life, Cole didn't need a plan; he didn't need to make a decision right this second. All he needed was Vivienne.

Epilogue

Nobody was more surprised than Vivienne when Estelle called her the following morning. At first, she assumed her former boss had heard about her job offer with A LaVish Affair and was calling to threaten to have her blackballed all the way down in Colorado. But the woman's voice was unusually raspy and even cordial when she announced her reason for the call. "Viv, I'd like you to buy me out."

"I beg your pardon?" Vivienne asked, pulling the bedsheet off Cole so she could cover her own nudity as she sat up.

"My doctor has been after me to retire for years and relocate to a warmer locale. I've been fighting it, but after you left, I realized that I just can't keep up like I used to."

"I'm sorry to hear that, Estelle, but I think your doctor is probably right."

"Meh. We'll see. I've got a sister in Phoenix who owns a funeral home and she said business never slows down over there. So I'll still want to take some event-planning binders with me, but maybe we can work out a deal for the rest of the office supplies."

Vivienne shuddered at the funeral-type events Estelle was hoping to plan. But she wished the woman well and agreed to meet with an attorney to go over the details. Really, there wasn't much to buy, since Vivienne could've easily just started her own company and taken over any outstanding clients and vendor contracts. But Estelle had given her a start in the business, and she didn't feel right not giving the woman some sort of fair compensation.

She also called Rich LaRue and told him she wasn't going to be able to take the job offer after all, since she would be moving to Rust Creek Falls once their wing in the main house was built on the Dalton property. The man was gracious and offered to give her the friends and family rate if she wanted him to plan her wedding.

"That's very kind of you, Rich, but Cole and I are planning to elope."

His gasp was sharp and a bit melodramatic. "Don't ever let me hear you use that word again, young lady."

Elopements were the bane to a wedding planner's business and it was an industry custom to never speak of them. She rolled her eyes as she attempted to placate him. "I know, but Cole and I both will have so much going on with me launching a new business and his family starting up their ranch."

That much was true. It ended up taking several months to get the main house built, and with Vivienne working at the office in Kalispell and Cole putting in long hours herding cattle at the ranch, they decided that once the lease was up, Vivienne would move everyday operations to the renovated train depot at Sawmill Station. And with all the referrals coming her way from his extended family and all their friends, Vivienne had to hire her own Junior Wedding Planner to cover for her while she and Cole finally got to have the destination wedding of their dreams.

Vivienne wore a simple white linen shift and a crown of wild orchids in her loose hair as she walked across a sandy white beach in Bora-Bora. Cole was standing on the water's edge, barefoot with his jeans rolled up to his calves, his casual white shirt unbuttoned at the neck and his favorite straw cowboy hat keeping the setting sun out of his eyes.

She'd once told him that every bride and groom wanted their wedding day to be a fairy tale. And on this day, she and Cole Dalton were finally getting their happily-ever-after.

* * * * *

COMING SOON!

We really hope you enjoyed reading this book. If you're looking for more romance, be sure to head to the shops when new books are available on

Thursday
28th June

To see which titles are coming soon, please visit
millsandboon.co.uk

MILLS & BOON

REUNITED AT THE ALTAR
Kate Hardy

Cream roses.

Brad had bought her cream roses.

Had he remembered that had been her wedding bouquet, Abigail wondered, a posy of half a dozen cream roses they'd bought last-minute at the local florist? Or had he just decided that roses were the best flowers to make an apology and those were the first ones he'd seen? She raked a shaking hand through her hair. It might not have been the best idea to agree to have dinner with Brad tonight.

Then again, he'd said he wanted a truce for Ruby's sake, and they needed to talk.

But seeing him again had stirred up all kinds of emotions she'd thought she'd buried a long time ago. She'd told herself that she was over her ex and could move on. The problem was, Bradley Powell was still the most attractive man she'd ever met – those dark, dark eyes; the dark hair that she knew curled out-rageously when it was wet; that sense of brooding about him. She'd never felt that same spark with anyone else she'd dated. She knew she hadn't been fair to the few men who'd asked her out; she really shouldn't have compared them to her first love, because how could they ever match up to him?

She could still remember the moment she'd fallen in love with Brad. She and Ruby had been revising for their English exams together in the garden, and Brad had come out to join them, wanting a break from his physics revision. Somehow he'd ended up reading Benedick's speeches while she'd read Beatrice's.

'I do love nothing in the world so well as you: is that not strange?'

She'd glanced up from her text and met his gaze, and a surge of heat had spun through her. He was looking at her as if it was the first time he'd ever seen her. As if she was the only living thing in the world apart from himself. As if the rest of the world had just melted away...

Continue reading

REUNITED AT THE ALTAR
Kate Hardy

Available next month
www.millsandboon.co.uk

LET'S TALK

Romance

For exclusive extracts, competitions
and special offers, find us online:

f facebook.com/millsandboon

◎ @millsandboonuk

🐦 @millsandboon

Or get in touch on 0844 844 1351*

For all the latest titles coming soon, visit
millsandboon.co.uk/nextmonth